MASTER'S CLAIM

Guy whirled, his hands shooting out, his fingers biting into her shoulders, his mouth on hers now, grinding cruelly. He drew back a moment, his breath rasping.

"Phoebe!"

"No, Marse Guy."

But he was not to be stopped. He forced her down upon the green earth, tearing at her clothing, searching her body with rapacious hands.

"Marse Guy," she wept. "Please don't—don't tear off my clothes. I'll take them off. . . ."

He was a planter's son and she was a field wench. She had no right to deny him—and he had no way to resist her. . . .

FAIROAKS

Frank Yerby

A DELL BOOK

Published by
DELL PUBLISHING CO., INC.
1 Dag Hammarskjold Plaza
New York, New York 10017

Copyright © 1957 by Frank Yerby

ISBN: 0-440-12455-7

Reprinted by arrangement with
The Dial Press
Printed in the United States of America
Previous Dell Edition #2455
New Dell Edition
First printing—August 1977

PROLOGUE

On the first of April, 1900, Lance Falks rode out from Fair-oaks in a driving rain. He was in a thoroughly bad humor, which, under the circumstances, was understandable.

"A fool," he growled to himself, "on a fool's errand, on All Fools Day! Drat Judy anyhow; the older she gets the more she grows like the old man. . . ."

The old man he referred to was the late Guy Falks, his wife's father. Judy being, it was believed, a distant cousin of his, had been born a Falks as well as married one, thus saving herself the slight trouble of having to change her name. Even pronouncing the words, Lance's tone softened. He had been tremendously fond of his father-in-law. It was a fact, he admitted to himself, that he had been far closer to that willful and brilliant old man than he had to his own father. When, two years ago, at the age of eighty, Guy died, in part from his loneliness and grief at the loss of Jo Ann Falks, his beloved wife and Judy's mother, who had preceded him six months before, Lance had wept openly. Though he complained of it, the fact that Judy was very like her father only endeared her to him the more.

The weather, as he put it, in his clipped Oxonian accent, was positively foul. And it was precisely this foulness that was the cause of his errand. The night before it had stormed thunderously; the floodgates of heaven had opened and the wind had reached gale force. Therefore, this morning, Judy had insisted that he ride up to the high ground above the Mississippi to see how the family burial plot had fared.

"Family graveyards," she said worriedly, "have been known to wash plumb away in these parts. Oh, for the Lord's sake, Lance, go see!"

She had been unable to accompany him herself, because she was occupied with the children. There were five of them now, three boys and two girls; for, as Judy said with an impish grin: "Since Dad had his heart so set on there being Falks at

Fairoaks always, we might as well do it up brown for him. Besides, kids are fun. . . ."

He was still thinking about them, and his own good fortune in having married a woman capable of producing offspring as full of hell as he had always wanted his to be, when he saw the graveyard before him. He pulled up his horse and sat there staring at it. He whistled softly in pure dismay.

Judy had been right. There were trees down all over the place; Guy and Jo Ann Falks' common headstone was noticeably out of plumb. A giant oak had crashed through the iron fence surrounding the burial plot, and knocked down the monument over Yvonne de Sompayac Falks' grave. It seemed to Lance, whom Judy had thoroughly steeped in her family's history, somewhat of a sacrilege that the wind had dared touch that stone.

He got down and hitched the horse to that part of the fence that still stood, and pushed open the gate. He clumped through the black Delta mud until he reached Yvonne's grave. The monument, in the form of a weeping angel, lay on its side, its furled wings half buried in the mud. He bent and tried to lift it upright again, but he could not. It weighed hundreds of pounds and the task was beyond even his considerable strength.

Have to get some of the blacks up here, he thought, with rope and tackle—He stopped dead, the thought half finished; for it was then that he saw the box.

It was quite small and made of bronze turned green with age and corrosion. It had been put in a square hole, cut by the stonemason to receive it, in the pedestal under the angel's feet. Then the monument had been placed over it, hiding it from all living eyes.

He bent and lifted it out by the handle set in the top of it. He shook it, but no sound came from within. Then, carrying it, he mounted the grey and rode down to Fairoaks. He placed the box in a drawer of his desk in the study, locked the drawer and pocketed the key. Then he went upstairs, told his wife of the damage, and sent a Negro to round up a gang of field hands to clear the fallen trees from the graveyard.

"I'd appreciate it, Judy," he said calmly, "if you'd keep these imps of Satan out of my way for a couple of hours. I've some accounts to go over, and I need quiet. . . ."

"Of course, love," Judy said. "And when you've finished them, bring them up here to me so I can go over them again.

Your arithmetic is a living disgrace. Now run along like a good boy. Can't you see I'm busy?"

He kissed her gratefully, went downstairs and armed himself with a hammer and chisel; and, having locked the door to his study, broke open the box. It contained only an envelope, faded, damp and moldy, and a leather-bound journal with ruled pages, in no better condition. In the envelope was a letter, written in French, by a man whose command of that tongue had been poor indeed.

"Ma chere Yvonne," he read, then automatically began to translate: "It is too late now, and nothing can absolve me of the want of courage that made me continue to lie to you until the very end. I know now I could have told you the truth and you would have accepted it. For you gave me proof ere you died, that it was the man you loved and not the name. What, after all, could the name Falks mean to you? A mouthful of air —a whistling upon the tongue. You could never even say it right. Samuel Mealey would have been as dear to you as Ashton Falks was. Vanity of vanities, sayeth the Preacher; and I, God help me, have lived a vain and empty lie.

"Here, in my journal, is the truth. I trust that in the vast and wind-swept space between the worlds, where all vanities fade away forever out of sight and thought, you will read it and forgive the man who loved you more than life, and who, throughout his years, was not one man but two. My duality extends even to this: that I, who loved you with the double love of my twin beings, must sign this with both my names.

. . .

> Samuel Mealey/Ashton Falks
> June 20th, 1820."

Damned curious, Lance thought, and picked up the moldy, leather-bound journal. On the flyleaf, the two names appeared again, written exactly as before: "Samuel Mealey/Ashton Falks: His/Their Journal."

Leaning forward in his chair Lance began to read. The script was crabbed and difficult; there were great gaps in the narration. But it was told with verve and a certain rude skill. Until almost the end, it contained no mention of the name, Ashton Falks.

"I, Samuel Mealey," Lance read, "and Jacob, my younger brother, were born in a back room over a tavern near the Wapping Old Stairs. Or, at least, it was somewhere in Wapping, for, as I was no more than seven or eight years old when

I began my homeless wandering about London, dragging my baby brother behind me to whatever likely spot I could find to beg or steal food for us both, my only recollection is of the Stairs themselves, not of the tavern or the quarter. I was born, by my own rough reckoning, in 1760, and Jake in 1762. We believed ourselves to be the sons of Dennis Mealey, a lifelong vagabond, drunkard and petty thief, whose one bumbling attempt at highway robbery resulted in his being hanged at Tyburn in 1764, when I was about four and Jake no more than two years old. Whether or not he was actually our father is open to question; for our mother who abandoned us shortly after Jacob's birth, thus granting me the right to speak so frankly, was a serving wench in the tavern, and customarily augmented her scanty earnings by the practice of the profession most available to such as she, said profession being scarcely conducive to nice distinctions over the delicate question of parenthood. Besides, she appears to have elected him, somewhat belatedly, to the honor, from among all the equally likely candidates for it, when his rather spectacular demise lent him a certain macabre grandeur in Watting by the Thames. . . ."

Deuced honest bloke, aren't you? Lance chuckled, though a bit heavy-handed with your irony . . . He read on:

"My first honorable employment, though in truth it must be said that it was scarcely a cut above my former occupations of beggar and thief, was to wander the streets of London with a mountebank, Hiram Henks, who, having discovered my native gift for mimicry, taught me to amuse the mob, for the sake of their tossed ha'pence, by my imitations of such men as Charles Townshend, whose tax on tea caused the Boston Tea Party, thus contributing to the birth of our new and happy nation; Lord North, the Prime Minister; Chatham, the great Whig, and Charles Fox, the leader of His Majesty's loyal opposition. Privately, I often imitated King George III, as well; but Messer Henks was too astute to allow me to do so in public. . . ."

Another gap; but Lance Falks read on, unheeding. What a tale was this. . . .

"In the early part of 1775, Jake and I were employed, surprising as it may seem, as page boys in the household of the Earl of Bloomsbury. It was I who made this possible with my perfect mastery of the accents and mannerisms of our betters, and the beautiful credentials that I bought for one,

8

ten and six from an unemployed forger temporarily out of his usual lodgings at Newgate Prison. I wished with all my heart to live in the warmth, cleanliness and comfort of our new home the rest of my life. But this was not to be. In 1777, we were dismissed for thievery, of which I, being too appreciative of my good fortune to risk it for the sake of a few pence, shillings, or even pounds, was completely innocent. I believed that Jake had been falsely accused as well; but he, street urchin to the bone, soon confessed his guilt to me. . . .

"The rest is soon told: A press gang kidnaped us into service as able-bodied seamen in His Majesty's Fleet, soon after our return to our usual haunts. As a seaman's life in any Navy, during the years of my youth, resembled at its best, purgatory, and at its worst, hell, in December, 1779, finding ourselves once more anchored in the Thames, we deserted and immediately put ourselves beyond the reach of the authorities by taking berths aboard the *Mermaid,* a merchantman bound for the West Indies, where we planned to jump ship, thus leaving England behind us forever. . . ."

Then it came: the day. That day. April 8, 1780, off the coast of South Carolina, precisely at eight o'clock in the morning. The day the miracle happened; the hour that Samuel Mealey seized his dream between his two rough hands and fleshed it with life. The prose became swift, racy. Details were added, direct quotations of the words spoken by the unwitting actors in Sam's tremendous drama. Descriptions of scene, of action; everything, full, and vivid, and complete.

Lance read it over four times. He sat there, the walls of his study fading out of time and mind; his imagination taking hold of it, pushing the years back, flooding all the world with sea and sky; and he, Lance Falks was there with them, seeing it, living it:

The two boys, Sam and Jake Mealey hung over the mizzen tops'l yardarm and stared at the people having breakfast on the poop below.

"Lord, but they be fine!" Jake said. "How did you say they was called, Sam?"

"Falks," Sam said. "Sir Percival Falks of Huntercrest, Lady Mary, and their two sons, Ashton and Brighton. Being sent out to Antigua as Governor, which is why they've got all their goods aboard. That youngish chap in regimentals is Sir

9

Milton Tarleton, their cousin—and he's the reason that we're so far North. . . ."

"Lord love us," Jake said. "I thought we was right on course. . . ."

"That we are," Sam told him, "but for Savannah in the Crown Colony of Georgia, not for the Caribbean. Have to put that bloke ashore there. Secret orders for Governor Wright and the Military—"

"Cripes but you do talk fine, Sam'l! Proper like a lord yourself. I know you could afore; but you've kept it up, even with nobody about but me since we was at Hedgecroft—"

"Where we could be yet," Sam said bitterly, "but for you. No matter, Jake. Mayhap I'll thank you for your folly one day. . . ."

"Thank me?" Jake said. "How you do change your tack, Sam'l. I'm bloody sorry over that. We had clean beds there, all the vittles a body could tuck away, and fine livery. And we could of kept 'em for all our lives, but for me. No call to thank me for that 'un, Sam. It was a rum trick. . . ."

"Yet I do thank you. Or I will. Because I was growing too content at Hedgecroft. Satisfied to spend the rest of my life at some blinking toff's beck and call. Now I'm not. I'll have duds like those meself one fine day; and liveried lackies to do my bidding. A man can go up in the isles; while at home—"

"A boot in the arse is all he can look forward to. I'm with you, Sam'l. But how do you think to manage it?"

"Don't know. Depends on what Antiqua's like. Work, of course, 'til we've a guinea or two laid by. Then open a grog shop. There's money in rum. After that, with the proceeds, a hotel or such like. Finally, land. Everybody who's great has his bigness based on the land."

"You'll do it," Jake said confidently. "Allus did have a head on your shoulders, Sam'l. Trouble with you is that you've got a sight too much nerve for comfort—"

"I know," Sam said quietly. "Don't know which is worse, my nerve or your want of it. Fairish part of the time, you're right, though—like that mutiny—"

"Don't!" Jake shuddered. "I can still see that poor blighter, Dan'ls, being whipped through the fleet. Beside that, them as was hung had it easy. Wasn't nothing left o' his back but blood'n bones by the time he got to us on the *Harvey*. Been dead more'n hour then, but the whipping still had to go on. And you'd of been in that, but for me. They'd of keelhauled you at the very least. Mayhap made you dance your last horn-pipe from a yardarm's end—"

"No wonder the colonists have kept it up so long," Sam mused. "Five years now, with us whipping 'em at every turn; and they're still full of fight. . . ."

"I don't sight your drift, Sam'l," Jake said.

"Things like that. Keelhauling, and hangings, and whipping through the fleet. Mayhap that's why they fight. Got a blinking bellyfull of us. And likely other, littler things: toffs like the Falks, dressed fair'n fine, dining off the best, while we wear rags and tap our mouldy seabiscuits to shake the weevils out of 'em. Some with too much and the rest with nothing. 'Tisn't fair, Jakie. A body shouldn't have to stay a pauper all his life—nor take so bloody damned much gaff from his so-called betters. Look at those boys. About our height'n build. Scrub us down, dig out the lice and dress us in their duds—"

"We'd give ourseln away the first time we opened our blinking mouths," Jake said.

"You would," Sam Mealey snapped. "I wouldn't. Listen: 'I say there, my good man; would you be so kind as to fetch me up a bit of fire? The room's deuced cold. And quick about it, lad. I cawn't wait all day!' "

"Perfect!" Jake laughed. "You allus could take off those toffs for fair. Now, if we only had the duds and the money to go along with them—"

"Sail ho!" the lookout called down from the masthead. "Three point off the port stem!"

Instantly, Captain Jenkins who had been breakfasting with Sir Percival Falks and his family, pushed back his chair. They could see him bowing to the distinguished company, then he rushed forward shouting orders:

"Bos'un, pipe all hands! Mr. Martin! Bend on more sail!"

"What's he so het up over?" Jake demanded as they scurried up the ratlines toward the mizzen royals.

"That sail. In these waters it's more likely a Colonial privateer or a Frenchie than any of ours. The fleet's up around New York where Sir Henry Clinton keeps it for protection. Risky business, coasting off the Carolinas. If it hadn't been for that Tarleton bloke, we'd have picked up the Southern trades off Portugal and run straight for the isles; but now—"

"Now?" Jake said.

"We'll likely have a fight on our hands with a vessel better armed than we—"

11

The sailors swarmed up the shrouds like so many monkeys. The *Mermaid,* with a spanking breeze a quarter astern, had been running under nearly a full press of canvas anyhow; but now, spurred on by the driving orders of the Captain and the Mates, the crew bent on everything including the cook's shirt.

But even under all that canvas, the *Mermaid's* speed increased only to a pitiful five knots. A beamy craft designed to carry all the cargo which could be crammed aboard, she simply was not built for speed. Worst of all, she was armed with only four ancient carronades, able to throw their round shot scarcely beyond cable length. They had, of course, a certain theoretical usefulness in repelling boarders; loaded with grape, and smartly handled they might serve to clear the decks of an enemy. If there be a man alive on deck when the boarding parties come, Sam thought grimly. Any half-way armed enemy could stand out of range and pound us to pieces without taking a shot of ours in return. . . .

"She's a Yankee!" the lookout called down from the mast-head. "Flying stars'n stripes! Privateer from the looks of her!"

Sam felt a renewed surge of hope. A privateer wouldn't sink them. She'd be too interested in the prize money and the goods aboard. And if the *Mermaid's* crew had any fight in them they stood a decent chance in a hand-to-hand struggle on the decks. Most privateers were small; they'd most likely outnumber any boarding party she could send.

"Issue small arms to the crew," Captain Jenkins ordered. Then, raising his speaking trumpet toward the lookout, "can you see any more of her?"

"Yes, Sir! Sloop o' War, schooner rigged. Twelve guns!"

They took up their stations and waited out the chase. The Falks and Colonel Tarleton had gone below; though the two boys, Ashton and Brighton, and Colonel Tarleton, had done so only at Captain Jenkins' direct order.

"I'm responsible for your safety, gentlemen," the Captain had said. "If anything happens to you the Admiralty will have my hide! Be off with you, now!"

It took the Yankee nearly all day to overhaul them. It was late evening before she was close enough to send a warning shot from her bow chaser whistling past them, while signalling to them to heave to and strike their colors.

"Return their fire, Mr. Martin," Captain Jenkins said. "We can't hit them from here, but we might as well let them know they're dealing with British seamen. Might cause those cowardly dogs to change their minds. . . ."

The four pitiful little popguns had long since been run out, the decks sanded and the fire pumps manned. Anybody with half an eye could see Captain Jenkins was an old Navy man. Sam wondered what he was doing commanding a fat-bellied merchantman. A seaman brought the smouldering linstock against the touchhole. The short, thick carronade bucked and bellowed, kicking backward against the guylines. It made an impressive amount of noise for so small a gun. Far out, the first geyser plumed skyward; there were secondary splashes as the roundshot skipped along the surface of the water. Then it plunged in and was gone, hundreds of yards short of the privateer.

The Yankee yawed to port, and sent a ranging shot over them. The shotsplash stood up as thick as a doric column a cable's length off their starboard bow. The second shot was short by the same length to port. Sam glanced at his younger brother. Any damned fool of a gunner should have the range by now.

The whole side of the Yankee disappeared behind a wall of flameshot smoke as she loosed her first broadside. All the portside boats vanished in one great crash. The air was filled with whining splinters. Sam saw a seaman go down, a full yard of planking driven clear through him like a spear. But the rigging, miraculously, was untouched.

"The fools!" Jenkins roared. "They're trying to sink us! Don't they have sense enough to demast us first?"

"Apparently not," Martin, the first mate said. "Look, Captain, Sir—there's dirty weather ahead. Beat for that and we might lose them. We can bear a line squall better than they can. . . ."

"Right," the Captain said. "Give the helmsman the heading, Mr. Martin. . . ."

Martin raced aft. Before he reached the wheel the second broadside caught them amidships. Men went down screaming. Flames leaped up from the splintered planking.

"Good Lord!" Sam breathed, "they're serving red hot shot!"

"Man the pumps!" the bos'un cried.

"Damned funny behavior for a privateer," Sam panted as he and Jake pumped away. "You'd think that the prize money didn't mean a thing to them!"

Jake didn't answer him. His face was bluish white. Like the sewer rat he was, Jake had no stomach for danger.

They put the fire out handily enough, but not before three of the starboard boats had burned upon their davits. They had to hurl them over the side. Sam wondered what in hell's fire they'd do if they had to abandon ship, with only two boats left for passengers and crew. Besides, it was beginning to run quite a sea by now.

The Yankee switched to solid shot, trying to pierce their hull. She succeeded notably. Down below, the seamen were pumping desperately, up to their knees in water. What saved them was the fact that by then the sea was running so high that no gunner could hold his aim. The privateer's shot shrieked harmlessly through the rigging as she rolled, or buried itself into the sea, yards short of the *Mermaid*. Then, just as they plunged into the midnight bosom of the squall, a chance shot splintered the foremast. The *Mermaid* listed dangerously to port.

The crew swarmed forward, armed with axes and cutlasses, hacking at the tangled rigging. In minutes they had the foremast free and over the side, and the *Mermaid* righted herself. They couldn't even see the Yankee any more, but that was scant comfort. For it was damnably apparent that this was no mere line squall into which they had plunged, but the outer fringes of a tempest.

"Reef all sail!" the Captain shouted; but the wind snatched away his words. There was no need for the order anyhow; the seamen knew what had to be done. The wind tore the royals, topgallants, and upper tops'ls from the mainmast before the crew ever reached the spars. Then, weakened by the Yankee's fire, the mainmast started to crack. It went, taking five sailors with it. As they chopped it free, Sam thought grimly: Mayhap those two boats will be enough after all.

But they weren't. By nightfall, the *Mermaid* was slowly sinking and every manjack aboard knew it. The winds had lulled somewhat, but the seas were mountainous still. Even with the Carolina coast plainly in sight to leeward, attempting to make land without being pounded to pieces by the breakers appeared to be as nearly impossible as anything in this world.

Then it was that Captain Jenkins showed his mettle. He ordered the two boats manned but let the crew draw straws for the places in them. Both Sam and Jake lost. Then he sent word below for Sir Percival Falks and his family to come up on deck. Once they were there, he told them the truth: that the ship's boats had one chance in a thousand of reaching shore, but that those who remained aboard the *Mermaid* had no chance at all.

Standing close to them, Samuel Mealey got his truest lesson in what being a gentleman meant. For Sir Percy turned to his wife and managed, despite the fact that he had to shout to be heard above the thunder of the seas, to make his query sound quite gentle:

"Well, Mary, old girl?" he said.

"We've come this far together, Percy," she shouted back. "We might as well go the distance. Dying's not so hard when one doesn't have to do it alone. . . ."

Sir Percy turned to his sons.

"We're with you, Governor!" they roared above the storm.

Sir Milton Tarleton behaved less well.

"I have to get ashore!" he shrieked. "My dispatches—Highest importance! I say, Captain, I must—"

A lull between the gusts enabled Captain Jenkins to speak with befitting quiet.

"A place has already been reserved for you, sir," he said.

"Good!" Sir Milton shouted. "Come along, then! Let's be off—"

"I," Captain Jenkins said, "am remaining aboard, sir. There is not enough room for us all. . . ."

They stared at him.

"Damn me, sir!" Sir Milton spluttered, "I—"

"Lower away, men!" Captain Jenkins said.

They got fifty yards to leeward before the wave came in. Sam saw it rising to the very heavens, curving downward over the two boats like the hand of God. Then it crashed down in a smothering broil of foam and grey-black water, and the two boats were gone. They could see black specks against the ocean's silver grey, hurling astern.

And that was the end of that branch of the Falks' family. Or it should have been.

They could hear the timbers of the *Mermaid* working as she settled. The bos'un came up to the Captain, his face grey with fear.

"Look, sir!" he shouted, "if we got to work now, we could make ourselves a raft from the wreckage! A raft's got a hell of a lot better chance than a boat in a sea like this! Lash ourselves to it. That way we might make it, sir! For God's sake,

Cap'n, give us a chance!"

"Very well," Captain Jenkins said tiredly. "Get to work, then. . . ."

They fell to with desperate will. In a miraculously short period of time, the raft was completed. They got it over the side and secured it with stout ropes; then they swarmed down the lines onto it. Sam put one leg over the gunwales; then something told him to look behind him. His brother was running away from the rail, racing for the hatchway. Sam dropped back to the deck and ran after him.

And thereby, because of Jacob Mealey's cowardice, both their lives were saved. For when Sam dragged his clawing, weeping, struggling brother once more to the deck, the raft was gone. Far astern they caught a glimpse of scattered timbers, riding the waves. But of the Captain and the crew, there was no sign. They were alone, aboard a sinking vessel. Or so they thought. But destiny had other plans for them.

There had been no time during the fight, or afterwards, to keep a leadsman in the bowsprit chains. So what the brothers did not know was that the *Mermaid* had already sunk—as far as she was going to. They were in shoal waters. And the vessel which ordinarily drew twenty feet had touched bottom only ten feet down, driven aground by the winds.

So they huddled there nightlong, under a tarpaulin, waiting for death. Shortly after midnight the wind died, but the seas ran high until morning. With the sunrise, they, too, abated; and the two brothers looked at each other with dawning wonder.

"Y'know," Sam said, "I believe we're aground. We aren't going to drown after all, Jake-boy. . . ."

"Oh, thank God!" Jake wept from pure relief. Then, seeing his brother heading for the hatchway, he cried out: "Sam'l, where on earth be you going?"

"I've things to do," Sam said darkly, and disappeared below. When he came back, Jake gaped at him in helpless wonder. He was dressed in scarlet velvet; he wore a powdered wig below his tricorne; a smallsword was belted to his slender waist. He looked every inch the young lordling.

"Blimey!" Jake got out. "What the devil do you—"

"Get below, my good fellow," Sam said crisply. "There're sails on the horizon, likely coming to salvage this vessel. By my reckoning, we are not too far from Savannah. And if we have to go ashore there, I mean to go in style. Get going now, change into Brighton's things. Incidentally, that's your name from now on and don't you forget it. . . ."

"Brighton—Falks," Jake whispered. "Lord luv me, Sam'l—"

"Not Samuel Ashton. Sir Ashton Falks, if you please!"

"But we can't!" Jake wailed. "Somebody'll know and—it's bad enough to rob the dead, but to take their names to boot seems to me—"

"Get going, Bright!" the new Ashton Falks spat. "You heard me, get along with you, now!"

They spent the next two hours hauling the Falks' possessions to the deck. Some of them, of course, had been spoiled by sea water. But most of them hadn't been. Sir Ashton Falks —for in his mind he was that now, wholly and completely— sat gripping the satchel crammed with banknotes and jewelry in his hands, and gloating over the pictures, the cases of which had been broken during the rolling and the pitching of the *Mermaid*. He stared at the curled and beribboned Restoration gallant with the grim face.

"How d'you do, sir?" he said politely. "Ancestor of mine, what? Don't worry, old boy, I'll take good care of you. . . ."

"You're mad," his brother spat. "What do you want to save a case full o' pictures for? They ain't worth a ha'penny and—"

"They're worth a bloody lot," he said serenely. "A man has need of ancestors in a new land. Come, Brighton, my boy; the cutter's nearly here. We'd better be prepared to greet our saviors in a manner befitting our station. Savannah's still loyal, y'know. And loyal British subjects, I'm quite sure, will display the proper respect that's due a lord. . . ."

Lance threw himself back against the chair and laughed aloud.

"Of all the gall," he chuckled. "Of all the pure, absolutely priceless gall!"

Then he sobered. I wonder if the old man knew? he thought. No, He couldn't have. Being a Falks was his religion and his life. Faith—that's what it was. A faith so pure as to be almost holy. And it didn't matter, did it, Guy, old man, that the whole bloody show was false? Believing, you made it so. You became what that nervy Cockney beggar dreamed for you: a gentleman to your fingertips. Bless you, wherever you are. For, being so fine, you bred my Judy finer still. . . .

He sat there frowning thoughtfully. The only thing that

17

bothers me now is: What the blazes do I do with these ruddy papers? Be a shame to burn them, yet. . . .

He sat there a long time before it came to him. Then, with a slow smile, he stuffed the letter and the journal into his coat pocket, and picked up the broken box. He rode over to the Bavarian settlement, and waited while the blacksmith brazed the broken hinges together again and fitted a new lock. He put the letter and the journal back into the box, locked it, and rode down to the river. He hurled the key as far out into the muddy waters as he had strength to throw.

He reached the graveyard just as the Negroes were levering the angel back into her place.

"Wait!" he called out to them, and galloping up to the iron fence he jumped down from his mount before it had stopped moving. He ran through the gate, and bending, with his body between them and the box so that they could not see what he did, placed it tenderly back in its final resting place.

"Now," he said, as he straightened up.

And the Negroes settled the angel back upon the pedestal, to brood forever over the far, lost years.

1

THE day it began, a sunwashed day in the Spring of 1832, had nothing to distinguish it from all the other days that young Guy Falks had already lived. The wash of sun through the pines, the lift of his native hills, the sound the wind made sweeping down the ravines, all these were old and familiar things.

Even his present activity, fighting with Mert Tolliver, was a customary, habitual pursuit. He and Mert fought every time they met, without knowing why. They accepted the fact of their life-long enmity without thought, holding it as natural as the antipathy between cat and dog. The only thing that was different about the present battle was its intensity.

Guy stepped back and glared at Mert Tolliver. It wasn't a very effective glare, considering the fact that one eye was already swollen shut and beginning to purple. His nose, too, was bleeding fiercely. But he didn't pay any attention to these trifles. He was consumed with one exceedingly simple, even primordial aim; and the name of that aim was—murder.

And it was then that Mert made his mistake. He was older, bigger, and heavier than Guy; and, so far, he had had all the best of it. Thus it was that now he dared to add insult to injury.

"Damn furriner!" he sneered. "You know how your fancy-dan Pa come up here, anyhow? Running like a cur dog with his tail 'twixt his legs! Him and his proper talk and his booklearning! Mouthing words like a lady schoolmarm! My Pa says—"

"Mert—" Guy whispered. But Mert was beyond all caution.—"that he must of been a hoss thief or a city slicker crook! Reading'n such! That's for wimmen! Menfolks got more important things to do. Hah! Holding himself so fine, looking down on everybody—calling us hill trash! And look what he married! Just you look! Your Ma! Why she—"

That was as far as he got. Guy came in then. Every ounce of his lean and sinewy frame—which, already, at fourteen, was reaching upward, long-boned and rangy, toward his father's six-foot-one of easy strength—was propelled by fury. His left fist buried itself to the wrist in Mert's blubbery middle, and, as the bigger boy doubled, Guy's right caught him flush on the chin in an uppercut that would have done credit to a professional.

Mert loosened all over going down. Almost before he struck the earth, Guy was upon him, sitting astride his belly, hammering his big head with both hands. In two minutes Mert's face was a bloody mess; but Guy continued to pound him, panting in tune to the blows:

"Don't—you—never—put—my Pa's name—in your filthy mouth! Don't—you—never—even think about my Ma—let alone—talk! You hear me, Mert? You big—fat—hill trash—bastid! You hear me?"

"I give up!" Mert whispered. "I give up, Guy—God, you aim to kill me or something?"

Slowly Guy got to his feet, and stood there looking down at Mert.

"Get up," he spat. "I won't whale you no more. Reckon I've learned you. But in case you forget: I'm a Falks. And nobody, not nobody, Mert, trifles with us. Now get up from there and get going!"

Mert got painfully to his feet. He hung there a moment staring at Guy. Then he turned and lumbered off, sped upon his way at the last moment by a well directed kick in the seat of his pants.

Watching him go, Guy smiled. His teeth were very even and white, and his smile was summer lightning in the darkness of his face. He had a good face, though it would have shamed him more than a mite had anybody told him so. The hill people were sparse with compliments. All they ever said of Guy was: "Favors his Pa. And that there Wes Falks is a mighty fine figure of a man. . . ."

But the smile was gone as quickly as it came. He touched his puffed eye with his finger tips and frowned. Have to do something about this, or Ma'll have the hide off me in strips for fighting. I'll go ask old Dan Riley for a piece of raw beef to put on this here shiner. That ought to take the swelling out some. . . .

He loped on, going downward until the cluster of unpainted shanties that made up the town lay before him. He crossed the dusty square and pushed open the door of Riley's General Store. Old Dan Riley sat in the middle of that flourishing, fly-specked disorder, perched upon a crackerbox, talking to a group of men.

"They be his folks from downstate," he said. "Got that Falks' look. Talk the same, too; all proper'n fine. Knowed it the minute I laid eyes on 'em. Said to myself, says I, Dan'l, them there quality is Wes Falks' kindred—"

The expression on his listeners' faces got over to him finally. He turned and saw the boy standing there, staring at him. But the fact that he had been overheard by Wes Falks' son embarrassed him not at all.

"Guy," he said sternly, "how come you ain't home? Youall's got company. Your kinfolks from downstate. Passed through here half a hour ago in the sweetest lil' carriage pulled by the finest pair o' greys I ever set eye to. You better skeedaddle, boy! Your Pa'll be fit to be tied if you ain't there to greet your kin. . . ."

Without a word, Guy whirled and left the store. By the time his feet struck the earth, he was running, all questions of black eyes and raw beef flown completely from his head.

When he came up out of the last bone dry gully onto the plateau where the house sat, and saw the throng of people gathered open-mouthed around the polished wood and rich

20

dark leather of the little landau, he was too out of breath and dizzy from running to clearly assimilate the details of what lay before him.

What the hill people were gaping at—the news having flashed from house to house as the dappled greys had whipped the little landau around the tortuous curves leading up to the Falks' place; and they, being unencumbered by the need to follow roads, flocking like raincrows over the most direct routes to Wes Falks' cabin, arriving, some of them, even before the carriage did—was the Negro coachman, sitting like an ebony statue at the reins, clad in livery which cost more money than any three hill families ever saw in a year.

Guy gave the black coachman scarcely half a glance, before his gaze, caught by some magnetism, fixed itself upon the tiny creature perched in a cloud of pink ruffles and lace upon the rear seat of the landau. She was then all of eight years old. She was pink and white and golden, scrubbed, polished and perfumed. And even at eight she knew who and what she was, for she sat there looking at the openmouthed tiers of hill-people with a calm that was nothing short of regal, with an indifference that bordered upon contempt.

All except Guy. For in two scant minutes he had shouldered his way through the crowd, and was standing there gazing up at her.

The tiny goddess stirred. She stared at him curiously, then: "You're Guy Falks," she said.

Guy gulped once or twice before he found his voice.

"How—how'd you know?" he said.

"You've got dark hair," the princess pronounced judiciously. "All Falks have dark hair. Except me. I take after my mother. Besides, you look like my daddy. We're cousins, you and I. Didn't you know that?"

"I—I reckon not," Guy said. "But it must be so—if you say so, Ma'am. . . ."

"Don't call me Ma'am. I'm not old enough. I'm eight. How old are you?"

"Fourteen," Guy got out; but before he could even think about what he wanted to say next, she had leaned closer.

"Why!" she said, "you've been fighting! Aren't you ashamed of yourself, Guy Falks! Go and wash your face this instant! It's all dirty and purply. You heard me—go wash!"

"Yes'm," Guy whispered and slunk away to the gate. But at it, he stopped. For the man who sat on the veranda chatting gaily with his father was beyond anything even his active imagination had been able to conjure up. He was as tall as Wes, but far slenderer—and he held his glass of mountaindew bourbon with a delicacy, a grace, that Guy, without understanding the reason, found strangely disturbing. And nothing that Guy had read about the regalia of princes had prepared him for the splendor of this man's dress.

Yet, beyond the frothy white of the stock that was wound about the slender neck, the foam of lace from shirt front, the gold brocade upon the fawn-colored waistcoat, the impeccable cut of his rust brown coat, the sculptured clinging of the pearl grey trousers to legs that would not have shamed a ballet dancer, there was something else: the face, smiling smoothly under the thatch of dark ringlets was, strangely, almost Guy's own.

The boy hung there, staring. Then his father's great voice boomed out:

"Come here, son, and meet your cousin! Don't hang back, boy, this is a great day!"

Guy, in the midst of a dream haze in which his feet moved with a volition not his own, his arms swinging awkwardly above hands grown suddenly and remarkably beyond all reckoning, gained the porch.

"Guy," his father said, "this is my cousin Gerald. He's come to take us away from here—back to where a man can live like a man!"

Gerald Falks stood up, the motion, like all his motions, having that aura of unreality about it, that curiously languid grace that somehow made the boy feel cold.

"I'm glad to meet you, Guy," he said, and put out his hand. To Guy's surprise, his grip was both warm and firm. Still holding the boy's hand, he turned slightly toward Wes.

"This one, I'm happy to say," he said gaily, "is all Falks. I was beginning to despair!"

Going down from the house for the last time in the big wagon drawn by the two mules of a size and strength inconceivable to the hillbred people, Guy looked back at his home as long as it was in sight.

"Some mules!" his brother Tom exulted. "Finest pair I ever set eye on. And this here wagon—"

"Real nice, ain't it?" his sister said. "Ain't it, Pa?"

22

"Shut up, will you!" Wes Falks snapped. "The nerve of him—"

"The nerve of who, Pa?" Mathilda said.

"Gerald," Wes rumbled; and from his tone, Guy knew he wasn't really answering Matty, he was simply letting off steam, speaking out a thing that was bothering him. "Sending a wagon. A wagon! For me!"

"Mighty fine wagon, if you ask me," Charity Falks observed mildly.

The way Wes turned upon his wife was like the swoop of a great eagle. His voice was vibrant with ferocity, rising from its usual bass rumble until it was almost shrill.

"Nobody asked you, Charity!" he spat. "When the hell are you going to learn to keep your trap shut until you've got something sensible to say?"

Guy turned away from his silent, lost-lonesome contemplation of the house and stared at his father. Guy had long been troubled by his father's apparent dislike of his mother. But now he saw that Wes Falks didn't dislike poor Charity: he openly and actively hated her.

Guy looked from one of them to the other, feeling the sickness coiling cold and wet inside his belly. It was a hard thing; and no matter how he tried to set it straight in his mind he couldn't make head or tail of it. Of course, he had been aware for a long time that his mother was no fit mate for his father. Still, it made no sense. When a man married, it was his bounden duty to love, honor and cherish his wife like the preacher said—or else why should he bother to take her at all? And especially have children by her?

It had something to do with the talk on the front porch that day, two weeks ago, when Cousin Gerald had come bringing little Jo Ann with him, descending upon them like a creature from another world. Remembering it, Guy permitted himself the luxury of reveling in pure hatred, though, for the life of him, he could not have told why, without motive or reason he already hated his cousin, to whom, according to his father, they were now boundlessly beholden.

Him and his finicky, womanish ways, he thought bitterly, holding his glass like that, and pushing the words out of his mouth like he was a-kissing 'em. Damn his too pretty soul, we was all right up here. Didn't need to be yanked off like this so's Pa had to sell the house and all our things for nigh onto nothing and—

But Gerald's words kept coming back, spoiling the unmixed pleasure of his hating:

"Yes, Wes—the last of them has gone. Young Burton broke his neck in a steeplechase—you know what a fool he always was about horseflesh . . . Timothy moved north this Spring to take a job in his uncle's bank. Plantation was played out, anyway. So you can come back now; there's nothing left to be afraid of. . . ."

"Never was afraid," his father rumbled. "It was just that I don't hold with needless killing. God, Jerry, don't you see that there never would have been an end to it? I'd done enough to those blasted Redfields. And seeing as how I didn't even have the right on my side. . . ."

"I must say you didn't," Gerald said. "Shooting a man after you'd pleasured yourself with his wife was—to put it mildly —crowding the mourners. . . ."

"He called me out," Wes said slowly. "It was done fair and square. But then I saw that I was going to have to fight 'em all, one after another. Hell, Jerry, I was a better shot than any of them; but how much blood can a man stomach having on his hands, 'specially when he's wrong?"

"Oh, I don't blame you," Gerald said. "The main thing is to get you started again. Knowing you, I thought it over a long time before offering you the job of overseer on the old place. Reckoned you'd consider it an insult. But it's not, Wes. In the first place, in two or three years you ought to be able to save enough to buy a few acres of your own. And, blast it all, man, I could get a dozen good overseers. It simply occurred to me that, as a Falks, I was honor bound to give you a chance—any kind of a chance at all—to make up for your having lost Fairoaks and having to live here."

"I," Wes said quietly, "am most humbly grateful, Jerry. You're right. I'd take a much worse job than driving your niggers to get out of this godforsaken hole. . . ."

Gerald stared at him.

"Your coming here, I can understand," he said. "It's isolated enough—and besides, nobody, knowing the Falks, would ever think of looking for you here. But what I don't understand is—"

"I know, I know. Look, Jerry, things look different to a man when he's lost and lonesome and—drunk—"

"And also," Gerald said drily, "if I may venture so much— when he is confronted with the quaint hill custom of enforcing the sanctity of the home and redressing the injured virtue of the female with a double-barrelled shotgun. . . ."

"Single," Wes grinned. "But one was more'n enough, Jerry. 'Specially when it's pointed at you by a bearded old coot, likkered up and so mad his trigger finger was already trembling. Besides, I'd been away from civilization a mighty long time by then, and she didn't look so bad to me even by daylight. But now——"

"Now?" Gerald echoed, his tone faintly mocking.

"I'd tell him to shoot and be damned," Wes said flatly. "Still, I got one good thing out of it. . . ."

"And what, may I ask, was that?"

"The boy," Wes said. "Like you said, he's all Falks. Don't believe I could have done any better with a real lady. . . ."

"To hear you talk," Gerald smiled, "you'd think he was your only child. . . ."

"He is," Wes snapped. "The two older brats haven't an ounce of Falks in them, Jerry—not an ounce. Pure hilltrash, knobby-kneed, washed-out, straw-topped, idiotic. If I didn't know for certain they were mine, I'd swear I had nothing to do with it. But they are mine, so every time I look at Tom and Matty, my own brood, I could weep. Hell, boy, to shoot those two would be a waste of powder and ball!"

The land was flattening out now and the pines were thickening. They rode on in silence, none of them daring to break into Wes' mood. The Negro who drove had not opened his mouth the whole way, and of them all, only Wes, in silent fury, understood why. He knew clearly and perfectly what the black man was thinking; he was trembling inside because neither by word or sign did the driver give him opportunity to let his rage escape.

But now, just before dark, the Negro began to hum a tune. Wes let him hum it through twice. Then he reached over with great calm and took the whip out of the socket. The Negro stared at him, startled. Wes reversed the whip, holding it butt outwards.

"Sing it," he grated. "You goddamned black bastard, sing the words!"

"Marse Wes——" the Negro began, but Wes was like a panther striking. The butt of the whip caught the Negro alongside the face, and big as he was, the impact of the blow rolled him out of the wagon into the dust.

25

Wes got down, holding the whip. His eyes were dancing with cold ferocity.

"Sing it," he whispered. "You heard me—sing!"

In a voice strangely high and quavering for so big a man, the Negro began:

" 'I'd ruther be a nigger, and work like heck'—Lord, Marse Wes, do I got to?"

"You got to, Cass," Wes said; "go on. . . ."

" 'Than be a—' "

"Go on, Cass," Wes whispered.

" 'Hill-trash cracker with a long red neck—' " Cass finished and stood there, waiting.

Slowly Wes smiled.

"All right, Cass," he said quietly. "Get back up on that wagon. If I were hill trash, I'd take the hide off you like you're expecting. Only I'm not, and you know it. Go on, get up there and drive. This is the end of it. 'Cause now you know I'm not to be trifled with. Or haven't you been on our place long enough to know what a Falks is?"

Cass scrambled back onto the seat. Suddenly, unaccountably, he began to talk.

"Reckon I knows, all right," he said. "But you see, Marse Wes, it's this way. Since yore pa died, ain't been nobody down there to take hold. Marse Jerry, he—"

"Go on," Wes said easily. "What about Marse Jerry?"

"This here is between us, ain't it, Marse Wes? You won't go and tell him what I said?"

"No, Cass," Wes said; "go on. . . ."

"Well, Marse Jerry, he ain't no proper Falks. He got the family looks, but there's something lacking. Kinda hard to put yore finger on it. He ain't like yore Pa—rest his soul, or yore Uncle Brighton, neither. He just don't seem to know how to get a grip on things. Warn't for Miz Rachel the place would of gone to hell by now. Shame to say so, Marse Wes, but Miz Rachel runs the old place and she runs Marse Jerry, too. . . ."

"Go on," Wes said.

"She's a mighty fine lady, Miz Rachel; but Lord, Lord what a temper she got! Reckon she's kind of disappointed like—after she done found out she ain't really got herself no man—"

"That's enough, Cass," Wes said quietly.

"But it's the living truth, Marse Wes! Tell you another thing. I'm certain sure that it was Marse Jerry what 'suaded your poor pa to disown you, when you got in that trouble. Old Marse was already sick then, and——"

"I said that's enough, Cass," Wes said once more; and though he did not raise his voice, it had in it the muted clang of well-sheathed steel.

"Yassuh," Cass said quickly. "I ain't talking no more, Marse Wes. . . ."

"Good; see that you don't, Cass," Westley Falks said.

In the morning, riding along beside Westley Falks, Guy sensed the lift and surge of his father's mood. For now, at long last, the pines had disappeared; here were blackgum and cypress and the lofty spread and reach of oak. And between the groves he could see the fields now, stretching out to the rim of the horizon and beyond, with the black people moving down the rows, singing.

"All this, boy," Wes said, "all this and more would have been yours, someday, if your pa hadn't been a bloody damned fool!"

"Pa——" Guy said.

"Yes, son?"

"You think what Cass said—I mean about Cousin Jerry 'suading Grandpa to——"

"Nothing to it," Wes said. "That's just nigger talk, son. Jerry, whatever his faults, is a Falks. And Falks, sinners and rapscallions, gamblers and whoremasters extraordinary though they be, are never wanting in honor. . . ."

"Wes!" Charity said sharply. "Talking like that to a boy!"

"He's got to learn sometime, Charity. Rather he had the family's natural taste for the fleshpots than some other faults like being smallminded, little of heart and mean. Look, boy, in another five minutes, you'll see the house——"

"Where we're gonna live, Pa?" Mathilda piped.

"Where we ought to live," Wes said sadly, "but not where we're going to, Matty. Never you mind, Missy; before you're wed we'll have one as fine; you've my word on it. . . ."

The wagon creaked on. Now and again, beyond the reach of fields, they could see the river coiling golden in the sun. A fast river packet panted down it, snorting black clouds from her twin stacks.

"Steamboat round the bend!" Tom exulted. "Whooo-Whooo! Whooo-Whooo!"

"For the love of God, stop that infernal racket!" Westley

said. "Reckon you can't help being a blinking idiot, considering your blood, but damn it, Tom, restrain yourself when I'm around, or I'll have your hide!"

Tom subsided into sullen silence. The wagon moved on.

It seemed to Guy that the very air was waiting, tense with expectancy. The mules pricked up their ears and quickened their gait with no whipcrack from Cass to urge them on. Then, suddenly, Cass hauled back on the reins, and pointed, his black face split by an enormous grin.

"Thar 'tis!" he said.

Guy felt the cold shivers racing up and down his spine as he looked at the house. It sat at the end of a two-mile-long alley of oaks, white with that whiteness which was like a cry in the darkness, stately with a dignity, even a grandeur, beyond even the sweep of his active imagination.

"Fairoaks," Westley said, and his voice, speaking, was that of a man pronouncing an invocation, or a prayer. Guy, caught by the tone, turned and looked at Wes. And for the first time in his life he saw tears, bright and unashamed, in his father's eyes.

Cass flapped the reins, and the mules' haunches tightened, pulling. The wagon moved off, turning into the lane under the giant oaks. In their shade it was cool, and a little talking wind ran before them, stirring the dust of the road.

Nobody spoke. They sat there watching Fairoaks grow bigger before their gaze, the Doric columns thickening to four times the width of a big man's body, soaring up, up, until their tops and the galley roof they supported, seemed to pierce heaven itself. The fanlight of window over the doors and above the little ironwork balcony high up under the roof, caught the sun, and poured back a golden flood in their faces. Roses, hyacinth, hollyhock and asters clustered about the pool, and pansy beds lined the flagstone walks and wound through the sweep of beautifully trimmed lawn, saturating the air with their perfume.

Guy could see the two garconieres, white temples themselves, flanking the manor; smaller, they retained all of its dignity and its grace. He turned to his father, his dark eyes wide with questioning.

"No," Wes said sadly, "not even those, son. . . ."

But now, from nowhere, a crowd of ragged, Negro children came flocking; they flew from all sides of the house, from

28

the gardens, running, their rags flapping jauntily behind them, screaming as they came:

"Company coming! Company coming! Comp'nee coming!"

At the sound of their clamor a tiny figure came out on the balcony. She was clad all in white, except for the rose-colored ribbons adorning her golden hair. Guy froze, staring. When he saw the white flash of her handkerchief waving, he had not the strength to lift his hand.

Then, pressed as he was between his mother and his father on the wagon seat, he felt the muscle of Wes' thigh tighten like steel against his own. He looked at his father. Wes was staring upward, too, now; the little knot of muscle above his jaw jerking visibly. Guy followed his gaze upward and looked into a woman's face, seeing her strangely, through his father's eyes, with the same lust and longing Wes must have felt, the same awe, the same aching wonder. . . .

She was bending over little Jo Ann, taking her arm to lead the child back inside again. But then, at that moment, her gaze met Wes' own; met and locked, so that Guy almost saw the lightning flash that passed between them; except that was wrong, too: lightning is a zig-zag thing, gone in an instant; while the ruler-straight lines of tension that flowed between this man and this woman, held and held and held while time, the world and human consciousness stood still, teetering upon the brink of—

Catastrophe, or gathering strength for an assault upon heaven itself.

"Wes—" Charity whined reproachfully.

He did not answer her. He was beyond the reach of any sound softer than a thunderclap, or any grasp less sure than black-robed death.

The woman straightened up proudly. Guy saw that her hair was redder than a sunset; and he knew surely, without being able, at this distance to make them out, that her eyes were the green fire of emeralds. She lifted her arm and pointed. The gesture was so brief that Guy was not sure he had not imagined it; but then, hearing the sob of his father's breath rasping out of his throat, feeling the absolute bottom-lessness of the rage that possessed Wes Falks at that moment, he knew that he had seen Rachel Falks' contemptuous gesture of dismissal, knew it even before Cass turned the team down the side road leading away from Fairoaks, before Wes' grating, involuntary murmur:

"You bitch. You goddamned hoity-toity bitch! Reckon I'll have to teach you the taste of crow. . . ."

"Wes!" Charity said furiously, "'pears to me you might have a smidgin of respect—"

Wes stared at her, his gaze choking off her words. When he spoke, his voice was the splintering of ice on a mountain pond.

"Respect?" he drawled. "For you, Charity? Well, I haven't. Not a bit. Not a miserable, goddamned bit. You ought to know that by now. I never made you any promises. When you tricked me into marrying you, all you got was my body. My heart stayed free, Char—and it'll take more than a scrawny hill slattern to put a bridle on it. A mighty, damned sight more—"

He whirled upon Cass, who had let the mules come to a stop.

"What are you waiting for?" he thundered. "Damn your black soul to hell and back again, move!"

"Yassuh, Marse Wes," Cass said, and brought the whip down, hard, across the backs of the mules.

The big animals leaped ahead. When Guy looked back, the dust cloud from their passage had blotted out the house.

2

THE overseer's house was a caricature, rather than a copy of Fairoaks. It was, of course, painted the same spotless white, and followed—from far off—the same neo-Grecian design. But, instead of being round, the columns that supported the roof were square, being formed of four planks with bevelled edges making a hollow box. The bevelling had been done with an adz, and by an unskilled or careless hand. There were gaps in the edges that Tom could and did poke a finger into.

Wes stood there looking at it, and swore, feelingly. Guy, as always, standing by his father, nodded in grave comprehension. All right, in comparison with any house he had ever seen before coming to Fairoaks, this was a regal palace; but it wasn't worthy of a Falks, not by a long shot. Fairoaks, itself, was; and, being himself and his father's son, he damned well wasn't going to settle for less.

The house Negroes had come out on the galley and stood there bowing and smiling their greetings. That is, they bowed and smiled to Westley Falks. But their collective gaze swept over Charity and the two fair-haired children like the flick of a whip, and Guy saw at once the insolence and the contempt in their eyes.

"Howdy, Marse Wes!" they chorused. "Mighty nice to have you back, suh! Yassuh, mighty nice. Shore Lord got yourself a flock of pretty young'uns! This here yore missus? Howdy, ma'am, might proud to make yore acquaintance. . . ."

The words were right, Guy saw; but the tone was wrong. They were the burlesque of courtesy, not the thing itself. But the timing was exact and beautiful; just before the lightning gathering in Wes Falks' eyes could flash, they had spoken, placing him upon his dignity as a white man not to notice the half-concealed mockery, and upon his honor as a member of the master caste not to retaliate.

"All right, all right," he said shortly. "Get the things out of the wagon, Rufe. You got supper ready, Bess? And I hope to hell you wenches have the place half-way clean. . . ."

"Yassuh," they chorused again. "Ever'thing's ready, Marse Wes. . . ."

Wes turned then, just in time to see Rufe staring at the ragged carpetbags he was handing down to Cass. His black face was twisted into an openly contemptuous grin. Seeing Wes' face, the grin vanished as though it had been wiped away by the hand of a magician. Wes looked at Rufe soberly, then at the bags.

"You're perfectly right, Rufe," he said at last. "They aren't fitten for anybody who's got even one drop of Falks' blood. Take 'em out back and burn 'em!"

"Pa!" Mathilda wailed, "I got my doll baby and all my things—"

"You'll have better, Missy," Wes said, not unkindly. "Go on, Rufe—take this trash out back and burn it. Cass—"

"Yassuh, Marse Wes?"

"You go up to the house, and tell Mister Jerry I want to see him. Right now. All right, you kids, go wash. Bess'll have supper ready in two shakes. . . ."

The furnishings of the house were plain but of good quality. But everywhere there were evidences that the last overseer hadn't cared very much. The Negroes had swept and dusted—as they always did when not rigidly supervised—the centers of the rooms, leaving the corners inches deep in dust.

Wes stared at his wife.

"All right," he growled, "tell them. After all, you are mistress here. . . ."

"It—it ain't cleaned very well," Charity ventured timidly.

"Blast and damn!" Wes roared. "It's not cleaned at all! Listen, you lazy, good for nothing black wenches! By this time tomorrow night I want to be able to eat off these floors! You hear me?"

"Yassuh, Marse Wes," the maidservants said.

"All right, all right!" Wes said. "You—what the devil are you called?"

"Ruby, suh. Ruby Lee, that is. . . ."

"You, Ruby, take these children and scrub them. All except this boy. And go tell Bessie, you—"

"Tildy, suh—"

"Tildy, go tell Bess I want my supper now, not next week!" He turned mockingly to his wife.

"Well, Charity," he said. "What do you think of it?"

"It's—it's real nice, Wes," Charity said.

They sat around the table, waiting. Bess and Ruby came in finally, bringing a huge tureen of soup. Ruby held the bowl, while Bess ladled out a generous portion into Wes' plate. Without waiting for the others to be served, Wes lifted a spoonful to his mouth. Guy sat there, staring at his father.

Wes came upright, his chair spinning backward behind him with a crash. Without a word, he seized the soup tureen from Bess' fat hands. In two strides, he reached the window. His arms came back, swinging. There was a hiss as the hot soup hurled through the window, a sodden splash as it struck the ground below.

Wes turned back to the cook, the tureen in his outstretched hands.

"Here," he said. "You know me, Bess. You damn near raised me. I don't eat slops. If you didn't know how to cook, it would be another thing. But you're one of the damn finest cooks in the whole blamed state of Mississippi. Now get back in that kitchen and start over. I'm going to be waiting. And I'm hungry. The longer I stay hungry the worse my disposition gets. You heard me, Bess, get going!"

"Yassuh, Marse Wes!" Bess wailed, and fled the dining room at a speed astonishing for one of her bulk.

The supper, when it again appeared—in so short a space of

time that Guy solemnly imagined that Bess must have summoned to her aid a legion of djinns and demons—was a miracle of culinary art. A true Creole gumbo-filé had replaced the soup, and mountains of golden brown fried chicken followed it, accompanied by beaten biscuits, lighter than thin air and so hot that Tom dropped his with a howl of anguish. There were candied yams and a dish of turnip greens with pieces of fat pork swimming in it. Ruby served everything, and by the time they were pushing back from the table, full to repletion, Bess was able to make a triumphant entrance, bearing the biggest peach cobbler Guy had ever seen in all his life. It also proved to be the best he had ever tasted.

Bess stood there beaming.

"Thar now," she chuckled. "You satisfied, Marse Wes?"

Wes stood up, his dark eyes twinkling. Solemnly he took Bess by the arm.

"You," he said, "have made a mighty big mistake, Bess. For the very first time you bring me a meal even a wee mite less good than this one, I'm going to have your fat hide off in strips. You hear me, Bess?"

"Yassuh, Marse Wes," Bess laughed. "But I reckon that's one thing neither one of us got to worry about. Nawsuh, not a-tall!"

Wes turned to his family.

"All right, Charity," he said pleasantly. "You and the kids go get some rest. Guy, you come with me. It's a long time before dark, and we'd best get started putting a hand to things. . . ."

"Yes, Pa," Guy said, and came to his father's side. As he did so he caught the hurt look in Tom's eyes, and, for the first time, he was sorry for his older brother.

"Couldn't Tom come, too?" he said.

"Well—" Wes hesitated, "well—all right. But," and this time he spoke directly to Tom: "you have to look alive, boy, and keep your mouth shut until you've got something sensible to say."

The three of them walked out of the house and stood in the front yard looking around them. The yard was a wilderness, overgrown with weed and brambles. It was, Wes could see, the growth of several years. No question about it; the last overseer had been slack indeed.

"We'll have to do something about this," Wes said. "Send up to the big house for seeds and cuttings, I reckon. Your mother's a pretty good hand at flowers. Once all this brush is cleared away, the place ought to look like something. . . ."

He moved off throwing one arm lightly around Guy's shoulders. As he did so, he saw Tom wince. He was conscious of a feeling of pity for his older son. After all, it wasn't really the boy's fault. He had long realized that much of Tom's backwardness was due to his own neglect of his firstborn. To have transferred, or rather extended, some of the resentment he had felt toward Charity to the child, the innocent instrument and forging of his personal slavery which bound him to Charity, as he had done since the boy's birth, simply wasn't just. And, above all, Wes Falks was a just man. So now he placed his other arm about Tom.

Tom straightened up, proudly. They walked like that around the house, past the poultry yards until they came to the stables. These, of course, were not the main stables of Fairoaks, but rather the smaller ones which housed the three or four nags grudgingly accorded by custom to the overseer's use. And nothing was more indicative of the lowly place of the overseer in Southern society than this: that in a land where a man was judged by his knowledge of horseflesh, the riding animals given to the overseer were universally fit only for the glue factory.

Wes was bitterly conscious of this fact. But he hadn't the slightest intention of letting his cousin treat him in such a fashion. So now, as he approached the stables, he was thinking how he could go about demanding decent mounts for himself and for Guy. It was a rankling thought. He had, after all, accepted of his own volition the inferior status of an overseer. By so doing, he had given up the right to demand anything whatsoever. But, damn it all to deep blue hell, he was still a Falks, wasn't he? And besides—

The land should have been his. He had lost it by his folly, by his lust. He had refused to listen to Cass' suggestion that Gerald, out of self interest, had influenced his father, old and sick and tried beyond his patience and his strength by the endless series of scandals, always involving some woman or another, in which Wes had figured. But, from now on, the idea was going to haunt him. It was, given Gerald's temperament and personality, well within the realm of possibility. Even as a child, when Ashton Falks had taken his brother Brighton— a failure in everything he had ever attempted—his ailing wife and weakling son to live as his lifelong guests at

34

flourishing Fairoaks, little Jerry had distinguished himself both by his open envy of Wes and the deviousness by which he had frequently triumphed over his more open-hearted cousin.

Wes pushed the thought aside. There was, after all, no way of proving it. And it didn't matter now. What was important was to begin the long climb back into the place in the sun that was rightfully his.

They came up to the stables. Even before they reached them, they heard the crash of splintering planking, the high, shrill neighing filled with wild savagery that to Guy, who was his father's son, was like a trumpet in the blood.

Wes took his arms from about his sons and ran forward. The great black stallion was already half out of his stall. One more assault on the bars and he would be free. The stable hand, his face grey with terror, had seized a pitchfork to defend himself. With one bound, Wes was beside him pushing him away.

"Marse Wes! Marse Wes!" the Negro quavered. "Don't go no closer, suh! That there ain't no hoss! That's a living devil! Done kilt one man already! Lord God, Marse Wes, don't go so close!"

"It's all right, Zeb," Wes laughed, the exultation vibrant in his voice, "I can handle him. . . ."

"Nawsuh, you cain't!" Zeb said. "Begging yore pardon, suh, cain't nobody handle that devil! He throwed Marse Jerry and bruk three ribs, so Marse Jerry give him to Marse Hently, the last overseer. First time Marse Hently tried to ride him he throwed him, too, and bruk his neck! Please, suh, don't!"

Guy could see, the stallion having subsided a little, that there was a rope around the animal's neck. The end of it hung loose, the great beast having broken it with his first frenzied lunge.

"Zeb," Wes said quietly, "come over here to one side and take down those bars. Gently now, so he doesn't hear you. . . ."

"Marse Wes!" Zeb wailed. "I cain't! I'm scairt! I'm plumb nacherly scairt!"

"I'll do it, Pa," Guy said, and stepped forward.

"Good!" Wes exulted. "Come on now, but careful, mind you. . . ."

Guy moved in close, stepping Indian fashion, silently, upon the balls of his feet. He took down the first of the remaining bars. Beyond that he had no occasion to do more. The stallion splintered them with one mighty surge and leaped free.

Guy saw his father seizing the rope and leaping, no, not leaping—for a motion as graceful, as beautifully timed, as perfect as his could not be confined to the explosive suddenness of a leap—but rather soaring up like a great and masterful bird of prey—onto the animal's back.

Wes leaned forward, buried his left hand into the black mane, tugging back on the rope with his right so that the noose tightened, shutting off the animal's breath. But the stallion had reserves of strength beyond those of an ordinary mount. He dug his hooves into the earth, his great haunches bunching and uncoiling smoothly, flying out of the stable yard, sending up clods of earth as big as a man's two fists behind him. The highgate was closed; the twelve-bar gate that no horse in the history of Fairoaks had ever succeeded in clearing; but the great black cleared it now, reaching upward in an arc, a trajectory as clean and sure as though it had been inscribed upon the naked air by a great compass.

Wes hung on. As the stallion came to earth again beyond the gate, Guy heard his laughter ring out, giant and booming. Then man and horse were gone, disappearing in a cloud of dust that diminished with incredible rapidity over field and hedge, crosscountry, steeplechasing; and long after their going, the boom of Wes Falks' laughter hung in the evening air like the half-remembered reverberations of a great brazen gong.

The two boys and the Negro waited.

"I'm scairt!" Tom whimpered. "That there wild horse gonna kill Pa! Then what on earth we gonna do?"

Guy stared at his brother with eyes filled with pity and contempt.

"Don't you worry, Tom, boy," he said kindly. "Horse what can unseat Pa ain't been born yet. . . ."

They stood there, waiting; then, down the road from the direction of Fairoaks, they saw a horseman coming. But as the rider came closer, they could see that this was not the black stallion and their father but a woman, mounted side saddle on a beautiful chestnut mare. Zeb ran and opened the gate for her. She rode into the yard and sat there staring down at them.

Guy heard the creak as Zeb closed the gate again; but he was only half aware of the sound. He was seeing that her eyes were as green as he had imagined them; her hair, with the light of the setting sun haloing it, the exact color of flame. Her beauty was regal; there was pride written in every line of her superb body, sitting tall and erect in the saddle.

"Come here," she said to Guy.

Guy came forward, straightening his body in unconscious imitation of Wes' princely carriage.

"Yes'm?" he said. There was not the faintest hint of humility in his tone. He was Wes Falks' son and he meant to be worthy of it. He could see the anger flaming in those ice green eyes.

"Where's your father?" she demanded.

"Out riding," Guy said, trailing a long and deliberate pause before he added, "ma'am. . . ."

"When he comes back," Rachel Falks said, "you tell him for me that my husband is unaccustomed to being summoned by his overseer. If he wants to see Mister Gerald he'd better ride up to Fairoaks and ask for him—at the back entrance. Now repeat what I told you. I want to see if you've got it right."

"No," Guy said.

"No?" Rachel snapped. "What's the matter with you, boy? Haven't you wit enough to remember a few simple words?"

"I remember all right," Guy said quietly. "Only nobody talks like that to my Pa, lady."

"Why you little hillbrat! I've a good mind to—"

"I wouldn't try it if I was you, lady," Guy said, still in that flat, dead calm voice. "I'm a Falks, ma'am. And people most in generally don't threaten a Falks. They most in generally knows better. Besides—" hearing now the thunder of the stallion's returning hoofbeats, "if you wait about half a minute, you can tell him yourself. . . ."

Rachel Falks whirled in the saddle. She was just in time to see Wes Falks, riding bareback, and with a rope halter for a bridle, lift the black stallion that no one up until now had been able to dominate, over the twelve-bar gate that also had never been jumped, with a soaring, effortless grace that beggared the imagination.

He drew the horse up with easy skill before her.

"Why Cousin Rachel," he said mockingly, "I'm honored. And what may I do for her ladyship, may I ask?"

Seeing her face, then, at that moment, Guy was aware of the warfare being waged inside her soul. But he didn't know the cause of it. This was a thing for which neither experience nor imagination had prepared him. But Rachel, being herself of the breed of the strong, very quickly mastered the confusion inside her; more, recognizing the tight dryness at the base of her throat, the hammering of the blood within her veins, the loosening, the slackening, the scalding of loins for what they were, she had to turn her fury at her own sudden weakness, her bitter self-contempt outward, purify herself of feelings that she, like all women of her time and of her station, had been taught to believe were beneath her, the attributes of the low, the fallen among womenkind. Unfortunately, never having known any other Falks beside her husband, and being far too outraged to analyze the character of which the mastery of the black stallion was but a single example, she turned her fury upon Westley Falks.

"I came to tell you," she said, "that my husband is unaccustomed to being summoned by his overseer. And further, any time you wish to see Mister Falks, you may ride up to the house and ask for him—at the back entrance. Do I make myself clear?"

"Perfectly," Wes said. "Clearer than maybe you even mean to, Rachel. Your husband's not accustomed to being sent for by his overseer, but he's damned well used to being ordered by his wife. I call that plumb, downright shameful. Then there're a couple of points you're forgetting, Rachie—or maybe you didn't know. I'll give you the benefit of the doubt on that—"

"Don't call me Rachie!" she spat. "Do I have to teach you your place, Wes Falks?"

"Don't reckon you need to, seeing as how I know my place a damned sight better than you do, Rachie," Wes said. "Now shut up and listen to me. I'll make it short. First: you're talking to a man. Second: the next time you presume to come down here to tell me anything whatsoever, I'll take a riding crop to you like Jerry ought to, if he were a man, which he sure Lord isn't. Third: My pa built Fairoaks, planted it, made it flower. Only mistake he ever made was to feel sorry for his good-for-nothing brother, my uncle Brighton, and let that slimy little weasel you married onto the place. I can't prove Jerry stole Fairoaks from me, but I wouldn't put it past him—"

"I won't listen to this!" Rachel got out. "I won't—"

"Look, Rachie," Wes said patiently, as though he were explaining a difficult matter to a backward child. "You keep

38

on making the same mistake. I'm a Falks—a real Falks, not a shoddy imitation like Jerry. And people don't tell a Falks what they won't do. 'Specially not women. The Falks' women speak when they're spoken to, and then quietly. I'm trying to be patient; but you're trying me sorely. Now listen like a good girl and don't rile me. I'll come to see Jerry if it suits my convenience; if it doesn't, I won't. I'll run this place for him, and run it damned well, however questionable his right to own it is; and believe me, Rachie, it's damned questionable. But I won't be treated like an underling; I won't be dictated to by anybody; 'specially not by a miserable little polecat who sends his wife to do errands he's not man enough to do himself. And I'll turn on a spit in deep blue hell before any goddamned woman will tell me anything whatsoever! And now, Missus Falks, I trust I've made myself abundantly clear?"

"Oh!" Rachel gasped, her mouth twisted, seeking for words. But they did not come. Wes turned to the gaping Negro.

"Zeb," he said mockingly, "please open the gate for the lady. I think she wants to go. . . ."

Rachel yanked her mount's head savagely around and thundered towards the gate.

"Tell Jerry," Wes called after her, "I'm still waiting for his visit. And I don't like waiting. . . ."

Rachel brought her riding crop down against the mare's flank so hard that the animal screamed and leaped forward, almost unseating her.

"Pa!" Guy cried out. "Pa, she's lost the reins!"

Wes clapped his heels against the black stallion's sides. As docilely as the tamest beast upon the land, the horse started out after Rachel. Guy was aware that his father was holding the great horse back. He could have caught Rachel in the first three bounds. But he didn't. The two horses stretched themselves out in a long, smooth gallop, cutting away from the road across the fields, racing toward the *chêne du bois,* the oakgrove, miles away on the border of the plantation.

The two boys and the Negro stood there watching the mounts and their riders diminishing, becoming diminutive with the distance, merging finally with the gathering dusk of the evening, with the lengthening shadows of the oakgrove.

"Funny," Tom said. "Pa could of caught her afore now. . . ."

Guy stared at his brother. The thoughts inside his mind

were vague and formless, but black and bitter for all that.

They stood there for perhaps ten minutes, waiting while the shadows extended themselves across the yard and the last patch of light dimmed into darkness. A star stood above the house and winked at them.

Zeb cleared his throat.

"You boys better fotch yoreselves long to bed," he growled. "Hit's gitting mighty late. . . ."

They moved off, then, to the house. Half an hour later Tom was already snoring, but, for the life of him Guy could not sleep.

He lay like that, miserably, until the first light of dawn was greying the windows. Then, at long last, he heard his father's booted feet upon the stairs.

Wes Falks came into the room and stood there looking down at his son. Guy had the feeling that his face was grey with weariness; or perhaps it was the quality of the light falling upon it—he didn't know. But what was unmistakable was the triumph in his father's smile.

Guy yawned and stretched as though he were just waking up.

"Pa," he said sleepily. "That ol' Miz Rachel—mighty mean woman, ain't she?"

Wes threw back his head and laughed aloud.

"Tell you a secret, son," he said, "and don't you ever forget it. Wild horses—and wild women—are always the best!"

3

Guy got up from the breakfast table and sauntered out toward the stables. His stomach was as tight as a drum from the mountain of buckwheat cakes, sausages and corn syrup he had eaten, the whole of it washed down with nigh onto half a gallon of the best coffee he'd ever tasted. He whistled as he went, finding the world a warm and good place where a body had more grub than he could possibly tuck away, a soft bed to sleep in and a whole new, st—ely magical life to explore. A life that bred men like Wes Falks, striding towering and unafraid across the sweep of fields, lords of all they surveyed. . . .

He found that Zeb had already saddled two nags, a bony roan and a diminutive grey. The grey really wasn't too bad, especially for him, but he knew his father would shout and damn the roof down the minute he saw that miserable roan gelding.

"Look, Zeb," he said firmly, "Pa'll never set himself astride that there hatrack. Come on, take the saddle off him and put it on the black. I'll help you—"

"Lord, Marse Guy," Zeb said, "I ain't gonna have no truck with Demon! Don't you know that there stallion'll kick us both into Kingdom come if we gits nigh him?"

"Not now," Guy said confidently. "Pa's plum broke him. Wait, I'll show you."

He marched straight up to the stall where Demon was. He put out his hand, and the great black shied a little. But something—curiosity, perhaps—made the stallion put his head forward again; and Guy stroked him gently. The horse jerked once more, but less this time. Then, apparently, Demon decided that he liked the feel of the boy's caress. He put his head forward, contentment in his eyes. Guy took hold of the rope and turned to Zeb with a grin.

"Take the bars down," he said.

Wonderingly the Negro did so, and the boy led the great stallion, as docile as any lamb, out into the courtyard.

"Well, I never!" Zeb gasped. "Who would of ever thought it!"

In five minutes they had Demon saddled. A minute or two later, Guy saw his father coming from the house. A body could never have guessed, from Wes Falks' appearance, that he had not slept at all. He walked with a jaunty air, humming a tune under his breath. When he saw the stallion, his dark eyes lighted.

"Good work, boy!" he said. "I came down here in a hurry for fear you'd try to saddle him. I reckoned he'd still be a mite skittish. But I should have known that you could handle him. Well, come on now. Reckon we'd better make the rounds. . . ."

They mounted then, and set off around the house at a brisk canter. But when they reached the front yard, Wes pulled Demon up and sat there, his face slowly purpling. Guy came up to his father and stared, seeing the same thing Wes did, but being unable to recognize what there was in it that should awake Wes' all too easily aroused fury.

Charity and Matty were in the yard, hoes and scythes in hand, busily attacking the overgrowth of brush. Guy watched while his father climbed down from the horse and walked toward them without haste, as controlled and silent as a great cat. When he was close enough, Wes' hands shot out, blurring sight with the speed of the motion. Charity cried out just once; but Wes wrenched the hoe out of her hand with one easy motion and hurled it into the brush. Then he turned on Matty.

"Pa!" Matty shrilled.

"Give me that scythe, Matty," Wes said quietly. "Come on, give it to me!"

Silently Matty handed it over. Wes sent it sailing, whirling like a boomerang, high over the tree tops. Then, once more, he turned to his wife.

"Reckon you can't help being a fool, Charity," he said, "seeing as how you were born one. But before you do anything around here, for the love of God have the simple horse sense to ask me if you ought to!"

"I wasn't doing nothing wrong, Wes," Charity quavered. "You said yourself that this here yard—"

"Listen, Char," Wes said, "I'm going to explain things to you, this once. I don't want to have to do it again, not ever. You are my wife, and, as such, you're mistress of this part of Fairoaks. You've got to forget that you're hill trash born and bred. You've got to learn to act like a lady. And ladies don't weed gardens! That's what we've got niggers for. A lady can sew and embroider and tend the sick. A lady supervises the housework and the gardening. But she does not do them herself—not even once! I'll never be able to straighten out these niggers now—once they've seen my wife and daughter doing field hands' work! Get back into the house, both of you! In a little while I'm going to send a couple of hands down here. Then you come out and tell them what you want done.

"Another thing—tomorrow or the next day, I'm going to call in a yellow wench I know to take yours and Matty's measurements for some dresses. Don't you dare tell her how you want 'em made, 'cause you haven't the faintest idea how a lady ought to dress. I'll tell her. And don't you invite her to sit down or have some tea or anything, for all that she's damn near as white as you are, if not whiter. She hasn't but one drop of nigger blood, but one drop's enough. Do you understand?"

"Yes, Wes," Charity whispered.

"Good. Next time you feel the urge to do some blame fool thing—you ask me. All right, boy—let's get going. . . ."

They moved out of the yard together, riding with the easy grace of men who have spent all their lives in the saddle, heading for the south acres where the Negroes worked under the sun. When they reached the fields the lead hand looked up and, without a word, increased his pace from a snail-like crawl to a speed approximating one-half the rate that any indifferent Ohio or Illinois farm hand could have managed without effort.

"You see, son," Wes said, pointing with his crop, "it doesn't make sense. I'm not a man to split hairs over the rightness or wrongness of slavery. But what it is, is economic nonsense. One thing I learned a long time ago is that a nigger's nobody's fool—for all that he's mighty damn careful to act like one most of the time. It's harder than old hell to get a good day's work out of a hired hand, let alone a creature who's got absolutely nothing to gain from the work he's doing. A man's got to have something to dream on: for instance that the land is his, or is going to be. That tomorrow he's going to have a fine house, the day afterwards a carriage; and that a little later on his son is going away to college to come back a lawyer or a fancy sawbones. We do the best we can, but cotton ruins the land in the first place, and the niggers don't half tend it in the second. And we can't make 'em. We can put a rawhide to 'em and get some action out of them for half an hour—or maybe half a day. But we can't beat 'em into matching the production of free labor—not by half, maybe not even by one third. We can't, because our arms would give out before we could whip 'em enough; and being decent folks at heart, we don't even have the stomach for it. . . ."

"Then why don't we just give up?" Guy said.

"Because we can't do that either. 'Cause we're caught up in it. We're the slaves, really—slaves to the system we created, to a system that the Yankees have crowded us into defending so hard that we can't back down now, neither in pride nor in honor. Yep, we're enslaved: to a system that doesn't make a damn bit of sense from the economic point of view, to a passel of burr-headed black bastards who don't give a damn, and who, when you think about it logically, hadn't even ought to

. . . Come on, now, let's move along and see what the rest of them are doing. . . ."

But, long before they reached the west acres, they saw Gerald Falks riding toward them, mounted on one of the dappled greys that were Fairoaks' pride. At his side, sitting side saddle on a milk-white pony as round as a barrel, his daughter rode. Wes pulled Demon up and waited, his dark face tightening. But Gerald's expression was the picture of serenity.

"Heard you had words with Rachel," he said easily. "Don't mind her, Wes. She's a bit high strung, and I have spoiled her. Incidentally, I didn't send her to chew your ears off; that was her own idea. Seems she found the ears tougher than she's accustomed to. Anyhow, forget it, will you?"

Wes Falks stared at his cousin, the contempt in his eyes unmasked.

"No offense taken," he said shortly. "I've met high-flown fillies before—"

"Good," Gerald said. "Now, what did you want to see me about?"

"An advance," Wes said. "My kids are plumb mother-naked. They could go round in calico and butternut breeches up there in the hills, but down here's another thing. . . ."

"Of course," Gerald said. "Any thing you need, Wes—you know that." He turned to his daughter. "Jo Ann," he said, "why don't you show your cousin about? His daddy and I have business to talk about. . . ."

"All right," Jo Ann said. "Come on, Guy—"

Wordlessly, Guy brought his grey alongside the white pony. They moved off, Guy holding the grey back to keep from outdistancing Jo Ann's diminutive mount.

"Don't you ever talk?" Jo Ann said.

"Sometimes," Guy said, "when there's something fitten to say. . . ."

"And when is that?" Jo Ann demanded.

"Don't know. It depends—"

"Depends on what?"

"Oh, you ask too many questions!" Guy said, and kicked his mount into a gallop. A moment later, he was sorry. Despite his best efforts the white pony was a hundred yards behind. Guy pulled the grey up and waited until Jo Ann caught up with him.

"You sure can ride!" Jo Ann said admiringly.

Guy reddened.

"Shucks," he said; "'t ain't nothing. . . ."

"Don't say ain't," Jo Ann corrected him, primly. "It isn't right. You're a Falks, remember. You'd better learn to talk like a gentleman . . ."

Guy leaned forward, all his hunger for knowledge vibrant in his tone.

"Will you teach me?" he asked. "Never had much book-learning, nohow. Will you, Jo?"

"Of course," the tiny goddess said. "Come on, let's ride down by the pool. . . ."

So it began, the first of many days of enchantment. They rode together, laughed together, swam, after Guy had taught her to swim, together in the pool; because, even at fourteen, Guy had not outgrown the innocence of childhood. Neither of them regarded each other's nakedness as anything very special.

But, beyond that, there was another thing, as resplendent as it was rare: Then, in the long days of that first summer—with the warm breezes drifting the Johnson grass, with the voice of the turtle mourning in the pinewood, and the hounds sorrowing through the oakgrove, bugling their ancient lament of pursuit and death, far off and sad like bells plunged in the wind, drowned in the immensity of air—they learned to love one another—long before their bodies' insistent demands could enter into it, years before they would stand pressing mouth to mouth bewildered by their blood. So, when the other should come to them, they already had something to base it upon; so that, the dark magic of seeking hands and entangled limbs would never in them entirely supersede the bright magic of companionship, of liking each other, of belonging. And this was a good thing, and very rare.

On a fall day they rode through the *chêniere,* through a shower of dead leaves, red and golden, wind-drifted.

"I can't come tomorrow," Jo Ann said. "I have to start my lessons again. Miss Branwell's coming—oh, darn!"

"I wish," Guy said, "I had some lessons to start. There's so much to learn; and a body wearies himself with nothing to do. . . ."

Jo Ann turned in the saddle, looking at him.

"I'll do it!" she squealed. "I'll ask Papa right now!"

"You'll ask your papa what?" Guy said morosely.

"If you couldn't come every day and have lessons with me! After all, you've got to be educated. Oh, Guy, come on! Let's go ask him, now!"

"He'd never," Guy said.

"Oh yes, he would!" Jo Ann said complacently. "My daddy will do anything I ask him. Come on!"

They rode up to the house together. One of the Negroes came out and took the reins.

Jo Ann seized Guy by the hand and started up the stairs.

"I don't know," Guy said. "I've never been inside . . . Maybe your Ma wouldn't like it. . . ."

"Oh, don't worry about her!" Jo Ann laughed. "She's changed a lot this summer. She doesn't yell half as much as she used to. Papa says he can't imagine what's got into her. . . ."

They went up the stairs into the gallery, and from there into the big hall. Guy hung back, staring. His unaccustomed eyes were stricken with the splendor of the immense cut-glass chandeliers, tinkling like a million crystal bells in the moving air, and the carpets into which his feet sank ankle-deep. There was the soft glow of furniture—richly sombre, polished by loving hands—the curtains and drapes, which alone cost more than the house he now lived in; and from the walls, row upon row, there frowned down the ancestral Falks, martial and stern, their dress changing generation by generation, back to the plumed, powdered, curled and be-wigged splendor of the chevaliers, resplendent in shot silks and laces.

Here before him were the materials for dreaming; here were his people—always, from the beginning, of the elect, lords and ladies, all of them, the men of commanding visage, the women of unsurpassed loveliness.

He felt the spur of pride rowel him all along his length. He stiffened, fire leaping and dancing in his dark eyes.

"I'm a Falks!" he whispered to himself. "I come from these people! From great folks like these, and I'm going to be—"

"Oh, come on!" Jo Ann said.

She pushed open the door to the study, and stopped. Her father's voice came over to them, clearly.

"But there must be some explanation, Rachel. You were never given to riding about all hours of the night. If you can't sleep, I'll have Doctor Williams prescribe—"

"But I like to ride in the darkness," Rachel said. "It's a wonderful, wonderful feeling, Jerry. Taking the onrush of darkness, the wind whirling backwards behind you—but you wouldn't understand that. You've always suffered from a certain lack of imagination—among the many other things you suffer from. . . ."

"Perhaps," Gerald's voice was ice suddenly, brittle as crystal, "I have more imagination than you give me credit for, Rachel. I've had to curb it a bit, here of late. Don't insist that I give it rein. The consequences might be—"

Then, startlingly, the silver peal of Rachel's laughter cut him short.

"Disastrous?" she laughed. "Perhaps, Jerry—but for whom? You've curbed your imagination, you say. And why, my little capon? Because at heart you're a coward, and you know it. Doesn't pay to imagine too much, does it? You're wrong, of course, in what you think—more's the pity—"

"Rachel!"

She went on serenely, as though she had not heard him.

"Or else you might have to learn just what a Falks is—and a man—"

"As you have learned?"

"I have not learned," Rachel said sadly, "anything more, Gerald Falks—if you have any right to call yourself that— than the shape and dimensions of a man's honor. Which is another thing you wouldn't understand. But don't crowd me, Jerry, or I might—"

"Papa," Jo Ann said, "I want—"

Her parents whirled, staring. Gerald caught his wife's eye.

"Do you think they—?" he began.

"No. And if they did, they didn't understand," Rachel said. "Come in, both of you. Now what the devil do you want?"

"I want Guy to come and have lessons with me," Jo Ann said firmly. Her mother did not awe her. There was between them, even then, the budding root of what might grow into pure enmity.

"Well," Gerald hesitated, looking at Rachel.

"Oh," she said, "let him. He is, after all, a Falks—and, from what I've seen of him, a real one."

She moved toward the children and suddenly put out her hand, letting it rest on Guy's dark head.

"You'll do," she said kindly. "In fact, you'll more than

47

do. I rather think you'll amount to something. After all, you do have the right stuff in you. . . ."

So it began: the second element that went into his being. Or in truth, continued rather than began. For his father had begun to teach Guy when he was eight years old—and already growing lean and sinewy—to spell out words before the intermittent flare and splutter of the pine knot fire.

In Guy there was that twin glory and curse: intelligence. He needed little teaching; in days, he was actually reading, his eyes flying across the lines of print too fast for his finger, which, until then, had led to keep up.

From then on, he had been limited only by the almost total lack of anything to read. But this, Jo Ann had ended, for the library at Fairoaks contained a world, an infinity of books. He waded through them, devoured them, gorged himself to repletion upon them. Then, when his mind could hold no more of the enormous quantity of undigested information he had crammed into it, in the unconscious desire to give himself time for reflection, or perhaps simply in surrender to the intense and contradictory duality of his nature, he would suddenly bang shut his books and disappear into the woods—still virgin at that time, even the trails that the Chickashaw had left were grown over again—carrying the rifle his father had bought him, with malice aforethought, as a medicine against the books. He would be gone for hours, days even, returning to lead the Negroes with unerring directness to the skinned, drawn and hung carcass of a deer.

And the forests, too, became his mentor. He learned to locate the North by the thickness of moss on that side of the oaks, or by the pole star; to read by the bend of brush the size and weight of the animal which had passed through it; to tell to the hour how long ago a hooved or claw-armed print had been pressed into the damp earth; even by some instinct to tell what a painter or a bear was going to do next, so that he could be there, ready at a stand when the beast appeared.

The day after his sixteenth birthday he was riding alone on the grey that Gerald Falks had given him as a birthday present, with the wry remark: "Anybody who can ride as you do deserves a decent mount . . ." Riding alone, because, by now, he had become aware of his body, and the childish presence of ten-year-old Jo Ann irked him in some vague and formless fashion he was unable to put words to. He was irked even more by the persistent invasion of his privacy by the younger serving wenches who found excuses to enter his room: "This the way you likes yore shirts pressed, Marse Guy? You wants me to bring you something to eat afore you goes to bed?"—letting their dark and slumberous eyes move lingeringly, caressingly over the whole lean length of him, as tall as his father now, though not yet as wide. And, upon leaving, they would give to their tight African buttocks a more provocative roll and sway, so that he was driven to an approximation of his father's fury, crying:

"I don't want anything! Goddamn it, get out of here!"

Alone. The grey stallion, very nearly pure Arab, was a marvel of speed and fiery, nervous docility. He took fences as though he were half bird; the air, as well as the earth, was almost his native element. It was for this that the boy had named him Pegasus; for he was, in truth, very nearly winged.

Guy had ridden far, coming now to the borders of the Mallory Place—a plantation almost as imposing as Fairoaks itself—and to which there clung an even darker increment of legend: of wives driven to madness and suicide by the male Mallorys' constant and spectacular adulteries with Negro women.

Guy had heard the stories—heard them and dismissed them as being clearly beyond belief. For, from whatever trace of Charity Nance's hill trash blood coursed through his veins, he had inherited the poor white's ferocious and icy contempt for Negroes one and all, and a very nearly perfect inability to see what any white man could find desirable in a black wench.

He was not thinking about that now. He was not thinking about anything at all, having surrendered with pagan completeness to the intoxication of the ride, soaring now over the last fence without ever recognizing that by so doing he had left Fairoaks and become a trespasser upon the Mallory lands, an act which the Mallorys had been known to resent with the furious impatience for which they were already famous.

Almost at once, he saw the girl. He drew the grey up and sat there looking at her. She was dressed like a house servant, but her skin was white, or very nearly. Rather, it was the color of hunters, of trappers, of all people who lingered over-long in the sun. Golden, his mind formed the words: golden on top with dusk rose underneath—Lord God!

Her hair was black, and plaited into braids like an Indian's; they hung loose, falling below her waist. She was the same age as he was, or perhaps a year older. She stood there, staring back at him; then, very slowly, the full-lipped, wine-red mouth shaped itself into a smile.

"Howdy," she said simply.

"Who're you?" he growled.

"Phoebe," she said.

"Phoebe?" he echoed. "Phoebe what?"

"Just Phoebe. Don't have no other name. Lessen you wants to call me Mallory. Reckon I got some rights to that one, too. . . ."

"Then you're—"

"Yep. One of them yaller Mallory yard children you done heard about. Now you know. But I might ask you the same thing, young master. Who you?"

"Guy Falks," he answered shortly. "Which way is the house?"

"That way," Phoebe answered, pointing. "Don't go yet. Set and talk a spell. Anybody ever tell you you's one mighty handsome man?"

"No!" Guy said furiously, "and I don't need to be told, 'specially not by the likes of you!"

He clapped spurs to the grey and bounded off, hearing behind him the silvery lift and soar of her laughter. It did not help the state of his mind at all.

He was so consumed with anger that he came upon the little group in the pasture almost before he saw them. They turned at the sound of the hoofbeats and stared at him. Their bodies, turning, broke the grouping so that now he could see the object they had been looking at: the calf lying there with its throat torn out, and beyond that the marks made by its having been dragged ten full yards by the marauding beast that had killed it.

He got down and walked over to it.

"What did it?" he said.

"Wolf," the boy his own age said. "Big one—look!"

Guy stared at the prints. Then he shook his head.

"Nope," he said. "There aren't any wolves in Mississippi any more. That there's a dog. Bull mastiff, I'd say. Maybe

50

one of those hound and mastiff mixtures they use to catch runaway niggers. Gone wild. . . ."

The boy turned to his father.

"You know, Dad," he said, "he's right! Remember that brindle bitch who was whelping when she disappeared three years ago? She was nearly pure mastiff anyhow. . . ."

"Too big," the father said. "That print's the size of a Great Dane's—even bigger. And the animal that dragged a calf that far must have been the size of a Shetland pony himself. . . ."

"Gone wild," Guy repeated. "Reverted to type. They'd grow bigger in the woods."

"You," Alan Mallory said, "know a mighty heap for a boy. Who the devil are you, anyhow? And I hope you realize you're trespassing. . . ."

"No," Guy said firmly. "Not trespassing—visiting. I'm Guy Falks, Mr. Mallory."

"Wes Falks' sprout," Alan Mallory said. "No wonder. Yes, it figures: the set, the looks, the carriage and the nerve. Glad to meet you, son. I'm Alan Mallory, and this is my son, Kilrain. . . ."

Guy shook hands with them both.

"If you don't mind, Mr. Mallory," he said, "I'd like to get that dog for you. If somebody doesn't get him he'll run through all your stock—and ours, too."

Alan Mallory stared at Guy a long, slow time.

"Yes," he said. "Reckon you could, at that. Your niggers have spread the word all over the county what a hunter you are. Go to it, boy, I've no objections. . . ."

"I'll come with you, Guy," Kilrain said.

Guy looked at the boy. Kilrain Mallory was tall and well muscled; but he wasn't a woodsman. Anybody with half an eye could see that. He'd be good enough in the saddle; but in the brush, where you had to walk and be mighty damned quiet about it, he'd be a nuisance—or worse. He'd get in the way, and make it impossible to ever find the dog. Slowly Guy shook his head.

"Don't reckon you know enough," he said. "It won't be play, Kilrain."

"Well, I'll be damned!" Kilrain exploded. "You got your nerve! Hill trash like you, coming onto my place, and play acting like a gentleman! I tell you—"

"I'm on your place, all right," Guy said quietly, "and as

51

such, sort of like a guest. Which is why I'm going to over-look what you said. But your father knows mine—and he can tell you that people don't talk to us like that—not ever. And anyhow, you've made me change my mind. I'll meet you here in an hour. Bring your gun. We'll go after him together. That way, maybe you'll find out what I am—or maybe what you are, yourself, though I hope you don't—'cause I don't think you'll like knowing. . . ."

He turned back to Alan Mallory.

"Good day, Sir," he said formally, and swung himself into the saddle.

Alan Mallory looked at his son.

"Go get your gun," he said coldly, "and next time, don't be so free with your insults. Because, whatever that boy's mother was, it's mighty clear that Wes Falks has bred himself a man. . . ."

When Guy cleared the fence again—clad this time in his hunting buckskins, powder horn slung about his shoulder, knife at his side and the long Pennsylvania flintlock in his left hand—the girl, Phoebe, was there, waiting.

"Howdy!" she called. "Howdy, Mister mighty handsome Guy Falks!"

"Oh, get out of my way!" Guy grated, and pounded on toward the pasture. Kilrain, having a shorter distance to come, was there before him. He was dressed in the finest hunting greens, and his rifle was scrolled and engraved all over. It was a good gun, Guy saw at once; and from the way young Mallory handled it, it was apparent he knew how to use it.

But, seeing his booted feet, Guy frowned.

"Haven't you got any moccasins?" he asked. "Boots make too much noise. . . ."

"No. Sorry," Kilrain said shortly.

"Reckon you'll have to walk in your socks when we get close, then," Guy said. "All right, now, come on."

They rode to the edge of the forest and dismounted, tethering the horses. Then they entered the woods, Guy leading and Kilrain a yard or two behind. Guy saw almost at once that he had misjudged the boy; the Mallorys, whatever else they might be, were neither fools nor cowards.

Kilrain, despite his boots, made surprisingly little noise.

52

Guy moved like a ghost, a shadow, his head bent above the great paw prints that went on and on, ever deeper into the forest. When it was too dark to follow the trail any more, they made camp. Kilrain pitched in, building the fire with expert skill.

Guy watched him, then, suddenly, impulsively, he put out his hand.

"I apologize," he said. "You're all right. I'm glad I met you. . . ."

"Me, too," Kilrain laughed. "And I'm sorry for what I said. Reckon we'll make quite a team, Guy. . . ."

Without talking they ate the hard tack and bacon from the knapsacks and then slept beside the fire, banked to keep going all night, until it was morning. Then they set out again, following the cooling trail until they lost it at a stream's edge. They could see the tracks going into the water, but there was no sign of their coming out.

"That's no dog," Guy said. "That's a living college professor. Knew damned well he was being tracked, so he went into the water, and came out a mile or two from here. And the hell of it is, there's no way on earth to tell if he went upstream or down. . . ."

Kilrain stood there frowning. Then he grinned.

"Got it!" he said. "You go upstream, I'll go down. The one who finds the tracks fires a shot and—"

"Nope," Guy said. "He'll hear that shot and get clean out of the county. Besides, we'd better stay together. We'll work upstream for a mile and a half. If we don't find the tracks in that distance, we'll backtrack downstream. One way or another, we'll get him. . . ."

They moved off silently. By late afternoon, having worked two full miles upstream and two down without having found the tracks again, they were on the point of giving up when they heard a crashing in the underbrush. Almost before they could bring their rifles to cock, a great stag burst into the clearing by the stream's edge, his eyes rolling in terror.

Kilrain's rifle came up, the motion easy, practiced, sure. He held his sights on the stag's chest a fraction of a second, then his finger caressed the trigger. The gun crashed, and the stag, dead on his feet, came on, propelled by a strength that for some moments exceeded life. Then he somersaulted and his great pronged antlers dug into the earth, causing him to roll head over heels. They could hear the bones of his neck breaking. The red-gold mass of his body completed the arc, going into the stream; the water rose from the impact like white wings, then folded again to receive him.

And before Guy could cry out his furious thought: You fool! Why didn't you hold your fire? Didn't you know it must be the dog? He wouldn't bugle, not being a hound, just would come on, silent and sure like. . . .

Now. Like a brindled ghost, bigger than any dog had any right to be, with eyes lambent and flamelike, absolutely wanting in fear. Not pausing, not breaking his stride, just rising up, soaring effortlessly up, graceful and sure, so that his weight, striking Kilrain in the chest, bowled the boy over. Guy, seeing the impossibility of firing even at that point-blank range without running the risk of hitting Kilrain, leaped upon the dog's back and thrust his left hand between its gaping jaws an instant before the long and yellowed fangs could close upon Kilrain's throat. He felt as though it were happening to someone else: the searing, the burst of pain, as the dog's teeth closed upon his hand, closed and held. . . .

Without haste, having all the time in the world to do it, he groped for and found the handle of the knife, while Kilrain rolling free from beneath the mastiff picked up Guy's rifle, and stood ready, being, as Guy had been before, unable to fire and for the same reason; watching helplessly while Guy reached around the furious animal and pushed the blade into its throat up to the hilt. He probed until he found both the jugular vein and the windpipe; and the dog, going down, the flame dulling in the lambent eyes, even then strangling to death in his own blood so that the red tide pumped out of his nostrils, still did not loosen the fangs which had passed entirely through Guy's left hand, not even when the great heart had given its last convulsive beat.

Not even in death. Guy knelt there, his face white.

"He's dead," he said. "Pry his teeth loose, Kil—"

Kil knelt beside him, working with his own knife. The jaws loosened finally, and Guy drew out his mangled left hand. When Kilrain saw it he vomited.

Guy walked steadily to the stream's edge, and bathed the hand. The cold water stung with all the fury of hell.

"Cut me a piece of your shirt tail, Kil," he said.

Shame-facedly, Kilrain did so, and even managed, with trembling fingers, to bandage the hand for Guy.

54

Guy walked back to where the dog lay, and stood there looking down at him.

"Sorry I had to kill you, ol' fellow," he said. "You and I would have made a pair—"

Then, for the first time, feeling the reaction—the weakness, shock and nausea—he moved over to a tree and sat down.

"Look, Guy," Kilrain said. "You're bad hurt. Come on, I'll help you. We'd better get out of here and to a doctor. . . ."

"No," Guy said. "Reckon I couldn't make it now, Kil. You get back to the house and bring your father and some niggers. . . ."

"And the doctor," Kilrain said. "That hand's bad, Guy—"

"If you like. But anyhow, get going. Before you leave, though, you better put that gun over here where I can reach it, in case the carcasses attract a painter. . . ."

Kilrain stood there staring at Guy, his face working. He wanted to cry, but he would have died before letting Guy see his weakness.

"Guy," he whispered, "You—you saved my life. Reckon that makes us friends for keeps—"

"Oh, for God's sake, get going," Guy said.

But he had reckoned without Kilrain's inexperience. Young Mallory, like any greenhorn, proceeded to get himself hopelessly lost before he had gotten five hundred yards from the clearing. He blundered about, circling all night long; and when he dropped, just before morning, under an oak, holding his head and crying, he not only was no closer to the field on the woods' edge where they had left the horses, but actually a mile or two further away.

Before daylight that same morning, already a little delirious with fever from the rapidly mounting infection those yellow fangs had caused, Guy, realizing what must have happened, set out on his own. Kilrain, having got up again, lacking, as he did, both the wit and the experience to stay where he was until his strength came back to him, was wandering, half dead of exhaustion, in ever widening circles, crossing and recrossing his own trail.

It was a measure of how sick he was that Guy, himself, lost the homeward path for a time. But when, in the first light of morning, he stumbled on the ruined cabin he had known existed, but which he never used because that part of the forest had been burned, cut over, and had regrown so sparsely that it was useless for hunting, both game and hunter despising its lack of cover, he knew both where he was and how to orient himself.

He leaned against a tree, feeling the pain in his hand bad, very bad. The hand was grotesquely swollen, and he, himself, close to despair, was resting before taking the trail once more. And it was then that a woman came to the window of the cabin.

She was naked. He had never seen a full-grown woman naked before in his life. She stood there like a pagan goddess, letting the first shaft of sunlight play over her body, so white that not even the dawn glow could yellow it; and raising her arms, she pushed back the heavy cloud of hair that was, in that light, like flame.

He hung there staring, protected by the forest gloom. Then the man was beside her, his dark and muscular arms, enwrapping that whiteness, and his voice known, beloved, booming:

"Come away from that window, Rachie—no point in showing yourself to the trees. They got no eyes; but I, praise glory, have!"

And he, the boy, fled from there, running, weeping, falling, cursing, getting up again, with rage and sickness deep inside his guts, crying:

"Damn her! Oh damn her damn her damn her and all women whatsoever to hell and back again, whores and bitches all of them, oh damn them all all all!"

4

HE had almost reached the edge of the Mallory fields when he knew he wasn't going to make it. He could see them from where he lay, in a great blaze of sun that danced before his fevered eyes between the wind-flickered curtain of the last trees. He tried to get to his feet, but he couldn't. He lay there, trying to focus his thoughts; but he couldn't do that either. Painfully, he turned over on his stomach and began to crawl. It took him an age, an infinity, to cover two yards. And all the strength he had left. He lay there staring at the fields one scant yard away, with the hot tears furrowing the dirt on his face. But that last yard might as well have been a thousand miles. He was done, and he knew it.

He closed his eyes. A half heart beat later, it seemed to him, though, afterwards, when he came to think of it, he guessed that it must have been much longer, an hour perhaps, or even two, he saw Phoebe standing at the field's edge, peering into the woods.

He called out to her. She did not move, nor did her expression change. He realized then, that though he had shaped her name, no sound had escaped his lips, no word at all. He tried again.

"Phoebe!" he got out. It was a dismal croak; but it was enough.

She dropped her gaze to where he lay; and, at once, with no interval at all, in that curious foreshortening of time that was a part of his delirium, she was kneeling beside him, her face gone white, whispering:

"You's hurt! You's bad hurt! Oh good Lord, Marse Guy—your hand!"

Then the darkness was around about him, within him, dissolving the world. . . .

When he came back again, his hand had been bandaged with a strip of petticoat. He felt something cool and wet inside the bandage, soothing against the wound. He looked up at her wonderingly.

"I put a leaf poultice on it," she said gently, "to draw out the pizen. You'll be all right, now. Put your arm around me, an I'll help you up, Marse Guy. I'll take you up to the big house, and Marse Alan'll send you home—"

"No!" he said furiously; "Can't go home now, Phoebe! My Pa—"

"What about your Pa?" she said.

"Nothing," he muttered. "Help me up, Phoebe. Then take me back into the woods. . . ."

"But you'll die!" she protested. "You needs a roof over your head and some real nursing. Them leaves ought to do some good; but a doctor—"

"No!" he spat. "No goddamned doctor! You do like I tell you, Phoebe!"

She stood there, considering the matter.

"Why can't you go home, Marse Guy?" she said. "Even if you's done something awful, your Pa—"

"Don't mention my Pa!" he screeched. "God damn it, Phoebe, get me up!"

She put her arm under him. He lurched up with all his strength. Then he hung there, clinging to her, while the trees performed a slow and stately dance above his head. They slowed at last into immobility, and he grinned at her.

"Good," he said. "Let's get going, now. . . ."

"I know," she said, talking mostly to herself. "I'll take you to them Richardsons, since you won't go home. . . ."

"Richardsons?" he croaked.

"Some po' shantyboat whitefolks I know. Kind o' looney, but nice. Reckon they's so poor'n downtrodden, they don't even care about a body's not being white. Leaseways, they's always been mighty nice to me—"

"All right," he said. "Let's go there, then. . . ."

It wasn't very far, just to the river's edge, through a shallow angle of the woods. But it took them more than an hour. Every few minutes, Phoebe had to stop so that he could rest.

Then he saw it: a shantyboat tied to the riverbank. Smoke curled lazily from a battered stove pipe; and on the deck, with a fat pig nuzzling contentedly against his side, an old man slept.

"Marse Tad!" Phoebe called out. "Marse Tad!"

"Haarrrumph!" the old man said, and settled quietly back into slumber. But the door, if that crazy collection of warped and broken boards could be distinguished by such a name, flew open, and a girl stepped out into the sunlight.

She was as slim and blond as a water nymph. And nothing, not even the rags she wore, the smudges of soot on her face, the dirt that caked her bare feet, could hide the fact that she was lovely.

"Miss Cathy," Phoebe said, "come here'n give me a hand. This here gentleman's hurt right bad—"

The girl, Cathy, stood there, staring at him with her enormous gazelle's eyes, of a shade between blue and green. Then, with a bound of indescribable grace she was ashore; and her grip upon Guy's arm was like steel.

The two of them got him aboard, and laid him down upon a pallet of rags in the cabin.

"You hongry?" Cathy said.

"Yes'm, thank you," Guy whispered.

"We got some stew. It were for Gramps; but no matter. He got into that jug o' busthead plumb early this morning. Reckon he won't wake up 'til night. Fix him some more afore then. . . ."

"Thank you, Miss Cathy," Phoebe said. "You reckon Marse Tad'll mind if he stays a day or two, 'til he's a mite stronger?"

"Reckon not," Cathy said, her great eyes fixed upon Guy's face. "Gramps most in general don't mind nothing I want to do. . . ."

"And you want to keep me here?" Guy whispered. "Why, Cathy?"

She shook her head, with a sudden motion of pure animal shyness, the long, pale golden hair, as straight as a horse's tail, flying out with the motion.

"Dunno," she muttered. "You's young and—and nice. I— I likes the way you looks. Reckon when you're sound, you must be something mighty fine. . . ."

The stew was good. He fell asleep with the last spoonful half-way to his mouth. When he woke, it was day again. He had slept around the clock. Cathy knelt by the pallet, staring at him. But Phoebe was nowhere to be seen.

"Phoebe?" he said. His voice was so strong it surprised even him.

"Gone. Last night," Cathy said. "Had to be gitting back or them high'n mighty Mallorys would put the pattyrollers after her. Hit's a plumb shame, white as she is, to be treated like a nigger—"

"But she is a nigger," Guy said drily.

"Foolishness. She's whiter'n you," Cathy said. "Want some more stew?"

Guy laughed aloud.

"Don't you ever eat anything but stew?" he asked.

"Sometimes—not real frequent, though. When Gramps sobers up long enough to shoot a deer or trap a 'possum, we have meat. And we eat fish nearly every day. But I reckon stew would be better for you 'til you're stronger. . . ."

She sat on a box, and watched him while he ate.

"Don't you have any other folks besides your Grandpa?" Guy asked.

"Nope. Ma'n Pa's dead. Don't even remember them, it

59

happened so long back. Got a uncle though. He's a sailor. Say—kin you read writing?"

"Yes," Guy said. "Why?"

" 'Cause Gramps got a letter from him. Leasewise we figger it's from him, 'cause he's the only kinfolks we got. Came nigh onto a month agone. Gramps has been talking about finding somebody to read it to us, but talking about a thing and getting 'round to doing it most in general takes Gramps a couple of years. I'll go get it and you can read it to us. . . ."

She was gone then, starting up with that peculiar animal grace of hers.

Half doe, Guy thought. Take a scrubbing brush and some lye soap to her, and she'd be something. . . .

When she came back again, the old man was with her.

"Howdy, son," he said. "You be looking right pert better. . . ."

"I am better, thank you," Guy said. "Your granddaughter says you want me to read you something, sir?"

"Yep. Letter from my boy, Tray," Tad Richardson said. "Mighty fine boy, only a mite wild. Me'n him had words, so he run away and went to sea. Ain't heard from him since afore this here gal was born. Lemme see now—yep—here 'tis. . . ."

He took the letter from his hip pocket. It was creased and so grease-stained that the writing on the envelope was illegible. The stamps were foreign. Guy opened it, and saw that it had been mailed in Havana, Cuba, nearly two months before.

" 'Dear Father,' " he read. " 'I met a Natchez man down here the other day, and he told me that Joe and Mary are both dead, and that you're living with their little girl on a shanty boat near the Mallory plantation. That's why I'm sending you this in care of the Mallorys. Hope they'll be kind enough to give it to you. . . .' "

"They did," Tad Richardson cackled. "Sent it down here by one of their niggers. Go on, son—"

" 'I'm mighty sorry to learn of my brother's death, and his sweet wife's, too. Of course, I didn't know her very well, but she always appeared rightly nice. But what I'm really sorry over, is to learn how hard up you are. Never thought you'd be forced down to that kind of life—' "

"Why, damn me!" the old man roared. "What's wrong with this life, I ask you? We got all the grub a body needs to eat; we don't have to work for nobody; and we got our free-

60

dom! Of all the tomfool notions! Read on, son. . . ."

"So, I'm coming to see you. I'll be sailing in about two weeks; but with schedules depending on the wind and tide, I can't rightly tell you when I'll get there, except to say I ought to arrive in about a month and a half—' "

"Lord God!" the old man whispered. "My boy's coming home!"

"Yes," Guy said, "and from the date of this letter, he ought to be here any day, now. There's not much more; he says: 'When I do, I'm going to buy you a nice little house, and a spread of ground, and pay little Cathy's board and tuition in a good school—' "

"School!" Cathy exploded. "I'll run away first!"

"Don't you worry, Cathy," the old man growled. "I'll soon knock them silly notions plumb out of his head. Me farm? Had enough o' that! Tied to the land, up to my eyes in debt, driving a passel o' worthless niggers. No, thank you! Living like this I'm free. May be a mite untidy, but—What do he say after that, son?"

"Nothing much. Just sends you his love. Reckon I'd better be trying my legs, though, sir. Your son might not like to find a free boarder here. . . ."

"Stuff'n nonsense!" Tad said. " 'Tain't none of his business, nohow. You stay right there, son, 'til you're good'n strong. Cathy, you change that bandage like Phoebe told you?"

"Yes, Gramps. Put them leaves on, too. The pizen's plumb nigh all gone. That Phoebe sure is smart—"

"She sure Lord is," Tad Richardson said. "Pity she ain't all white. . . ."

The next afternoon, when Phoebe came to see him, Guy was up and about again. He was sitting on the prow of the shanty boat, with the old man, fishing. Already the two of them had caught nearly a dozen catfish. Guy lay back against a box, the very picture of contentment.

"Hi, Phoebe," he said lazily.

"Just look at you!" she said wrathfully. "The picture o' health, and yore po Pa half out o' his mind from worrying over you! I didn't dast tell him the truth. But sure as shooting, Marse Guy, if you don't skedaddle home right now, I'm agoing to tell where you's at! And I'll bet he'll whale the living daylights outen you when he catches you!"

"Pa's worried?" Guy said. "Why? He ain't got no call to

carry on. I've stayed away two, three days before now, and—"

"They found Marse Kil half dead in the woods," Phoebe said, "and he told 'em how bad you was hurt. So now they thinks you's dead. Yore po Pa is plumb, downright pitiful. Keeps on saying it's all his fault. . . ."

Guy sat there, frowning. Reckon I'm being too hard on Pa, he thought. Should have known he'd take on over me. In a way, I'm all he's got. And he's my Pa. A whorish woman like that Rachel can drag any man to—

"All right, Phoebe," he said. "I'll go home tonight, first dark. Don't you let on until then. I want to surprise, Pa. . . ."

"You better—" Phoebe began, but Cathy interrupted her. "Phoebe," she called. "Come here a minute. . . ."

Phoebe turned and went over to where she sat. Looking over his shoulder, Guy could see them talking earnestly, their heads close together.

Wonder what they're talking about? he thought; then he surrendered once more to the laziness of the day, and dismissed them from his mind.

"Son," Tad Richardson said. "Will you go get my chawing tobaccy? Hit's in a can on the shelf in the cabin. . . ."

"Yes sir," Guy said, and got up. The cabin was dark for all its flimsy construction and the cracks through which the sunlight poured. He found the tobacco finally, and was putting the can back in place, when he heard Cathy through the thin walls, say his name. He stood there, listening.

"But," the girl wailed, "he don't pay me no 'tention a-tall, Phoebe! You say I'm pretty. Can't see where it do me a mite o' good with him . . . Oh, for the Lord's sake, Phoebe-honey, tell me what to do!"

Phoebe's voice, answering, was endlessly sad.

"He sure Lord is one good-looking boy," she said. "And, like I said, you's mighty pretty, Miss Cathy. Reckon I could tell you a thing or two, if you promises me you won't git mad. . . ."

" 'Course not!" Cathy said. "Go on, Phoebe, tell me!"

"You—you ought to wash more frequent, for one thing," Phoebe said, " all over. . . ."

"All over?" Cathy gasped. "I couldn't! Gramps says I'd catch my death—"

"Your grandpa's rightly old," Phoebe said, "and he don't know everything. Quality like the Mallorys washes all over

once a week in w[...]
when it's real hot—"

"Every day!" Cathy ma[...]
nice!"

"They do. So you wash all o[...]
good soap. I'll bring you some. Was[...]
and put some ribbons in it. Put on a [...]
fewer holes . . ."

"But—but this one's all I got," Cathy said.

"Bring you a couple of the old missus' dr[...]
Alan won't miss 'em. He ain't been in her room [...]
died. Be a mite long for you, but I'll take a tuck in the[...]
and—Lordy, Cathy, youall's got a visitor! My, my but he[...]
look fine!"

Guy, the warm, heady feeling of his first conquest lost
in the excitement of the news, flew out on deck. He was in
time to see old Tad Richardson embracing the stranger.
Despite the mass of dirty white whiskers that hid half the old
man's face, Guy could see the resemblance between them.
The stranger clearly, was the old man's son.

Guy hung back, staring at him. Travis Richardson was in
his late forties, a rough-hewn, square-cut, solid-looking man.
He was quite short; but what he lacked in height, he more
than made up in breadth. Guy was sure that one blow from
those enormous fists would flatten a mule. His clothes were
good, but a trifle gaudy; and everything about him: the
wrinkles at the corners of his eyes, his piercing glance, the
slight roll to his walk, bespoke a man who had spent years at
sea.

"Lordy, Tray!" the old man was babbling. "Lordy, but you
do be fine! Cathy! Come here and meet yore Uncle! You, too,
son! Great jumping balls o' fire, but this here's one happy
day!"

Guy waited until Cathy had been presented, and received
her uncle's kiss upon her forehead, before he started forward.
As he did so, he saw, out of the corner of his eye, Phoebe
skipping lightly ashore. A moment later she had vanished into
the woods.

Poor little thing, he thought; hell of a way to have to
live. . . .

Then he went forward to be presented in his turn.

Captain Travis Richardson listened gravely to his father's
somewhat exaggerated account of the hunt that had almost

but tell me,
t be fair fit

Pa are a little
dn't go before
eed each other.
with your own

on the good side
s son. When I left
th a sizable spread
t have come down

ose at my houseboat,
a sight happier here
than ... arm! Besides, you ain't
got no call to ... yourself. That were one
o' the main reasons w... dead set on going to
sea—"

"That's true enough, Pa," Captain Richardson said. "But I was young then, and a fool. Knowing what I do now, I'd have stayed. . . ."

"You mean you're tired of being a sailor, sir?" Guy said incredulously.

"No, son. The sea's a lovely witch that a man never gets entirely shut of. Man and boy, it's held me. Fifteen years before the mast, and five aft, most of them as Master. That's a long time, boy; and part of it was glorious. But it don't pay you back for all the things it robs you of: a snug haven, a wife, kids. . . ."

"Reckon it would be mighty fine, sailing with a Cap'n like you, sir. . . ."

"And I'm a thinking that you'd make a good sailor," Captain Tray said. "I'll be belayed and keelhauled if I don't!"

"Then take me along with you when you go!" Guy said eagerly. "I'll work hard—and I'll learn—"

Captain Tray let his heavy hand fall on the boy's shoulder.

"I'd be glad to, lad," he said gently, "but for two things: first, I may be quitting the sea for good before the year's out, if that little black-haired angel I left behind in Cuba will have me. Aim to run a cane plantation down there. Second, I'd never give any man's son a berth aboard a vessel

I command unless I had that man's permission in writing. Now square away, lad, and look me in the eye: Do you honestly think your pa would let you go?"

"No," Guy said miserably. "Not now, leastwise. Maybe later on, when I'm older. . . ."

"Just as I thought," Captain Tray said kindly. "Tell you what, son. If ever you do get permission, beat your way down to Havana and ask for me. In any waterfront saloon they'll know Cap'n Tray and plot your course for you, direct. Even if I'm beached high'n dry for good by then, I've friends who'll take you aboard on my word. But think well before you embark upon seafaring; for a seaman's life is an uncertain thing. . . ."

"Tell me about it, sir," Guy said.

"Later. Right now I've got to try to knock some sense into my old man's head. Get on with your fishing, lad; while the skipper and I go aft and talk things over. . . ."

"Yes, sir," Guy said, and picked up the pole. A moment later, Cathy sat down beside him. She didn't say anything for a long time, so Guy could hear the muffled roars of old Tad Richardson as the argument went on behind them.

"But I don't want to farm, dang blast it! This here life suits me! Look, Tray, you want to kill yore ol' pa from over-work? What's that? Niggers? Lord God, son, hit's a sight less trouble to work a place yourself than to whup them burr-headed black bastids into doing it. I tell you—"

"Guy," Cathy said shyly.

"Yes, Cathy?" Guy growled.

"Do you—think I'm pretty?" she whispered.

Guy studied her critically. She was a wild woods creature, doe-eyed, sylph-like.

"Yes," he said cruelly. "From the little I can see of you under all that dirt, you are—"

"I—I'm going to wash," she said quickly. "From now on I'm going to be clean. Going to put ribbons in my hair and dress nice and—"

"Why?" he mocked. "Why should you, Cathy?"

She stared at him, her eyes wide with hurt.

"So—so's you'll like me a little, Guy," she said candidly. "I'd do anything to make you like me—"

"Anything?" Guy said flatly. "Tell me, Cathy—just how much territory does that anything take in?"

"Why," she said, and her voice was so brimful of innocence that he felt ashamed; "anything you want me to, Guy—"

"You don't know what you're talking about!" he said gruffly, and turned away from her. He heard her sob and looked at her. But before he could find words of comfort, Captain Richardson and his father were coming forward again.

"He's too tough for me!" Captain Tray sighed. "Besides, I reckon he's right. Farming is rough work for such an old party. This is a nice life—or it could be . . . Can you do me a favor, boy?"

"Yes sir," Guy said at once.

"Hire me a couple of good hands trained to carpentry from one of the neighboring plantations. I'm going to fix this shantyboat up into snug living quarters. Cathy'll have some decent clothes and she'll have to go to school—"

"Oh, no!" Cathy wailed.

"Cathy," Guy said gently, "remember what you said before?"

"Y-y-yes . . ." she sobbed.

"Well, this is a thing you can do that would please me a mighty heap. Go to school. Learn to read and write and cipher and talk like a lady. . . ."

"Yes, Guy," Cathy whispered.

"Know how to handle wimmen already, don't you, son," Captain Tray said. "Can you get me those hands, boy? And a dressmaker?"

"Yes sir," Guy said.

"All right. Be off with you then and get them. Tell their master that I'll pay any reasonable fee—What are you waiting for, lad?"

"I can't get you the niggers before tomorrow, Cap'n," Guy said; "and you promised to tell me about a sailor's life . . . About your own adventures, sir. . . ."

"All right," Captain Richardson said. "First off, I'm a slaver —and I'm not ashamed of it. Seems to me a man's cut to mighty small measure who holds niggers himself and then scorns them as supplies him with 'em. Besides, the tales you hear of cruelty during the middle passage are lies, boy, cut from the whole cloth. Stands to reason, if folks would or could think about it: there's no profit to us in dead Bumboes. We treat 'em as tender as you please. . . ."

He rumbled on, making Guy almost see it: the coffles winding down to the barracoons; the canoes of the Kroomen leaping the broiling surf to bring the slaves aboard, with the

66

great sharks waiting for an upset; the white-winged slaver receiving its cargo, taking the Negroes below, fastening them with leg irons to the lower decks, then moving out, silently, watchful for the Mixed Commission cruisers hovering off shore to lay a shot across their bows. . . .

It was exciting, stirring, and even partially true. Guy was saddened when the tale came to an end. He shook hands with the Captain solemnly, saying: "I'll try to join you, sir, in a year or two. . . ."

"See that you do, Master Falks," the Captain said.

Guy came back that same night to a house plunged in deepest mourning over his supposed death. He pushed open the door of his father's study, and saw Wes sitting there, his back to the door, belaboring with whiskey both his grief and his sense of guilt; linking the two things, making of them, the unrelated, cause and effect, weeping inside his heart the terrible hurt of the strong, the tears of brine and blood, thinking: I did it. I killed my son. Because of whoring after another man's woman God took him away from me to teach me—

Guy tiptoed around the table, and stood there staring at his father's great figure bowed over the bottle.

"Pa," he said. "Pa—"

And Wes, seeing him, rose up, taller than the mountain, than thunder, than cloud, saying:

"Son. My son." Then, crushing the boy in his great embrace, and turning his bloodshot, whiskey-hazed eyes toward heaven:

"My beloved son, with whom I am well pleased. Oh, thank you, God!"

5

Guy sent the Negroes to rebuild the Richardson's shanty boat. as he had promised, and a seamstress to make the dresses Captain Tray ordered for Cathy. But, after a week, when Captain Richardson announced his immediate departure for Cuba, Guy didn't go there any more. His reasons did him credit. At six-teen he already knew the source of the dark and savage hungers that scourged him.

Cathy, no. Be a dirty shame. She's little and sweet, and she don't know what she's saying. Can't get mixed up with her—can't. Be like Ma'n Pa all over again. I'm aiming a sight higher than a river rat's granddaughter. A real lady, like Jo Ann will be. Get stuck with Cathy, and she'll be a millstone around my neck. But, Oh Lord, I want me a girl! A body can't go on this way, fair burning up, and—

Phoebe . . . Phoebe . . . The name entered his mind un-bidden. She's so damn near white; and nobody gives a hoot up a hollow stump about—that. Folks take it as a matter of course that a planter's son has got a yellow wench to pleasure himself with. No danger in that—no danger at all. 'Sides, she likes me, and—I'll go find her now!

But she wasn't in the field beside the fence. Guy rode deeper into the Mallory place, but she was nowhere to be found. He guessed she must be in the house itself and finally, in despera-tion, threw discretion to the winds and sent a Negro to find her. She came almost at once. He sat there on Pegasus, glaring down at her.

"Get up behind me," he growled.

She obeyed him without a word. He turned Peg towards the woods, and followed the stream bed until he came to the clearing where he had killed the great mastiff.

"Get down," he said gruffly.

She did so, and he dismounted, tying Pegasus to one of the smaller trees.

"Didn't 'spec to see no more of you," Phoebe said, "what with Miss Cathy being so sweet on you like she be. . . ."

"Let's not talk about her," Guy said.

"All right," Phoebe said. "What can we talk about, Marse Guy?"

"You. Me. Us. Never thanked you properly for saving my life. I'm mighty grateful, Phoebe. . . ."

"I was glad I could help, Marse Guy," Phoebe said.

There was a silence between them. It went on and on—to the crack of doom, and beyond. Guy sat there cursing him-self for forty-seven different kinds of a fool until, finally, the rage inside him was great enough. He whirled, his hands shooting out, his fingers biting into her shoulders, his mouth on hers now, grinding cruelly. He drew back a moment, his breath rasping.

"Phoebe!" he croaked. His voice was strangling.

"No, Marse Guy," she said quietly.

But he was not to be stopped. He forced her down upon the green earth, tearing at her clothing, searching her body with rapacious hands.

"Marse Guy," she wept. "Please don't—"

"Why not? Why not, Phoebe?"

"Wait. Don't tear my clothes, Marse Guy. You wants, I'll take 'em off myself. But first you got to listen. . . ."

"I'm listening," he said grimly.

"I—I could love you, Marse Guy. For real—like a true woman. But I don't want things—like this. I don't want to be hurt'n torn and shamed. You listening, Marse Guy?"

"Yes," he stormed. "What the hell do you think you are, Phoebe—white?"

"My heart is. And my mind. I ain't no little she-thing, bitch-thing to be used and tossed aside when you's done. This here's my body; and it don't even belong to me. I knows that. I knows it's there for whatever young white master's hot and honing. Only—I reckoned you was different, Marse Guy—"

"Different?" he said, furious at himself for having asked the question, recognizing in it the beginning of defeat; "different how?"

"Finer. Nicer. More gentle like. With a heart what can sympathize, and a mind what can understand—"

"Understand what?" he growled.

"That I'm a woman for true. Be so easy just to let you, Marse Guy . . . Reckon maybe I even wants to, really. But what's between a man'n woman ain't just bodies atwisting'n ascrambling in the dark. It's more than that—it's easing each other, comforting each other, bringing each other peace. Man I bed with's got to like having me around, Marse Guy. Like talking to me, or even not talking to me, a feeling good all over just 'cause I'm there. Like I'll feel 'bout him. Want him with me all the time being good to me not just that way but in all ways. Loving'n cherishing me, like the preacher says. Being with me all the time, eating, sleeping and when we goes down together on our knees, real reverent-like afore the Good Lord, Hisself, in prayer. My man, all my life long, 'til death do us part. That's why I can't be yore little she-thing,

69

bitch-thing, playtoy gal. That's why I can't open up my heart and love you like I could. There's too much 'twixt us, Marse Guy, 'twixt yore folks an' mine—too much death'n hell and misery—"

"Phoebe," he croaked.

"So, if you wants to take me, force me, go right ahead, Marse Guy. I won't fight. But I 'spects you'll wake up tomorrow feeling mighty 'shamed and sick 'cause once in life you wasn't really a true man. You wants it like that, go ahead. You wants to get me with child, who under the law will be Mallory property; your own son, with your own hot, sweet blood in him, a owned thing what can be sold like a mule—"

"Phoebe!"

"Go right ahead. I'll even forgive you. What I don't reckon is—that you'll ever forgive yourself. . . ."

And it was not until then that she saw the rush of anguished tears that were flooding his dark face.

"Oh!" she wept, "I'm sorry! Didn't mean to hurt you, Marse Guy! I'm sorry, so sorry—love me if you wants, do what you wants if that'll make you feel better—"

"No," he said gruffly. "It's me who's sorry, Phoebe. Sorry and ashamed. After all you've done for me. I had to come out here and jump on you like a wild animal and—"

"Don't blame yourself, Marse Guy. You's just young, and you needs a light o' love. They's plenty who'd be happy to give you all you wants whenever you wants. Wish I wasn't such a crazy fool. Be better if I could just turn loose. Specially since what I wants I ain't got no hopes of never getting—not never—atall . . ."

"Why not? You could marry one of your own kind. Not a nigger. One of those good-looking mulatto or quadroon boys. God knows Malloryhill is full of 'em. . . ."

"No," Phoebe said simply. "I couldn't. I need a man, Marse Guy."

"And they?" he prompted.

"Ain't. You's a man. Young as you is you's already a man. Them boys won't never be. Not even if they lives to see ninety. It's plumb different. . . ."

"I don't understand you," he growled.

"Don't need to," Phoebe smiled. "Just be nice to me, Marse Guy—that's enough. That's all I ask. . . ."

She took his left hand gently, and raised it so that the

70

crescent of ragged fang scars, still red and angry against the darkness of his skin, showed.

"This," she said, "this here's part of it. This here scar. It's a badge, a sign of glory, Marse Guy. . . ."

"You're plumb crazy!" Guy said, and tried to draw away his hand; but she held it fast.

"Reckon I am," she said, "but it ain't a thing I can help. This here is the mark of a man. A man don't count costs. He ups and does what's got to be done, and makes the reckoning afterwards. Between your hand, and Marse Kilrain's throat, you didn't need to reckon up; now did you? Just done it; 'cause what it took to do it, you was born with. Now you see?"

"No," Guy spat. "I don't see. Why can't you accept a boy you can have a proper wedding with? I don't—"

She rested her head against his shoulder. He could smell the good smell of her hair, its cleanness.

"Listen," she said flatly. "Lemme talk. Don't stop me. A woman's a lonesome thing. A mixed-up, sorrowing thing. A puny thing needing strength, Guy. Needing, like I said—a man. And a man ain't never no slave. A man can't be bought'n sold like a mule, whipped to work in somebody else's fields. Not never. Critter what can, got no right to claim manhood; don't even know what the power and the glory is. . . ."

"They haven't got a chance," Guy said. "What could they do?"

"Die," Phoebe said simply. "You would, first. Man take a black snake whip to you, tell you go plough, go chop cotton, you kill that man, right now. Knowing they going to kill you afterwards, you kill him. The dying wouldn't make no never-mind to you. You take it to your bosom, put your arms out to ol' raw head'n bloody bones like to a sweetheart; but not never you bow your proud head to no man living; not never you reckon up the costs and bed you down with shame. Now, would you?"

"No," Guy said. "I wouldn't. But what good is a dead man to a woman? Tell me that, Phoebe?"

"Better'n a live coward. 'Cause then she got the memories to look back on. 'Sides, dying ain't the only choice. A man could run away'n take me with him. That's his right. What ain't his right is to bed with me and get children other folks is going to own like you own your grey hoss, Peg, and what other folks can sell, like they can a litter of pigs. . . ."

Guy straightened up and stared at her.

"Lord God, Phoebe," he said, "how can you think like that?"

"I'm a true woman, Guy, just like you's a true man."

She leaned over and kissed him.

"Let's don't talk no more sadness, Marse Guy," she said. " 'Sides we better start back now—it's getting mighty late. . . ."

"What's your hurry?" Guy said. "It's a long time before dark."

"It's Marse Kil, Guy," she said. "He's gitting plum suspicious. This morning, he followed me. I had a real hard time getting away from him."

"Well, I'll be damned!" Guy said helplessly. "What's it to him? Be blessed if I can see why he should care one way or the other—"

Phoebe shrugged.

"Just curious, I reckon. Don't make no never mind, but all the same—"

"All the same?" Guy said.

"I'd just as soon he didn't know. Come on, now, please, Guy—"

They rode out of the woods with Phoebe sitting behind Guy on Pegasus, her slim arms wrapped about his waist. And he, lost in the murky depths of his own thinking, his vision turned inward, did not see the other horseman until he felt the convulsive tightening of Phoebe's grip, heard the soft, explosive outrush of her breath shaping the words, thrusting them out upon the moving tide of her terror:

"Lord Jesus!"

Then he lifted his head. But it was too late now. Nothing to do, but to keep on riding, sitting tall in the saddle, pulled erect by that thing in him that all his life would keep him facing squarely all dangers, disasters, threats of shame, the thing whose labels, affixed to it by men, must remain always but approximations, pride, perhaps, or honor; and these it was; but also something more—something bred into the very fibre of him, bone deep, gut deep, so that he would never have to think about it; never on occasions like this one, or even those involving greater perils, have to make decisions; the decisions, themselves, having all been made for him long before he was born, stamped irrevocably, and ineradicably upon the very stuff of his being, so that always he would do at once and without wavering what he had to do, because he was what he was.

Kilrain waited, his face the picture of malicious glee.

"Why, do tell!" he mocked. " 'Pears to me that we Mallorys aren't the only ones with a taste for dark meat! Tell me, Guy, how is she? Noticed a long time ago that she knew how to wiggle her—"

"Kil," Guy said. That was all. Just that one word, flat, expressionless, soft-spoken. But it was enough.

Kilrain sat there staring.

"Lord God, Guy!" he spluttered. "You needn't take on so about it. I won't tell. If you want to pleasure yourself with one of our wenches, it's no skin off my nose. Amuse yourself all you want. And if you breed her, it'll only increase the value of the stock. An octoroon filly is worth four times the price of a prime field hand. . . ."

"All right," Guy said wearily. There was no use to talk about it, and he knew it. No use for even anger. There was not anything to be said that Kil would or could understand. Not even the avowal of the fact that nothing had happened between them, which no planter's son would ever believe.

"All right," he said again. Then: "Get down, Phoebe."

"Yes sir, Marse Guy," she said.

They sat on their horses watching her scampering away toward the quarters.

"God, boy," Kilrain said. "You're sure stuck on her, aren't you? Bad business."

Guy said, "Let's not talk about it, Kil."

There was a silence between them. There would always be from that moment on, a silence, a gulf, a chasm between them, which the years would only widen.

"Reckon you're getting in some practice by now," Kilrain said.

"Practice? For what?"

"Jo Ann's birthday. Biggest event of the year, hereabouts. Jerry sure spreads himself high, wide and handsome for that kid."

Guy was still struggling to break through the mood that gripped him.

"Still don't see," he said, "what there is about a birthday party that a body needs to practice for—"

"Not *a* party, Jo Ann's party. It lasts all day. There's horse racing for a prize. A turkey shoot. Fox hunting and a ring tournament. Man who gets the highest score in all events is crowned king and sits on a throne beside Jo Ann. I was king for the last two years," Kilrain added complacently. He stared at Guy in sudden puzzlement.

"It's funny," he went on. "You should have been there. It's been nigh onto two years since you came here. . . ."

Slowly Guy shook his head.

"There's some mighty long distances in this world, Kil," he said, "but I reckon the furtherest stretch there is must be the one between the Big House and the overseer's place. Further even than the distance between the house and the quarters—else there wouldn't be any—Phoebes. . . ."

"But you're always up at Fairoaks. You study with her, and—"

"Because she asked them, herself. Pity for the poor relative, I reckon. But a birthday party's another thing. That's speaking out loud, acknowledging—"

"Oh, I don't know—"

"The relationship," Guy went on imperturbably. "I was out hunting her last birthday. I heard all the whooping'n hollering—all the Buckra quality in pink coats, riding like mad after one little fox. Wonder how many of 'em it would take to get a painter—or a bear?"

"You don't understand," Kilrain said. "It's a sport like any—"

"No. A sport's where the animal's got a chance. But twenty-five horsemen and a hundred hounds after one little fox—whatever it is, Kil, sure Lord is not sport!"

"Reckon you're right," Kilrain said. "Sorry I brought up the subject, Guy. I didn't know. I thought that seeing as how you're kissing kin, the question of your father's being your cousin's overseer wouldn't matter. Besides, Fairoaks should be yours by right. Many's the time I've heard my father say that anybody not an absolute fool would have to realize that Jerry influenced your grandfather when he was too sick to care—'cause that was right after the Creole died—"

"The Creole?" Guy said.

"His second wife. Didn't you know? Old Ash Falks married again back in '15, right after the Battle of New Orleans—a Creole girl he met down there while he was serving under Andy Jackson. Her name was Yvonne something or other. I don't remember the rest of it—'cause all folks ever called her was la belle Creole, the beautiful Creole. All the old folks still rave about how beautiful she was. Funny you didn't know—"

"I didn't," Guy said. "What did she die of?"

"In childbirth. Baby was born dead, too. She was too delicate, I reckon. And old Ash, your grandfather, was plumb nigh sixty when it happened. He built Fairoaks for her. Took him five years to do it. Before that the house you live in was Fairoaks. Built that one, too—"

"You were saying that your father said that Jerry—"

"Stole Fairoaks from your father. Of course Wes was wild and crazy; but what young man of good family hereabouts isn't? Lord, we Mallorys make the Devil himself blush! There's no way to prove it one way or another, but what my father thinks makes a lot of sense. He doesn't even believe that Jerry influenced ol' Ash. Look, Guy, a father doesn't get too worked up over his son's sins of the flesh. More likely to chuckle over 'em in secret, though a daughter's another thing. No. And specially not a man like ol' Ash, who was nobody's plaster saint, himself ... A man who, at fifty-five, marries a girl young enough to be his daughter and gets her with child at sixty, ought to be able to understand the itch his son gets when a filly twitches her tail at him, right?"

"Right," Guy said. "Go on, Kil. . . ."

"That's why my father thinks, what with Wes being away—'cause he left here the year before the battle; and it's one more proof of what an old heller your Grandpa was that he felt called upon to fight. At fifty-five years old, when he sure Lord could have got out of it, he not only felt called upon, but distinguished himself in the battle so that Andy Jackson decorated him, holding him up as an example to the younger men—"

"Lord God, Kil," Guy said, "you do wander about! No wonder you got lost in the woods. Get to the point, boy!"

"I'm getting there. A man like your grandfather wouldn't have disowned his son for a little plain and fancy whorehopping; and certainly not for responding to a duel when he was called out. So my father thinks that Jerry changed the will himself, or maybe forged the old man's signature to a new one he had prepared. And that, Guy Falks, makes sense!"

Guy shook his head.

"Not quite," he said. "Why should Jerry go to the trouble to come looking for us up there in the hills? Appears to me that if he'd done such a thing, my father would be the last man on earth he'd want anywhere near him. . . ."

"Guilty conscience, for one thing. Another was that Jerry sure Lord is nobody's planter. Wasn't for Rachel, Fairoaks would have plumb gone to rack'n ruin by now. Reckon he figgered that if he got Wes to run it for him, he could get Rachel off his neck, take credit for Wes' work, sort of. Besides, it was smart. Knowing Wes, as he does, he knew your Pa would reason just like you're doing now. 'Can't be guilty, or why have me back?' Jerry'n Wes were raised together, remember. He knows Wes' mind backwards. Reckoned from the very first that your Pa wasn't the kind of a man who'd go down to the county seat and ask to see the probated will. Even if he did, what could he prove? Living with your grandfather, he never had the occasion to get a letter from the old man in his life—after they broke, both 'em were too damned proud to write, and anyhow ol' Ash didn't know where Wes was. So, apart from the ledgers, which the overseer on a plantation like Fairoaks most likely kept anyhow, merely showing them to your Grandpa for inspection, Wes probably never saw enough of ol' Ash's handwriting to be sure whether Jerry forged the will or not. Besides which, being sick like ol' Ash was, Jerry could always claim the old man's hand was shaky—"

Guy sat there, looking at Kilrain. It was all there, every bit of it: the desire, the opportunity, even the traits predisposed toward the underhand, the cunning, the stealthy; everything except the essential: the proof.

But, he thought hotly, I don't need proof. I'll get it back for Pa. I'll get it back and make that womanish little bastard eat crow in the bargain. . . .

And then, quite suddenly, he knew, uninvited or not, he was going to that party, he was going to show them, once and for all. But Kilrain was talking again:

"Say, Guy, I almost forgot why I came looking for you. There were more tracks down by the pigpen last night! So there must be more than one of them. Lord God, boy, think of it—that brindle bitch could have whelped a litter of a dozen! And if she did, we've got our work cut out for us!"

"I," Guy said, "wouldn't like to kill any more of 'em. Doesn't seem right, shooting a dog—"

"But, Lord God, boy—if we don't, they'll run through the stock! I'd swear there were three different sizes of tracks around that pen—maybe more—"

"We don't have to shoot them, Kil. We could try trapping them. Think of it, boy, we'd have the best damn bear'n painter dogs in the state!"

"If we can tame them," Kilrain said dubiously. "I wake up nights dreaming about those yellow eyes coming at me through the dark. We'd better kill them off, Guy. And I promise you I won't shoot 'til I'm sure it's dog, not some other breed of critter. Besides, I'll bring along a brace of pistols for each of us. That way, we can get in three shots apiece. . . ."

"All right," Guy said. "We'll thin them out. But I want to save a pair of 'em for breeding. Make a noose snare and bait it with a deer carcass, and we'll get ourselves one. Then, later on, we can get the other one, too—how, I haven't figured out yet. Because that breed is so smart the same trick sure Lord won't work twice. Agreed?"

The hunt was a failure. They killed three of the bull mastiffs, but two, a male and a female escaped both the trap and their fire. They trailed them to the river's edge; and saw their two heads far out, black against the silver track of moonlight on the dark waters, swimming strongly for the Louisiana side. The threat to the stock was ended, but Guy was disappointed. With dogs like those, he thought, I could—

Then he turned and saw the rebuilt shanty boat, a little below them, trim and glistening with paint that was milk white under the moon.

"You ride on home, Kil," he said. "I got to drop in on those shanty boat folks. They nursed me while I was sick with my hand, and I owe 'em a call—"

"Some shanty boat!" Kil said admiringly. "I could come along, you know. . . ."

"No," Guy said. "They aren't your kind of folks, Kil. Be seeing you, boy. . . ."

After making sure that Kil had really gone, he leaped aboard the houseboat. On the deck, as usual, Tad Richardson snored, a jug of rot gut cradled in his arms.

"Cathy!" Guy called softly. "Oh, Cathy!"

She came out of the cabin in a rush. She had on a ruffled nightgown. A blue ribbon tied back her shining hair. She was spotlessly clean and achingly lovely in the moonlight. Guy stood there, staring at her.

"Guy!" she whispered. "Oh Guy, I'm so glad to see you! Come on in!"

"No," he growled, stiffening himself against the clamor in his blood. "You slip on a dress, and we'll go for a walk, Cathy. Too nice a night for that pokey ol' cabin. . . ."

"All right," she said. "Just you wait a minute, Guy. . . ."

When she came back, she was a sight to see. Her dress was white and she had white slippers on her feet. She moved close to him and took his arm. As she did so, a cloud of perfume rose dizzily about his head.

Lord God, he groaned inside his heart, oh good Lord God!

"Let's go a long ways from here," she said. "A mighty long ways. Gramps won't wake up 'til tomorrow afternoon—and the moon's so pretty! Makes a body feel so . . . so. . . ."

"So what, Cathy?" he said.

"Oh, I don't know!" she laughed. "Never did feel like this, before—all a-tickle, like goose skin on a frosty morning. Come on, Guy, take me for a ride on your pretty horse. . . ."

"All right," he muttered, thinking: I shouldn't, I mustn't, I—

But he knew he was going to. There was no hope for it, now. It's all Phoebe's fault, he thought darkly. If she hadn't been so damn finicky. . . .

He rode in silence until he came to the clearing. Cathy cried out in delight when she saw it.

"Oh, Guy!" she said. "It's so—so pretty!"

Pretty, Guy decided grimly, was her word for everything. He got down from the grey, and lifted her to the ground. Instantly, she wiggled out of his embrace, and raced for the stream's edge. She sat down beside it and kicked off her slippers. Then she splashed her feet in the waters, gaily, like a child.

Guy frowned. This was beginning badly. Or maybe, he thought morosely, it was beginning well. Sweet and innocent as the child was, it was a crime and a sin to even think about— *that.* But he was thinking about *that.* He purely couldn't help it.

The flash of her legs as she splashed made a sickness in him. He turned his face away from her. It was one of those nights when you could read a newspaper by the full moon, so she saw the gesture.

"Guy," she said plaintively, "ain't you happy?"

"No," he growled.

"Why ain't you, Guy?" she whispered. "Did I do something?"

"No. I'm just lonesome, I reckon. I'm plumb grown up, now, Cathy and I—I just plain need a girl. . . ."

"But you got a girl, if you wants her, Guy. You . . . you got . . . me. . . ."

He turned to her, his brow like a thundercloud.

"You mean that, Cathy?" he said, thickly.

"Yes, Guy. I'll kiss you to seal the bargain. There—"

"Call that a kiss?" Guy said mockingly.

She stared at him in purest astonishment.

"Well—warn't it?" she said.

"Come here, Cathy," he said, and gathered her into his arms.

When at last he released her, she still clung to him.

"Guy," she breathed. "Oh, Guy, honey, kiss me like that some more—I never knowed—I purely never reckoned—Oh Lordy, Guy. . . ."

She lay there in his arms.

"Please, don't!" she babbled. "Give me a minute . . . I feel— I don't know how I do feel. . . ."

He laid her gently back upon the green sod and kissed her endlessly, his fingers working at the buttons of the dress, letting the night air in, the sudden coolness.

"Guy!" she moaned, the words muffled, distorted by his pressing mouth. "Don't! Please, don't—"

The sudden coolness was gone now, vanquished by the heat of his searching hands.

She moaned once more very softly, then she was still. She lay there with her great eyes reflecting the full moon, startlingly silver, staring at him with no outcry or protest as he drew her garments from her one by one. . . .

She cried out shrilly, sharply, in pure pain.

She moaned a little, the choked-back moans of hurt, of shame. Then the sounds coming from her throat changed. Pain no longer. No longer pain.

Then, at last, one great cry, hurled up in triumph to the watching moon.

"Guy," she whispered. "Oh Guy—oh honey I—"

"Hush!" he said, the reaction upon him, the shame in him— bone-deep, gut-deep—the slow, sick coiling of remorse. "Hush, Cathy! Listen to me. I'm sorry. I didn't mean to—oh, Cathy, honey, I'm so damned ashamed and sorry. . . ."

Her fingers were slivers of silver in the midnight of his hair.

"Sorry?" she said, her voice low, throaty, warm. "For what, Guy? This happens to every gal sometime, don't it, love? Just means I'm a woman I reckon. And since it had to happen, I'm plum, downright glad it was you. . . ."

He moved a little away from her, groping for his scattered clothes.

"Guy," she whispered, contentment bubbling through her tone, "lie still! Didn't I tell you Gramps won't wake up 'til tomorrow afternoon?"

He saw, as he headed Pegasus toward the Mallory place, the slim little figure coming toward him mounted on the fat white pony.

Damn, he thought, I won't be able to see Cathy, now . . . But then he brightened. Jo Ann's birthday was not far off, less than a month; and this once he was prepared to forget his pride, exchanging it for the chance to show Gerald, and especially cousin Rachel, the stature and dimension of a man of Falks' blood. He drew the grey up and waited.

"Guy," she said plaintively, "it's been so long! 'Course, I know you're grown up now, but it appears to me—"

He sat there, smiling down at her. At almost ten, she was a white birch sapling, slim and formless, having inherited the Falks' length of limb. Grown, he would not dwarf her as he would nearly all other women; though she would never have her mother's Junoesque proportions, she would be taller— willow-tall, and lovely. She was very nearly born to be the mate of such a man as Guy would be, as, in fact, he already was. Not that he knew it, then. At fourteen he had been all dreamer, all child—and the distance between him and the eight-year-old pink and white goddess who had appeared out of nowhere in the very first elegant carriage he had ever seen, had not been great. But now, at sixteen, those six years had become an impassable gulf. He loved her still; but with the warm, impatient, occasional and desultory love of an older brother for a small sister. He did not mind riding with her from time to time; but his books and his hunting now came first. Given a chance to spend a day in her company, or in Kilrain's, he would have chosen the society of young Mallory without a second thought. And if, on any other occasion, she should have interrupted his lovemaking with his poor-white sweetheart he would have sent her packing without either a qualm or a backward glance.

But now . . . He had what his father lacked—a strain of old Ashton's shrewdness: the quality that had enabled the old man to build Fairoaks and found a new dynasty, so that in the space of a few years he became what he knew perfectly well he was not—all his stolen ancestors parading the walls of Fairoaks to the contrary—an aristocrat and a gentleman. . . .

Guy did not speak of her birthday that day, or the next, or the next. He simply rode with her every day for a week, leaving poor Cathy to weep her eyes out while Jo Ann herself existed in a seventh heaven of perfect bliss. It was on that fateful Saturday that he broached the subject finally, saying:

"Jerry ought to get you a real mount, now. You'll never learn to ride properly on that fat tub of guts. After all, you'll be ten very soon now—and if you had one of the greys, a gelding, say, or a mare, I could teach you—"

"Oh, Guy, would you?" she cried.

"Of course. Why don't you ask Jerry to give you a good horse for your birthday?"

"I will!" she said. "I will, sure! Then I could ride him in the fox hunt—"

"What fox hunt?" Guy said blandly.

She stared at him.

"Didn't you know?" she said. "Every year on my birthday, we—"

"But I've never been to your birthday party," Guy said brusquely. "Come on, let's ride."

"Guy," she said plaintively, "I wanted you to come. I did so want you to. Only I was afraid that Mama might—Oh, fiddlesticks! This time you're coming! I'm going to tell Papa to send you an invitation, right now!"

"No, don't," Guy said. "If your mother doesn't want me I'm certain sure that I don't want to come. . . ."

"She never said that, Guy," Jo Ann said rapidly. "She always says that you're smart and manly and just like your father. It's just that she and Papa quarrel so awf'ly. Papa thinks she likes your father too much. And when she gets mad she says such mean things to everybody. That's why I didn't ask for you last year. But this year, it'll be different. You'll see. . . ."

"I don't have to come, Jo," Guy said slowly. "I wouldn't want to be the cause of anything—"

"You won't be. Last year I missed you frightfully. Oh, I do want you to come, Guy! Please say you'll come—promise?"

He looked down at her, frowning. Then he relaxed.

"All right," he said. "I promise—if I get a proper invitation from your father. Come on, little one, let's ride. . . ."

6

HE RODE back from the houseboat on the river, bent over with pure weariness. As he jogged along—

"Guy!" the voice was a hoarse whisper, edged with pain. He pulled the grey up and stared.

"Phoebe!" he got out. "Child—what happened to you?"

"Marse Kil," she moaned. "He—he tried, Marse Guy. When I fought him, he took his riding crop and—"

Guy was off the horse at once. He took her in his arms. He could see the great, purplish welts crisscrossing her shoulders. He tightened his hold about her waist and she cried out, briefly.

"My back—" she whispered. "Hit's plumb in ribbons, Marse Guy—"

"The bastard!" Guy grated. "You just wait 'til I get my hands on that mangy, stinking, polecat bastard—"

"No," she said with a flash of tired mockery, "he was inside his rights, Marse Guy. A master can always whip his slave. . . ."

"I don't care!" Guy raged. "I'm going to teach him how a taste of leather feels! You come with me up to the house, and after Bess fixes you up, I'll—"

"No," she said again. "Can't, Marse Guy. You ain't heard the worst of it. . . ."

"You mean," Guy said, "that there's something worse than this?"

"Yes. Marse Alan heard the noise and come arunning. So Marse Kil he said that I—that I—" She gave way to a storm of weeping.

"Hush, baby," Guy said gently. "It's all right now—or it's going to be. . . ."

"No," she said. "It's never all right when you's black, or even when your grandma was— And what's done happened now don't leave nobody no room for hope. . . ."

"What did happen? Tell me, Phoebe."

"Marse Kil had to get out of it somehow. So he told his Pa that he was whipping me 'cause I—I made 'vances to him and it made him so mad—"

"Alan Mallory believed *that?*"

"No," Phoebe said. "Marse Alan ain't nobody's fool. He warn't taken in for a minute. But hit didn't make no difference. He 'lowed the family's got a bad enough reputation for wenching already . . . So he's done sent Marse Kil up to Dierdre, the upriver plantation. Swears he's going to keep him up there with his tutor'n his books 'til come Missy Jo Ann's birthday time. As for me, he's done sent word for a slave trader to come by Malloryhill, tomorrow. He—he's going to sell me South, Marse Guy! That's how come I run away!"

"Didn't run very far, did you?" Guy said. "Come on, I'll take you down to the Richardsons'. Then I'll get some money out of my Pa to send you North—"

"No," Phoebe said. "If the pattyrollers find me at the Richardsons', they'd be in a mighty heap o' trouble. And they're my friends. . . ."

This, Guy reflected, was quite true. If the night patrols which scoured all the roads and fields searching for runaway slaves, found her on the houseboat the Richardsons would be in trouble, indeed. Aiding and abetting a runaway was one of the most serious of crimes. He stood there, frowning. There was only one other half-way secure place of shelter; the cabin. And his father and Rachel did not go there every night . . . The only trouble was, he had no way of knowing whether or not this would be one of the nights they planned to meet there. Still, it had to be the cabin. There simply wasn't any other place.

"Look, Phoebe," he said, "I'm going to take you to that old ruined cabin in the woods. You'll be safe there." He looked at her speculatively. "If you hear horses, get out and hide in the woods. But don't worry if somebody comes. It'll only be my Pa—or Miz Rachel—"

Phoebe found the strength to smile.

"You can trust me, Marse Guy," she said.

"I know. That's why I told you. You hole up there for tonight and tomorrow. I'll pack you some grub, and a white girl's dress'n hat. Cathy'll give me some of her things. She's got lots of clothes now. Dressed like that, you can pass. Mighty heap of white people no lighter'n you anyhow. Then I'll get boat fare to Cincinnati out of my Pa. Reckon you know enough about sewing and such like to get yourself a job—"

"Thanks, Marse Guy," Phoebe whispered. "You see, I was right. You's just like I thought: fine and nice and a real gentleman—"

"I'm not," Guy said flatly. "I'm as big a bastard as the next man, I reckon. But there are some things I can't stomach. Come on now, let's get going. . . ."

Getting the money out of his father proved easy. Wes Falks was an open-handed man. Besides, Guy knew exactly how to approach him, for his father's mind was his own mind; the two of them being, actually, very nearly the same, except that Guy was colder of head, not given to Wes' bluster and rages; even at sixteen he was more man and less child than his father would ever be.

"It's a debt of honor, Pa," he said. "I bet Kil fifty dollars we could get all those bull mastiffs with one volley, and I lost. You always told me that a Falks' word is sacred. So I won't feel right until I pay him—"

"Lord God, boy!" Wes spluttered. "You think money grows on trees? Let me tell you one thing: it's true that a man pays his gambling debts at once, so that folks'll know his word is his bond. But that's exactly why he ought to avoid gambling in the first place, so's not to get himself in situations where—"

"Pa," Guy grinned. "You never did."

Wes had to smile. He put his hand on his son's shoulder.

"You got me there, boy," he said. "But one more thing: as an example, your ol' Pa exists in a state of the world's worst poverty. Listen to me, son, carefully. A smart man doesn't have to make mistakes to learn by. Got any gumption, motherwit, or even hoss sense, he profits from the mistakes of other folks without getting burnt himself. Your Pa, son, in the pursuit of pleasure, robbed you of your birthright, and—"

"No," Guy said, "not you, Pa—Jerry stole it from us. . . ."

Wes stared at his son.

"Who told you that?" he growled.

"Kil. Mr. Mallory believes Jerry forged Grandpa's signature to a new will, or changed the old one. And, knowing Jerry, that makes sense to me—"

Wes shook his head.

"If I could prove that, I'd—but don't you go 'round listening to gossip, son. It doesn't help matters, even when it's true. Besides, it's impossible to prove one way or another, now. That was all of seventeen years ago, and—"

"Pa, ever thought of riding down to the county seat and looking at the probated will?"

Wes stood there, looking at his son.

"Guy," he said, "you make up to me for all the misery, all the—hell, that's sense—or it would be if I had ever been anything but a young buck rampaging the countryside. I don't recollect having seen Pa's signature in my life. Never would interest myself in book-keeping, or such like. Anyhow, it was Wil Stevens who kept the books. So, how the hell," he went on, his voice strangling in baffled rage, "how the hell would I be able to tell that Jerry forged the old man's hand—if I saw it—or prove it, if I could tell?"

"Couldn't you find an old letter of Grandpa's to compare the writings?" Guy asked. "That way, we could—"

"No. Pa never wrote letters. His only kin was his brother, Brighton, and he lived here. Apparently they were orphans. Leastwise, neither one of them ever wrote to anybody in England—and that's where they were born. . . ."

"Too bad," Guy said. "About that money, Pa—"

"All right, all right!" Wes said. "But don't do it again, boy! You youngsters are all getting a mite too big for your breeches. Like your pal, Kilrain—"

Guy stopped dead.

"What about Kil, Pa?" he said.

"Al caught him dead to rights, hayrolling with a wench. Sent him upriver, and sold the filly South. Natchez trader took her away this morning. . . ."

"You say," Guy whispered, "that a trader took—the girl—away—this morning?"

"Yep. She tried to make a getaway last night; but the patrol caught her. She was wandering around in that burnt-over section—"

"Pa," Guy said bitterly, "you were out a mite late last night, weren't you?"

Westley Falks stared at his son.

"What the devil do you mean by that, boy?" he growled.

"Nothing. Only you can keep your money now, Pa. I don't need it any more."

Wes' face was like a thundercloud.

"You," he said, "you wanted that money to help that yaller wench get away!"

"Yes, Pa," Guy said.

"Look, son," Wes said quietly, "I don't cotton to that. Never thought you'd get mixed up with a nigger wench—yellow or not. We're not Mallorys, son. Falks are proud enough to steer clear of the quarters. Among other things, you breed a wench and your own son, your own flesh and blood, is part nigger and a slave. And that shouldn't be done to a man of Falks' blood—we shouldn't ever mix it with inferior strains, for one thing, or condemn a child with our tendency to pride, to force, to arrogance, even, to be an owned creature like a horse. . . ."

"Or maybe not a child of any blood, eh, Pa?" Guy said quietly.

Wes whirled upon him.

"God damn it, boy!" he roared. "Don't go talking no abolitionist cant to me!"

"I'm not," Guy said. "Free 'em—and where would they go? What could they do? They'd starve to death in a month without us to take care of 'em. That's not what I'm saying, Pa. I'm saying that what we've done, what we're doing, is plain dead damned wrong, and every manjack of us knows it, if we had the guts to admit it. Only we're stuck with it. Sins of the fathers, I reckon. . . ."

"Lord God!" Wes said. "Never thought a mite of hay-rolling with a yellow wench could unhinge a son of mine's reason! I tell you, boy—"

"No, Pa, I'm telling you. I never had anything to do with Phoebe, that way. I'm just grateful to her for saving my life. I never told you before, but she found me in the woods, bandaged my hand and took me down to the Richardsons' shantyboat. Seemed little enough for me to do to help her get away before they sold her off to warm an old man's bed. . . ."

Wes sat there, his head bowed with the weight of his thoughts.

"A pity," he said at last. "You're right, son. Only you went at it, wrong. Should have told me. Then I'd have bought her from Alan Mallory, and sent her North with a written pass.

Legal that way. What hurts is you didn't trust me enough to tell me. . . ."

"Wasn't that, Pa. I just didn't think of it," Guy said.

7

"WES, we'd better not go to the cabin for a spell. What with them catching that runaway wench there, the patrol's going to keep an eye on it now. Maybe we'd better stop seeing each other—at all—at least for a while. . . ."

"The hell you say!" Wes growled. "Ask me to give up breathing, Rachie. That's easier. . . ."

"I know. For me, too. But, Wes, I'm scared!"

"Don't be, Rachie. There're lots of other places. For instance, I know the sweetest lil' clearing right down by the stream, with trees all around, safe as in church and private as a boudoir. . . ."

Rachel hesitated.

"You're sure it's safe, Wes?" she said.

"I'll show you, Baby," Wes chuckled. "Come on!"

They left the horses some distance from the clearing, and made their way quietly through the woods on foot. Wes was just about to step out into the open place beside the stream, when suddenly, convulsively, Rachel caught his arm.

Then he saw it: The two of them swimming together in the moon-washed pool of water just above the little cataract. He hung there, frozen, hearing Cathy's voice ring out, clear and silvery:

"Come on, Guy! It's mighty late and Gramps just might wake up!"

They came out of the stream together, the droplets on their bodies bejeweled by the moonlight. On the stream's edge, they embraced, Cathy's birch sapling whiteness blending into Guy's dark oaken form.

"Oh!" Rachel whispered, "how beautiful they are! How beautiful and young! Oh, Wes, I—I envy them!"

Her voice broke the spell, releasing his pent-up fury. He surged forward, but Rachel locked her arms about him, and held him back with all her strength.

"No!" she hissed. "What right have we, Wes? Tell me, what right?"

Wes stopped still. He was trembling all over.

"Damn it all," he groaned, "I haven't a leg to stand on, have I, Rachie? Only I happen to know the gal is old river rat Richardson's granddaughter. And, by God, before I see Guy make the same mistake I did, I'll see him stretched out dead!"

Rachel stared at them, fondly.

"Is it a mistake, Wes? Lovely as she is—"

"Charity wasn't bad either, when she was young," Wes growled. "Come on, Rachie—I'll take you home now. Seeing this has drove me plumb out of the mood. . . ."

The minute Cathy saw the tall man on the great black horse she knew he was Guy's father. The resemblance between them was like a cry in the thickets of her fears.

"Yes, sir?" she whispered.

"I said where's your grandpa, gal?" Wes growled.

"He—he's sleeping—sir," Cathy said.

"Go wake him up," Wes said flatly.

"I dasn't—" Cathy got out. "Wake Gramps up and he'll be meaner'n a sorehead bear!"

"I said wake him up!" Wes roared. "Damn it, wench, I ain't got all day!"

Cathy scurried forward, her face white with terror.

When she came back, Tad Richardson was with her.

"My name's Wes Falks," Wes said, "and I'm a plain-spoken man. What I came down here to talk over with you, old man, ain't pretty. But first I want your word that you'll go light on the wench. She don't look strong enough to stand much of a hiding. . . ."

"What the devil be you talking about, Mister?" Tad Richardson said.

"Listen, you goddamned ol' river rat, you be careful how you speak to your betters! I'll put it to you straight: this here gal of yours is messing around with my boy. And I damn sure don't want him putting in a crop afore he's built a fence. 'Specially since, to my thinking, this particular ground ain't worth fencing off, nohow. . . .

"Tell me, gal," Wes said to Cathy, "you pregnant?"

"Pregnant?" Cathy whispered. "What's that, sir?"

88

"Big. Knocked up. With child. Oh, hell, gal, what I mean is: You going to have a baby for my boy?"

"No, sir," Cathy whispered.

"Good," Wes said. "Then I'll make it short. I'm not a rich man, but I got two hundred dollars right here in my pocket. That's more than you ever see in a year, old man. And it's yours the minute you untie your fancy shantyboat from that there stump and drift down the river so damn far that my boy'll never see hair nor hide of this little wench again. . . ."

Tad Richardson stood there, staring at him. When the old man spoke, his voice was very quiet.

"Never had much dealings with your kind of folks, and from what I sees now, 'pears to me I ain't missed much. Maybe 'mongst you Buckra quality in your big houses, your word and your wimmen's honor be for sale. Mine ain't. Not neither one. . . ."

Wes sat there on Demon, eyeing him steadily.

"You mean you aim to hold out for a proper wedding, old man?" he growled.

"No. Took a liking to that there boy of your'n. But seeing as how he's got your blood in his veins, I reckon now he ain't fitt'n for my granddaughter. When she's wed, it'll be to a good man and a true, not to no Buckra whelp grown great and fat off nigger sweat—"

"Why you old bastard!" Wes roared. "Wasn't for them white hairs, I'd—"

"Don't let them white hairs bother you, son. Tell you one thing, though. I got a old double-barrelled twelve-gauge lying right here in this box. Loaded with scrap iron and rusty nails. Didn't haul it out, 'cause I don't like to make no false motions. But varmint shooting pleasures me a mighty heap, son. So afore you gits down off'n that there horse, think a mite. Be a damn sight better if you just turned him around real quiet like and rode off right now."

Wes' anger died. He had always had a real admiration for pure guts. And this old man had them to spare.

"All right, old man," he said. "You win. All I want to know is what you aim to do?"

"Nothing," Tad Richardson said. "The boot's on the other foot, son. My filly don't go nowhere looking for yore whelp. You just keep him up there a-wallowing around the quarters, and everything will be just fine. . . ."

"I'll do that," Wes said. "I like your nerve, old man. Maybe

I did come down here hind end to. I'll keep the boy away—and you keep an eye on the wench. Shake on it, old man?"

Tad Richardson took his outstretched hand.

"Gramps!" Cathy wailed. "You can't! I tell you, you can't! You do that and I'll drown myself in the river! I swear! Can't live without him, can't—"

"Shut up, Cathy," the old man said. "Save your blubbering for the hiding I'm a going to lay on you just as soon as this gentleman leaves!"

That night, Tad Richardson came into the cabin with the lantern in his hand. He held it up and bent over his granddaughter, asleep in her bunk, her face still streaked with bitter tears.

Poor lil' filly, he thought, poor lil' loning thing. The heart ain't easy to tame, I reckon. Hard to learn that aiming high don't always catch the best. There be rottenness in high places, baby, and goodness among the lowly. Still—I kinda liked that boy. Better you don't see him no more, baby—much better, child. . . .

Then he went back on deck, stepped ashore and untied the house boat from the stump. He shoved it off the bar with all his strength. Then, climbing back aboard he poled it slowly and quietly out to midstream. The current caught it, drifting it southward. He sat in the stern, puffing his corncob pipe and looking up at the stars.

There be other snug heavens, he thought, and I got to see my baby through to hers. . . .

Because Jo Ann's birthday was only a week off now, Guy was too busy to ride down to the shantyboat. So he did not know that Cathy Richardson had drifted forever out of his life. Nor could Wes have told him, if the subject of the affair had been raised. For, depending upon his agreement with Tad Richardson, Wes did not ride that way again.

The very next day after the Richardson's departure, Guy rode out to the South acres where he knew Wes would be this time of day. He pulled up the grey alongside of his father's black stallion, pushed his hat onto the back of his head and said:

"Howdy, Pa. You still got that old pink coat? Maybe if it was narrowed a mite in the shoulders it would fit—"

Twenty years later, some of the Negroes who witnessed it would still be telling the story:

"Marse Wes he just set there a looking at that boy. Didn't nary a living word pass his lips for nigh onto ten minutes. Then he opened his mouth and started in to swear. Man'n boy I done heard me some cussing in my time, but Marse Wes' swearing that there day was purely an admiration and a glory! Looked up and the leaves on that ol' oak tree forty foot overhead was curling up'n turning brown! The head o' steam he got up would of drove a steamboat upstream from N'Awleens to Natchez and fair broke all records adoing it!

"An' all that time, young Marse Guy, he sat there on that grey hoss o' his'n, listening to his Pa and grinning. And when Marse Wes plumb run clean out of breath, he opens up his mouth and says:

"You finished, Pa? Now, as I was saying, I reckon Brutus, that nigger tailor on the Mallory Place, could cut that coat down, and make it fit real fine. . . ."

Wes glared at his son.

"You just drop the subject of that coat," he growled, "and come along to the other side where the niggers can't hear. You'n me have a mighty big crow to pick, boy—"

Guy rode away with him. He was very calm. Wes' rages didn't frighten him.

Wes sat there, looking at the boy, and slowly working himself up to the proper pitch of fury.

"Ought to take a rawhide to you!" he roared. "Sneaking out at night to hayroll with that white trash wench! And with that on your conscience, you come riding up to me as big as life without a word of apology, and ask me about a pink coat damn near before you say 'howdy, Pa!' Damn it all, boy, what have you got to say for yourself?"

"Nothing, Pa," Guy said.

"Nothing! Great jumping balls o' fire! Now I am going to lay a good dozen onto your tail! You young whippersnapper, I tell you—"

"No, Pa," Guy said gravely. "No, you ain't. In the first place, I'm a man grown and lambasting me would add up to quite a proposition. In the second, as far as Cathy is concerned, I just plain don't see where I owe you any explanation at all. . . ."

"You don't owe me an explanation?" Wes said, spacing the words out in deadly quiet.

"No, Pa. Cathy is mine. Maybe her folks ain't much, but for that matter one side of my family sure Lord didn't come

91

into this world dressed in silks and velvets. And she's a true girl, Pa—good and sweet and loving. I tried every way I could, but damned if I'm able to see where her poor white blood makes any difference. Besides, you aren't really worried about my having her; all that's eating you is that I might be forced to—even might decide to—marry her. Either way, it's purely my business, Pa. And I'd thank you mighty kindly to stay out of it. . . ."

"Your business is my business 'til you're a man grown, boy!" Wes howled. "And anyhow there's the whole question of right and wrong—"

"For God's sake, Pa!" Guy said, "don't bring that in. I love Cathy—I'm going to go on loving her as long as I can—right or wrong be damned. You shouldn't even bring that subject up. I'll match Cathy, not tied by her own word to any other man, against your Rachel, sneaking away to meet you in that there ruined cabin in the burned-over section, any day in the week!"

Wes' face was a thunder cloud, purpling into fury.

"You—" he whispered—"you god damned little spy!"

"No. I wasn't spying, Pa. And I never breathed a word to a living soul—not even to you, up 'til now. I just come out of the woods with my hand chewed half off, sick to my guts, and burning up with fever, and then I saw you and Rachel. Could have called out to you for the help I needed damned bad—only I didn't want to embarrass you, didn't want to hurt you. And, being a man, I even understood what you see in Rachel. So I went on without you. Went on and almost didn't make it, so you could enjoy your own sins in peace. So—"

"Guy—" Wes pleaded.

"Don't go calling me down on account of mine. White trash or not, Cathy is mine, and I love her in a true way. And whatever I do, now, or in the future, has got to be my business, Pa. What's more, I promise you one thing, right now: Being myself, I'll never be a plaster saint. Reckon I'll top my share of women like every other Falks born from the beginning of time. But Pa—and here's my word on it—no son of mine'll ever have to ask me for a worn-out coat because I cost him his birthright, his place in the world and brought him down to the job of assistant nigger driver because I couldn't let other men's women alone!"

Wes looked at his son a long time and very slowly. Then he turned away his face. Sitting there on the great black stallion, his head bowed, the whole of his big frame loosening into defeat, into surrender, he epitomized abject shame in every line of his powerful body. It was not a thing to be borne. Not by Guy, whose love for his father was truly the strongest emotion he possessed. . . .

"Pa!" he got out. "Pa!"

Wes did not answer him.

He pulled the grey over and put his arm around his father's massive shoulders.

"Pa," he choked, "I'm sorry. That was dirty rotten of me. You're the best damn pa anybody ever had, and I'm proud of you. I'm glad and proud to be—"

"No, Guy," Wes whispered.

"Your son. There're things a man can't help. I can't help Cathy—and you can't help loving Rachel. She's your kind of a woman, and Ma sure Lord ain't. Even Rachie can't be blamed. So I want most humbly to ask your pardon for saying that. A man oughtn't to fight with his tongue, no matter how riled up he gets. That's plumb womanish. I'm sorry, Pa. I won't, ever again—"

Wes turned once more to Guy, and his slow smile was painful to see.

"It's all right, boy," Wes said. "Let's ride into town for some pink velvet. On the way back, Alan Mallory's nigger can take your measurements. A man's got a right to stand up to his fellows, even when it comes to a fox-hunting coat. Come on, boy, let's ride!"

The day after the first and last quarrel they ever had in their lives, out of something more than shame—pride, perhaps, or the need for self justification, the desire, even, to see his son stand up tall in those exalted ranks out of which his own folly had ejected him—Wes Falks offered Guy the use of Demon for the fox-hunt or the steeplechase, not because he did not think Guy's own grey was not good enough, but because he knew that no one horse could stand up under the pressure of the day-long events which Gerald had scheduled.

"It's this way, son," he said; "with Demon you'll have a sure win in the first two trials, because they mostly call for speed and strength. In the afternoon, in the ring tournament, the turkey pulls and such, Peg'll be better; he's lighter and he's got more control."

"Thanks, Pa," Guy said.

"Another thing. I'd like to see you win. It would mean a

mighty lot to me, if you did. But I'd rather see you lose than to win by cheating. Wait! I know you don't lie and you don't cheat. But there'll be a fair to middling heap o' cheating done by the others. The temptation will be there to fight fire with fire, if you understand me, boy. Don't do it. What another man does is never justification for what you do. And two wrongs never added up to a right from the beginning of time. Which is," Wes added, smiling, "maybe what I ought to have answered you with yesterday when you were chiding me about Rachie. Only it didn't come to me, then——"

"Pa——" Guy began.

"Forget it. Besides, here comes Jo Ann alooking for you. Nice kid. Maybe when she grows up, and fills out—heck boy, 'twixt a man and a woman six years are less than nothing. . . ."

"I've thought about it," Guy said slowly, "but only if we suit each other by then, Pa. Not to get Fairoaks back. But I will get it back—or build another place upriver that will make it and Mallory Place and all the rest look sick. They got us down now; but it's only for a spell. Falks don't stay down; 'cause there's nobody big enough to hold us. So long, Pa——"

He rode out to meet Jo Ann, seeing the pure delight dancing in her blue eyes, the wonder, the near worship.

"Guy!" she said, "I was so worried. I haven't seen you in so long and—my goodness gracious! Look at you! Why you're as skinny as a rail fence—and brown as a berry. Where have you been? What have you been up to? You men! I just naturally do declare!"

Guy sat there looking down at her and smiling.

She's sweet, he thought, real sweet—and maybe she will do, later on. Hard to tell now. Like a colt—all legs and arms. But later, maybe . . . maybe. . . .

"Come on, little one," he said as usual. "Let's ride——"

"Don't call me little one! I'm ten—or I will be day after tomorrow. And you know what, Guy? Daddy's going to give me one of the greys, like you suggested! Isn't that wonderful? When I asked him, he hemmed and hawed and pretended he didn't think much of the idea; but I know he just did that so it'll be sort of a surprise. Besides, I saw Rufus grooming the prettiest little mare yesterday—oh, Guy!"

"Good," Guy said. "But what do you want to do, now?"

"Go up to the big house and see if we can get Aunt Becky to let us lick the pots she's making icing for the cakes in. No—it's too early for that. Let's ride down to the landing and watch the niggers unload the ice from the steamboat."

"Ice? This time of year?"

"Of course, silly. It comes from up North, all packed in straw. We have to have it, or else how could the darkies make ice cream for my party? Very few people down here ever use it 'cause it costs so much. But Papa says my birthday's very special and therefore it's worth it. . . ."

He had, of course, seen ice before. In midwinter, in the hill country, it formed a film over the ponds which lasted until ten o'clock in the morning. Twice, within his nearly seventeen years of existence it had even snowed, once so heavily that it had taken all of two days for the last of it to melt. But in the furthest sweep of his imagination he had not been able to conjure up anything like the glistening, immense bars of ice that the Negroes were bringing ashore—protecting their hands and shoulders with thick paddings of burlap bags—and loading into the waiting wagon.

Riding over to the wagon he took up a jagged chip of the ice and handed it to Jo Ann. She popped it into her mouth. But she spat it out quickly.

"My, it's cold!" she gasped. "My mouth's all frozen!"

"Is ice cream that cold?" Guy said.

She stared at him.

"Haven't you ever had any?" she whispered.

"No," Guy said gruffly. "Never."

"Never you mind," Jo Ann said. "You'll have some day after tomorrow. It's not nearly so cold as ice—and it's delicious! I always try to eat all I can of it—since we only have it once a year, on my birthday. Come on, let's go up to the kitchen and see what we can beg out of Aunt Becky. Have to be careful, though. She gets in an awful temper when she has so much to do. . . ."

They swung their mounts about, and headed toward Fairoaks, circling around the house to reach the kitchen. Ten feet away, Jo Ann halted, her face the picture of childish mischief.

"Guy," she whispered, "you're real tall. Reckon you can reach that tin of pralines? Aunt Becky put it in the window to cool. . . ."

Guy stared at her.

"But," he said, "that would be stealing. . . ."

"Of course not, silly!" Jo Ann laughed. "She's making them for me. That makes them mine. Tell me, Guy, how can a body steal from himself?"

Guy stood there, puzzling over the thought. He did not know it, then; but he had lost his first battle with the one absolutely invincible quality in the world: feminine logic. Though, be it said, this was not a pure example of the workings of the female mind, Jo Ann's argument, on this occasion, having elements of reason acceptable even to a man. But later, he would learn to his bafflement and his wonder, that women add apples and pears as a matter of course; that they consistently erect such a towering structure of glittering irrelevancies, cemented together with flat contradictions, the whole mounted upon a foundation of deviousness, so vast and complicated that mere man retreats before it in abject defeat, especially when he is convinced that his mate believes every part of it: the contradictions, the irrelevancies, the plain, utter nonsense. And when, as often happens, this giddy structure stands up, achieving results that his plodding masculine logic can never attain, his defeat becomes utter rout. For women are born with the instinctive knowledge that life is not logical; that the history of man's days has been one long and bitter chronicle of illogic, and that the world and time have always rejected the foolish consistency of the human mind with fierce hostility. So, in wonderment and fear, he will go on watching his mate adding two and two to arrive at six or at three, as the notion strikes her, rejecting with bland kindliness his stubborn insistence that the total is always four—knowing as she does in her secret heart of hearts that nothing is *always* anything.

"Here," he said. "Take this." He handed her his hat and was off on tiptoe, angling toward the kitchen window so that Aunt Becky could see him only by putting out her head.

A moment later, he had lifted the still warm tin and the two of them were flying toward the willows which bent over the creek. They sat there, stuffing the still soft pralines into their mouths and half choking with silent laughter. When they had eaten them all, Guy lay back on the mossy bank, staring upward at the sky.

Jo Ann sat there looking at him solemnly, her small face, despite the cold water she had used to wash away the traces of candy, strangely flushed.

"Guy—" she whispered.

"Yes," he said. "Yes, Jo?"

"Would you—would you like to kiss me?"

He jack-knifed into a sitting position, his brown eyes widening.

"Well," she said a little crossly, "would you?"

"Good Lord!" he exploded. "You don't know what you're saying! You're only a child and I—"

"You're six years older. I know. But my daddy's ten years older than my mama, and yet they're married. 'Sides, I'm not a baby; and I *want* you to kiss me. Will you, please?"

She closed her eyes, and sat there waiting, her lips puckered expectantly. He sat there staring, then laughing a little, bent forward and kissed her lightly on the forehead.

Her eyes flew open, flashing azure fire.

"Not like that!" she said. "I'm old enough, Guy!" Then her two little hands flew up and seized him by the ears, dragging his face down level with hers.

"Now, kiss me!" she commanded.

It was like running into a fence post, Guy reckoned. Her tiny lips were closed and tight and icy cold from the creek water. But she turned his ears loose and sat back, beaming with evident satisfaction.

"Now, we're engaged," she said, "and if you ever even look at another girl, Guy Falks, I'll horsewhip you and—and scratch out her eyes!"

"Well, I never!" Guy whispered, but she had already risen and was tugging at his hand.

"Come on!" she said gaily. "I want to show you my party dress! It's the prettiest thing!"

He followed her, with amiable condescension, up to the house. They entered the vast hall, tiptoeing past the frowning visages of the ancestors; but, at the door of the study they stopped, for it was open, and from within it anyone could easily see them as they started up the stairs.

Guy moved forward cautiously, all the silence he had learned in the woods at his command. Then he turned and beckoned to Jo Ann, and the two of them fled past the door and up the stairs.

But he had mounted no more than four or five of them before the strangeness of what he had seen halted him in his tracks. He turned and stared once more, his heavy brows knitting into a frown. It was a curious thing. More than curious. It was downright strange.

For Gerald Falks sat at his desk, his back turned to the door, whittling busily at a piece of white oak with a pen knife. Before him, on the desk, lay an open, velvet-lined case containing his dueling pistols. From where Guy stood, on the

97

stairs, he could see that nearly everything was intact within the case, the bullets, patches, ramrods, brushes for cleaning, the small container of oil, the box of percussion caps, everything, in fact, except one of the heavily ornamented powder flasks. It was propped up against the case, while the white oak block rapidly took the shape of it, under the skillful strokes of Jerry's knife.

Strange. Most men hereabouts whittled in their idle moments. But not in their oak and walnut studies. And mostly they whittled aimlessly, not making anything in particular beyond a pile of shavings. But Jerry was carving a duplicate of the silver powder flask with real skill—making it, however, considerably smaller than the original.

Wonderingly, Guy shook his head. It didn't make sense that Gerald Falks with his hands as soft as those of a woman should be carving wood in his study. Some other man maybe, but Jerry—never. . . .

He felt Jo Ann tugging fiercely at his arm.

"Oh, will you come on!" she said.

The pink coat fitted him marvelously well. So did the fawn-colored breeches and yellow waistcoat his father had generously added. It was after midnight when Brutus delivered them, but the time didn't matter. Guy was far beyond sleep anyhow.

In the morning, before it was light, he got up and dressed in the first really fine clothes he had owned in all his life. Wes came to his room, and aided him in winding the snowy stock about his thin throat. Then he sat the beaked hunting cap at a jaunty angle on his son's head.

"God damn it, boy!" he growled, "but you look fine!"

Guy stared solemnly at his image in the mirror. The transformation was startling; no longer did the gangling farm boy clad in linsey shirt and jeans look back at him, but a young lordling, fit to take his place alongside the frowning ancestors on Fairoaks' walls. He tried to duplicate their look of severity, of command, with the result that Wes, seeing his expression, said gruffly:

"Now, what the devil, boy? Don't you like these duds?"

"Very much, Pa." Guy grinned suddenly. "I was just trying to look important, I reckon. . . ."

"Don't have to try, son," Wes said fondly. "You *are* important, and don't you ever forget it. Come on now, Zeb's got Demon ready."

They went out to the stable together. The great black loomed up before them, his satiny coat glistening in the first light of morning. Guy put up his hand and patted him, and the big horse nuzzled the boy's cheek affectionately. Guy swung into the saddle, and sat there, looking down at his father and the Negro.

"Here," Wes said suddenly, and handed him a small, tissue-wrapped package. "It's a present for Jo Ann. Locket—gold, real gold. Reckoned you wouldn't want to be outclassed in that, neither. . . ."

"Thanks, Pa," Guy whispered, and put the gift in his pocket. Then, partly to conceal his emotion, he whirled Demon about and thundered toward the still closed gate.

"Wait!" Wes roared. "Lord God—boy!"

But Guy lifted the great black effortlessly, soaring up between the two men watching and the pale dawn glow, clearing the big gate, perhaps because of his lesser weight, by a wider margin than Wes had ever done. The horse came to earth again beyond the gate, then in an explosion of great clods torn up by his hooves, he stretched himself out along the road, running.

"Lord," Wes whispered.

"He sure kin ride!" Zeb exulted. "Most good as you, Marse Wes—"

"Better," Wes said proudly. "But then, that boy's already a better man than I ever was. . . ."

When Guy drew Demon up in the curving drive before Fair-oaks, most of the others were already there. Kilrain stared at him, seeing the impeccable cut and splendor of his clothes, and frowned angrily. The source of his anger was obscure, even to himself. But the whole thing was really quite simple: It is easy to forgive those who have wronged us; but those whom we have wronged are a living goad in the flesh, causing us to bleed in our tenderest spot: our self esteem.

"Why do tell!" he said mockingly. "Togged out like a gentleman, and mounted on Demon, too. Anybody would think—"

Guy danced the great black over to where Kilrain sat.

"What would any body think, Kil?" he said coldly.

"Now look, you two!" Jo Ann said, "I won't have any quarreling! Specially not on my birthday. You behave yourselves, you hear?"

The two youths subsided, glowering at each other.

The bugling of the pack saved the situation, as the Master of the Hounds appeared from the kennels in the midst of a rush, a broil of yapping, short-legged beagles. Behind them the taller fox hounds gave tongue now, sounding from sheer exuberance. Then two horsemen stood up in their stirrups, the silver circle of their instruments catching the light, and wound the horns, the notes winging far and clear over hill and forest and echoing back far and faint and sad. Now all of them moved out in a slow line of horsemen and women, with Gerald and Rachel leading, and the others following, two by two.

The hounds were silent now, noses down, fanning out, quartering the woods, the beagles yapping feverishly and tugging at their leashes, and the horsemen moving out, slow and silent, while the winding horns sounded now and again, silvering the morning.

Then the hounds gave tongue, far off and deep, bells plunged in the wind, sounding their ancient dirge of pursuit and death; and the horsemen, leaning forward now, using whip and spur, raced over the broken ground, still silent, the faster horses pulling away in a symphony of hoof beats, beagle yapping, horn notes and the far off belling of the hounds.

It was, Guy found, intensely moving. He found himself surrendering to the magic of it, knowing at last that there were some things beyond mere sport; that this was high drama, pageantry, inevitable tragedy, pagan and barbaric: this sacrifice of the small, furry beast, this clothing of savagery in music and splendor; this glorious ceremony in honor of man's old and bloody gods . . .

He was, of course, in at the death. The fox went down under a smothering rush of the fierce little beagles; and he, rising in the saddle, whipped them off, and bending down, lifted the torn and broken carcass, draping it across his saddle horn.

The others came up to him, and ringed him round about. Wordlessly, Gerald passed him over the leather-covered whiskey flask, in silent accolade, in the recognition that the boy was now a man. As Guy tilted it skyward, he caught a flash of Kilrain's face, dark with anger. Letting the fiery liquor run down his throat, he thought coldly, clearly:

All right, you bastard. This is just the beginning. I'm going to show you. And when it sticks in your craw, reckon you'll crowd me. There's mighty damn little I'll take off you, any-how. You cost me Phoebe, got me one hand half ruined for your sake, and now—

They trailed back through the woods, Jo Ann riding at his side on the saucy grey mare and looking up at him in unconcealed adoration.

"After breakfast's the steeplechase," she said. "You going to ride Demon again—or is your groom going to bring Peg?"

"Demon," Guy said. "Going to save Peg for the afternoon events. Hope that coffee's good'n hot. I could use some. . . ."

It was. And the buckwheat cakes were a golden mountain, swimming in cane syrup and melted butter, surrounded by the rich, dark semicircle of sausage. Guy fell to with the wholehearted appetite of healthy youth; but after a time, he noticed that Kilrain was eating scarcely anything at all.

Starve, he thought grimly; reckon your craw's plumb full already. But wait, boy, for the race—just you wait. . . .

The course was laid out over the worst of the badlands, sweeping over fallen trees and ditches and abrupt precipices, pounding through woodlands where low hanging branches waited to sweep the incautious from the saddle. The winner would be, indisputably, the best horseman among the twenty-five youths lined up at the post, and mounted just as indisputably, upon the best horse.

Guy lounged in the saddle, the picture of contemptuous ease, waiting as Gerald lifted one of the dueling pistols skyward, holding it there as he stared downward at the hands of his watch.

The gun jumped in his hand, the sound of it curiously soft. As he clapped his knees to Demon's sides, Guy found himself unaccountably thinking about the wooden powder flask Jerry had been carving.

Must have used it to load, he thought. It was a damned sight smaller than the silver one, and that there gun sure Lord does sound undercharged—

Then he forgot it in the first smooth rush as he pulled away from all the rest except Kilrain, mounted on a great roan stallion, the two of them thundering neck and neck towards the first obstacle, a white rail fence, propped up alongside a stretch of creek. The two of them took it easily, clearing the false fence and the creek beyond it in one long, reaching leap, coming to earth again, flying toward the fallen giant oak, hearing behind them the splashes as some of the others failed to clear the stream, and even, high and clear, the scream of an injured horse, like that of a woman in pain.

The rail fences between Fairoaks and Malloryhill were nothing: he had jumped them a dozen times. But there was one place that was bad: a cane brake towering up to a height of six or seven feet, and beyond that, an abrupt falling away of the earth to an ancient, dried-up creek bed, so that the jump that started out to be no great shakes even for the average jumper, changed terribly in midair, the horseman, lifting his mount up and over, finding at the very top of his arcing trajectory that instead of the green sod directly below, waiting comfortably for the flying hooves, there was nothing below except the void dropping away to a depth of fifteen or twenty feet into a jumble of rocks and sand. Horse and rider, having already committed themselves to the steeper arc of a high jump, being unable in full flight to change it to the broad, shallow arc this jump actually required, had to wait long seconds ticking away into an eternity, until they crashed sickeningly among the rocks, to lie there until the rider could be carried away to mend his broken bones and the horse shot where he lay.

The cane brake jump was not obligatory. Out of consideration for the youth and inexperience of some of the riders, Gerald Falks had mapped out an alternative route which crossed the ancient creek bed on a level half a mile further upstream. But nobody who took the alternative route was going to win this race; that Guy knew. He was not afraid of the jump, itself; both he and Kilrain and half a dozen other youths among the steeplechasers had cleared greater ones. What worried him was that he might fail to recognize it among the three or four other cane brake jumps, and discover his error in midair, when it was too late to change the pattern of flight to which he had already committed Demon.

Take 'em all like they were broad jumps, he thought grimly. A mite of cane scraping Demon's belly isn't going to do him any harm. But break his legs and Pa'll never forgive me. "Easy, boy! Up'n over—that's it—that's it. . . ."

They had left the others behind from the first. The race was between him and Kilrain. He had known it would be like that. For, whatever faults he might have, Kilrain Mallory was one damned fine horseman.

Guy pulled ahead now. Then he turned in the saddle and looked back at Kilrain. He hadn't meant to pass young Mallory yet. It was far too early in the race to extend his mount, even so great-hearted a horse as Demon. So he looked behind him to confirm a suspicion, seeing at once that it was correct: Kil was holding the roan back, letting Guy take the lead; and he, facing forward again, saw the first of the cane brakes looming up before him.

Smart, he thought grimly. Either wants me to lead him over them, or—Hell, he knows them better than I do. Won this race three times already. No—what he wants is to see me break my neck, and not profit from his knowledge. Going to fool him, though . . . take 'em all the same: low and broad, just scraping the tops. That way, when I come to the right one—

He lifted Demon well back of the first jump, not clearing it entirely, scraping through the cane tops, coming to earth with yards to spare. And the second. But when he came to the third, he knew that this was it, not knowing how he knew, from what source the recognition came, it having exactly the same look as all the others. For the first time in the whole race, he clapped spurs to Demon's sides and went thundering toward it, entering the jump with that strange combination of exaltation and serenity that a man has when he realizes he is doing a thing right, beautifully, perfectly, from the very beginning. The cane brake dropped away below Demon's belly, the dry stream bed was far beneath, yellow in the sun, rolling down and back . . . and the green patch of the opposite bank came up now with dreamy slowness, until Demon's hooves bit in and they were away, and free. . . .

Glancing back, he saw that Kilrain had made the jump as easily and as well, as he. The rest of it was nothing; all he had to do now was to hold his lead; and that, riding Demon, was no trick at all.

Still, it was surprising how fast Kilrain's roan was. He was half a yard behind Demon all the way, so when they came back into the home stretch, over the same ground that the race had covered in the beginning, jumping the fallen oak, coming up to the stream's edge, out of nowhere, Kilrain thundered past, his crop ceaselessly belaboring the roan. Then rising in the saddle, he slashed down, and backward, catching Demon full across the eyes, and the great black recoiling, rising up, rearing, pawing the empty air, crawfished sidewise and fell heavily. Guy, having half a heartbeat to do it, got his left leg up and out of the stirrup at the exact instant before the stallion's weight would have crushed it, and half rolled, half fell, free.

The fall stunned him. When he got to his feet, he saw that Demon was already up again and unhurt, so he hurled himself into the saddle and started after Kilrain. It was too late, of course; but he crossed the finish line only two lengths behind the roan. Coming up to Kilrain and sitting there Guy looked at him wordlessly.

"What's the matter, boy?" Kilrain mocked. "Don't that nag know how to keep his feet, yet?"

"Later," Guy said. "I'll settle with you later, Kil." Then he rode away from there.

The rest of it he went through with cold ferocity, so that all of them there knew they hadn't a chance. He won the gander pull easily; mounting Peg, now, and riding down the list at breakneck speed, jerking the head off the goose suspended by its feet above the track, very cleanly, although the tough neck of the old bird had already yanked four other riders, including Kilrain, ignominiously out of the saddle. After that, the exhibition of horsemanship, displaying his mount's gaits, jumping in the ring without a fault over the difficult and close-placed barriers without even scraping a bar, let alone knocking down any; and last of all, and most difficult, the ring tournament, in which the horseman while riding at full gallop, threads his lance through a series of twelve rings hanging upon strings from above.

He drew Pegasus up, and saluting, dumped the twelve rings into Jo Ann's lap. Alone, of all the contestants, he had not a miss; and, but for the steeplechase, a perfect score.

"Luck," Kilrain said. "Pure coon-nigger luck! Just wait until next year, and I'll—"

"Later," Guy said grimly. "When it's over, Kil. . . ."

"Ladies and Gentlemen!" Gerald Falks called out. "Now we will have the ceremony of crowning the new king! After that, refreshments will be served!"

The children cheered.

Slowly, his face flushed scarlet, Guy got down from the grey and approached the big arm chair, covered with white cloth, which served Jo Ann as a throne. Jo Ann stood up smiling, her crown of gilt paper nestling among her golden curls. She was enjoying every minute of the spectacle.

"Kneel!" she commanded, imperiously. "Kneel, Sir Guy— my very gentil, parfit Knight!"

Clumsily Guy knelt on the edge of the wooden platform on which the throne stood. Gerald handed his daughter a wooden sword. A second later, Jo Ann brought it down on Guy's shoulder with a whack that very nearly knocked him over. The crowd roared with laughter. Then Jo Ann took another paper crown and placed it on his dark head.

"Rise, King Guy the First!" she cried out gaily. "Rise, Your Majesty, and greet your subjects! People, salute His Royal Majesty, King Guy the First, and my Liege Lord!"

Then she kissed him, not on the forehead, as was the custom, but full on the mouth. It was still, Guy reflected wryly, like butting into a post. But he saw Jerry and Rachel staring at each other. Went too far, that time, Jo—baby, he thought. Then he saw the Negroes coming with the ice cream and the cake.

He felt in his pocket and came out with the little package. "Here," he said gruffly. "It's for you."

"Oh, Guy!" she breathed, her slender fingers tearing at the wrappings; then, again, when she had it open: "Oh, Guy!" Softer now; her eyes bright with the rush of tears.

"Now, what the devil?" Guy said wonderingly.

"It's—it's so sweet," Jo Ann said. "I'll wear it always—'til the day I die. And even then I'll be buried in it, I reckon. 'Cause don't you see, Guy darling, it's our pledge! 'Til death do us part, you know. Now put it on me."

Guy draped the little gold chain around her neck. But for the life of him, he couldn't get that tiny catch fastened. His fingers were too big and rough from work and hunting. She had to do it herself, finally. Then, suddenly, impulsively, she leaned over and kissed his cheek.

Gerald Falks shook his head angrily.

"That child," he said to his wife, "is growing up, too damned fast!"

"Or is all Falks," Rachel said dryly. "And I don't know which is worse. . . ."

It was over at last, the cakes destroyed down to the last sticky crumbs, the ice cream vanished, the plates so cleaned that Aunt Becky swore she wasn't even going to have to wash them; and one by one the guests took their leave.

Seeing Kilrain marching toward the hitching rail in the company of several youths, Guy got up from his throne without a word and raced toward them. The rail itself was around the corner of the house, out of sight of the remaining guests. Which was, perhaps, fortunate.

Kilrain had already put one foot in the stirrup of the roan, when Guy reached him.

"Kil," he said quietly, "I reckon you'n I have a crow to pick. . . ."

"Oh, forget it, Guy," Kilrain snapped. "You won after all, so what have you got to complain about?"

"Not the race," Guy said. "Not even the fact that you cheated to win. That makes no difference. You've always been a liar, and a cheat and a coward, too, I reckon. Not even the way you've been so free with your mouth all day. But Phoebe, Kil. Reckon you thought I was going to forget that?"

"I," Kilrain said, "didn't give much of a damn about what you remembered or forgot, Guy. That yaller wench was my property, mine to do with what I damn well pleased. And furthermore," Kilrain looked about him for the approval of his fellows, being, as he was, the type who gathers a sort of artificial courage from the support of the crowd, "I don't see where I have to stand here jawing with an overseer's son, and hill trash to boot!"

Guy stared at him, soberly, solemnly.

"You don't, Kil," he said flatly. "You don't have to put up with that—nor with this!"

Then he slapped Kilrain stingingly across the face.

"Why you—!" Kilrain roared and lunged forward.

Guy stepped back, his face cold and still.

"Don't aim to fight you with my fists," he said, "for all your big mouth about hill trash. And you've taken a blow in the presence of witnesses. I'd like to know what you aim to do about it."

Kilrain hung there, his face whitening. Then, suddenly, he stiffened. A slow smile lighted his eyes.

"I'll meet you," he said. "Although, considering what you are, I ought to have you caned by my niggers. Only that wouldn't teach you anything, bullheaded as you are. I aim to teach you a real lesson—maybe even a permanent one. . . ."

"When?" Guy said.

"In about an hour. My place, edge of the forest. You got a second?"

Tyre Wilson stepped forward. He, like many another of the boys present, had suffered from Kilrain's arrogant bullying.

106

"I'd like to ask that honor, Guy," he said.

"All right," Guy said. "Thanks, Tyre—"

"Don't mention it. It's a pleasure—"

"You, Bob," Kilrain said, "will be my second. All right?"

"Right," Bob Dixon said.

"Just one more thing," Kilrain said slowly, savoring the words: "As the challenged party, I have the choice of weapons. And I choose—"

They waited, staring at him.

"Rapiers!" Kilrain said triumphantly.

"You bastard!" Tyre Wilson spat. "You know what a shot he is, don't you? And although you're a damned fine shot, yourself, you don't aim to play fair and give him a chance. God damn it, Kil, I'll second a duel, not an execution! Guy probably never had a smallsword in his hand in his life."

"He can always apologize. I'll even accept the apology. Running a man through is a messy business. . . ."

They all swung their gaze to Guy's dark face. Slowly he shook his head.

"No, Kil," he said. "I don't apologize. In an hour, then?"

"Right," Kilrain Mallory said.

Guy hadn't a chance and he knew it. The half-hour lesson Tyre Wilson gave him, with foils borrowed from Fairoaks on a pretext, clearly showed that. Despite his superior height and reach, Tyre touched him at will; and Kilrain, everybody knew, was the best blade among the planters' sons, better than Tyre Wilson would ever be.

But Guy was waiting at the appointed place before Kilrain came. Both the seconds made one last attempt.

"Apologize, Guy," young Dixon pleaded. "It's no skin off your nose. We all know you're not a coward."

"Hell, Guy," Tyre Wilson almost wept, "there's a difference between being yellow and being a fool! And you're being a ring-tailed, double-dyed, cross-eyed fool!"

"No," Guy said quietly.

"On guard then!" Kilrain laughed.

Then, to his great surprise he was borne backward by the fury of Guy's attack. He was driven back to the woods' edge by that whipping, slashing, whining blade. So great was the ferocity of Guy's onslaught that it took Kilrain nearly five minutes to realize its clumsiness, its lack of skill.

When he did, it was over almost at once. Kilrain parried *en terce;* parried once again *en quince,* bringing Guy's sword wide of his body; then, in a stinging *riposte,* he stretched himself out long and low, lunging upward toward Guy's unprotected heart. But Guy Falks had the eye of a woodsman; and it was this that saved his life. He parried the thrust, too late and incompletely, so that the rapier's point ripped along the shoulder of his sword arm, opening it almost to the bone and making a gash ten inches long, from which the slashed flesh rolled back like a cavernous mouth.

They had brought neither bandages nor a doctor; and not one of them had ever seen that much blood before.

"You bastard!" Tyre wept. "You stinking, murdering polecat-bastard! You'll meet me for this! I tell you——"

"No," Guy said wearily. "No, Tyre. It was a fair fight and I lost. Now, if one of you gentlemen will be so kind as to lend me his shirt-tail. . . ."

They knelt beside him, binding up the wound with strips cut from their shirts. The blood soaked through the clumsy bandage in seconds. Kilrain stood there, his face ghost-white.

"God, Guy!" he whispered.

And to his vast astonishment, Guy saw that Kilrain was crying.

"Help me up, Kil," he said.

Kilrain and the others got him to his feet. Kil eased Guy's left arm around his own shoulder.

"I'm sorry, Guy," he whispered. "I'm damned sorry. I only meant to pink you a little. And right now, before you fellows, I want to humbly apologize. . . ."

"It's all right, Kil," Guy said. "Bring my coat, Tyre. . . ."

"Take him up to the house," Kilrain said. "Pa'll kill me for this, but that wound's bad . . . You, Bob, ride for the doctor. . . ."

"No," Guy said. "No doctors. Help me into my coat and up onto Peg. Then stay with me 'til I'm most home. We'd better hush this thing up. No need to cause more trouble than necessary. Bess'll take care of me. But I'd rather my Pa didn't find out for as long as possible. . . ."

"Look, Guy," Bob Dixon began, "you're——"

"God damn it, do as I say!" Guy spat.

They rode with him almost to the door of the overseer's house. Then they sat there, watching helplessly as he straightened up and rode into the yard as though nothing had ever happened.

108

Wes Falks was sitting down at supper with his family when Guy came in. He saw his son's pallor, but put it down to fatigue.

"Well, boy?" he said. "How did it go?"

"I—I won, Pa," Guy whispered, "all but the steeplechase and that was pure bad luck. Took a fall, and Kil beat me—"

"Great!" Wes roared. "Knew you would! Put her there, boy!"

Guy looked down at his right arm, dangling helplessly. The slow red streams were still stealing down the back of his hand.

"Can't, Pa," he whispered. "Kind of banged up my arm in the fall. . . ."

"Lemme have a look at it, son," Wes said, his voice darkening. "Maybe you broke the bone—"

"Later, Pa." Guy managed a grin. "Nothing but a bad sprain, and right now, I'm plumb starving. . . ."

"Tom!" Wes snapped. "Pull up a chair for your brother. Don't you want to take off that coat, Guy?"

"I reckon not," Guy muttered, and put out his left hand to steady himself against the chair. He was too late. Going down with the wings of darkness engulfing him, he heard his mother and his sister screaming, and through it Tom's terrified babble:

"The blood, Pa! Lookit th' blood!"

And after that Wes' bull bellow:

"They've killed him! Some bastard's killed my boy!"

He revived quickly enough, to find his head pillowed in his father's arms. Wes was rocking him back and forth in a frenzy of grief, great, hot tears splashing into Guy's face.

"Going to get him!" the big man was roaring. "Going to get him! Going to chaw out his liver with my teeth, gouge out both his damned eyes, and—"

"Pa," Guy said clearly. "You're damn near strangling me!"

Wes stared at his son.

"Great God Almighty!" he whispered. "Tom! Ride for the doctor! Matty! Go get me your Maw's scissors. Have to cut this coat off of him. Char, god damn it, just don't stand there —go call Bess! She's good at nursing. . . ."

He looked at his son, unaware or uncaring of the tears still pencilling his sun- and wind-browned face.

"Who was it, son?" he rumbled. "That's all I want to know—Who was it?"

Guy smiled up at his father, proudly, tenderly.

"It was a private matter, Pa," he said, "and fair fought. Let's leave it like that, shall we?"

8

THE next day, Doctor Wilson came, and sewed up the great gash. And, although the boy was only semiconscious from the whiskey and laudanum they had given him, it was intensely painful. But he lay there without a murmur and took it, his lips whitening, refusing by so much as a grimace to surrender to that blinding, physical anguish, while his father sat beside him, gripping his left hand and sweating.

In the midst of his task, Doctor Wilson looked up.

"God damn it, Wes," he growled, "if you're going to faint or something, get out of here! Anybody would think it was you I was stitching on. . . ."

"Faint?" Wes rumbled. "Me?"

"Yes, you. I've seen it before—mostly in childbirth cases. Men whom I've set broken legs for and fished pistol balls out of their guts with nary a groan nor a murmur out of 'em, keeling over like green fillies because their wives were suffering a mite of natural pain. Everybody knows what a fool you are over this boy. Go on—get out of here. Sit in the kitchen with a bottle. Git drunk. Do anything you want—only get out of my sight and stay there. Send me Bess. She's worth ten of you in a case like this. . . ."

"No," Wes said flatly. "I'm staying, Joe. That there's his right arm you're messing with, you ignorant sawbones! And if I don't watch you, you'll leave him lame for life!"

Joe Wilson grinned at his friend.

"Aw, let me stay, Joe," Wes pleaded. "I've got a grip on myself now."

"All right," Joe said; "but if you start feeling squeamish, for God's sake—leave!"

Joe Wilson bent to his task. There was no sound in the

110

room except the rasp of Wes Falk's breathing. Finally, the doctor straightened up.

"There, now," he said. "That there arm ought to be as good as new in a few weeks. Maybe a mite stiff, but after the wound's fairly healed, he'll be able to exercise it. Won't do to favor it or the strength will never come back. That's the trouble with this sort of thing: gets stiff and a little painful in damp weather, so folks try to nurse it along, and then they do end up lame. This really ain't too bad. Opened up the muscle lengthwise, so that even with the scar tissue, it'll still function properly. Crosswise, a gash like that would have left the arm paralyzed. Wes, I'll take a snort of that rotgut of yours, if there's any left by now. . . ."

"It's all right to leave him?" Wes said dubiously.

"Why sure. He's all right, now. Just needs some rest and good food to build him up again. Have Bess look in on him from time to time during the night. Expect he'll have some fever. That's normal. But if he has too much, and gets delirious, send for me. I'll stop in every day for the first week. But a strong healthy kid like this one usually isn't any real problem. . . ."

The healing, as Doctor Wilson predicted, was both rapid and normal. Three weeks later, Guy was up and about again, looking like the ghost of his former self. The arm remained stiff and painful; and even after it had gained back most of its former strength, Guy found that his right hand, due, perhaps, to some damage to the nerve patterns, had lost much of its former dexterity. He didn't say anything about it, however, but with quiet concentration he went about the difficult business of teaching himself to write, eat and shoot with his left hand. It was slow work, but in the end, he mastered it.

But what he did not, could not, master, was the void left in his life by the loss of Cathy. As soon as he was able to mount a horse he had, of course, ridden down to the river bank to seek her out. He had borne himself with great courage during his encounter with Kilrain; he had supported the pain of his wound with patience and fortitude; but, standing there by the Mississippi, gazing out over the desolate stretch of empty waters, he found, after all, that he was neither too brave, nor too old—for tears.

He charged his father with his loss, naturally enough; but Wes, his face gone dark with shame was able to say with something like conviction, and even partial truth—though

111

the credit for his truthfulness belonged to old Tad Richardson, not to him—

"Yep. I told him, all right. Only it wasn't agreed for him to take the filly away. We only said that we'd try to keep you two apart. Reckon he figured it was the best way. But 'twas his doing, not mine, boy—"

The void was impossible to fill. Jo Ann's childish companionship was no compensation. The gap between ten and sixteen can only be measured in aeons, in light years. . . .

Guy, for all that he was solitary by nature, found his loneliness a burden. And it was the simple companionship he had enjoyed with Cathy that he craved far more than the appeasement of the hungers of the flesh, which, be it admitted, weren't very strong during his long, slow convalescence.

He missed, too, more than he would have ever admitted, the company of Kilrain. But he was too proud to take the first step toward the restoration of their former friendship; and Kilrain was occupied all that autumn with his younger cousin, Fitzhugh Mallory, orphaned by one of New Orlean's outbreaks of yellow fever in which Alan Mallory's brother Timothy, one of the Crescent City's greatest cotton factors, and his wife had perished, leaving nine-year-old Fitz to become his uncle's ward. But beyond his preoccupation with his suddenly acquired cousin-become-younger-brother, it was shame and fear that held Kilrain back.

In his extremity, Guy was moved to try to form some sort of relationship with his older brother. But this was simply impossible; one week of trying showed him that. Poor Tom, he thought. He's plumb, downright pitiful. Reckon I'll have to take care of him and Matty all their lives. . . .

So it was that Guy fell back into his old habits, driven in part by a lingering weakness from his wound that made riding and hunting noticeably tiring. And the chief of these was spending long hours in the library of Fairoaks, reading the masterly collection of books that his grandfather had accumulated. He read them now with true appreciation, having at last the background of passion and sorrow to understand the emotions set down on paper by the masters. There is a time in the youth of a man when his intelligence and his imagination—if he possesses these qualities—catch fire. And Guy Falks, bone and blood and flesh and spirit of his grandfather, possessed them in far greater measure than any other Falks ever born.

He devoured the books with insatiable hunger; and whatever he read became a part of him, materials for his growth. When Hope Branwell arrived from Boston for the winter's instruction of Jo Ann and Guy, she found the change in him astonishing. He soared through the Latin and Greek like a hungry eagle; and, when, having come upon the French and Spanish novels that had been his step-grandmother's joy, he demanded that Hope teach him those tongues as well, his disappointment at her inability to do so was acute.

But he was not one to be easily defeated. Learning by chance that Tyre Wilson was going down to New Orleans for a two weeks' visit with relatives, he charged the boy with the purchase of dictionaries and grammars of the two languages. By spring, he had a fair reading knowledge of them both, though, sadly, he hadn't the faintest idea of how they were pronounced.

That winter, too, he completed the mending of both his speech and his manners, taking Gerald Falks as his model; for despite his contempt for Jerry, he recognized his qualities, being saved from his cousin's preciousness by his own sturdy maleness. Jerry, in etiquette and speech, was an admirable model; educated in the North and in England, he actually possessed the polish that his fellow planters talked about and fondly imagined they had.

It was a strange thing, something more than coincidence, stronger than chance, that young Guy Falks devoted the winter of 1834-35 to such intense intellectual labors. It was as though he sensed the approach of the time when he would need all the weapons of mind and spirit. And though he did not know it, that time was already upon him. For the fatal spring of 1835 was already at hand.

He was sitting on the grey beside his father, supervising the work of the Negroes when he saw Gerald riding toward them. As always, on such occasions, he stiffened, the cold feeling of dread running along his spine like a ghostly hand. Dread—not fear. His contempt for his cousin was great. He did not for one moment believe that Jerry would take the usual step required of any man of honor in his position; Jerry would never dare to challenge Wes. Besides, in the exceedingly unlikely event of a duel, Guy had unshakable faith in his father's ability to take care of himself. What he dreaded was something much worse: that as a mere employee of Gerald's, Wes Falks could be sent packing any time the legally recognized master of Fairoaks took a notion to dismiss him. And Wes hadn't saved any money, could not, in fact, being what he was—a man completely openhanded and generous, not able to keep a dollar in his pocket for as long as a half hour. It would be back to the hills for them; and now, having tasted the fruits of good living, the idea of such a fate was, to Guy, very nearly insupportable.

He sat there, studying Jerry's face. Wes had not yet become aware of his cousin's approach. And, for one moment, Jerry's eyes were unmasked, and naked. The hatred in them was absolutely venomous; but it was mingled with something else —a thing the boy was hard put to define: fear, certainly, but something more: a confused mixture of pitiful self-contempt, and an admiration, a respect for Wes Falks that was curiously feminine.

So, Guy thought, you know. You know, and you shut your eyes and your ears, because the one thing you couldn't stand would be proof. Being sure, being certain, you'd have to do something—and you don't dare . . . don't want to be forced into playing the man, do you, Jerry? Can't stomach having to look over the muzzle of Pa's pistol into his eyes. I pity you. Must be hell in the nights knowing she isn't there; knowing perfectly damn well where she must be, and what she must be doing. Hope life never gets that precious to me. Funny—the only way a man can live really, is to always be ready to die before bedding himself down with shame. . . .

"Wes," Gerald said easily, pleasantly, "I wonder if you'd lend me the boy for a while? I'd like to give him a permanent job that'll put a little spending money in his pockets. . . ."

"What kind of job, Jerry?" Wes asked.

"Oh, nothing too difficult. I had a talk with Captain Morris of the Cincinnati Steamboat Lines in Natchez last week. The captain says his line would appreciate it if we'd establish a refueling station at Fairoaks. Thought I'd put Guy in charge. First he'll have to supervise the building of a dock off the old section—you know, where your father diverted the river to make it flow past Fairoaks—and after that keep a gang of niggers at work every day, cutting cord wood for the boats. I think he's grown up and responsible enough for the job. And he can keep ten per cent of the money he'll be paid for the wood. What do you say?"

Wes Falks turned to his son.

"What do you say, boy?" he said quietly.

"I'd like to have a whack at it, Pa, if you don't mind," Guy said.

"Good!" Jerry said gaily. "Guy, you come with me, and we'll pick up a gang from the south section. After they're outfitted with axes and saws, I'll take you out to the old section and show you where I want the dock built. Then I'll leave you entirely in charge. Nothing like a little responsibility to build character, as your grandfather always said. . . ."

"All right," Guy said. "So long, Pa. . . ."

"S'long," Wes said gruffly. "Thanks, Jerry. . . ."

"Don't mention it," Jerry said.

Guy rode with Jerry at the head of the line of ten Negroes. He did not know what his cousin meant by the old section, but he didn't want to ask. He had an instinctive dislike for too much talking; and, besides, he'd find out in a few minutes anyhow.

He realized suddenly that their route was going to take them right by the old cabin in the cut-over clearing. He frowned. Then he shrugged. Wes was in the fields with the hands, and Rachel, more than likely, up at Fairoaks. Jerry certainly must know that the old cabin was there. And since there was nothing about the cabin itself to attract a body's attention. . . .

He rode on, thinking: Wish Pa would give her up. A man oughtn't to get himself mixed up in a thing that no good can come out of. Though I've no room to talk. What good could have come out of bedding with Cathy? Even if Pa hadn't ruined things, something else would have happened, more than likely. A kid, maybe. That would have been bad. I'd have to marry her then—and Lord knows I wouldn't want to be hitched to a woman who couldn't even read or write her name. . . .

He stopped suddenly, jerking the reins so hard that Pegasus almost reared. He cast a sidelong glance at Jerry, trying to decide if he had seen it, too. But his cousin's face was impassive and serene.

Maybe I'm wrong, he thought, maybe—

Then he clapped spurs to Peg, riding on ahead of the others. He was not wrong. That glint he had seen was the flash of sunlight on windowglass. And those—Lord God— were curtains in the windows! Flowerpots. Women, he groaned inside his heart. Sweet Lord Jesus—women!

He brought Peg about and cantered up to Gerald.

"Cousin Jerry," he said, "you planning to build that dock at Niggerhead Point?"

"Yes," Jerry said. "Why?"

"Don't think it's a good place," Guy said quickly. "Last highwater, river took damn near half that point away. Next flood, it'll all go. You know what the river's like. You told me yourself how grandpa made that cut-off by digging a little ditch in flood times, and the whole blamed river cut itself a new channel to his door. . . ."

"Well," Jerry said thoughtfully. "What would you suggest, Guy?"

"Plum Bluff. I know it's high, but that's the beauty of it. We can slant the dock down from the top, and even the highest water anybody ever heard tell of won't be enough to carry it away. . . ."

Gerald considered the idea. He had great respect for Guy's knowledge and woodsmanship. In fact, his hatred for Wes Falks, having as it did, much justification, did not include his son. Gerald liked Guy, seeing in the boy the force and manhood proper to a future master of Fairoaks. He had long ago resolved not to oppose a match between Jo Ann and Guy, for among all the sons of planters in the district, he was acutely aware there was not the boy's equal.

"All right," he said pleasantly. "We'll have a look at Plum Bluff, first. Lead on, Guy—"

Guy turned his horse at a sharp angle away from the cabin. The Negroes swung into line behind him and Jerry. He was about to let his breath out in a long relief-filled sigh, when he looked back. Then he whirled his mount, thundering toward the cabin.

The Negro was bent over, peering through the window, shading his eyes with his hand. Guy stood up in the stirrups, lifting his crop, bringing it down across the man's back with all the force he could muster. It cut through the linsey shirt like a knife. The Negro fell back, howling.

"Marse Guy!" he moaned. "Lord God, Marse Guy, I was just—"

Guy swung the crop again, sidewise, slashing across the man's face.

"Get," he said. "Get back into line, you burr-headed black bastard! Go on, catch up with the rest! You heard me, get!"

"Yassuh, Marse Guy," the Negro said sullenly. "I thought I saw a light in there and—"

116

"You," Guy said with cold fury, "didn't see anything. Not a blessed, living thing. And if you open your mouth to Marse Jerry or anybody else about this cabin, they'll find your black carcass floating—you understand?"

"Yassuh, Marse Guy," the Negro said. But there was a thing in his tone that Guy didn't like. Something more than resentment, a nuance, a timbre of—defiance, perhaps, but the boy couldn't be sure.

"What was he up to, Guy?" Jerry said after the boy had again caught up with him.

"Nothing, I reckon," Guy growled. "Straggling and looking for a chance to steal, most likely. But there's nothing in that old cabin. Hasn't been occupied for years, far as I know..."

"Strange—" Jerry mused, "there seemed something different about it—something changed...."

"I sleep there sometimes when I'm out hunting," Guy said. "Fixed it up a mite to make it more comfortable. Hope you don't mind, Jerry?"

"Not at all. You're welcome to it. Though I must say I've never been able to see what pleasure there is to be found in the slaughter of animals...."

If you were a man, you would, Guy thought; but aloud, he said:

"Not the killing, Cousin Jerry. The hunting—matching your wits against their instincts, their cunning. I only kill when we can use the meat at the house. I've tracked hundreds of animals clear to their dens and let 'em go without a shot when we didn't need 'em for eating. It's a hard thing to explain: you like it or you don't—and that's about all there is to it...."

" 'One man's meat is another's poison,' so the saying goes, eh, Guy?" Gerald said. "Guess I'm too finicky. Prefer to have other people kill them for me. Well, here's your bluff, boy. Let's see how you manage it...."

Time and again, during that long day, Guy could feel the eyes of the Negro he had beaten, burning holes in his back. But whenever he looked, the man dropped his gaze. Guy kept watching him, but the black worked steadily and well, outpacing the others.

Doesn't want to give me another chance at his hide, Guy thought grimly. He'll tell Jerry what he saw, first chance he gets. Good thing I thought to say I fixed that cabin up. He can talk and be damned now, for all the good it'll do....

Yet there was a thing he couldn't define, working inside him, a feeling cold and still, tugging at his brain. There was something wrong, dreadfully, deadly wrong; but for the life of him, he couldn't put his finger on it.

The nigger would tell—but that didn't matter much. All he had to do was to warn his Pa not to go to the cabin again, in case Jerry had it watched. That, and get rid of those damned flowerpots and curtains. Even Jerry would see through his story, if he found them there. He'd have to do that right away—tonight, as soon as he'd gotten the niggers back into the quarters. Because, sure as shooting, Jerry would ride out to have a look. . . .

They got the line of poles in, cross-timbered and braced, starting with the ones on shore, and ending with those driven into the river bed at a depth where a man could still stand up with his head and shoulders out of water . . . Then they started working backward with taller and taller tree trunks until they had the last ones in, reaching up to the crown of the Bluff. Tomorrow, they'd connect the pole tops with a line of beams, then plank the whole thing over with heavy, rough-hewn planks laid crosswise. Then, last of all, they'd have to put in the last two poles of all, those which would support the dock at steamboat depth, which would have to be driven into the river bed from a raft. Only, first they'd have to build the raft itself. Two, three days more, Guy figured.

Guy had a fair idea how docks were built, for, last year, when a shifting sand bar had made the one before Malloryhill useless by blocking the approach to it with tons of sand, he had helped Tom Stevens and his son, Brad, the Mallorys' overseers, build a new one further upriver where the water was deeper. Tom Stevens, the son of Ashton Falks' overseer and friend, Old Will, was a fine practical engineer, though none of his knowledge came from books. Once he got started, Guy remembered very well how it had been done.

It was well after dark, before he had the Negroes back in the quarters. Jerry, of course, had ridden home long ago, seeing that Guy knew what he was doing better than Wes would have; leaving Guy to pray helplessly that he wouldn't take the route past the cabin. Which, he realized, wasn't likely—unless Jerry already suspected something. From Plum Bluff, the trail past the cabin was the long way around. . . .

Guy sat there on the horse, frowning. He couldn't decide whether it was better to ride home, call Wes aside and warn him, or ride out to the cabin and get rid of the tell-tale evidences of feminine occupancy. Better go to the cabin first, he decided. Pa won't ride out there 'till real late, and I can catch him at home at supper, or a little after if I don't get back home on time. . . .

Still, it was a long way to the cabin. When he got there, he found it locked and the new, glass windows jammed shut. He wasted three-quarters of an hour trying to get it open before he gave up the attempt to work his way in and boldly smashed the windows. He yanked down the curtains and rolled the flower pots in them. Then he ripped the fine, poplin sheets, with the Falks' coat of arms on them, off the cot, and added them to the bundle. The pewter coffee pot and the Fairoaks dishes followed; when he was satisfied he had overlooked nothing, he rode down to the river's edge and tied the whole thing into a bundle, weighting it with rocks—although the flower pots themselves would have been weight enough—and hurled it in, watching with grim satisfaction as it sank beneath the moon-washed waters.

But it was already late, terribly late, he knew that. The only comfort he had was that if his Pa did come, Wes would take warning from the destruction and pilferage he had wrought in the cabin . . . But would he? Wouldn't he put it down to some thieving nigger, and rest secure in the belief that the black's own guilt would prevent him from mentioning the matter to Jerry?

The boy started home at a gallop, riding full tilt through the shadowed woods, leaping fallen logs and ditches more from memory than from sight, until he burst out of the pine dark into the moon-silvered fields, lifting Peg over the fences, riding, going on . . . He swung himself down from the saddle before the grey had stopped moving, his feet already running as he struck the earth, tearing the door open, flying down the hall, crying: "Pa! Pa!"

"He ain't here," Charity Falks said tiredly. "He ain't never come home—"

And he, turning, racing back for the door, the yard, the horse, hearing her voice high-pitched and whining: "Wait— don't you want your supper?"—ignoring the question, being beyond all considerations of hunger, of fatigue and even of filial piety, hurled himself once more into the saddle, taking Peg once more out of the yard, into the moonlit splendor of

119

the fields, now gone grey for him. He was sick with terrible thinking:

Too late too late too late. He's there by now and maybe that nigger's already put Jerry up to watch to spy—And Jerry can shoot from ambush which doesn't take nerve and no jury in the land would—"God damn it, Peg, come on!"

It was very quiet in the clearing before the cabin. There was a pinkish glow from the broken windows, a fire in the grate, perhaps burning more for light than for warmth, because the nights were already warm enough now. And he, leaving the horse, crossing the clearing on foot, standing before that cabin door, lifted his hand to knock; but he could not, seeing their night-shadowed, flame-washed figures locked in close embrace, and he, backing away from there, feeling in his guts the death sickness, feeling profaned at the sight of Rachel's nakedness, that was a blasphemy in the temple of his private gods, whirled, tear-blinded, and ran straight into the arms of one of the five or six men who had accompanied Gerald Falks upon this final, deadly errand of vindication of the honor he did not possess, but must now defend as though he did.

"Hold him," Jerry said quietly. "Tie him up if need be. All right, the rest of you, come on."

Guy did not struggle, but stood there between the two big men who had pinioned his arms, knowing in his heart that it was now too late for struggling, calling out, flight. Too late for anything at all, but the ancient, atavistic drama of two men facing each other across the pistol barrels, linked by chance, by the ludicrous tragi-comedy of their pretensions to honor, condemned equally by their folly and their pride.

It had come to that, Jerry had had the nerve. Tomorrow, Guy thought bitterly, the Mississippi's going to run up stream from New Orleans to Cincinnati; the moon'll rise at dawn and the stars will fall. . . .

He saw them draw back, gathering for a rush. Then they hurled forward, smashing against the door. It crashed inward, splintering against Rachel's screams and Wes' bull-bellow: "Who th' living hell—" Then it was quiet for a long, slow time, until Gerald Falks, his voice high-pitched, but controlled for all that, said clearly:

"You see, gentlemen, that I have ample grounds to petition the superior court for a divorce from this woman. . . ."

"You little bastard!" Wes roared, "I'll break your god damned—"

"You, Wes," Gerald went on imperturbably, "are hardly in a position to threaten. Besides, you have, I believe, some claim to gentility. Let's dispense with this bluster, shall we? I'll meet you on the sand bar at dawn, tomorrow. You have some fame as a shot, so I imagine you won't object to pistols. The choice is yours, of course, though, actually, I'm being generous. I'm aware of the fact that you've had no training with sabres or smallswords, while I have. Come man, what do you say?"

"I should choose bowie knives across a handkerchief at three paces," Wes growled. "But you've always been such a dainty fop, that I'd rather leave your carcass fit for the mourners to look at. Pistols it is. Now get out of here, you sneaking, spying little bastard, and let us get dressed. . . ."

"Don't bother," Jerry sneered. "We shall leave you in peace for the rest of the night. What does one more occasion matter, when you shall pay for them all, tomorrow, my dear cousin? Enjoy yourselves my children, with my blessing—if you can!"

He turned then, and led the raiding party back to where the two men waited with Guy. In the moonlight, the boy could see the other men looking at him in wonder, then with grudging admiration. Gerald Falks had behaved well, better than any man who knew him could have expected.

I, Guy thought bitterly, am going to pistol that nigger. But they were upon him once more.

"Turn the boy loose," Gerald said gravely; then, to Guy: "I'm sorry, son, that you had to witness this. But even you have to admit that I have the right on my side—"

Guy stood there without answering him.

"You'd better come along with us, boy," one of the men said, not unkindly.

"No," Guy whispered. "I want to wait for my Pa—"

"You might have a damned long wait," one of the men chuckled.

"I doubt it," Gerald said icily. "They'll be out of there in ten minutes or I miss my guess. There are some things, gentlemen, that can only be accomplished when the mind's at ease. Well, Guy?"

"I'm staying," the boy said doggedly.

"Very well," Gerald said gently. "And—I'm sorry Guy."

"You should be!" Guy burst out. "Been any kind of a man, you could have kept your woman at home! Letting her run around loose, ruining everything for everybody—"

"That," Gerald said coolly, "was my mistake—but also my privilege. Goodnight, Guy—"

Guy stood there, and did not answer him.

Jerry was, of course, right. In less than ten minutes Wes Falks came out of the cabin, with Rachel on his arm. She was sobbing convulsively.

"You mustn't Wes you mustn't you can't he's been practicing with the pistols for months and I've seen him hit targets so small and far away you could hardly see them and—"

"Pa," Guy said, "may I have the honor of seconding you?"

"Great balls o' fire!" Wes roared. "What in hell's name are you doing here?"

"We passed here with the niggers this morning," Guy said. "I saw the window panes and the flowers. So I made an excuse to turn off from the trail so Jerry wouldn't see 'em. But one of the niggers did. I whipped him away from the window, Pa. Maybe I did wrong. Maybe if I hadn't beaten him, he wouldn't have told Jerry. After work, I came back here and broke in and got rid of the things that would have given you away if Jerry'd come tomorrow by daylight as I figured he would—"

"Only Jerry jumped the gun," Wes said musingly. "Come busting in as brave as a fyce dog bearding a painter. Lord God, who would have thought it? But why'd you come back, boy?"

"Ma told me you hadn't come home for supper. So I figured I'd better warn you. I was too late. Sorry, Pa—"

"Guy!" Rachel wept, "tell him he mustn't fight! Tell him, son—he loves you better than anything in this world, far more than he does me; oh, Guy, for God's sake tell—"

"No," Guy said flatly. "He's got to, ma'am. But don't worry your head over it—Pa can take care of himself. Besides, it won't be you he'll be fighting over anyhow—"

"Guy!" Wes said, warningly.

" 'Cause it appears to me you aren't fitten for any man to risk his life for," Guy went on imperturbably. "No woman ever is, I reckon—"

Wes' great hand came down on his son's shoulder like a hammer stroke.

"God damn it, boy!" he roared. "You'll apologize for that!"

Guy shook his head.

"No, Pa," he said. "I don't apologize for speaking Gospel truth. You won't be fighting over her. You'll just be defending your sacred honor as a man. But don't go yelling at me because I don't cotton to your fancy woman, who's already cost us the best home we ever had or ever will, and all my chances to boot, and tomorrow, maybe even your life—"

"Guy!" Wes thundered; but Rachel laid a restraining hand on his arm.

"No, Wes," she said. "He's right. I'm not worth it, never was worth it, nor ever will be . . . Besides, how it was—the reasons—he doesn't understand. He's too young and. . . ."

"I'm old enough," Guy said flatly. "I've waked in the night with my guts aching from wanting a woman. And when I found her, they took her away from me. But she was mine, and no man had a rightful claim on her. I'm more man than my Pa, I reckon, 'cause I don't bend my head nor shame my body by bedding down with used and borrowed goods. Not out of fear—but because it's a filthiness and an abomination, and what I am wasn't made for sneaking and hiding and prowling like a thief in the night—"

"Guy!" Wes' voice had death anguish in it. "Good Lord, boy, I—"

"You didn't think that way. I'm not trying to shame you, Pa. You're you and I'm me. I would have walked out of Fairoaks first. But I'm done preaching. Like I said, Pa, I'd like to be your second—"

"No," Wes said gruffly. "That no, son. Get along home— I'll be there directly—"

"Guy," Rachel whispered. "Guy, please—"

But he turned like a soldier, and marched towards the waiting horse.

In the morning, he lay in the brush at Niggerhead Point, looking at the sandbar, ten yards out from the shore. He knew what his father planned to do, because Wes had told him:

"Going to wing him, boy. Thought about shooting in the air; but he's too good a shot for me to take the chance. And I can't kill him—not over this. Nor get myself killed and leave you and your Ma and the kids. I'm good with a gun— better'n he is, and a damned sight faster. So don't you worry your head about it none a'tall. . . ."

But he was worried. The thing, the curious part-memory, part-fear, buried deep below the layers of his consciousness, tugged at him for recognition, begging to be brought upward into the light; but he could not remember. He worked it over in his mind: Jerry was too brave. Wasn't like him. He's not brave by nature. He's an arrant, womanish coward; and for him to stand up to Pa so cool and manly, there must be a reason something I don't see, can't remember, Lord God in Heaven help me remember before it's too late—

It was already too late. He could see the boats putting out for the sandbar from a little below the point. His father's face, he could see, was cool and serene; but so, amazingly, was Gerald's—and that was wrong, terribly, dreadfully wrong. It fitted his worry too well; Jerry ought to have been afraid to challenge Wes, and he hadn't been; Jerry ought to be afraid now to meet his cousin, and he wasn't. Something was fatally out of joint, but what? What?

They were on the bar now, facing each other. Doc Wilson was with them, and the two seconds. He could see Joe Wilson's lips moving in an impassioned plea for them to cease and desist from this murderous folly, but he could not hear the words. The wind took them, snatched them from the doctor's mouth.

He saw Jerry turning to say something to Hank Towers, Wes' second. Apparently what he said was not entirely to Hank's liking, because he got up and spoke to Wes about it. Wes nodded briefly.

No, Guy wept. No Pa—you mustn't agree to anything! It's a trick a trick I tell you and if only I knew what it was I'd—

But Hank came back and proceeded to load the pistols. He put them over the crook of his arm, and tendered them to Jerry. Jerry hesitated, then Hank nodded towards one of the pistols. Jerry took that one. That was it, that was where the trick lay! But Hank had loaded them and Hank was a true man and one of the best friends his Pa had and he had done the loading in plain sight of everybody so how, how—?

Gerald and Westley Falks were standing back to back now, the pistols pointed skyward. Guy could see the seconds counting off the paces as they moved out from one another. He counted them, twelve and a half: twenty-five yards. Lord God, any fair shot could take every spot out of the nine of spades at that distance! And both Gerald and his father were better than fair: they were excellent marksmen.

He hung there, his knuckles whitening as he clung to the brush. The seconds were counting, now: One—oh Dear God in Glory help him, don't let him miss, please God!

Two—Don't let him, guide his aim, he's not killing, just

defending himself trying to save his life his home his—

Three—God, God! The puff of smoke spitting out of Wes' pistol, flame-pierced; the sound of it curiously soft; and Jerry spinning half around; but hanging there, miraculously not falling; straightening up now, bringing his pistol up, sighting coolly, precisely, taking all the time in the world about it, until he, Guy, heard his own voice screaming:

"Shoot, god damn it, shoot and get it over with! Oh, dear God don't let him don't let—"

The flame-shot smoke burst, and the slow following sound, short and sharp like somebody breaking a board across, cut through the boy's voice; and he, Wes, stood there like an oak, unmoving a long, long time—so long that Guy breathed: "Oh, thank you, God!" just as the pistol slipped from Wes' nerveless fingers; and his big hands coming up, clawed at his middle. The seconds and Doc Wilson, rushing toward him, caught him by his massive shoulders, easing him down upon the sand; and Guy, unable to bear it, stood up, hurling himself into the shallow water and splashing toward the bar, wading, coming up on the bar, crying:

"Doc, he's not—for God's sake, Doc, tell me he's not—"

"No, son," Joe Wilson said. "But he's gut-shot. 'Pears like the big intestine's perforated—and with this hot weather coming on. . . ."

He turned to the others.

"Help me get him into the boat. I've done all I can here. Better get him home where I can tend to him right. . . ."

And that was all, except the forty-one days it took Wes Falks to die, fighting with his giant's strength for life until the heat of August hung like a smothering blanket over the Delta; nursed all that time by his son, Guy, who stood guard over his father with fierce will, protecting him from the well meaning interference of Charity and the Negroes, doing everything for the big man, feeding him, bathing him, changing bedpans, dressing his wound, going without sleep and very nearly without food for weeks on end, listening to Wes' raving, until the very end; until that day Wes woke up—his eyes clear and serene, but with death already in them—and stretched out his big hand and lay it on his son's dark head, whispering:

"It's no good, boy—I'm going. Tonight or tomorrow. I've done my best. Only one thing I'd like to know, just one thing: I hit him squarely right where I aimed, and he spun around but he wasn't hurt. Nary a scratch on him, Joe says: but I hit him I tell you, I hit him and—"

Guy stiffened, staring at his father.

"Pa," he breathed. "Those were Jerry's pistols you used?"

"My Pa's. Jerry had them. Makes no difference. They're good pieces, and I saw Hank charge 'em. I don't see—I can't understand—"

"Pa," Guy said, the tears strangling his voice, "you hold on! I'll be right back! Don't you go, Pa! I've got something to show you!"

He was back within the hour with the pistol case, having stolen it from Jerry's study with great ease, nobody being there; for, by that time, the divorce case was being heard in the superior court at Natchez, and Jo Ann had been sent away to the Mallory place.

He laid the case on the table beside his father's bed, and opened it. He took the two silver powder flasks out, and shook them. Wes followed his every motion with mute and wondering eyes. One of the flasks made no sound; but the other— the other—

Guy put it down on the table, and going to his room, came back with the hunting knife and a mallet. He turned the flask edgewise, resting the blade of the knife upon it; then bringing the mallet down upon the blade, he split the flask with one clean blow. Slowly his fingers closed over the block of white oak, carved to fit the inside of the flask, only slightly smaller than the interior itself, so that any pistol charged therefrom would be—

"Undercharged," Guy wept. "Not even enough powder left in that flask—with all the space taken up by that block—to send a ball through a silk shirt, let alone a man's frock coat! And the flask would weigh and feel the same. And I saw him carving that block, Pa! I saw him! I can get proof, too! Jerry had to split that flask, just like I did, to put that plug in it; but he damned sure couldn't solder it back together again. Had to get Wil, our blacksmith for that! And Wil can testify—"

"No," Wes whispered. "A nigger's word's not acceptable against a white man in a court of law. . . ."

"But wait 'til I show Judge Griffiths this!" Guy said. "I'll see Jerry Falks dancing on air yet, by God!"

But he saw then, the slow, slight shake of Wes Falks' head. Wes' lips moved, forming words, but they were so low that

126

Guy had to put his ear almost to his father's lips to hear them.

"No. Been enough killing. Forgive him, son. Let him go in peace because I wronged him and whatever, however he—I forgive him. You too—got to. Say you will. Promise—"

"Lord God, Pa!"

"Promise!" Wes Falks' voice came clear. "Promise—no vengeance! Word of honor, as a Falks." His voice died down again. "My dying wish, boy," he muttered. "Promise me. . . ."

"I promise, Pa," Guy said, and sat back, his eyes too blinded to distinguish his father's face.

He sat there while the shadows lengthened in the room. He was very weak and tired from having slept only in snatches in four days and nights, and having eaten only a few scattered mouthfuls in three. It was dark now, and he could hear the whippoorwills calling, far off and sad, over the fields and the river. It was very still in the room, and, after a time he put his head down on the coverlet beside his father's feet and slept. He slept a long time and very soundly.

Then, some time after midnight, a screech owl cried out in the adjacent wood. Guy jerked upright, staring through the darkness at his father's face. From the courtyard at Fairoaks, a hound lifted his head and bayed the absent moon. The sound hung quaveringly on the night air, anguished and lost, echoing against the oakwood, lingering on along the twanging harpstrings of the boy's nerves long after it had died out of time and mind.

"Pa," Guy whispered. "You all right, Pa? Pa, answer me! I said you all right?"

He got up and approached his father's pillow.

"Pa—" the tone was exploratory, sliding down the scale, out of belief, out of hope. Then: "Pa—no. Please, Pa—no— you can't. You mustn't. Don't leave me, Pa, please Pa, stay, stay—"

He hurled himself upon the still form, screaming. When the others came into the room, he was still there, embracing all that was mortal of Wes Falks and crying in such an absolute intensity of pure grief that Matty and Tom fled from the room. It took both Bess and Charity to tear him away from his father's body. Bess led him away, and put him to bed, sitting beside him, cradling his head in her enormous black arms and crooning to him as softly as to a child.

He lay in bed two days and would not eat or speak or even open his eyes; lying there with the tears stealing out from under the closed eyelids and penciling his gaunt cheeks. But he got up for the funeral, dressed himself neatly and with care. He stood beside the grave, dry-eyed, and listened while Reverend Morton spoke the final words of comfort, not even hearing his mother's unrestrained sobbing and Matty's idiotic wails. He had gone far beyond such childish tokens and showings of his grief. . . .

But, as they were placing the flowers on Wes Falks' grave, he turned and saw Rachel standing there, a bouquet of roses as red as blood in her hands. She knelt and placed them beside the others, but Guy bent and snatched them up, flinging them beyond the gate. Then he turned upon her, saying in a voice that rasped through her heart like a rusty file:

"Get out. You've no place here. A man's burying is for his wife and children, not for his whore. You heard me, Rachie. Get out of here."

And she, standing there, looked into his face with love and longing and with grief. Then she turned and walked beyond the iron gate, beyond, in fact, all gates and doors and griefs and memories. . . .

This much is known:

When Rachel rode away from Fairoaks that night, she left her personal maid to pack her things; she instructed the Negroes to have all her valises, trunks, hatcases and bundles at the steamboat landing, in time for the southbound boat. She did not say goodbye to Gerald, which was hardly strange, since he, having been granted both the divorce and the custody of the child, had given her three days in which to leave Fairoaks forever. Nor did she ride up to Malloryhill to say farewell to Jo Ann. . . .

What is certain is that she rode out in the darkness—rode out to meet the darkness—the night before she was to leave Fairoaks for good and all, and she did not come back. A searching party of slaves, headed by the master of Fairoaks, found her riderless horse standing in mute and patient waiting before the door of the cabin where she had found love. They followed the hoof marks, backtracking into the woods, and found her crumpled body—the neck broken very cleanly, so that she must have died at once and without pain—in a dried-up creekbed. The bruise on her forehead showed where the low-hanging branch had swept her from the saddle as she took the dry creek jump.

Yet, Rachel had taken that same jump hundreds of times,

most of them in the dark—a fact which those who held she had added self-murder to her other sins were quick to point out. But never, replied the more charitable, with unthinking minds and tear-blinded eyes.

Her horse still stood before the cabin when Jerry and his Negroes came out of the woods bearing her body. And Gerald Falks, seeing this, remembering, had the Negroes dig her grave before the cabin door, and laid her to her final rest without priest or chant or prayer or even a headstone to mark the place. At his orders, the blacks leveled the grave even with the surrounding earth, and razed the cabin to the ground. And in a space of years no man could tell with any certainty where the cabin had been, or the grave. . . .

It was, perhaps, better so.

9

THERE was only one thing left, one small detail, which didn't matter now; but Guy had to know it. So he sought out Hank Towers, who had served as his father's second, and asked him flatly:

"Did Jerry make a choice between the pistols when he killed my Pa, Mister Towers?"

Hank Towers stared at the boy.

"No," he said. "It was fought fair, far as I could see. . . ." He stopped, and a puzzled light came into his eyes. "There was one thing a mite odd, though, now that you've called it to mind. Jerry comes up to me and says as cool as you please: 'Load mine from the lighter of the two flasks, Hank. I've found these pistols throw truer when they're slightly under-charged. . . .'"

"Then what?" Guy said.

"I asked Wes if he had any objections, as was fair. Wes allowed he didn't care, saying he could hit a squirrel in the eyes at that distance, no matter how the guns were charged. So I balanced the flasks in my hands, and sure enough, one was lighter than the other. So I loaded Jerry's pistol from that one. It didn't strike me as odd at the time. Many marksmen are a wee bit fussy about the charge they put behind the ball. I'd of paid more attention if he'd asked for the heavier one; a duel can be rigged by undercharging one of the guns. But the difference in the weights of those flasks was slight, and he favored Wes with the heavier charge—"

"Thanks, Mister Towers," Guy said, and turned Peg away.

"Wait, son," Hank Towers rumbled. "If there was something wrong—if you know something—"

Guy sat there upon the grey, looking down at the man. His eyes were flat, level, still.

"No," he said. "Nothing wrong, Mister Towers." Then he rode away from there.

Back at the house, the packing was going on in funereal silence. Out of pity, out of friendship for the deceased, Alan Mallory had offered Wes Falks' widow a house and ten acres of land from his upriver plantation. It really wasn't too bad a stretch of ground, if a body knew what to do with it, which was precisely the catch. Of them all, only young Guy Falks was intelligent enough to manage a farm, and he, with this thing inside him like fire, like poison, had not the slightest intention of sinking forever into the yeoman-farmer class. So he accepted the two thousand dollars' blood money that Gerald Falks offered his mother, and bought three prime hands with it. Tom, he reckoned, was hill man enough to keep niggers working; and the blacks, themselves, knew how to farm. He sternly warned Tom against putting all the land to cotton:

"Grow stuff for eating: corn, potatoes, collard greens, cabbage, beans. Get some stock with your first cash crop: pigs, cows, and chickens. And, God damn it, Tom, if I come back and find you haven't done what I said, I'll have your hide!"

"Where you going, Guy?" Tom said fearfully.

"Away. I got things to do. And I don't want to have to worry my head about youall while I'm gone. It'll be a long time before I get back, and I want to know you're eating. And for God's sake, try to keep the house whitewashed, and in good repair. I don't want folks saying we're nothing but hill trash. Promise me, boy?"

"All right, Guy. I promise," Tom said.

Guy stayed barely ten minutes, watching the packing for the move to the new house. Then he rode over to Malloryhill and sought out Kilrain.

"What'll you give me for Peg, Kil?" he said without preliminaries.

130

"Lord God, boy!" Kilrain said. "What you want to sell your horse for? You'll need him at the upriver place and—"

"I'm not going upriver," Guy said flatly, "and where I am going will take money to get to. Come on, Kil, make me an offer. . . ."

"A thousand dollars," Kilrain said at once; "that is, if Pa'll back me up. You come along and help me convince him. I can win back twice that in the first season, racing him, but Pa's a mite tight-fisted. Where you aiming to go, boy? 'Pears to me, farming that upriver place right, you could make something out of it in a few years—"

"Don't aim to be a farmer," Guy said. "None of my folks ever were. By the way, how's your little cousin, Fitz? Haven't seen him but once since he came here. . . ."

"Oh, him?" Kilrain said scornfully, "he's all right—in his way. Always reading and studying—like you. But he can't ride worth a damn, nor shoot not even that good. And he ain't even interested in learning. Books, books, books! Wouldn't mind that so much if he were good for something else. You, for instance, are a real scholar; but you're a hell of a man, too, but Fitz— Lord God!"

"Like to say goodbye to him, too," Guy said. "I liked that kid, the little I saw of him. And anyhow, it takes all kinds of people to make a world. . . ."

"All right, all right," Kilrain said. "You'll see him. But quit trying to change the subject, Guy. Tell me, what are your plans?"

"I," Guy said, "am going for broke, Kil. Either I come back here rolling in money, or I don't come back at all. . . ."

"But where are you going?" Kilrain insisted.

"Cuba," Guy told him. "I've got connections down there. . . ."

"Connections?" Kil said. "Far as I know you've never been out of Mississippi in your life. So how could you have connections in Cuba? Tell me that, Guy—"

"You," Guy said, "are more curious than an old woman. I've got a friend in Cuba and that's a fact. The how's, why's and wherefore's make too long a story, which, considering your bell clapper tongue, I wouldn't tell you, anyhow. Come on, Kil, let's go see your Pa about the money. . . ."

Kilrain stared at him a long moment. Then he shrugged.

"All right, then, let's go," he said. . . .

Guy could hear Alan Mallory's voice clearly through the door of the study.

"A thousand dollars! For a horse? Have you lost your wits, Kilrain? Besides, I've already done enough for those people. Allowed myself to be carried away by sympathy, appears to me now. What's that? Oh, I see—you'll pay me back with the money you win racing this miraculous creature. No thank you, son. I've other plans cut out for you beyond the life of a gentleman jockey—and that's that. No more arguments now!"

The door opened, and father and son came out together. Seeing Guy there, Alan Mallory's face darkened.

"I suppose you overheard," he said. "I'm sorry, Guy—"

"It's all right, Mr. Mallory," Guy said easily. "You're within your rights. But now I'd like to hand Peg over to you, sir, in part payment for that farm, since you're sorry for what you've done. You make me out a due bill for the rest of it and I'll sign it. Don't know how much that house'n land are worth, nor how long it'll take me to pay it all off; but you'll be paid —you have my word on it."

Alan Mallory looked at the boy. Then he put out his hand and laid it on Guy's shoulder.

"You're a man, son," he said gravely; "more man, and more gentleman than this sprig of mine will ever be. No, Guy— I won't take your mount, nor a bill on that land. It's a pleasure to be able to do something for Wes Falks' family—even if I did run off at the mouth a moment ago. The pressure of business, son. So keep your horse and your pride, boy. Perhaps you can sell him advantageously to some other, more sporting planter than I am. . . ."

"No," Guy said. "I won't sell him, now. I'd like to make sure he'll be in good hands after I leave. So with your permission, sir, I'd like to give him to Kil. That way I can be sure he'll be well treated. . . ."

Kilrain stared at his father.

"For God's sake, Pa!" he burst out, "how small are you going to make us look?"

"All right," Alan Mallory sighed. "You win, both of you. But I'll tell you frankly that I can't afford a thousand dollars. When you boys have become planters yourselves, you'll understand why. Even the biggest and finest plantations, like this one, are run on credit. We're rich in land and slaves, but poor in cash. If you, Guy, will accept five hundred dollars, I'll take your horse off your hands. If not, you'll have to look elsewhere, questions of honor and delicacy be damned!"

Guy stood there a long moment, thinking it over. But, in reality, he hadn't any choice, and he knew it. He could get down to New Orleans, walking and living off the country; but beyond that lay the open sea. Stow away on a Havana-bound vessel? He rejected the thought as soon as it was formed. He might have to wait weeks in New Orleans before such a ship put into port; and be without a copper in his jeans to buy food. Besides, he didn't want to appear before Captain Richardson like a starving mendicant; and there was the likelihood that he might have to wait months for the Captain's return if the slaver were off on a voyage to Africa.

"All right, sir," he said. "I'll take it—because I have to. And—thanks, Mr. Mallory; thank you very much."

"Don't mention it, boy," Alan Mallory said.

"Lord God, Guy," Kilrain said as they walked away; "you sure know how to handle people. I couldn't have got five hundred dollars out of my Pa even by going down on my knees in prayer. Anyhow, I'm glad you brought him around. I was feeling kind of small and—"

"Forget it," Guy said shortly. "I'm the one who feels small now, Kil. Your Pa is mighty white—if you only had sense enough to appreciate him. Besides, even if he weren't, it still means a whole lot to have a father at all. . . ."

"I'm sorry, Guy," Kilrain said softly. "Didn't mean to remind you. That was awfully bad business. Folks hereabouts are swearing that there was something crooked about that duel. Nobody—absolutely nobody at all, Guy, believes Jerry could outshoot your Pa. Half of 'em are saying that there was some trick; and the others—"

He stopped short, confusion in his eyes.

"Go on, Kil," Guy said.

"Me and my big mouth!" Kilrain groaned. "Well, I might as well finish it. The rest of them, Guy, are saying that your Pa, knowing himself guilty, didn't even try to hit Jerry. Fred Dalton, Jerry's second, had to threaten to call out one man who kept insisting that Wes fired into the air. . . ."

"Fred's right," Guy said quietly. "I saw the duel, Kil. I was hidden in the brush at Niggerhead Point. My Pa didn't shoot in the air. . . ."

"Then, *how* in the name of God?" Kilrain whispered. "I've seen your Pa shoot. Hell, at twenty-five yards, he could have cut the wings off a fly! And he shot first—everybody knows that—"

Guy stood there, staring at his friend, his eyes bleak and sombre.

"I'd like to go say goodbye to Fitzhugh, now, Kil, if you don't mind," he said.

Kilrain stopped, his mouth open, the words trembling on his tongue. Then he clamped his jaws down, hard.

"All right, come on, then," he said.

They found the boy, sitting in an armchair, reading Suetonius' *Lives of the Twelve Caesars* in Latin. At ten years of age, Fitzhugh Mallory could read both Latin and Greek. He was a born scholar, one of those oddly gentle people who from time to time appear as mutations even among the horse, dog, and gun-worshippers of the sporting gentry. This, Guy, no mean scholar, himself, was prepared to accept, and to appreciate.

Seeing them, Fitzhugh stood up and put out his hand with a smile. He was an extraordinarily handsome boy, lithe and slender, with a pre-Raphaelite sort of face, under a mass of soft-curling, golden hair. But his eyes were still sombre from remembered grief. And that, too, Guy understood only too well.

"Hello, Guy," Fitz said, as Guy took his hand.

"Came to say goodbye," Guy said gruffly. He had a sudden, aching realization that this was the kind of brother he should have had—not Tom with his pitiful want of wit, nor even one like Kilrain with his bluster and arrogance, but a little brother like this one, gentle, intelligent, and fine—whom to lead and teach would have been a delight.

Fitzhugh's eyes darkened with apparent disappointment.

"You're going away?" he said. "I'm sorry, Guy."

"Why?" Guy demanded. "You haven't even had a chance to get to know me. . . ."

"That's what I'm sorry about," Fitz said. "I would have liked to have been one of your friends. . . ."

"Then you are," Guy said. "Shake on it, boy. I'll see you when I get back. But, in the meantime—"

"Yes, Guy?" Fitz said.

"Let Kil teach you to ride and shoot," Guy said.

"But I don't like those things, Guy," Fitz said, "so why should I learn them? I like animals as pets, not to kill them. And where I have to go, I can walk."

134

Guy considered this point of view, not with the mocking derision apparent upon Kilrain's face, but seriously.

"You don't have to like them," he said slowly, "any more than you liked the medicine your ma gave you for a stomach ache. Only they're necessary——"

"Why?" Fitzhugh said.

"Because you've got brains," Guy said. "Brains are mighty rare, and mighty valuable. Kind of like a treasure. A man's got to be able to protect them. 'Pears to me you've got something to give to the world, Fitz. And you don't have the right to rob yourself or other folks of your talents just because you can't shoot straighter than some blustering idiot who's taking up the space and breathing the air that ought to go to a better man. . . ."

"You've got a damned peculiar way of looking at things, Guy," Kilrain said.

"It's not my way—or it wasn't. I'm just saying over again what my Pa told me, many's the time; but it's true, Kil. Another thing Pa always used to say is that the only kind of aristocracy that counts is the aristocracy of brains and talent. Look what this kid's reading. Could you read it?"

"Hell, no!" Kilrain said.

"I can—but not easy. When we came in, he was plumb flipping his eyes over the lines, fast as you please. I tell you Kil, this kid's got more brains in the left side of his hind-quarters than you and I have in our heads. And our kind of folks don't cotton to brains. He'll be bullied, tormented, insulted, if by the time he grows up he hasn't taught 'em a mite of respect with their own damned weapons. They'll even accept brains when they're yoked cheek to jowl with force. So he's got to learn to beat the tom-tom and stomp around the campfire with paint on his face, howling at the top of his lungs —if that's what's generally done; 'cause that's the only way——"

"Lord God, Guy," Kilrain said. "You sound so bitter——"

"He'll be let alone long enough to do what he wants to do, what he damned sure ought to be allowed to do. So he's got to learn to ride'n shoot and hold his liquor like a gentleman; bet on the turn of a card, and be gallant to the ladies. He's got to learn all that, and whatever other kind of damn fool nonsense we judge a man by. 'Cause nothing's free in this world, and that's the price he'll have to pay to be his own man in the end. Now I'm done preaching. What do you say, kid? Will you try?"

"If you want me to, Guy," young Fitzhugh Mallory said.

Forty-five days later, Guy Falks stood on the deck of the schooner *Bonita*, looking out over the harbor of Havana. Nothing he had ever seen before had prepared him for the sight. Behind him was the grim pile of the Morro Castle, and the frowning batteries of the Cabanas lay guarding the seaward approaches; and, as the *Bonita* dropped anchor before the sleepy village of Regla, it seemed to him that truly he had entered into paradise. The water was as still as glass, changing from indigo far out, to clear sapphire closer inshore, and shading off finally into a pale, milky green. From its edge, hills, themselves greener than jade—than emerald—made an amphitheatre for present or departed gods. They were splashed here and there with the foam-white lacework of villas, broken with the blood-purple of bougainvillea, the scarlet cry of frangipani, half-hiding the weathered grey of fort and castle, until on the port side at the land's end, the city basked in the sun like a jewel, while on the starboard, the dark and silent muzzles of the guns brooded over the ever-changing bay.

At that time, in 1835, those niceties of civilization, passports, and customs officials waiting to paw the traveler's belongings into shreds were, happily, still far in the future. So Guy slung his carpetbag into a waiting launch, and went ashore. At once, he was confronted with a difficulty he had proudly imagined was already solved: no one could understand a single syllable of his painfully acquired Spanish. What the heavy Yankee accent does to the lovely, lisping Castilian language—even when acquired with the aid of native teachers—is at best, a disgrace; but the assault, battery, mayhem and murder that young Guy Falks inflicted upon the language he had learned solely from books without ever hearing it spoken, was very nearly a hanging offense.

The good-natured Cubans greeted his efforts with roars of laughter, and dispatched a flock of small boys to seek out a compatriot who spoke English. Guy waited, thinking darkly: I have to learn it right. I know the words. It's the sounds I haven't got. And if they wouldn't rattle at me like a volley of musketry, maybe I could make head or tail of what they're saying. . . .

The flock of small boys was coming back now, whooping around a tall man in rumpled, tropical whites. He wore a

136

straw hat on his head and was impressively mustacheoed.

"Good day, Señor," he said. "What can I do for Your Excellency?"

"Howdy," Guy said. "I'm looking for an American named Richardson. Captain Travis Richardson. You know him, sir? They call him Cap'n Tray. . . ."

At once the small boys set up a howl.

"*El Capitan* Tray! *El Capitan* Tray! *Seguro, Señor! Venga con nosotros y—*"

"Silence!" the interpreter roared, and removed his broad-brimmed panama despite the sun's blinding heat. "Your Excellency has then the honor of being a friend of the Great Captain Tray?"

"Yes," Guy said. "I'm a friend of his. Where can I find him?"

"That, Your Worship," the interpreter said, "presents a certain difficulty. Captain Tray no longer lives in Havana. Since his recent marriage, he has retired from the sea and bought a *finca* some miles from here. But if you care to undertake the expense of renting a pair of horses, I will gladly indicate to you the location of the *finca*. It is this that you desire, no?"

"Yes," Guy said, "that's where I want to go, all right. Just take me to the nearest livery stable, and we'll get started—if it's not taking you away from your business. . . ."

"Ah—but my business is but a small thing and of no importance in comparison to the pleasure of serving any friend of *el gran capitan* Tray!" the interpreter said. He turned to the largest of the small boys: "Thou, Miguel, take up the equipage of the señor and come with us. No! No! I said Miguel alone. We have not necessity for more!"

The boy, Miguel, picked up the carpetbag; and, for the first time, Guy was able to distinguish the words, accompanied as they were by gestures and actions. But his heart sank to his boot tops as he recognized the vast difference between the way they were pronounced, and the way he would have said them, himself. All that time wasted, he thought bitterly; got to start all over now—

They rode out of Havana, with Señor Rafael Gonzalez, as the interpreter was called, carrying, at his own insistence, the carpetbag. They wound up into the blessed coolness of the hills, while Don Rafael chatted away, giving Guy many details about Richardson he had not known:

"Ah, but your great and noble friend is one of the most beloved of men in Cuba, for all that he is a foreigner. It is the contrast, I think, between his behavior, and that of most *estrangeros,* Your Worship understands? In the first place, he has troubled himself to acquire a most excellent command of our language—a policy, if I may dare to suggest it—Your Worship would do well to imitate—"

"I mean to," Guy said. "Go on—"

"Good! In the second place, the Captain has been most splendid in his generosity to the poor. His kindness is proverbial; and it is this, I think, which enabled him to make so brilliant a marriage. It is true that Doña Maria Carmen del Pilar Ortega y Basset was not, herself, of great wealth; but no lady of our land stands higher in social category . . . A brilliant match, and most romantic. For when Doña Pilar expressed a most understandable repugnance for the profession of our good Captain—*amor de Dios!* How I do talk!"

"Doesn't matter," Guy said. "I know Cap'n Tray's a slaver. . . ."

"Ah, what a relief! I should not have liked to betray the Captain's secret. But he earned the respect of all Cuba when he agreed without hesitation to give up the slave trade and the sea, and become a respectable *ranchero* for Doña Pilar's lovely sake. Not that the sacrifice was too great. Any man at all would have done as much for a woman so beautiful!"

Damn, Guy thought; I sure have the most confounded luck! Here I was aiming to sail with Cap'n Tray and some damn fool woman has to come along and ruin everything . . . Oh well, maybe the Cap'n will introduce me around so I can find another ship. . . .

They came, finally, to the gates of the *finca.* At the sight of Don Rafael, a Negro leaped to open them; and the interpreter and Guy continued to ride down the drive for a full two miles before they came to the house. It was a lovely, Spanish colonial *casa grande.* As they drew up before it, a horde of grinning, jabbering blacks surrounded them, holding the horses for them to dismount, struggling for the honor of being allowed to carry Guy's carpetbag, and crying out incomprehensible greetings.

A neat mulatto serving maid came out on the veranda.

"No," she said to Don Rafael, *"El Señor Capitan* is not at home. But the young *Americano* is a friend of the *Capitan?*

138

Surely my Señora will welcome him. Wait a moment, if you please."

They waited on the veranda. In a few minutes, Guy heard the click of high heels accompanying the whisper of the maid's sandals. Then he stiffened; for the damn fool woman he had been busily consigning to hell and beyond for the ruination of his plans, stood before him.

Buenas tardes, Señor," she said. *"Haga el favor de entrar—"* Then seeing his blank expression, she switched at once into very nearly flawless English: "Please do come in, young sir. You are, I have been told, a friend of my husband's?"

But Guy Falks was beyond the possibility of answering. He stood there helplessly, seeing, not the fat, middle-aged woman he had calmly assumed a man of Travis Richardson's years would have married, but a slender girl, with grave, dark eyes, and hair that was not black, but something more, the very absence and negation of light, glowing, where the sun touched it, not with a brownish tinge, but blue. His gaze fastened upon her lips, moving, full-fleshed and warm, like the petals of some great, exotic flower. She smiled at him then, gaily.

"I know," she said. "You had been expecting a woman much older, no? But do not let my appearance deceive you, Señor. I have ten years more than you, if I guess correctly that the young *caballero* has less than twenty years. . . ."

"You're right, Ma'am," Guy got out. "I'm—I'm nineteen."

She laughed once more at the boy's clumsy attempt to add two years to his actual age.

"Or, *tal vez,* not so much?" she teased. "Do not be offended, young sir. Please have the goodness to come in. But first, tell me your name?"

"Guy Falks," the boy said.

"Guy Falks? I've heard that name it seems to me," Doña Pilar said. "Did not you know my husband before he came to Cuba? No; that is not possible. You are much too young. . . ."

"I met the Cap'n," Guy explained, "when he came back to Mississippi to visit his folks. . . ."

"Oh, I remember now!" Doña Pilar said. "You're the boy who wanted to become a sailor. Welcome, Don Guy. Although this is an ambition I am much opposed to, I am glad to meet you. My husband has spoken of you, many times. . . ."

Doña Pilar had turned to the interpreter.

"And thou, Don Rafael," she said in her native tongue,

139

"how cameth thou to encounter this so gallant young caballero of whom my husband has spoken much?"

Don Rafael told her the story, at length and with many gestures. By staring at him intently, Guy found he could follow his words. The thought cheered him. I'll get the hang of it yet, he vowed.

The maid came back with cakes and wine; after which Don Rafael took his leave, leading the horse that Guy had ridden from Havana back to the city; and Guy, to his intense discomfort, was left alone with Pilar.

"My husband will return after the inspection of the *finca* and *los ingenieros,* the sugar mills, is finished, *tu comprendes,* Don Guy," she said. "Meantime, permit me to profit from the occasion and learn something about you. You have, without doubt, a family?"

"Yes'm," Guy said. "But my Pa's dead now. He was killed two months ago in a duel. . . ."

"Oh!" Pilar said, her dark eyes speaking fire, "it is this that I hate! This stupidity and pride of men! What right had he to do it? What right, I ask you, Don Guy, has any man to get himself killed over this folly that you men insist upon calling honor? For us women, it makes nothing, you understand? Nothing, and again nothing, and beyond that, nothing! Except the tears you leave us to shed, and the burden of sorrow you put upon us to carry—" Then, seeing the blank astonishment in his face, she took his hand, suddenly, impulsively.

"Forgive me," she said gently. "My husband says that I have *pajaros en la cabeza*—little birds inside my head, and also that I am more crazy than a watering pot. . . ."

"Why," Guy asked her, "should a watering pot be crazy?"

"I don't know. But it is a thing we always say in Spanish. At least, Don Tray admits with pride that I am a very advanced woman; and this, I think, is true. There are many things in the world I would change, if I were permitted to set up a government of women—"

"Of women!" Guy laughed. "Ma'am—lead me to the next boat!"

"You men!" Pilar said, pouting in mock wrath. "You think we count for nothing except love and motherhood and to be your pets. But you mistake yourselves, I think. Such a government of women would never countenance this barbarity and

140

stupidity of war, for instance, nor the injustice and cruelty of human slavery. . . ."

"But you have slaves," Guy pointed out.

"My husband has," Pilar corrected him gravely; "all of whom shall be freed by his testament upon his death. I had wished to free them at once; but my husband pointed out, justly, I believe, that to do so would be a greater cruelty, unprepared as they are to take care of themselves. So it has fallen upon me to teach them to read and to write and to cipher; while my husband has brought in trained artisans of their own race to instruct them in useful skills. When he dies, they will be able to take their places among civilized men. . . ."

"But suppose they learn all those things before Cap'n Tray dies," Guy said. "Would you still keep them as slaves?"

"Yes," Pilar said sadly. "We will have to—as the government is not kindly disposed toward those who free their Negroes. Hence my husband's will. For not even the government can set aside its own laws regarding the sacredness of a man's final testament. But we have talked enough of these things, I think—and it is time I saw about putting some flesh upon your long bones. You have hunger, no?"

"Yes'm," Guy said, perfectly at ease now. "I have a most canine hunger." And this time he got the words almost right.

"Ah!" Pilar laughed, clapping her hands like a child; "so you do speak Spanish! It was not nice of you to deceive me."

"Not a word," Guy said. "I can read it, though—"

"Then I will teach you to speak it, also. This afternoon, after the siesta, we will begin. . . ."

They sat down to a meal of *arroz con pollo*, that universal Hispano-American dish of rice, chicken, olives, shrimps, clams—and whatever else there happens to be in the kitchen—cooked together. After which the servants brought an endless variety of fish, and after that a heaping platter of pork, all of which was washed down with several kinds of excellent wine, and accompanied by yams, plantains, onions and other vegetables. The dessert was a mountain of fruit; but, when Guy, out of curiosity, tried the two kinds which were new to him: mangoes and papaya, he found that he could not eat them. But there were enough oranges, tangerines, grapes and bananas to fill him to repletion.

Rising, with some difficulty, from the table, he saw the point of the Spanish siesta. After all that food and wine, sleeping during the daylight no longer seemed strange to him. He followed the trim *mulata* to the bedroom which had been assigned to him. The walls, of course, were profusely decorated with crucifixes, statues of the Virgin, and pictures of the saints. Around one bedpost hung a rosary. He lay there, glaring at them; because, according to the hard-shelled Protestantism of his native hills, these things were abominations.

But, already that morning, he had received a sharp and bitter lesson on the folly of fixed ideas; and, being as he was, both alert and imaginative, he began now his first adventure into independent thought. So he lay there, thinking: *No.* Reckon God's not so narrow as to close all roads to his grace, except one. There're millions of peoplẽ who think like we do, but many more millions who don't. And our way of doing things produced Rachie—and theirs, Pilar. So, who's to judge, really? Not me—that's sure. I've done the last judging I'm ever going to do—

So thinking, he drifted off into sleep. He was awakened, late in the evening, by the heavy clump of Captain Tray's riding boots, and his great voice booming out in Spanish:

"And so, my life, what's this about your entertaining a strange man in my absence? Where is he so I may cut his throat, notch his nose, and shear off his ears?"

Guy heard the musical tinkle of Pilar's laughter, and the glissando rush of her reply; but he could not make out what she said. Captain Richardson's delighted roar, however, spoken as it was in English, was clear enough.

"That boy? The kid from back home who—great guns a-roaring! Where is he? Where have you put him, *mi vida?*"

Guy swung his long legs down from the bed, just as the door burst open.

"So you did come!" Captain Tray boomed. "Put her there, son! What the deuce took you so long? I'd just about given you up!"

"Couldn't before now, Cap'n Tray," Guy said, flexing his fingers to make sure none of his bones had been crushed by the captain's grip. "But here I am—a mite too late, it appears, ·seeing as how you've given up the sea. ... ."

"Not too late," the Captain said. "There're other and better ways of making a living. We'll talk about that later. The point is, you're here. Finally persuaded your folks to let you come, eh? Good! Tell me, son, how long can you stay?"

"I didn't have to persuade them," Guy said sadly. "My Pa got killed, and I sort of took french leave from the others. So

142

Antilles, presented no difficulty at all—to return in the dawn with trembling limbs and greying face, spent, exhausted, but with the hunger within him abated, not appeased. Until, at last, he had to give that up as well, for her face, from nowhere, intervened between his and that of his casual partner of the night. . . .

There were no substitutes, not fatigue, nor drink, nor cold baths, nor dangers eagerly sought, nor even the limb-entwined writhing, sweat-glossed and panting in the tropic dark. . . .

Beyond this, he was haunted by the feeling of having betrayed a trust, of having turned aside from his private holy cause: regaining Fairoaks, and taking vengeance on his father's murderer. And though, as the adoptive son, the heir, and one of the island's richest men, he could look forward to a life of ease, a university education and marriage to someone of a family in his own new-found high station in life, he could not rid himself of the idea that to accept those unearned increments of glory, was in fact, a denial of self, a betrayal of what he was.

So he began to spend more time in Don Rafael Gonzalez' company. Don Rafael, by profession an interpreter, had his finger in many pies, among which, Guy was sure, were the sleek and rakish slavers that came beating into port. Finally, after weeks of dropping hints not markedly distinguished by their subtlety, which Don Rafael ignored with matchless calm, the boy burst out:

"Why don't you tell me the truth, Rafe? You know I'm dying to have a try at it. I can't stay here forever, living off the cap'n like this. I want to go to sea—sail to Africa, make myself a fortune in my own right. So why don't you help me, tell me what I want to know?"

Don Rafael contemplated the end of his fragrant *puro*.

"Because," he said, "your father, the good captain, would flay me alive, if I were to put you in contact with the slavers. . . ."

"But he was a slaver, himself!"

"A fact he now regrets. He has much right, my son. Blackbirding is an ugly business. Someday, my own conscience—when I am wealthy enough to afford it—will overcome my greed for gold. And you do not need money. The Captain is rich. . . ."

"I've got things to do," Guy said flatly, "that I sure Lord can't do with the Captain's money. I'll keep you in the clear,

145

Rafe—all you got to do is show me where I can accidentally get in touch with one of the captains or their backers. Come on, you lazy bones—let's take us a ride!"

Rafael smiled, ever so slowly.

"No," he said. "That I am a *vago*—how do you say it in English?—ah, yes, a lazybones, is true. And since it is true, I dislike doing things uselessly. Today, we could ride from one end of Cuba to the other—and we would encounter no one, not even by accident. While, tomorrow—"

"Tomorrow?" Guy growled.

"Si Dios quiere—if God wills, perhaps—who knows? Tomorrow, the possibility of a fortuitous encounter exists—slightly. Very, very slightly; but still it exists. Today, it does not. Not at all."

"Then we will go for that ride, tomorrow," Guy said. "Have I your word on that much, Rafe?"

"Ah—yes. On that much," Don Rafael said; "but on nothing more. Remember, I am opposed to this. I will introduce you to no one. We are merely going riding. Should we stumble upon some of those unwashed and ill-smelling creatures you so ardently desire to meet, it will be purely an accident, and not of my doing. That is, if we encounter anyone at all. . . ."

Guy stood up, grinning at the interpreter.

"Did anyone ever tell you, Rafe," he said, "that you're one very slippery character?"

"Yes," Don Rafael said complacently, "many times. *Seguro,* you will not change your mind?"

"No," Guy said. " 'Til tomorrow, then?"

"Si—hasta mañana, Guy," Don Rafael Gonzalez said.

10

THEY rode out of Havana at a brisk trot, circling the bay until they came to the village of Regla. Two schooners and a brigantine lay at anchor before the town, all of them blackbirders by their looks, and unmistakably by their smell. But Don Rafael did not give them a second glance. He turned his horse's head toward the wooded hills behind the village, and Guy followed him.

146

They broke out of the woods into a cleared field, and suddenly Guy saw some three or four hundred African Negroes, all jabbering at once, laughing uproariously, dressed in trousers put on hind part before, or wearing only shirts, with the trousers draped over their shoulders like a cloak, staring in unconcealed awe at the carriage which stood before them, and flocking to surround the black postilion who at that moment was climbing down from his superb mount.

The postilion cracked his whip for attention, and opening his mouth, shouted a phrase in what was unmistakably an African dialect. At once he was almost smothered by the rush of the Negroes, who pranced around him, snapping their fingers in his face.

The postilion snapped back at them cordially. Guy looked at Rafael in wonder.

"They don't shake hands," he explained. "It's their way of greeting. . . ."

The postilion then launched into a long discourse, cracking his whip at the end of every phrase. The Africans received his message with roars of delight.

"What the devil is he saying?" Guy demanded.

"I don't know, truly. I don't speak Whydah. But I imagine he is telling them what his master instructed him to: what a glorious thing it is to be a white man's slave—"

"But suppose he were to tell them to revolt," Guy said. "I don't reckon there's anybody about who'd know the difference. . . ."

Rafael tilted his head toward the edge of the forest.

"I'm sure those *hombres* would," he said. "I'm certain that among them you'll find men fluent in Ashanti, Mandingo, Soosoo, Whydah, and Kroo. . . ."

Turning, Guy saw the white men standing at the border of the field. One of them, from his dress and bearing, was unquestionably the Grandee who owned the *finca;* but the others were of every species of villainy that the nations of western man is capable of producing. Their captain was American, Guy felt sure.

"Reckon I'll mosey over and hold a palaver with those *hombres*," he said to Don Rafael. "That is, if you don't care to introduce me. . . ."

Don Rafael smiled at him, blandly.

"That, I'm afraid, would be impossible. I am, regrettably, unacquainted with the *caballeros* in question. In fact," he went

147

on, still smiling, "I'm afraid I've even lost my way. I do not recall ever having seen this place before. . . ."

"And you won't remember having been here tomorrow, eh, Rafe?" Guy said mockingly. "Don't worry, *amigo*—far as I can recollect, I haven't seen you in the last three weeks or so either—" Then he moved off, trotting over to where the slavers stood.

"Howdy," he said to the Captain. "Could you use a good navigator, next trip?"

The Captain studied him a long time, and very carefully.

"And you," he said, with a marked New England twang, "be the navigator, I take it?"

"Right," Guy said evenly; "and a damned good one at that. Well, could you?"

"That I could," the Captain snapped, "if I could find one. Cabin boys are ten cents a dozen, though, no matter how much navigation they talk!"

"I beg your pardon, Captain Rudgers," the Grandee put in suddenly; "you mistake yourself, I think. This young man is the adopted son of Captain Tray, and was taught navigation by him."

"Tray's kid, eh?" Captain Rudgers growled. "Well, that does put a different face on things. Look, son, you ride into town with me, and we'll talk the matter over—"

Before Guy could answer, a Negro on horseback came galloping into the field.

"They come, Señores!" he yelled. "The Lancers come—and the Dragoons!"

Instantly, the Grandee disappeared inside his carriage and was driven away at breakneck speed. The villainous crew swarmed out into the fields, cracking their whips. In an amazingly short time, every Negro had been driven back into the dense brush.

Don Rafael lighted a fresh *puro*, and waited while Guy cantered over to his side.

"We'd better get out of here," the boy said.

"Why?" Don Rafael said coolly. "I rather think we should wait in order to give the Captain General's Dragoons the information they shall require. . . ."

Guy looked at the interpreter. If you've got to be a crook, he thought, this is the kind of crook to be!

The Dragoons came prancing into view. As soon as they were close enough for him to distinguish their faces, Guy saw that they weren't looking for slaves or slavers, at least, not very seriously. The young Lieutenant commanding them lifted his hand, and the column came to a halt in a jingle of harness and a clanging of sabres. Then the Lieutenant rode forward, saluting, his hand drawn up against the gleaming brass of his helmet under the fiery glory of his plume.

He stopped a yard away from where they sat, and his smile flashed brilliantly under the inevitable mustache.

"I suppose my Negro reached here in time?" he said. "I see the blackbirds have flown. . . ."

Don Rafael stared at him with that icy contempt a master conspirator always has for a bumbling amateur. Then he smiled coldly.

"I am quite sure," he said, "that we haven't the faintest idea of what the Lieutenant is talking about; have we, Major?"

"Major?" the Lieutenant gasped. "Major who?"

"Major John Hennersy," Don Rafael said impulsively. "Of His Brittanic Majesty's Investigating Service—here at the special invitation of our good Captain General to aid in stamping out this nefarious business of slave trading . . . Major, may I present Lieutenant Jose Maria Garcia-Monbello, who, in his way, is upon much the same errand as ourselves?"

"Delighted," Guy growled, his gruff tone being due as much to the fact that he was strangling with laughter, as to any desire he had to take part in Rafael's masquerade. "Seems a likely spot here for a meeting of slavers, doesn't it, Don Rafael? Perhaps if Lieutenant Garcia would have his men beat about the woods. . . ."

Dutifully Rafael translated Guy's suggestion into Spanish. The Lieutenant's confusion was a joy to behold.

"No—no!" he got out. "This is—private property. And the owner's a—a friend of the Captain General's. I'm afraid the Captain General would not like it if—"

"Too bad," Guy said. "Then we must seek other means, eh, Don Rafael? Good day, Lieutenant—"

He turned and rode away. Don Rafael followed him. The Lieutenant came up to them at a gallop.

"Please—" he almost wept, "Don Rafael, you will have my undying gratitude if you do not permit any knowledge of this indiscretion to reach the ears of the Captain General!"

"Indiscretion?" Don Rafael said. "I was not aware of any indiscretion on your part, Lieutenant. Perhaps if you would stop talking in riddles and make yourself a trifle clearer, I would be able to—"

"No, no thank you!" Lieutenant Garcia said happily, falling back. "I bid you both a very good afternoon, *caballeros!* Go with God!"

They rode on, doubled over with laughter, until the sound of the Dragoons leaving the woods at a gallop in the opposite direction, had died entirely away. Then they turned back to the *finca.* A few minutes later, it was exactly as they had found it in the first place, swarming with grinning Africans listening to the speech-making of the postilion, while the Grandee and the slavers lounged against the trees at the edge of the field.

But now, the Grandee's own overseers moved among the Negroes, leading them away to be fed and to commence their training. And the slavers climbed awkwardly aboard their rented nags. The business was over—at least until the next voyage.

Captain Rudgers called Guy to his side.

"Come with me, son," he said. "I got a little call to pay on the Captain General. You can come along, and after that, I aim to find out how much or how little you know about navigation—which, if you listened to Tray's teachings, ought to be considerable; but knowing as I do what thick skulls youngsters have got, I'd rather find out for myself. . . ."

"Aye-aye, sir!" Guy said, and brought his mount alongside the Captain's. They all rode into Havana together; but long before they reached the Captain General's residence, the group dispersed, leaving Guy alone with Captain Rudgers. The Yankee seemed disposed toward silence, so Guy made no attempt at conversation.

Not until they rode up to the imposing *casa grande* and dismounted before the door, did the Captain open his mouth. When he did, what he said was short and to the point.

"You're Tray's kid," he growled, "or else I wouldn't take you in here. I expect you can be trusted. Whatever you see or hear, you're to forget ever happened—understand?"

"Aye, aye, sir!" Guy said.

"All right, then, come on," Captain Rudgers said. He strode up the stairs and knocked, boldly.

As soon as the door was opened, Guy realized that this was not the first time Captain Rudgers had visited the highest official of the land. The guard ushered them imperiously past the long line of people waiting to see the Captain General.

But they were not taken into the main office; rather it was the smaller office of the secretary into which they were shown.

And here, again, Guy Falks obtained a lesson in the methods by which affairs are actually conducted in the world of men. The Yankee captain sat there a full half hour, chatting casually with the secretary. They discussed the weather, the crops, the beauty of Havana, the price of rum and sugar in Massachusetts, everything on earth except slaves and slavers. It should have been, from Guy's point of view, horribly boring; but it wasn't. There was an undercurrent of excitement, of tension, even, moving like lightning through the smoky room. Guy couldn't put his finger on it, nor upon its cause; but it was there. Captain Rudgers made a slight motion as if to rise. The secretary lifted a warning hand.

"Don't go," he said suavely. "I fancy his Excellency would like a word with you, himself. . . ."

At that moment, as though by some prearranged signal, a door opened, and his Excellency, Captain General of the Island of Cuba, stepped into the room. He was a tall man, with enormous hands and feet, and the exaggerated heaviness of chin and jaw that bespoke Hapsburg blood. He was blond, and his little green-grey eyes didn't focus very well. He kept blinking them in a convulsive, involuntary manner that was almost hypnotic to watch.

"Ah," he said, "my good Captain Rudgers! I trust all goes well with you?"

"Just fine, your Excellency," Rudgers grinned.

"And this of the contraband?" the Captain General said. "No difficulties there, either, *amigo mio?*"

"No, sir," Rudgers said. "None. Your boys have been nice and blind, as usual."

"Good. But the English Commissions grow increasingly suspicious. I'm afraid that expenses in that regard will have to be increased. . . ."

"I guessed as much," Rudgers said drily. "Incidentally, speaking of expenses reminds me; concerning that gambling debt I owe *your secretary here,* I'd like to pay it in your presence, so Don Jaime can't claim forgetfulness as he did once before. . . ."

He took a leather drawstring bag out of his pocket, and began to count out the golden *rouleaux* on the secretary's desk. Guy watched in fascination as the pile grew. Then, at long last, the Captain General nodded, almost imperceptibly, and the secretary swept the *rouleaux* into a small bag of his own.

"I," the Captain General said with a smile, "will take charge of those, Don Jaime. Your amiable señora will thank me, if I do not permit you to gamble them away. . . ."

They enjoy this play-acting, Guy thought. Everybody in this room knows what's going on. But they have to pretty it up. For my benefit? Hardly. The Captain General knows I wouldn't be here with Captain Rudgers if I weren't in on things. . . .

The comedy required a few minutes more of desultory talk to round it off. They shook hands with his Excellency and started towards the door. The secretary, Don Jaime, laid a detaining hand on Captain Rudgers' arm.

"You, good Captain," he said, "have a reputation for generosity. As you must know, my salary as secretary is scarcely sufficient to provide my wife with sufficient *servidumbre* about the house. I wonder if, on your next trip, you might bring me a *Negrito*—a small one, who would not eat too much?"

"Or," Rudgers grinned, "his equivalent in *rouleaux*, Don Jaime? How would that suit you?"

"Far, far better!" Don Jaime said. Whereupon Captain Rudgers counted out two or three of the golden coins into the secretary's hand. Then, having said their *'adios'* he and Guy sauntered down the long corridor to the street.

The entire next day, Guy spent sailing about the islands in his foster father's sloop, with Captain Rudgers as passenger. The old Yankee was a sharp seaman. He commanded the boy to take him to several exact spots on the off-shore islands, and even in the open sea. Upon their arrival, he would check their bearing with the sextant. Guy knew perfectly well that he could do these elementary exercises in navigation blindfolded; but not by word, gesture, or expression, did Rudgers indicate either approval or disapproval. He sat there like a massive heathen idol carved of mahogany or teak, and watched Guy display his seamanship, and his navigator's skill. Finally he growled:

"You'll do. We sail with the tide tomorrow. See that you're aboard, Master Falks."

Now that it was done, Guy was conscious of the enormity of the sin he was committing against his foster parents. There

152

was no doubt that Captain Tray loved him like a son. And Pili, by which affectionate diminutive Guy addressed her, even in thought, loved him better than a son—like a beloved younger brother, or even, subconsciously, something more. . . .

Like many another sea-struck lad, he sat down and penned a farewell note, rather than say his goodbyes in person. His bravery was physical; he lacked this higher kind of courage. But, perhaps with subconscious intent, he blundered about so long and made so much noise packing his things, that he woke Pilar up. This is, of course, difficult to believe in a boy who could steal through the woods so silently he could come within bowshot of his prey without being detected. Nevertheless, it was so: Guy Falks, deft, silent, sure, upon the night of his departure became all thumbs, knocked over his footstool, searched frantically for things whose exact location he knew, or should have known. A man's mind is much less the servant of his will than he is ever willing to believe.

She came into the room, wearing her nightdress. She held a candle in her hand. And her hair, streaming loose, billowing about her small, angelic face, was like the darkness upon the deep, like a night without stars, like time before light was.

She stood there staring at him, her lips pale and trembling in the candleglow.

"You—you're leaving us," she whispered. "Why, Guy?"

He stretched himself up tall before her, the light of the candle hurling his shadow black and gigantic against the ceiling. He stood there, looking at her, a long, long time. When he spoke finally, his voice was strangling in rage and passion.

"You ask me that, Pili?" he whispered. "You?"

"I—I don't understand," she said. "What have I done? Have I not been kind to you. Loved you like a son?"

His eyes were bleak as death.

"Yes," he said flatly. "So kind. So loving . . . Only I'm a man, Pili—with blood in my veins. And you're a woman—the kind of woman that no man coming here like I did, with what I've got behind me, inside me, could ever make a mother of—"

"Guy—" she whispered.

"Mothers are old, Pili. They've got white hair. They don't have mouths that make a fellow wild with wanting to kiss 'em, nor bodies like young palm trees in the Spring trades . . . Nor a walk that sets up a pounding like a brush nigger's tomtom inside my blood—"

"Guy!" her voice was imploring now.

"No. You've been kind, all right—only that kindness has been killing me by inches. And loving—which was pure hell and damnation, 'cause the only kind of love I want from you would shame you forever, and stop me from looking at my own face in a glass for the rest of my life, considering how fine the Cap'n's been to me. So you see—"

"Guy!"

"I got to go. Maybe I can forget—if it's possible to forget you, Pili—loving you like I do—"

He whirled, suddenly, stumbled blindly across the room and sat down in a chair; and, as she came toward him, she saw, in the flick and splutter of the candle flame, his shoulders heaving with the anguish of his sobs. He was, after all, only seventeen years old.

"Guy," she said, her voice drowning in the bitter tides of grief, "listen to me, *hijo mio*, my great and fierce son—if I have wronged you, I humbly beg your pardon for—"

He looked up, then; his eyes red in the light of the candle. He reached out and seized her hand, kissing it hungrily, tenderly, with something beyond passion, something more akin to pain.

"Beg my pardon?" he croaked. "Pili! I should go down on my knees to you to pray that you can forgive me for the things I've said! I've been a dog—a miserable, mangy hound dog critter who ought to be shot and—"

"No," she said tenderly. "You are a man, Guy, and very male. And the woman who becomes yours will be blessed. Perhaps it is my fault that I loved you beyond even my own reckoning . . . Calm yourself. I have no anger at you, but only sorrow at losing you."

He stared at her through the darkness. She bent to him and kissed his mouth, tenderly lingeringly, but without passion.

"*Adios, mi* Guy," she whispered. "*Vaya con Dios*—Go with God!"

Then she turned and left him.

In a little time, when he had gathered his forces, he went. As he rode through the darkness toward Regla, he was sure that he had left his heart with Pilar forever. . . . Later, like all men, he would accept, implicit in its beginning, the end of each new love—and with but little sorrow. But that would be later. Now he had all he could do to keep from crying his grief and pain aloud to the empty sky.

11

THE *Susan R.*, Captain Rudgers' vessel, was a brig; that is, she had only two masts instead of three, like a ship. She was very narrow of beam, and had a prow like the blade of a knife; for, if greed dictated a large, beamy craft with a capacity for many Negroes, prudence—since the almost universal outlawing of the slave trade by the great powers—dictated a racer that could, as Captain Rudgers put it: "outfoot a British cruiser with a couple of hands stationed forward and amidships to breathe into the jibs and dolphin strikers. . . ."

Which was, of course, an exaggeration; but it was a fact that the *Susan R.* could manage a knot or two in air so light that even a wetted finger held upward would fail to distinguish from which quarter the wind came. She was also equipped with three different sets of papers, and as many flags: Portuguese, since that nation was the sole great power which had not outlawed the trade, and had the right, by treaty, to pursue it south of the Equator; American, because in the not unlikely chance that she should fall in with a British cruiser north of the line, the still smarting memories of 1812 greatly decreased the possibility that his Majesty's officers would attempt to board her; and Spanish, because she was, in fact, Cuban-owned, the syndicate which purchased and outfitted her being headed by no less a personage than the humble, apparently poor interpreter, Don Rafael Gonzalez.

How much of Guy's privileged position aboard was due to the fact that he had been "introduced" by Don Rafael, and how much to his being Captain Travis Richardson's adopted son, was an open question among the crew. Nobody—among that collection of scum and scourings of the earth, swept aboard by the pressgangs or bought out of prison by Don Rafael's payment of their fines on condition that they take a berth—not even those who signed up to escape capture for thievery or an occasional casual murder—had either the wit or the breadth of view to appreciate the simple truth: James

Rudgers, hardbitten Yankee master that he was, was not impressed by either of these considerations. The reality was much simpler: Captain Rudgers had not had a first-class, precisely-trained navigator in many a year; and the sense of relief at not having to do his own calculations in order to correct the mistakes of the ruined and drunken swine who were the only type of officers who would ship aboard a slaver, was great. Besides, the contrast between Guy's manners and bearing, and those of the other officers was enormous; James Rudgers had been a gentleman; he found in the boy a nostalgic reminder of his own lost youth.

So, with gruff kindliness, he gave Guy the run of the ship; and thereby, unwittingly, endangered the boy's life. For he placed him in too intimate contact with the crew. Sailors instinctively resent any newcomer who appears to be the Master's favorite; and to that offal and ordure of Havana's jails and crimping houses, everything about Guy: his youth, his good looks, his personal cleanliness, his mode of speech, bespoke a world, which they, being unable to enter, longed, with that black envy that is the capstone of the worthless, to destroy. . . .

On the fifth day out of Havana, standing at the lee rail, and watching the ponderous upsweep and decline of the sea, as the *Susan R.* rolled with infinite slowness, Guy Falks was unaware of danger. Everything about the brig delighted him: her trim lines, the rush of spume foaming backward from her prow as she knifed through, the taut swelling of the sails, the crewmen swarming like monkeys high amid the rigging, the vast emptiness of the ocean itself. . . .

He looked down at the grating which admitted air to the slave deck below. Bending, he tried to peer through it; but he could see nothing. Down there, the blackness was abysmal.

On such a day, blue-white and drenched in sun, the hatches were not battened down. There was no need to close them, since the *Susan R.* carried only the trading goods and ballast. Guy took a quick look around. The foredeck was empty; no one was near the forward hatch. He glanced aloft; the seamen were busy, since the wind had veered to a quarter astern, in cracking on all sail. He dove for the hatch. A moment later, he disappeared below.

It was, he found, impossible to stand or even sit upright on the slave deck. As his eyes became accustomed to the darkness, he made a quick, but accurate estimation that the space between the two decks was less than a yard high. He crouched there, on his hands and knees, peering at the row after row of footirons and chains, laid out, and ready.

He knew that two slaves were fastened together at the ankles by leg irons, a device like handcuffs fastened to the deck with a short length of chain. By counting the number of leg irons, and dividing by two, he could arrive at the exact number of Negroes who would be placed aboard on their return voyage. Grimly he started crawling. He was drenched with sweat before he was one quarter of the way across the forward hold. He had to start over several times, because the lack of air, even with all the gratings open, made his head swim. But he kept at it, doggedly. As nearly as he could figure it, they would bring back two hundred and twenty Africans. He lay directly under one of the gratings, where it was possible to breathe, in the same position that one of the Negroes would be chained, and made mental calculations:

The deck's four hundred and four square feet. I know that from the ship's papers. And that divided by two hundred and twenty gives—less than two square feet of space for a full-grown man!

He tried to imagine how it would be, but he could not. Such abysmal, callous cruelty was beyond his experience or his imagination. Directly under the gratings, where he was, he could breathe with some comfort; but a few feet to either side produced the panicky symptoms of suffocation. And this while the slave deck was empty. How would it be when hundreds of blacks were competing for every breath?

He started crawling back toward the hatch, noticing, as he did so, that the space through which he crawled was scrupulously clean. It had been hosed down, scraped, and holystoned. Still, for all that, a faint, but almost unbearable aroma clung to it—a combination of sweat, urine, and human excretia. If it smells like this now, Guy gasped, how in hell's fire are we going to be able to stand it when it's jam-packed with niggers?

He came up on deck to be confronted with the lifted eyebrows of Jorge Sanchez, the mate.

"And what, Don Guy," Sanchez demanded, "were you doing below?"

"Looking around," Guy told him flatly. "Don Jorge, you can't keep that many people down there—they'll all die!"

"Not people," Jorge said, smiling: *"Butos Negros.* There is

157

a distinction, my charitable young friend. And they won't die—at least not all of them. . . ."

"But," Guy protested, "there's no space—and no air. . . ."

"We set up the windsails on the homeward voyage to pour air into the holds when there is a breeze," Jorge said. "When there is not, we remove the gratings entirely, if the behavior of *los Negros* permits it. We even bring them up on deck in rotation for exercise, food, and air. Besides, only men are kept below. Women are put in the cabin, and boys and girls upon deck, always. At night, once we have tried their temper, the women are allowed to wander about the deck at will, and this—since for reasons of hygiene they are kept quite naked, and often, though they have the faces of ancient monkeys, they have also the bodies of ebony goddesses—can be quite interesting. . . ."

Guy stared at him.

"You mean," he said, "that you bed with Negresses? How could you, Don Jorge? It would make me heave up my rations to touch one!"

Sanchez threw back his head and laughed aloud.

"Ah, my young puritan!" he chuckled. "This is a point of view very rare, and one which, doubtless, will change with time. Of course I bed with *las Negras*. And why not, my saintly Don Guy, since they have exactly the same equipment as other women and rather more aptitude in the use of it? You will find that they are vessels of fire—and as much more enjoyable than our fair Cubanitas, who, at least, have warm blood in their veins, as our women are more pleasing than your icy *Nordicas*, who, one and all, I am told, hate men, detest love, and produce their offspring by some undiscovered method of immaculate conception!"

Guy moved away, shaking his head. He was too preoccupied with his thoughts to notice that Jean Lascals, a scarcely human object spewed up from the sewers of Marseilles, a city which can dispute on even terms its right to the title of the world's wickedest city with any other city known to man, had deliberately thrust his huge, muscular leg across the deck, directly in the boy's path.

Guy crashed to the deck. But he was up at once, his dark eyes flaming.

"Morbleu!" Lascals swore. "Damn your eyes to deep blue hell. You think, then, that you 'ave the right to step upon people?"

158

"You did that with malice," Guy said slowly in French. "Get up, you species of a pig, before I kick your teeth down your throat where you lie!"

"Ah!" Lascals breathed delightedly. "How he crows, this young cock! *Voila, mes gars! Regardez* while I pluck him!"

He came up, a short, square man of tremendous strength, and started toward Guy with his arms outstretched. Guy recognized at once that matching muscle with Lascals was foolish. But skill was quite another matter. He backed away from the man's bear-like rush. Then, as Lascals hurled forward, Guy threw himself backward to the deck, so suddenly that Lascals would have fallen upon him, had not Guy lifted his feet, planting both of them into the Frenchman's stomach. Then, straightening his legs with tremendous force, he flipped the man up and over his own body to crash into a gun carriage with such an impact as to render him speechless. Lascals got up on one knee, shaking his massive head. Guy stepped to the rail, and snatched up a belaying pin. As Lascals swayed to his feet Guy sent him down again with a blow which would have split a less solid skull. This time, Lascals did not move.

Guy stood there, looking at him. Then, lifting his head, he saw the villainous faces of the crew ringing him. Staring from one of them to the other, he knew quite clearly and coldly what he must do. With deliberation and precision he proceeded to kick in three of Lascals' ribs.

He was no longer angry. He did this soberly, out of the icy calculation that it was better to do one fine job on Lascals now, than have to contend with that prize collection of blackguards during the entire voyage. He saw, as he stepped away from his fallen foe, that he had made his point. The crew gazed at him in awe and in fear. Brutality superior to their own was the only language they understood.

He was, of course, called before the Captain and the first and second mates, to render an account of his behavior. But Don Jorge, the first mate, defended him stoutly, remarking, among other things:

"It seems to me that the interests of discipline were well served by this fiery young fighting cock here. He has, *con permisso,* Señor, introduced a little sorely needed respect among those swine. I vote that he be acquitted with the warning to control himself better in the future. This of the belaying pin was enough; that of the feet was, *quiza,* excessive. . . ."

Captain Rudgers looked at Guy. The Captain's face was set in stern lines, but there was a hint of a twinkle in his eyes.

"Very well," he growled. "Master Falks, I hereby fine you the equivalent of his daily salary for every day that Lascals is laid up. Case dismissed!"

On the forty-first day out of Havana, they sighted the shores of Africa. They crawled along off shore, past the three interminable lines which made up the Slave Coast: the white line of surf, the yellow line of beach, and the green line of jungle. They came to the mouth of the Rio Pongo, and started in. Guy was standing at the bow, watching the mangrove swamps and cottonsilk trees and tamarinds growing slowly larger, when a bearded sailor poked him in the ribs.

"Look, kid," the sailor said, and pointed downward.

Guy looked down. He did not say anything. But his knuckles, gripping the rail, whitened.

They were floating in the surf, about fifty of them: women and men, staring with sightless eyes into the brilliant sky. They washed backward and forward with the roll of the surf, and the sharks flashed among them, nuzzling them aside, being too gorged by now to feed any more.

"Why?" Guy got out. "Why?"

"Cruiser cornered 'em," the old tar chuckled, "so they had to get rid of the evidence. Them Johnny Bulls can only convict you when they find you with Bumboes actually aboard—"

Guy stood there, staring.

"Still think you can be a slaver, me pretty lad?" the old tar cackled.

Guy turned and looked at him. When he spoke at last, his voice was the splintering of ice on a mountain pond.

"Yes," he said. "I'm sure I can."

This was his introduction to Africa.

12

THEY moved up the river through the dense and steaming growth. From tree limbs spreading far out over the Pongo, the inverted cones of weaverbirds' nests swung, attached always to those branches too limber to permit the monkeys and snakes to reach the precious eggs. Simians, scampering and chattering through the tree tops, paused from time to time to delouse each other, then swirled off again to send the multicolored flocks of birds exploding into flight.

The river was golden under the sun. Guy saw that it had more than a few half-sunken logs floating in it. But at that moment, a sailor aft, threw some refuse overboard; and the "logs" leaped into vicious life, arrowing toward the spot with incredible speed.

"Crocodiles!" he said aloud; and the old tar, who, for some strange reason, had taken it upon himself to complete the boy's education, laughed aloud.

"Aye," he cackled, "that they be! Mark it, lad, where ever there's slave barracoons, there be crocodiles. Them ugly beasts seem to know where the pickings are going to be good—"

Guy turned and looked at the old sailor.

"From what you tell me," he said, "I don't see how there can be any profit in the trade—if everybody seems to be bent on killing off the niggers in wholesale lots. . . ."

"No, lad, you've taken what I say wrongly," the old tar said seriously. "All I've been trying to point out to you is that it's a rough life, and the likes of you should get out of it as soon as possible. You impress me as being a scholar and a gentleman. I've seen such-like before, starting out all fresh'n fine. And in a few years, Africa ruins 'em. They get the fever and the ague; they have to soak themselves with rum to keep the shakes down. They take up with black wenches, who drain away their wits through their loins and feed 'em stuff prepared by the Ju-Ju Man. Then, when they're shrunken down to trembling wrecks, no longer any good for a woman's pleasure —a dose o' sassy-wood poison in the night, and afore morning the crocodiles has another meal—"

"But," Guy said, insistent upon getting back to the original point, "What about all those niggers we saw floating this morning? I still don't see how there's a profit made if so many die. . . ."

"Profit," the old man said mournfully. "Reckon ye'll make a slaver, all right. To be sure, lad, there be profits right enough. In the first place, the captains insure their cargoes against loss with the marine insurance companies—so a few dead Bumboes don't matter. In the second, a black who costs us anywhere from twenty to forty dollars, brings in from three to five hundred dollars in Cuba. So we can lose half our cargo by death, and still make a profit. What's more, we do everything possible to bring our black ivory home not only alive, but fat'n sassy. Stands to reason, lad. You can't make any money out of a dead Cuffee. . . ."

"Still," Guy said, "there were more than forty floating back there. . . ."

"Accident. More than likely a cruiser'd been hanging about the mouth of the Pongo, and hid to draw the black-birder out. Cap'n was a fool, and scairt to boot. So he got rid of his cargo. Seeing as how there weren't more'n fifty dead Bumboes, it must have been a very small craft—a rank amateur. Regular cap'ns have more heart than that. Never heard of a regular blackbirder deliberately killing slaves unless they mutinied. Nope—it's pretty nigh always some accident that causes deaths. 'Member one time, I put out in a Por- tugee from Bahia. Cap'n was a rumpot. We come out from Brazil with the water kegs filled with salt water as ballast, intending to change 'em for fresh when we had the niggers aboard afore sailing. I replenished the water for the crew; but that damn fool Portuguese forgot to give the order for the niggers' water. Since the Bumboes are only given two water rations a day on most slavers, morning'n night, we'd been out twelve hours before we found out that we only had fresh water for the crew, and none for the Cuffees. And the Cap'n was drunk as usual. Couldn't get him to put back. He cut down our water ration to almost nothing, trying to keep the blacks alive. Finally when we was half way across, when it didn't make no difference whether we put back or kept on, the boatswain let slip that at the rate we was using it, we'd be out of water ten days afore we sighted land—"

"So?" Guy said.

"We mutinied. Even the officers was with us. In the excitement, the Cap'n was killed. After that, we stopped giving water to the Bumboes. Even so, we'd been dry two full days when we sighted Rio—"

"And the Negroes?" Guy said.

"Dead loss. We had twenty-five days sailing afore us when we mutinied," the old tar said. "But such things is rare. Most in general we lose niggers when we have to batten down for a storm, or in a chase—by suffocation—or by them killing each other fighting for the space near the hatches. Once in a great while the surgeon gets drunk or careless and lets a nigger with smallpox aboard. If we find it out in time, we do in the poor devil with laudanum, and heave him over the side, because smallpox is the worst of all. Bye the bye, lad, you been inoculated against it?"

"No," Guy said.

"Better have it done when we get back to Cuba. Don't hurt much and only makes you a wee mite sick. Never can tell when you're going to be exposed in Africa. But here we be! That there is Pongoland, where we'll take aboard our black ivory. . . ."

Guy stared at the low cluster of buildings that lay in the jungle by the river's edge. They were all built of bamboo, thickly plastered with mud. One or two of them had been white-washed. Before them, another vessel lay at anchor, while canoes plied back and forth between her and the dock, loading her with slaves. Guy read her name, *Le Louis*, and turned his attention once more to the slave factory before him.

"I take my leave of ye, lad," the old sailor said. "We have to get the trading goods in order for dealing with his nibs, Mongo Joã . . ."

"Who the devil is Mongo Joã?" Guy demanded.

"The owner of yon factory," the old tar said. "He's a Portugee nigger named Joã da Coimbra, and prouder'n old hell. You'll meet him soon enough. Be seeing you, lad—"

Guy leaned over the rail. As he did so, he heard the whisper of footsteps, as though someone were tiptoeing with elaborate caution across the deck. Raising his head, he saw Jean Lascals, who, on yesterday had groaningly protested his total inability to move, creeping toward the port rail. Lascals leaned far over, and began a rapid exchange with the Negroes in one of the canoes who had come out to demand *bungies* or *dash*, as gifts were called on the Slave Coast. He spoke in Soosoo, so Guy hadn't the faintest idea what he was saying.

From the river below, the Negro boatman replied. In a moment or two, the bargain was struck, and Lascals hurled over a bolt of white cloth, stolen, Guy realized, from the ship's stores. Then, from under one of the boats, he brought forth his seabag, where, obviously he had hidden it the night before. Immediately thereafter, with an agility astonishing in a man who for the past forty days had been proclaiming that he was crippled for life, he swung himself down a line into the canoe. The black boatmen dug their paddles into the muddy gold of the river, and the craft shot straight as an arrow for *Le Louis*.

Guy had a momentary impulse to report this desertion to Captain Rudgers; but he thought better of it. Good riddance, he told himself cheerfully. Now I can sail home in peace—

A few minutes later, the crew lowered the Captain's gig to the river. Captain Rudgers and Don Jorge came out of the cabin, and went down the rope ladder into the boat. Guy watched them being rowed ashore, cursing the sudden shyness that had prevented him from asking to be taken along.

They were gone all day. When they returned to the brig, Senhor da Coimbra, the Mongo of Pongoland, was with them. Guy stared at the gigantic mulatto with frank curiosity. Joã da Coimbra was well over six feet tall, and powerfully built. But now, after years of inactivity, his great muscles were slackening into fat, and his face, which in his youth had been considered handsome, was now heavy-jowled and puffy with dissipation. In color, he was only a little darker than a white man long exposed to the African sun; but his hair was very nearly as kinky as a pure black's; and his lips—in astonishing contrast to his high-arched, aquiline and perfectly Caucasian nose—were thick and fleshy, giving to his whole face an aspect of cruel sensuality.

He was clad in spotless tropical whites, but his snowy shirt was open to the navel; and he constantly mopped his big belly with a huge handkerchief of the finest silk.

Captain Rudgers ordered a table set up on deck, as the heat in the Captain's quarters, even so late in the evening, was very nearly insupportable. Oporto, sherry, and a selection of the finest French and Italian wines were set out, and the best meal the ship stores could afford were served.

Guy stared at this performance in utter astonishment. At Fairoaks, he had seen octoroon tailors and quadroon business men, whose physical appearance was absolutely indistinguishable from pure whites, sent around to the back door for the simple reason that their almost infinitesimal touch of the tar brush was known. It was inconceivable to him that any white man would receive a Negro at his table; and to him, a Negro was a person having any degree of Negro blood whatsoever. But now Captain Rudgers and the mate were not only eating with this big, burly mulatto, but chatting with him in the most affable and respectful fashion possible. The conversation was carried on in English, which the Mongo spoke perfectly with a marked British accent. From time to time he dropped asides to Don Jorge in Spanish equally as pure; and now and then in his native Portuguese, a tongue which resembled Spanish enough for Guy to follow the drift with ease.

The trade goods, consisting of cloth, firearms, Cuban cigars, and doubloons to the value of fifteen thousand dollars, had been inspected and approved before the meal began; so now, at its conclusion, the Mongo Joã lit a *puro* with evident enjoyment and spread wide his big, powerful hands.

"I hope," he said, "that you are not averse to spending a few days with us, Captain Rudgers. Unfortunately, that stupid animal of a Frenchman has quite depleted my stock. I am some fifty Negroes short of your capacity, thanks to his want of foresight. . . ."

"How so, Senhor?" Captain Rudgers said.

"You saw the bodies floating in the surf? Well, three days ago, I completed his consignment. When the blacks were aboard, the ruddy fool battened down his hatches! And in this heat, at that. The next morning, fifty Negroes were dead of suffocation, so, of course, I had to replace them—"

"Why, Dom Joã?" Don Jorge said. "It seems to me that you were under no obligation to do anything more for him—"

"Nor was I," the Mongo laughed, "but the frog-eater whined so piteously that finally I consented to supply him—at one hundred dollars a head! Naturally, gentlemen, when he accepted such an outrageous price, I could no longer refuse him. After all, I am not in this business for my health—"

Frenchman or not, Guy thought hotly, that's a *white* man he's talking about! Why the goddamn yellow nigger bastard! And the Cap'n and Don Jorge sitting there, letting him! I'd like to have his fat carcass at Fairoaks for a week. Reckon I'd teach him the respect that's a white man's due!

"Incidentally," da Coimbra went on, "you've lost a member of your crew to M. Oiseau. Did you know that, Captain?"

"Hell, no!" Captain Rudgers spat. "Which one?"

"A burly brute out of Marseilles, name of Lascals. He came aboard *Le Louis* this morning, complaining of ill treatment. Seems one of your younger officers administered him a terrible beating—which, I have no doubt, he richly deserved. I'm curious to see the man powerful enough to batter that animal. He seems made of solid oak—"

"Wait," Captain Rudgers grinned, "and I'll present him. Master Falks, come here, if you please!"

Guy came over to the table.

"This boy!" the Mongo roared. "But that's impossible! How in the name of heaven—"

"Pure guts," Captain Rudgers said, "and superior quickness and skill. Anyhow, I'm glad to be rid of Lascals. Oiseau is welcome to him. And now, Senhor da Coimbra, may I present my navigator, Master Guy Falks—"

Mongo Joã stood up and put out his hand.

Guy stood there, staring at it in stony silence.

"Master Falks!" Captain Rudgers thundered. "What's the meaning of this?"

"I'm from Mississippi, sir," Guy said flatly. "We don't shake hands with niggers. No kind of niggers, sir; not even fancy yellow ones who talk fine."

Captain Rudgers stood up, his face like granite.

"Master Falks," he said icily, "you may go below. Consider yourself under arrest."

"No, Captain," the Mongo laughed; "this kind of nerve I like. I beg you to pardon the boy. He's young and has a lot to learn. I've met Southerners before. Awfully stubborn people, but rather damned decent, once they've been taught the facts of life. In fact, I'd like you to bring Master Falks ashore with you tomorrow. Perhaps, in my humble way, I can even contribute to his education—"

"Very well," James Rudgers said; "but only on condition that you apologize at once, Master Falks!"

Guy stared at the Captain.

"Is that an order, Sir?" he said.

"Of course!" Rudgers thundered.

"Then I do apologize," Guy said.

"Very well, you may go," the Captain said coldly.

The Mongo, that next night, spread before them an African

166

repast that was very nearly fit for a king. There were suck-ling pigs roasted whole, with stuffings of yam and cassava, followed by chicken stewed in fresh grape juice, served in a sauce of whole grapes and almonds; then came bowls of rice, accompanied by force-meat balls of mutton, minced with roasted ground nuts. For dessert there was a dish of boiled rice, dried in the sun and then pounded to a powder which was then boiled again with goat's milk and mixed with honey —or, for more delicate palates, slices of oranges, sprinkled with sugar and dried coconut, floating in rose water amid the crushed petals of the roses.

All this was washed down with palm wine, brandy, sherry, port, whisky, gin, crème de cacao, absinthe, and a dozen other liquors that Guy had never heard of before. He sipped his wine sparingly, remembering his father's admonition not to get drunk in the presence of a man he didn't trust.

He noticed that even the Captain was three sheets to the wind, while Don Jorge Sanchez was roaring out Castilian drinking songs at the top of his lungs. The Mongo, himself, had put away a prodigious amount of liquor; but as far as Guy could tell; it had had absolutely no effect upon him at all. He lifted his enormous hands and clapped twice, and a group of African musicians appeared in the room. They were equipped with harps made of triangles of wood, strung with the fibers of cane; banjos of gourds, with a drum-tight skin stretched over the opening, and strung with animal gut: a marimba or vibraharp with boards of mahogany strung upon cane fiber, making the keys, while gourds, fastened below made sounding chambers. Of course, there were the usual tom toms.

At a signal from the Mongo, they set up a most unearthly din, which Guy was hard put, at first, to recognize as music. But, presently, a recognizable beat began to emerge from the screeching discord. The drums took it up, emphasizing it; then the curtains separating the dining hall from an alcove drew back; and, in one long, soaring leap, the Timbo dancing girl appeared before the orchestra.

In her, the strong Arabic strain present in the Fulahs of Timbo, predominated over the Negro. Great black brows met over a hawk-like nose. Her flamed eyes were as yellow as coals. Her lips were full and of the color of darkest wine, moist and inviting in her mahogany face. Except for the clanging ropes of bangles, she was naked to the waist. Her breasts were a glory, high and out-thrusting, glistening with the perfumed oil with which her whole upper body had been coated. Below her harem sash, she wore Turkish trousers that were like scarlet mist, while her slim ankles were encircled with bracelets of beaten gold. Hoops of gold dangled from her ears; and, as she whirled closer, Guy saw that her nose had been pierced, and a pearl as big as the egg of a small bird had been set in one nostril.

She spun dizzily, whirling a scarf of scarlet silk about her head; and her night black hair foaming beneath it made dark smoke for its flame. Then, as the beat of the drums slowed, she spun to a halt directly in front of Guy. She planted her feet wide apart, and raising her arms toward the ceiling, she stood absolutely motionless, except that her slim trunk from the hips upward was possessed of an independent life of its own; a slow, undulating tremor seized it; the muscles beneath her mahogany skin rippling upward in waves, crawling upward like snakes, while her proud breasts described bright circles against the smoke-filled air. She moved now, with short, jerky steps, until she was inches away from the boy. Then she swooped toward him, her sinewy body weaving about him like a great, dark, incredibly graceful serpent, but miraculously never touching him. Guy's face flamed redder than a sunset, and great drops of sweat burst out upon his forehead, gleaming in the light of the oil lamps.

The music crashed to a halt. And abruptly as though the life had gone out of her with the cessation of the sound, the Timbo girl loosened all over into bonelessness, collapsing into Guy Falks' arms. He sat there, stiff as a ramrod, holding her with an expression of such absolutely ludicrous surprise and dismay upon his youthful countenance, that the entire company dissolved into helpless laughter. They roared, they whooped, they guffawed; they pounded each other upon the back, pointing with laughter-shaken fingers at the petrified youth.

God damn 'em! Guy thought; god damn 'em all! I'll show 'em!

He bent suddenly, forcing the Timbo girl downward; he found her mouth, kissing her savagely until her eyes flew open, flaming into his, then fluttered closed again, dissolving into the exquisite languor of surrender.

The laughter died. Guy was aware of a heavy hand upon his shoulder. Whirling, he looked into the Mongo Joã's smiling face.

"I am sorry, Master Falks," he said ceremoniously, "but this one you cannot have. She happens to be my number three wife. However, because you are a very brave lad, and also because I have taken a liking to you, I will offer you a substitute. . . ."

He turned to one of the Negroes. "Nimbo," he commanded, "bring Beeljie here!"

The big black salaamed, and disappeared through the door. In two minutes he was back, dragging another Timbo girl behind him. He thrust her roughly into the room; and stood behind her, folding his black arms impassively.

The child, for she was no more than fourteen, swayed there, trembling all over, the great tears streaking her dark, copper face. She had not the fierce, hawk-like beauty of the dancer. Instead, she was lovely, with a soft, childlike loveliness that was wonderfully appealing. Under the heavy brows characteristic of the Fulah girls of Timbo, her eyes were light grey, startling in the the deep mahogany of her face. The face, itself, was finely chiseled and aquiline. Arabic, for all her darkness, the mouth soft and tender, seemed made for love, not lust; her body, just budding into womanhood, was sweet-curving and slender—or it would have been, had it not been for the fact that she was noticeably, shockingly pregnant.

"Well, Master Falks," the Mongo said, "how do you like her?"

"She's—she's—" Guy got out.

"I know. But you needn't worry about that," da Coimbra said suavely. "I am aware of your distaste for the darker brethren. The child should be nearly as white as you are, Master Falks—perhaps even whiter—for you're rather dark and the man who fathered it is a striking blond. . . ."

"Then it's not yours?" Guy said bluntly.

"Of course not. Poor Beeljie's condition, Master Falks, is a prime example of the superior morality of the superior race. I bought her from her ex-master, though technically she was free and could not be sold. Her ex-master, you see, Master Falks, is a trader from your country, and an abolitionist. Beeljie was supposed to be the personal maid of his daughter, who is two years older than she is. Naturally, the good Caucasian gentleman could not afford to keep her until her condition became apparent to his daughter. And as I am always most humbly grateful for the opportunity to do a service for my racial betters—I bought her from him for enough rum to keep him in the most exalted state of drunkenness possible for a month. . . ."

"You," Guy flared, "shouldn't talk about white people that way!"

"I venture to suggest," the Mongo said blandly, "that white people shouldn't act the way they do. Come, Master Falks, what do you say?"

"No," Guy said coldly, and got to his feet. "You've had your little joke, Mongo. Keep her—and enjoy yourself."

Then he stalked out into the night.

The next morning, he was awakened by the crash of gunfire. He rolled from his hammock, and rushed to the window of the bamboo hut the Mongo had assigned him. In the middle of the square, da Coimbra's Negroes were firing off muskets with great gusto; pointing their muzzles toward the empty sky. Guy felt a surge of disappointment at the fact that they were not engaged in repelling an attack, which had been his first thought upon hearing the volleys. They were grinning broadly, evidently enjoying the devilish racket they were making.

In the hills, between the volleys, Guy thought he heard echoes floating back over the jungle; but, after a moment he realized that the faint, far-off sound was the firing of other guns. He dressed in some haste, and came out into the square.

"What the devil's going on?" he demanded of one of the blacks.

"Coffle coming, Cap'n," the Negro said cheerfully. "Cap'n sabby coffle? Much nigger, fat, strong—worth much musket, tobacco, cloth—Cap'n sabby?"

"Yes," Guy said. "I savvy, all right. But why are you shooting?"

"Say 'em good day. Say 'em glad they come. Send out *fanda*. Send out *bungee*. Make *colungee*. Make grand palaver!"

"All right," Guy said; "easy, boy. You send out what?"

"*Fanda*—eats, wine—make 'em plenty drunk. Send out *bungee*, too. Like *dash*, give 'em things, make 'em glad. . . ."

"You send out food and wine to the caravan," Guy said; "then you send them presents. But those other things you said —what were they?"

"Cap'n no sabby? Cap'n plenty new, plenty young. We make *colungee* here. Plenty eats, plenty wine, plenty dancing . . . Then we hold grand palaver. Everybody talk. Coffle chiefs

170

make their *dantica*—say why they come. Then we trade. . . ."

I sure have one hell of a lot to learn, Guy thought. . . .

He had, even more than he realized. First of all, he had imagined, or had acquired somewhere in his reading, the idea that the slavers of the interior of Africa, as opposed to the seagoing merchants in human flesh, were Arabs. Now he saw this was not so. The only difference between the leader of the coffle, his whip-armed guards, and the men and women bound throat to throat by ropes, was that the leaders walked free and were damned handy with the lash. Fully ninety per cent of the blacks sold into slavery in foreign lands, he afterwards learned, were sold by their own people. . . .

He saw Don Jorge coming out of his hut, yawning luxuriously. He went up to the mate at once.

"Look!" he said. "They're all niggers! I thought—"

"That we went into the woods and hunted them ourselves?" Don Jorge said. "Hardly. This is not necessary, my boy. Negroes have been slaves since before the dawn of history. Long before the white man came to Africa, they held each other in bondage and sold their captives to the Arabs and the Egyptians. Now, of course, it's worse. With us to stimulate their greed, they've made slavery the punishment for every crime: thievery, murder, adultery, witchcraft, rebellion against paternal authority. . . ."

"You mean they sell their own children?" Guy said.

"Of course. And their own brothers, sisters, wives they're tired of, a father whose power they wish to usurp. Did you not know, that in most African languages there is no word for good in the spiritual sense? They can say that food tastes good, or that a wench feels good in the dark. But they cannot say that a man is good. The very idea is foreign to their minds. . . ."

"Minds!" Guy snorted. "Never met a nigger yet who had anything like brains. . . ."

"Ah—there you are wrong, my son. Some of them are extremely intelligent. The men driving that coffle are in no way inferior to white men in intellect. They are Fulahs, a Moslem tribe. They can read and write Arabic, are good mathematicians, and are among the finest workers in gold and iron in the world. . . ."

"But I thought," Guy said, "that dancing girl was a Fulah. And she wasn't a nigger. These are!"

"The girl was also a Fulah. The Fulahs are a mixed race.

171

Many of them tend to inherit the traits of their Arabic ancestors, especially those from the town of Timbo, who, by close intermarriage, have kept the Negro strain to an absolute minimum. You will notice that, black as they are, they have the noses and lips of Caucasians, rather than of Africans. . . ."

Guy studied them carefully.

"Not all of them," he said.

"No, of course not," Don Jorge said. "The Fulahs, are, after all, Negroes, for all their Arabic blood. The surprising thing is how many of them, after all these centuries, look Moorish instead of Negro. Their neighbors, the Mandingos, who are also Mohammedans, are pure blacks—perhaps because they made no effort to preserve the Arabic strain . . . but here is our good Mongo, come to *dash* them, snap fingers and make the palaver—"

Guy watched the curious ceremony of African greeting. Everybody cracked fingers with great enthusiasm. Then the Mongo "dashed" his visitors, with bolts of white cotton cloth, German mirrors, beads, and rum. Then the Fulah chieftain made his *dantica*, declaring the purpose of his visit. The Mongo listened with grave courtesy, although the purpose of the visit was distressingly obvious since they were standing in the naked flesh, in bonds and tethers, just beyond the chieftain as he spoke.

Guy was sure that now the business of bargaining over the slaves would begin. But he reckoned without the African love for ceremony and show. No business was transacted until after the *colungee*, or great feast. It lasted all day, and far into the night. Guy became thoroughly sick of it finally, and slipped away to his hut as soon as he could, to sleep.

Noise kept him awake a long time. He was just drifting off into slumber, when something, a whisper, a hint of sound, brought him upright in the hammock. There, in the darkness of the hut, was a shape of deeper darkness; it moved now, coming toward him. Guy put down his right hand and groped for his pistol. But, at that moment, the shadow crossed the window, and the light of the flaring camp fires fell upon her face.

"Beeljie!" Guy breathed.

She put her finger to her lips.

"Do not speak, Master!" she whispered in astonishingly good English. "The Mongo Joã must not hear!"

She came closer. Now Guy could see the tears on her dark

172

face, red as drops of blood in the firelight.

"Why you no take me, Master?" she whispered. "I good girl. I work hard. I make Master many man child, yes! Don't leave me, Master. Mongo cruel. Mongo beat Beeljie when he drunk. Maybe kill baby, yes. Please, Master—you take me?"

"Beeljie!" Guy got out. "I can't. You don't know what our ship is like. In your condition, you'd die, sure!"

Beeljie digested his words, slowly.

"Ship bad?" she said.

"Very bad," Guy said rapidly. "There's no place to sleep. The food is awful, and it rolls and the wind howls, and the sailors are cruel. You understand, Beeljie? You understand why I can't take you?"

Beeljie nodded. The kindliness of his tone was enough to cheer her.

"Aw right. I savvy. But Master, him kind, he come back after baby born and take poor Beeljie 'way?" She smiled suddenly, her teeth like pearls in her dark face. "Master him one damn fine pretty man!"

"Thanks, Beeljie," Guy chuckled. "You're pretty, too. Tell me, how come you speak English?"

"Ol' master teach Beeljie."

"What was your old master like?" Guy asked her.

"Big. Pretty, too, for all him old. Hair like yellow grass, like sunset. Eyes like sea. And lil' Missy, her! Pretty! But ol' master have to sell Beeljie, so lil' Missy no see big belly, no see baby damn near white like ol' Master. Now Beeljie want to go 'way, over sea, far from bad, ugly, fat, cruel Mongo! Master come back and take her, yes?"

"Yes," Guy said quickly. "I'll come back, Beeljie."

"Master give 'em Beeljie kiss to make bargain?"

Guy stared at her.

"All right," he said gruffly. "Come here. . . ."

Her lips were wonderfully warm and soft. And salty with the taste of tears. But it wasn't unpleasant. It wasn't unpleasant at all.

Lying there in the darkness after she had gone, Guy cursed himself savagely. Poor little thing, he thought; poor little nigger wench! But what else could I do? Never would have got rid of her if I had told her the truth. . . .

It was a long time before he slept.

Three days later, the *Susan R.*'s consignment of Negroes was complete. Guy aided Don Jorge in supervising their preparation for the voyage. For the prevention of lice, the head of every man and woman was neatly shaved; then the sailors, with a relish that sickened Guy, branded each of them with hot irons bearing the marks of the various owners of the cargo. The brand was not pressed deeply into the flesh, but touched quickly and lightly so as to merely raise blisters. Before sailing day, Don Jorge assured Guy, the brands would be entirely healed.

On the day of departure, all of the Negroes in the barracoons were given an abundant feast, made up of the special delicacies of their various tribes. They were issued enough palm wine to make them gay, but not drunk. Then, when the eating and singing were over, they were loaded in canoes and rowed to the *Susan R.*'s side.

As they came aboard, rough hands ripped their scanty garments from their shining bodies. Naked as they came into Africa, they went out of it. The men were fettered below, lying on their right sides, doubled into the S form, so that each reposed in the lap of his neighbor. The women were put into the cabin, and the boys and girls allowed the freedom of the deck.

When they were all safely stored away, the Mongo Joã came aboard to say goodbye. He shook hands with the Captain and the Mate. Then, once more, he offered his hand to Guy.

This time, Guy took it.

"Bon voyage, Master Falks!" the huge mulatto boomed. "Should you ever tire of the sea, come to Pongoland. You can have a position as my secretary—and little Beeljie, too—if you like. Think about it. I assure you that no man below the rank of captain ever got rich aboard a slaver—and precious few captains have. The factories are another thing. Think about it, my boy. . . ."

"Thank you, Mongo," Guy said. "I will. . . ."

It is probable that had that first inbound voyage been anything like those which followed it, Guy would have quit the slave trade at once. But it was, in fact, exceptional. The Negroes were docile; the weather ideal. None of the slaves attempted suicide by strangling themselves, or throwing themselves into the sea, or even by the subtler method of self-starvation. No dread sickness appeared to carry off half the cargo. And by these things was young Guy Falks deceived.

Life aboard settled rapidly into routine. At ten in the morning and four in the afternoon, the men were brought topside to be fed. They were separated into messes of ten, and forced to wash their hands in salt water. Then to the cry of *"viva la Havana!"* and a great clapping of hands, a *kidd* of rice, farina, yams, or beans, according to which tribes the Negroes came from, was placed before each squad. A sailor, armed with a cat o' nine tails, stood before each mess. At the first whipcrack, the blacks were allowed to dip their hands into the common bowl. Another crack, and they lifted the food to their mouths and swallowed. If it were not done thus, the old tar explained to Guy, the greedy would wolf down the food, and the slow would starve.

Twice in every twenty-four hours, each black was given a half pint of water. And after their periods of exercise upon the deck, boys passed among women and men alike with pipes, allowing each Negro a whiff or two of tobacco smoke, of which they seemed inordinately fond. Three times a week, their mouths were rinsed with vinegar, and each morning they were forced to drink a dram of it to prevent scurvy.

Once a week, the ship's barber scraped their chins and pared their nails to the quick—this last being a precaution against serious injury in the fights that occurred every night as each slave tried to take as much sleeping space for himself as possible, struggling ferociously for every inch of the deck to which he was glued by his own sweat and that of his neighbor.

During the day, men and women were allowed to talk to one another; but a strict watch prevented these conversations from ripening into intimacy. At night, when, with much cursing and whip cracking, the men were stored below, the crew had their sport of the women without let or hindrance. Like nearly everyone else, Guy had to sleep on deck, because the junior officers' quarters, as well as those of the crew, were now occupied by the women; he finally, after a week or two out, managed the trick of sleeping soundly through the noise of close-coupled bodies thumping against the deck a few feet from his ears.

The voyage went on, with the boatswain making his incessant patrols of purification. The crew washed and swabbed the deck; hosed down the Negroes themselves, daily. A squad of Negroes scraped and holystoned the slave deck during the times their fellows were above. Still the rank, fetid smell lingered, until the boy got so used to it he no longer realized it was there.

He became, unfortunately for him, accustomed to the life, itself. He had had, before shipping aboard the *Susan R.*, some lingering scruples about the blackbirding trade. His memories of Phoebe inclined him to pity Negroes in general. But on that first voyage, he began to lose his scruples, forget his pity. He saw blacks, appointed as guards during the night to watch over their fellow slaves—being for their services rewarded with an old shirt and a pair of tarry trousers, and given a whip to enforce their commands—lash their own companions in misery with a mercilessness and a relish that was sickening to behold. He learned that two or three of the Negroes chained below were free men, paid to pose as slaves and to report the first hint of mutiny to the crew member on that watch. He saw the complaisance of the black women, the readiness with which they submitted to the sailors' lust, the frequency with which they deliberately provoked the white men's carnality.

By the time they reached Cuba, his contempt for the Negro, as a race, was complete. And, sadder still, was his acceptance of his new rôle in life. Although his eighteenth birthday had passed, unnoted during the outward voyage to Africa, he was still too young, and not analytical enough to realize that he was, in fact, adding apples and cabbages. He was, perhaps, not to be blamed for judging a whole people, by the scum and scourings of it with which he came in contact. To him, a Negro was a Negro; he had no way of distinguishing between the Whydahs, Eboes, Congos, Gullahs, Veys, and Folgias—slave peoples from the beginning of time, in whom the slave traits of brutality, moral cowardice, lack of either racial cohesion or loyalty, were so fixed that in the three hundred years of American slavery, only one of the many attempted rebellions would even partially succeed—and the proud and lordly Masai, Kaffirs, Dahomeans, and Ashanti.

Had young Guy Falks been possessed of clearer vision, he might have seen that human ethics cannot be reduced to algebraic formulae: equating wrongs with wrongs to cancel each other out. Whatever the people were whom Guy helped to buy and sell, whatever the greed, cupidity, selfishness, lack of pride, want of loyalty—that fitted them admirably for the role of walking beasts of burden they afterwards became—the fact remains that to stifle mercy, drown scruple, harden one's heart into a stone, reject brotherhood, rejoice in cruelty and become calloused to the sight of almost unimaginable suffering as young Guy Falks did between his eighteenth and his twenty-second birthday, has no justification whatsoever. . . .

The voyage was eminently successful. Only three Negroes died of suffocation on the way home. They were thrown into the sea. Best of all, Captain Rudgers did not take Lascals' pay out of Guy's wages, so that walking down the quay at Regla to Havana he could feel the silver jingling in his pockets, and know at last that he was on his way. . . .

13

ON THE third day of September, 1842, the clipper *Martha Jean* put out from Whydah with eight hundred Negroes aboard, thus averaging sixteen inches of lateral space and five feet, two inches lengthwise, for each slave. These measurements are noteworthy; for they had been achieved by a degree of crowding unusual even among slavers, and over the sturdy protest of Second Mate, Guy Falks.

But rock-ribbed New England captains of Baltimore-built clippers take somewhat less than kindly to gratuitous advice from their junior officers, especially when the junior officer in question is a mere stripling of twenty-four.

"Blast and damn ye for a lubber, Mister Falks!" Captain Peabody roared. "One more sample of your lip, and in irons ye go! No more from ye now, or I'll be tempted to add a taste of the cat as well!"

"Very well, sir," Guy said stiffly. "But begging your pardon, sir, it's not your seamanship I'm calling in question. If I did that I'd deserve to be punished. You, Cap'n, are the best master I've ever sailed with, and I've shipped with quite a few. It's the trade, I'm talking about, sir! I've been in this business six years; and I happen to know that this is the first time you've ever commanded a slaver—"

"Mister Falks," the Captain said, his voice dangerously quiet. "I'm going to give you five minutes in which to have your say. I'm going to hear you out—this once. Afterwards, if one word other than aye, aye, sir, passes your lips, except in response to a direct question, in irons ye go! Do I make myself clear?"

"Perfectly, sir," Guy said. "I'll abide by those conditions with pleasure. I realize that eight dollars per head is an awful temptation; but then, sir, so is the two dollars per head that me'n the boatswain get. All I'm saying, sir, is that it's better to take fewer Bumboes, and to deliver them alive. That way, you'll keep the good will of the owners and stay in the trade long enough to make some real money. . . ."

"All right," Captain Peabody growled. "You've had your say. I'm master aboard, and by heaven and hell, I won't have my judgment questioned! Mine's the authority, and mine's the responsibility. And now, will you be so kind as to give the helmsman a heading? Time's a wasting! Be off with ye, and look alive!"

"Aye, aye, sir!" Guy said, and moved aft.

They stood out from Whydah with the wind almost dead astern, under a brilliant sky. All day the wind held, while the clipper heeled over hard before it, taking the bone in her teeth, racing toward the setting sun. The night came in cloudless, spangled with stars and the crescent of the new moon. It was one of those white nights, in which all the sea is silver and the rush of a taut ship through the darkness is an intoxication and a glory.

But Captain Josiah Peabody, walking the deck, came upon the boatswain coupled with one of the Whydah women. He had the woman whipped, and placed the boatswain in irons. By morning the *Martha Jean* was a doomed ship, and everybody aboard knew it.

The swinish scum who made up a slaver's crew had to be directed with a firm hand; but the kind of discipline natural aboard a man o' war or a first-class merchantman, would not work with them. The blackbirding captains knew this, or soon learned it. So they closed their eyes to drunkenness and lechery; paid more attention to sanitation than to seamanship, and thus got their ships home despite the cut-throats, thieves, drunkards and madmen who made up their crews. But Captain Peabody had an exceptionally hard head, and was, in sober fact, too good a man for the trade upon which he was now embarked. Worse still, he was a martinet by nature. So a glorious sun rose upon a ship whose crew was already sullen, muttering and half disposed to mutiny. Meanwhile, below deck, eight hundred Africans scalded in their own sweat and that of their neighbors, as the rolling of the ship poured pools of it from man to man. With the boatswain in irons, nobody had thought to rig the windsails to force air below to where the Negroes lay.

No purification patrol was organized that morning. That, too, was the boatswain's duty. So by noon, with hundreds of blacks wallowing in their urine and excretia, the stench became offensive even to nostrils hardened to it by years in the Middle Passage.

A seaman approached the Captain and saluted.

"Begging your pardon, sir!" he said, "but them Bumboes is making an awful racket below!"

Captain Peabody considered the matter. He was a stubborn man; but he was no fool.

"Ask Mister Rodgers and Mister Falks to step here a moment," he growled.

The two mates appeared, saluted, and drew themselves to attention.

"What the devil's going on?" Captain Peabody said.

"Well, sir," James Rodgers said hesitatingly; "there're a good many things that haven't been done, sir—"

"Blast and damnit, sir! Why haven't they?" the Captain said.

"Because they're the boatswain's duties, sir," the first mate said crisply, "and you ordered him placed in irons, sir!"

"That I did and there he stays 'til I see fit to release him! You, Mister Falks, what hasn't been done that should have been?"

"First, sir," Guy said slowly, "the windsails haven't been rigged, so the niggers are probably dying of suffocation. Second, it's noon, and the blacks are generally fed at ten o'clock. Third, unless the slave deck is washed, scraped, and holystoned every day, they'll all die of the diseases bred of filth. Fourth, it is customary to exercise them upon the deck during the day. Fifth—"

"That's enough, Mister Falks! Why in the name of the green sea witch, knowing these things as you do, didn't you order them done?"

"Begging your pardon, Captain," Guy said mildly; "as third officer aboard, it is hardly my place to give orders apart from those relating directly to my duties, while both my superior officers are alive and aboard. . . ."

"Impertinent pup, aren't you! And you, Rodgers, why didn't you give them?"

"I considered it indiscreet, sir," James Rodgers said. "Most of those things should be done under the direction of the boatswain—so, I would either have had to beg you to release him, or appoint someone to take his place. And, quite frankly, sir—seeing the temper you got into over the small matter of his topping a black wench—I didn't dare. . . ."

"Small matter!" Peabody roared. "I'll have you know, both of ye, that I'll not have my ship converted into a floating whorehouse! From now on any officer or member of the crew whom I catch consorting with those Negresses is going to get thirty of the cat, well laid on!"

"Then, sir," Guy said crisply, "I hope you are prepared to quell a mutiny."

"Mutiny! Mutiny! Falks, I thought I told you to speak only when you're spoken to! Mutiny! I'll see the whole bunch of these goats and monkeys in hell if they so much as dare to lift a hand!"

"Begging your pardon, sir," Rodgers said, "but Mr. Falks is right. I've made many a voyage with you, sir; but I also made two voyages on the *Congo Queen,* a slaver, that year you were laid up, so I've learned a few things about it. Slavers' crews are always permitted the freedom of the women. It is one of their most ancient privileges. They're not first-class seamen, sir, or naval men. It would be wiser to bear with their human failings than to have to stand off the lot of them—"

"Enough!" Captain Peabody screeched. "Out of here, both of you! Out, I say! Release that blackguard of a boatswain! Have the niggers fed! You, Falks, set up a system for the management of the blacks, and have it on my desk in writing in an hour! Now to your watches, both of you, and look alive!"

Guy prepared his report carefully. And Captain Peabody, be it said, accepted it with good grace. But it was too late; the harm had been done. The sullen crew, held to a discipline beyond their endurance, took out their savage disappointment upon the blacks. From stem to stern, the *Martha Jean* echoed with whip cracks. Worse still, since Captain Peabody had not known enough about the slave trade to take interpreters aboard, and nobody among the officers and men could speak Whydah, the Negroes' complaints and grievances could not be adjusted, so the whining crack of the cat served as answer to everything.

One day out, the first symptom appeared. A Negro wrapped a chain about his throat during the night and strangled himself to death. During the next morning's meal, with a wild

180

screech, another climbed the netting that had been rigged high above the gunnel to prevent just such a thing, and hurled himself into the sea.

The third day out, the boatswain sought out Guy Falks and whispered:

"Nine of them Bumboes ain't eating, sir. You better tell the Cap'n—"

Guy went aft, and saluted the Captain.

"Good day, sir," he said stiffly. "I'd like the Captain's permission to speak, sir—if I may. It's important."

"Then speak and be damned!" the Captain roared. "What is it now, Falks?"

"Nine of the niggers are refusing to eat, sir," Guy said. "If something isn't done, this thing will spread, and we'll have a whole wave of suicides on our hands. . . ."

"Do you, Mister Falks," Captain Peabody said soberly, "know what to do in a case like this?"

"Aye, sir. But it's not pretty—"

"Pretty or not, order it done! 'Fore God, this ship is bewitched! Every damned thing goes wrong! Come, lad, I want to see those Negroes fed. . . ."

It was not pretty. The boatswain and a squad of fifteen men brought the nine Negroes up on deck. Then a brazier was brought, and one of the men blew the coals into fiery redness with a hand bellows. Two of the men seized a Negro, forcing him to his knees. Then the boatswain took a live coal out with the tongs, and applied it to the Negro's lips. They sizzled and broke; blood gushed over his chin; instantly, as the black opened his mouth to scream, another crewman forced the *speculum oris,* a great funnel with a wedge-shaped tube at its end, into the Negro's mouth. Then another shoveled a sticky mess of mashed horsebeans into the bell of the funnel, while the butt end of a cat, punched into the black's Adam's apple at intervals, forced him to swallow.

It was indicative of the desperation or the stubbornness of the Negroes, that they had to feed four in this fashion before the others gave in. Three of the blacks, however, vomited up the food at once. From experience, Guy knew there was no hope for them; in a short time they would be dead. . . .

Six days out, just after dark, Captain Peabody caught three more of the crew copulating with the Whydah women. He ordered them to be whipped upon the deck at high noon the next day.

181

Guy moved among the crew, searching their eyes for some hint of what might be expected of them. To a man, they turned away their faces. He had spent six years aboard various slavers; he didn't have to guess any longer: he knew.

It was still early in the evening, so he sought an audience with the Captain. But that strait-laced, pious, bad-tempered New Englander blasted and damned Guy from his door without giving him a chance to speak. Thereafter, Guy chased a covey of black wenches out of what had formerly been the mate's cabin. Then he called a council of war with James Rodgers, first mate, Paul Tully, the boatswain, and Pacho the big Negro cook.

"They're going to mutiny," he said flatly. "I've summered and wintered with these bastards, and I know them. I tried to warn the Cap'n; but he sent me to hell in a longboat. Besides, he can't keep a cool head, anyhow. Reckon that makes you chief of this party, Jimmy, so I'll step aside and listen to your palaver. . . ."

"No, you don't, Guy Falks!" James Rodgers said. "I rank you; but you've forgotten more about this business than I'll ever know. Why the company decided to join up with that Cuban outfit of yours, and put us in the slave trade is more than I can see! You've got the floor, Falks; tell us what we should do. . . ."

"All right," Guy said. "But first I've got to find out something. You, Paul, have suffered at the captain's hands. How do you feel about it? You with us, or against us?"

"Well—" the boatswain said, "he's a stiff-necked old ass, but he's a good Cap'n. And seeing as how it'll be me who'll have to lay on those stripes tomorrow, them johnnies ain't going to have no love lost for me, neither. . . ."

"Good. And you, Pacho?"

"With you. Those white devils never forget I am a Negro. I have suffered much at their hands—"

"All right, then. First of all, thank God it's a dark night. You, Pacho, strip off your clothes and at midnight, crawl to the arms chest. Bring all the firearms here, and a cutlass per man. You, Jimmy, will order the watch off deck, on the pretense that all's quiet, and that you and I can keep the watch. You might even express sympathy for those boys who're going to get it tomorrow. Say you're going to try to persuade the Cap'n to pardon them. And give Pacho the key to the arms chest. You, Boats, keep those wenches out of here. I'll bet they're planning to attack during the whipping, so as to catch us off guard. But this will be a good enough place to store the arms—"

But fate kept its grip upon the *Martha Jean*. Pacho returned to report he hadn't had to use the key. The arms chest had already been forced, perhaps days ago, and nearly all the pistols, which, because of their size, could be more easily concealed, were gone.

James Rodgers and Guy looked at each other soberly. Four men against the entire crew were very long odds. Guy turned to the boatswain.

"Load all the muskets with buckshot," he said. "When that's done, pipe all hands! We've got to attack—it's the only chance we've got. . . ."

The shrill piping of the boatswain's whistle brought Captain Peabody roaring to the deck. But not a crew man showed his head.

"What in hell's fire's going on here?" the Captain roared; and, as if in answer to his voice, an orange tongue of flame stabbed the dark from the forecastle. The Captain spun heavily, and crashed to the deck. The mutineer who had fired put out his head, and Guy Falks, aiming one of his own pistols with icy care, put a ball directly between his eyes— which was luck, because he had seen only the outline of the man's head, silhouetted against the white bulkhead.

Instantly a howl arose from the forecastle, and a volley of pistol shots illuminated the dark. By their brief flare, Guy saw the Captain writhing on the deck.

"Cover me," he said. "I'm going out to get the Captain. He's still alive. . . ."

He reloaded his pistol, stuck it and its mate in his belt, and began to crawl from stanchion to coil of rope, to gunwales' shadow until he was close to the Captain. He eased his arms under the lean and leathery old New Englander. Then he stood up and lifted powerfully. He started off then, running toward the poop while pistol balls whistled past him. He heard the Captain jerk and groan, and knew that the old man had received another ball.

He reached the cabin unhurt. They cut the Captain's clothing from his wounds. The second shot was not bad, having lodged in his shoulder; but the first was a bluish hole from which blood oozed sullenly, just below his navel. And the surgeon had either joined the crew, or had been imprisoned by them. It made no difference in either case. In the 1840's a gut-shot man was nearly always as good as dead.

Josiah Peabody's eyes came open. They were like those of a great eagle.

"Falks?" he rumbled.

"Here, sir," Guy said.

"Want to beg your pardon, lad," the Captain said clearly. "You were right. Forgive a stiff-necked old fool, will you?"

"It's—it's all right, sir," Guy said gently.

"No. Not all right. Boats!"

"Yessir," the boatswain said.

"Get me the log, ink, pens, sand. Want to enter my will— and commendation for three damn good officers I hadn't sense enough to appreciate. The Nigger, too. Get the log, Boats!"

"Aye, aye, sir!" the boatswain said.

The Captain had stubbornly maintained his quarters in the cabin, stationing a sailor before his door to keep the black women quiet with a whip during the night. So the boatswain was able to go directly to it and return with the log, without exposing himself to the fire of the crew.

James Rodgers wrote the will, as the Captain dictated. Josiah Peabody left his entire head money to Guy Falks, a sum amounting to some sixty-four hundred dollars. To Rodgers he willed his half share in the ownership of the vessel —about five thousand dollars—because Jimmy had been his mate for a long time. The boatswain was rewarded for his pains to the extent of a thousand, and Pacho received five hundred. Other bequests to his wife, his daughter and a brother, disposed of thirty thousand more. The old man had found the sea a profitable calling. . . .

Hardly had he signed the document with a shaking hand, and had it witnessed by the two mates, when the Negro whispered:

"They're coming out—going to rush us!"

"Good!" Guy said. "Hold your fire 'til they're abeam of that stanchion. Then let 'em have it. Aim low—for the legs. We'll need these bastards once they're licked."

The four men took up their muskets. Pacho placed three extra loaded guns by each man's side. They waited, quietly.

"Now!" Guy Falks shouted; and every porthole spoke flame. Six men went down, howling. The rest broke; but Guy's group snatched up fresh muskets and dropped four more before the crew reached the safety of the forecastle. Then it was quiet,

100's smokers!
Compare your brand with Kent Golden Lights 100's.

FTC Report Dec. 1976

Regular 100's	MG TAR	MG NIC	Menthol 100's	MG TAR	MG NIC
Kent Golden Lights	10	0.9*	Kent Golden Lights	10	0.9*
Vantage Longs	11	0.9*	Merit	12	0.9*
Merit	12	0.9*	Salem Long Lights	12	0.9*
Parliament	12	0.9*	Virginia Slims	16	0.9
Winston Lights	14	1.0*	Silva Thins	16	1.1
Virginia Slims	16	0.9	Pall Mall	16	1.2
Tareyton	16	1.2*	Eve	17	1.1
Silva Thins	17	1.2	L&M	18	1.1
L&M	17	1.1	Salem	18	1.2
Viceroy	18	1.3	Kool	18	1.3
Raleigh	18	1.3	Belair	18	1.3
Marlboro	18	1.1	Benson & Hedges	18	1.0
Benson & Hedges	18	1.0	Winston	19	1.2
Lark	19	1.2			
Winston	19	1.2	Lowest of all brands sold	0.5	0.05
Pall Mall	19	1.4	*FTC Method		

Kent Golden Lights 100's
Real smoking satisfaction at only 10 mg tar.

B

10 mg. "tar", 0.9 mg. nicotine av. per cigarette by FTC Method.

except for the moaning of the wounded on the deck. The night wore itself out. The day came in with mist and cloud, and thunderous seas. Then, just at full dawn, it happened: With a screech like all the fiends of hell, a hundred gibbering blacks poured out of the hatches onto the deck.

They were armed with the billets of wood they had been given as pillows. And now, screaming, yelling, dancing, they attacked both the forecastle and the cabin simultaneously. There was nothing to do but shoot. Between the crossfire of the officers and the crew, the Negroes dropped like flies.

"Look!" the first mate said; and Guy saw the white flag waving from the forecastle. But it was to their officers the crew was surrendering, not the blacks. Under this new and deadly danger, they preferred to forget their mutiny and make common cause with the only men brave enough and intelligent enough to lead them.

Cutlass and pistol in hand, Guy Falks led his little band out on the deck; then, with a cheer, the crew rushed out to join them. It was soon over, after that. The buckshot blasts drove the blacks inch by inch back to the hatches. Handspikes, belaying pins, and the whining cat o' nine tails forced them below. Then the sweating, bleeding officers and crew faced each other.

That is, Guy Falks and Paul Tully faced the crew; for James Rodgers lay stretched out on the deck, his head stove in by a Negro's billet. The dead, among the whites, amounted to two: the sailor Guy had shot through the head, and the mate. None of the Negroes had been killed. Some lay with buckshot and pistol balls in their legs upon the decks, the rest still ranted and raved below.

Guy gave sharp orders. In the galley, Pacho brought huge caldrons of water to a boil. These were poured through the gratings upon the slaves. Anguished howls rose up, then silence. At one of the gratings, two big blacks still howled and shook the bars. Guy nodded to the boatswain. Without a word, Paul shot both of them.

So ended the first double mutiny of crew and of slaves that Guy Falks had ever heard of. But his problems did not permit him time to ponder two mysteries: how the Negroes had succeeded in freeing themselves of their shackles; and why Whydahs, universally known as the most docile of Africans, should have revolted in the first place. His responsibilities were too great: he had become Captain of the clipper by default; he had to decide what to do with his mutinous crew.

Fortunately, Captain Peabody solved this last problem for him. The old skipper commanded Pacho to carry him to the deck. There, lying on a mattress, and covered with a tarpaulin, he ordered every man who could still walk to file by him. He took each man's hand and freely pardoned him for his crimes, on condition that he would obey the new master implicitly.

It was probable that he had James Rodgers in mind when he spoke, for Guy had concealed the first mate's death from the dying skipper. In any event, it made no difference; for the thoroughly cowed and chastened crew were disposed to obey anyone with a loud voice and a firm hand. Guy faced the crew.

"All right," he said. "I'm Master, now. Mr. Tully is Mate! You, Martin—" he called out to the one half-way decent member of the crew, "are Boatswain! Now look alive, men! To your watches, and clew up all sheets except jibs, spankers, and the foretopgallant. We're in for a blow, so move!"

That evening, clad in oilskins, with the prayerbook soaked into near illegibility in his hand, he read the service for the dead over the bodies of the mate and the sailor he, himself, had slain. Then their bodies and those of the two blacks the ex-boatswain had had to kill, were slid over the side. The sea took them, hurling them aft like so many chips. . . .

Two days later, under exactly the same conditions, he performed the service over the body of his Captain. Then he settled down to wait out the storm.

It blew for nine days without letup. During all that time, the hatches were battened down, and the Negroes were fed with rations of sea biscuit and cold horsebeans, brought to them, where they lay, by small boys from the cabin. But for the wind and the driving rain, the stench would have been unbearable.

On the sixteenth day out of Africa, the clouds broke, and a dazzling ray of sunlight poured through like a beacon. Seeing it, young Guy Falks had the feeling that it was a symbol, a benediction from above, marking the end of their troubles.

But he was wrong. That same afternoon, scudding to leeward under flying jibs, spanker, topgallants, tops'ls, royals; but with the big mainsails on the fore, mizzen and main still reefed, under a sky rapidly becoming cloudless and a sea slackening into calm, Martin, the new boatswain came to him with a troubled face.

"Cap'n, sir," he said. "Three of them Cuffees down there is dead. What's more, they've been dead so long, I can't tell what killed 'em. But there's eight sick; and if I ain't beating on the wrong tack, what they've got is smallpox. . . ."

Guy's face greyed under his tan. When he spoke, his voice was very quiet.

"You sure, Boats?" he said.

"Certain sure, Cap'n," Martin said. "Got all the symptoms: pulse high, quick'n hard; face'n eyes red and swollen. Fever. Rosy pimples on neck'n chest. If that ain't smallpox, it's its first cousin, sir—"

"All right," Guy said, feeling the weariness down to the soles of his feet; "first of all, get those bodies out of there and over the side, then—"

"Begging your pardon, Cap'n," Martin said, "that's another thing—don't nobody want to touch 'em. They's—they's plumb putrid, sir. And the poor niggers what's chained to 'em is out o' their minds. Look, Cap'n, I want to put it to you, squarely. The crew ain't disposed to mutiny no more. But I hope you won't order 'em to drag them dead Bumboes out. It's awful to have to handle a corpse whose flesh comes off on your hands—"

"I see, Boats," Guy said; and stood there, lost in thought. Then he turned once more to the boatswain. "Look, Martin," he said. "I've got an idea: most men will follow an example where they'd resent a command. Can't blame them for it, either. It's bad to be ordered to do the dirty work by some spit'n polish officer who doesn't even get a mite of tar under his fingernails. . . ."

"I catch your drift, sir," Martin said. "You mean you're going down there yourself, and—"

"Yes, Boats. And I hope you'll go with me. That's not an order. This is a thing I wouldn't order any man to do. What do you say?"

Martin's face was the most rueful sight in the world.

"Well, sir," he said at last, "I'm game if you are. But the two of us can't bring out three dead'n rotten niggers. One trip, and we'll be too sick to go back. . . ."

"I'll fix that," Guy said. "Pipe all hands to stations, Boats. . . ."

That the crew already knew what a disaster they were facing, Guy saw at once from their sullen, hangdog faces. But, even at twenty-four, Guy Falks knew how to handle men.

"We're in trouble," he said. "I won't try to conceal from you men how bad that trouble is. It's smallpox—and at sea there's nothing worse than that. So there are certain things that have to be done. First, those three dead Bumboes below have to be heaved over the side—"

A sullen mutter greeted his words.

"I know," Guy went on calmly. "It won't be pretty. Which is why I'm not going to order a man jack of you to do it. Boats and I are going below to bring the first one out. But in fairness you men have to admit that three are too many for any man's stomach. So I'm asking for volunteers, but only from those of you who've been inoculated against the disease, or who have had it and recovered. . . ."

The crew stood there in stony silence.

"Well, Boats," Guy said cheerfully, "we might as well get started, seeing as how there's not a man aboard. . . ."

At his words, three of the men stepped forward.

"Issue those men a double ration of rum," Guy said, "and put them down for a raise in pay, Mr. Tully."

With a roar, the entire crew stepped forward at once.

"I only need three more," Guy said. "You Jiminez; you, Stocatetti, and you, Johnson—" Then to the rest of the crew, he said: "I'm taking these men because they're pock-marked, which means they're immune. The rest of you report to the surgeon for examination. Those who've been inoculated will handle the niggers from now on. The rest of you will have to stay clear of both the blacks and the men in charge of them. And that includes the women. I don't think a black piece is worth a man's life; do you?"

"Hell no, Cap'n!" the men roared.

"Issue a ration of rum to all hands," Guy commanded, "Now, you volunteers come with me. . . ."

A half hour later, with cloths soaked in vinegar over their mouths and noses, and thickly tarred gloves on their hands, Guy, Martin, and the six volunteers went below. Two of the men had to hold the crazed Negroes down while the masses of putrefaction were unchained from their sides. It wasn't pretty. It wasn't pretty at all . . . After they had flung the corpses into the sea—and the gloves with which they had handled them—the eight men hung over the gunn'ls and gave way

188

to the racking spasms of nausea that seized them, until they were purged of pity, terror, and disgust.

The reek clung to them, their hands, their clothes, their hair. As soon as he had strength enough to speak, Guy ordered the men to strip. They did so, and their clothes, too, were cast over the side. Pacho brought hot water, strong soap, and brushes. Then the eight scrubbed each other mercilessly until their hides were as red as blood.

When they were dressed in fresh garments, Guy heard the surgeon's report. Among the non-immune of the crew, two men were already infected. Guy ordered the women out of the cabin, and sent men to scrub the walls, ceiling and deck with hot water, lye soap and disinfectants. Then he turned it into a sick bay.

Silently blessing the old tar who had advised him long ago to seek the protection of vaccination, Guy ordered those members of the crew still susceptible to contagion well forward, and then had the Negroes brought on deck. Besides the eight that the boatswain had already reported, thirty others proved to have the disease in its most virulent form.

The next fifteen days were the ones that Guy Falks could never bear to remember afterward. Thirteen members of the crew, among those who had not been immunized against the disease, came down with smallpox. Of the thirteen, three survived. Two of the men who bore the marks of inoculation on their arms sickened and died, also. As for the blacks, what happened to them was horror.

They overflowed the sick bay the second day of the epidemic. Guy tried the desperate experiment of keeping the apparently healthy below; but day in and day out, from the slave deck, and from topside, the bodies were hurled into the sea. A gang of slaves, aided and directed by volunteers from the crew, all of them, blacks and whites alike, soaked in rum in order to enable them to stand the stench, dragged the putrefying masses that had been human beings to the rail, and threw them into the sunlit, benign, sea.

The tenth day, of the fifteen days it lasted, a lookout becried a sail. It came on, gaining rapidly upon them, because Guy simply had not the men left to mount the rigging and crack on more canvas. By noon, he was able to discern that it was an English cruiser, stripped down and squared for action.

He looked down at the deck which crawled with black,

naked forms, unable to stand; he heard their guttural moans, saw the slime of blood and pus they left behind them as they moved, saw even the raw patches of flesh that clung to the deck after the bodies had been heaved over the side. The stench was around his head like a sickening blanket; it burned inside his nostrils; he could taste it down to the very pit of his lungs. He stood there, gaunt, skeletal himself, his eyes sunken into his head, his skin grey from fatigue, and from hunger. For although they had plenty of food, he could not force it down.

Let 'em come, he thought, in the midst of that bone-deep, soul-deep weariness that possessed him utterly; let 'em come. I'm done. I can't—I can't—

It was then he heard the whistling crack of the first shell crossing the *Martha Jean*'s bows.

"Mister Tully," he whispered. "Strike our colors and heave to—"

He stood there, watching the boatloads of Her Majesty's Royal Marines crawling toward them over the sunlit sea. The Mate ordered the men to throw down rope ladders to them, and they—at least the first three of them swarmed aboard. The big, red-faced Lieutenant of the Marines was the first to reach the deck. He gave one look, and flew to the rail, roaring:

"Avast there! Steer off! In God's name stay clear! This bark's a pest hole!"

The two men who were directly below him poked their heads over the gunwales. One of them released his hold on the lines and dived, uniform, carbine, boots and all, straight into the sea. The other fled down the ladder like a frightened monkey. Only the Lieutenant was left, standing there looking over the *Martha Jean*'s deck.

"God!" he whispered.

Then he whirled to the rail and followed the others. Guy saw them beating back to the cruiser, double-stroking, racing for safety. . . .

There were five more days of horror. Then it was over. No new cases appeared, and the lightly infected began to recover. Guy ordered the ship cleansed from stem to stern. It was easy to do that now; there was plenty of space. Of the original crew of fifty hands, thirty-eight men were left alive. Of the eight hundred Whydahs, two hundred and ninety-two greyish, walking skeletons survived.

He allowed them to remain unshackled. With the surplus of

water and food the dead had left, he was able to permit the blacks to slake their thirst at will, instead of submitting them to the torture of the customary two drinks daily. The crew had no heart to swing a cat any more, so minor infractions of the rules were overlooked. The Negroes, in the three more weeks it took to reach Cuba, recovered both health and spirits. So did the crew. Guy allowed them two rum rations a day and turned his eyes away from their nightly sport with the few women who had survived. It took him nine days to completely rid the *Martha Jean* of the smell of death. But as she dropped anchor off Regla, no cleaner slaver ever existed in the entire history of the trade. . . .

14

GUY FALKS sat with Don Rafael Gonzalez on the cool patio of Don Rafael's villa, high above Havana. Here, all the elaborate camouflage of the rumpled tropical whites and the pedantic mannerisms of a port interpreter were dispensed with. Don Rafael was magnificent in white silk shirt, Parisian pumps, and the smartest drills that money could buy. The villa was nothing short of a palace; no less than five slaves were busy about the simple business of clearing away the afternoon meal and bringing liquors, coffee and cigars.

"Well, Guy," Don Rafael said, "how does it feel to be the hero of the hour?"

"It doesn't feel like anything," Guy said slowly. "I don't sleep any better—and I can't get the smell of dead and rotten bodies out of my nose. Besides, that hero business is plain nonsense. I was scared spitless, most of the time. I just did what I had to do, like any man would—"

"As many a man would not, or could not have done," Don Rafael corrected him, smiling. "The company's exceedingly pleased with you, Guy. You saved us a fine ship under almost unimaginable difficulties; you brought back enough Africans alive and in marketable condition so that we still, despite everything, made a profit—small, but a profit for all that. Those mutinous blackguards of a crew, are singing your praises all over Havana. Quite a feat for a man twenty-four years old. . . ."

"Thanks," Guy said dryly.

"Therefore," Don Rafael added grandly, "I have been empowered to confirm you in the captaincy of the *Martha Jean*. *Mis felicitaciones, hijo mio*—you are now the youngest Master on the seven seas. . . ."

Guy took the outstretched hand; but there was no joy in his face at the news.

Don Rafael, whose fortune had been made upon his ability to read men, saw the look.

"This does not please you," he said quickly. "Strange. I had thought it would. . . ."

"It does," Guy said. "It's a great honor, and I'm more than pleased. Only—"

"Go on," Don Rafael said. "Please do speak frankly, Guy—"

"All right. Being a captain's mighty fine at any age; I know that. A year ago, hell, even six months ago, I would have thrown a celebration at the thought of making the grade by the time I was forty. But not now. I've seen a mite too much. Not just the *Martha Jean*—other things. Like good old Cap'n Rudgers, the first skipper I ever sailed with, being in jail, because a Yankee cruiser bottled him up as he came out of Dahomey. Like Nelson, my second skipper, having his throat cut by Folgias, because he was fool enough to take on twenty Ashantis among the lot, warriors who'd been sold by their own people because they'd revolted against their king. One Ashanti is too many. They don't know what fear is. I honestly believe you could flay the flesh off their backs with a cat and they'd still mutiny. And Nelson took on twenty. Naturally, with that much guts and brains to lead them, even those bastard Folgias were able to pull it off—"

"I heard about that," Don Rafael said. "Still—"

"Still a Bible-kissing abolitionist judge in Massachusetts, freed 'em—after they had murdered Nelson and his whole crew except the mate, whom those cunning devils of Ashantis knew they needed to steer and plot their course—and sent 'em back to Africa. That was one thing. But I don't need to tell you what the risks are. Nor that I'm not afraid of risks—if there really were any profit in this business for the men who sail the Middle Passage and do the dirty work. But there isn't. In six years at sea, Rafe, I've been able to save a little over six thousand dollars—and that includes the two thousand three hundred and thirty-six I made in head money this last trip. In other words—a thousand a year. I'll die of old age before getting rich at that rate—"

"A captain's head money is much greater," Don Rafael said.

"I know. That's what I got last trip, remember? Eight dollars a head, if he gets the Bumboes back alive, if he isn't captured by the cruisers—which, since last year, Rafe, have had the right to seize a cruiser outward-bound and empty on the basis that she's equipped for slaving—and if all the profits of a voyage aren't eaten up in bribes. If all of a million and one disasters don't happen. Tell me, Rafe, apart from Cap'n Tray, how many rich slaving captains do you know?"

"Two or three," Don Rafael said.

"Two or three out of all the hundreds engaging in the trade. And the rest? Down on the quay, old and broken, cadging drinks, selling toy ships in bottles, and dying slowly of hunger. There's a fatality in this business, Rafe—"

"So you want to get out of it," Don Rafael said. "Remember what I told you?"

"You were right. But I don't want to get out of it—not yet. What I want to do is to get into it deeper, into the place where the big money is made. In other words, I want to be a factor, Rafe—in Africa."

"Hmmm," Don Rafael mused. "That's not a bad idea . . . If you cooperated with us, and we backed you, say, it would mean that we would have control at both ends of the voyage; and thus thieves like Pedro Blanco, da Souza, and da Coimbra could not rob us blind, as they are doing now. Still—a slave factory is a complicated business, requiring much experience. Tell me, how many African tongues do you speak?"

"Soosoo and Mandingo. Of course, they're nearly the same. Lengua franca, which is mostly French, anyhow. Been studying Arabic; but I can't make much headway without practice. I plead guilty to a want of experience; but I know how to correct that. On my first trip over, that arrogant mulatto son of a bitch, da Coimbra, offered me a job as his secretary. I propose to take it, spend a year or two with him, learn the business inside out and watch him all the time so he can't cheat us. Then I'll set up my own factory, in, of course, direct partnership with you and the company. How does that strike you, Rafe?"

"I like it," Don Rafael said slowly. "You have much head, Guy. I'll send you out as supercargo on the *Aerostatico,* which sails next week. Once in Africa, you will have to arrange matters yourself. It would hardly help things if da Coimbra knew you were representing us. . . ."

"You," Guy said slowly, "are going to hear some damned funny rumors, Rafe. The *Aerostatico*'s crew are going to pick up the news in those waterfront rum shops that I was passed over for the captaincy of the *Martha Jean* on account of my age; and that the company refused to pay me Cap'n Peabody's head money. I'm madder'n hell over the foul way you've treated me, so, naturally, if, when I get to Pongoland, I just happen to jump ship and join the Mongo Joã, nobody's going to be greatly surprised—"

"Excellent!" Don Rafael laughed. "You have the makings of a conspirator, my boy! I'll advise the other members of the syndicate as to our plans, so that they will not deny or contradict what's being said . . . Incidentally, you ought to go see Captain Tray. He let drop a strong hint in my presence that he's forgiven you. In that matter, Guy, it seems to me you behaved exceedingly badly. . . ."

"I know," Guy said soberly. "But I couldn't help it, Rafe. There—there was something else—"

"Doña Pilar? I guessed as much. She is an exceedingly beautiful woman. And boys of the age you were then are—well—impressionable—"

"Boys of any age," Guy said dryly, "up to and including ninety. Trouble was, I just couldn't get it through my head that she was at least thirteen years older than I. She looked like a kid. But she was a true woman, Rafe. Kind and loyal, and good to me. That was what hurt most. Young fool that I was, I couldn't stand her treating me like a child. . . ."

"Yet you were a child," Don Rafael said kindly, "in many ways. Now, you aren't. I think now you should be able to visit them without—"

"No. I'm not that grown-up, yet. It wouldn't be pleasant. You don't forget women like Pili, Rafe. You replace them. With somebody else, somebody different in every way. Not better—because there isn't any better. . . ."

"Still bad, eh, son?"

"Bad enough when I think about it; which isn't often. Time and distance have a funny way of curing all kinds of feelings, even that one. But, to visit them might start over an emotion that I've nearly dominated. So you tell them I'm sorry I left, and that I hope to make it up to them someday. . . ."

"All right," Don Rafael said. "I'll do that. Shall I have a chamber prepared for your siesta?"

"No thank you," Guy said cheerfully. "I've got some rumors to spread. Be seeing you, Rafe. . . ."

During the entire thirty-nine days of the crossing, for the *Aerostatico* lived up to her name, Guy was careful to present a sullen face and a surly mood to officers and crew alike. Among her crew were men who had sailed under his brief command on the *Martha Jean*. Slavers, like other seamen, were constantly changing ships for real and fancied grievances, and for the truer reason that they are by nature a restless breed. Guy, himself, mostly to widen his experience, had served upon four different vessels in his six years at sea. But it was the fact of the presence of members of his former crew that enabled him to learn how beautifully his plan was working. One and all, they sidled up to him sometime during the voyage, and whispered, gruffly:

"Damned shame! Best bloody cap'n we ever had—that you was. You understand how a seaman feels about things, which none of these barnacled old oaksides we generally gets ever took the trouble to learn. If you ever gets a command, you just let me know; I'm your man, Cap'n, to hell'n back again!"

"You'll have a mighty long wait," Guy told each of them. "A man has to blame near die of old age before they'll make him a skipper in this trade. . . ."

By the time they anchored in the muddy mouth of the Rio Pongo, Guy was entirely confident. Nevertheless, he waited until after the Captain had granted the majority of the crew shore leave, before descending upon Pongoland himself. Further, he clinched the matter by asking Martin, his former boatswain, a man whose talkativeness he could depend upon, to convey his greetings to the Mongo Joã. That da Coimbra would pump Martin dry of information within the first five minutes, there was not the slightest doubt. Thinking about it, Guy smiled through the smoke of his *puro*. He had adopted the pleasant vice of smoking early in his career as a slaver, partially to counteract the smells arising from a blackbirder's hold.

When Martin, not too unsteady from drunkenness, returned

aboard, he brought with him a note from the Mongo himself. It was written in English, though with so many curlicues and flourishes of expert Spencerian penmanship, that Guy had some difficulty in reading it. It said, among other things:

"If you can pay me a visit, you might find it advantageous, as well as pleasant, to have a chat with me over a bottle. Despite our differences of opinion in the past, you will find in me a man who appreciates sterling worth as, sadly, some other people"—these three words were heavily underscored —"have failed to do. Will you send me word by one of the Kroomen?"

As soon as he had deciphered the Mongo's difficult script, Guy stepped to the rail, and called to one of the Kharoo Monoos, or Kroomen, as the slavers called them. A rapid exchange in Soosoo—which was enough like the Kroomen's own dialect to be understood by them—and a fist-full of cigars completed the matter. Tomorrow, when Guy Falks went ashore the Mongo Joā would be expecting him.

He was. After the feast, for it was that, the Mongo, considerably fatter now, and noticeably the worse for wear, waxed affable over a bottle of brandy.

"I think I can speak frankly," he beamed, rubbing his huge hands together. "Your friend, Martin—and please don't chide him for this—let slip the story of how badly those Cuban swine treated you. In a way, I confess I'm glad; for perhaps it will incline you to accept the proposition I have in mind. . . ."

"Could be," Guy said noncommittally. "You're talking, Mongo. I'm listening. . . ."

"It is a most attractive proposition," da Coimbra said. "How would it strike you, Guy Falks, if I were to offer you the post of—junior partner?"

"Damned strange," Guy said flatly. "You offered me, once, I remember, the job of secretary. To tell the truth, I came ashore prepared to take you up on that. But this promotion is a hell of a sight too sudden. And it doesn't make sense. Partners, Mongo, bring capital into a business—or important connections, or something else of value. But I haven't a copper; and whatever connections I have had, sure Lord haven't shown much cordiality on my behalf. So let's deal squarely, cards face-up on the table. You just tell me one simple thing: why in the name of holy hell fire should you make me a partner?"

"That, my boy," the Mongo said, "is simple. You have one exceedingly valuable asset as far as I am concerned: the color of your skin. Wait—I'll explain it to you. More and more, the blackbirders who put into the Pongo are beginning to be Americans. In dealing with them, my color is a handicap. They try to cheat me on the bland assumption that I am a Negro, and hence, an idiot. When I call their hands, they resent it—furiously. If you were my partner, I could turn all dealings with your prickly fellow countrymen over to you. I would gladly and willingly pose as your secretary or assistant in their presence. I have no false pride. In the rôle of an underling, they would accept or ignore me, which would be jolly fine as far as I am concerned. The main thing is to get business done, however we can—"

"But," Guy said slowly, "you must, in all these years have known some other white man who—"

"No. The fact of being white is not, of itself, enough. I need a man of cleverness, decision, force—qualities rare in any race. Your average Caucasian, if I may risk offending your sensibilities, is a stupid animal. His very bland and childish assumption that the accident of race makes him unquestionably superior to all other men proves that. You, however, have precisely what I need here, even if you do share this Anglo-Saxon folly. In time, I think you will outgrow it. But this has no importance. What is important is that you could be very valuable to me, and, incidentally, to yourself. Come, Guy, what do you say?"

"Listens good," Guy said. "And the salary?"

"Five prime niggers a month—of your own selection. You can trade them for specie or goods, as you like. At the very least they'll bring you two hundred dollars a month; if you play your cards right, as much as five hundred. And don't tell me you ever made that much aboard a slaver, for I know better—"

"Well—" Guy hesitated.

"A house, of course. Clean, and well furnished. Your meals. Materials for your clothing. The services of my own tailor. . . ."

"And—Beeljie?" Guy demanded suddenly, more for the sake of watching the Mongo's reaction than for any other reason.

Da Coimbra frowned.

"That, no—" he said heavily. "I have taken her as my

fourth wife, as a good Mussulman should—"

"You're a Mohammedan? But I thought—"

"That I was a good Catholic like all men of Portuguese blood. I know. But what does it matter what species of Ju Ju palaver a man listens to? It's all nonsense. And my dealings are principally with the Mandingos and Fulahs, staunch followers of Allah; so, for business reasons—"

"And," Guy said dryly, "also to justify your harem, eh, Mongo?"

"Not for that. Polygamy is practiced among nearly all the tribes, and doesn't have to be justified. Besides, four wives are not just four times as much trouble as one, but at least eighty times as much. I'd like to toss them all to the crocodiles, more than half the time. . . ."

"Yet, you married little Beeljie," Guy pointed out.

"A whim of the moment. She has become, in the nearly five years since you saw her last, really quite striking. But do not mistake me. Women have no importance. I would give her to you were she twenty times more beautiful than she is—if this were possible. But it is not. There are things a Mongo cannot do. I could present you with the fairest of my concubines without causing the slightest surprise among my subjects. But to give away a wife would cause me to lose face. Even if I divorced her and allowed her to come to you, they would look upon me as a cuckold and my dominance over them would end at that moment. So forget Beeljie, won't you? I will provide you with a substitute just as fair. . . ."

"No, thanks," Guy laughed. "I've got too much of that Caucasian stupidity you were talking about a little while ago. I prefer my women white, and smelling of soap and perfume—"

To his surprise, the Mongo appeared to take the remark seriously.

"That, my boy," he said gravely, "is a rather difficult proposition in Africa. But if you will accept the post, and really take hold, I will take my long deferred vacation in Europe, and bring you back a little Parisian girl. How would that suit you?"

"Excellent!" Guy laughed, willing to play along with this nonsense. "I like 'em small, Mongo. The color of hair doesn't matter—though I'm kind of partial to blondes or redheads. But as long as she's pretty, and damned good at what a woman's for, I'll be satisfied. . . ."

"I'll make a note of your requirements," da Coimbra said. "Then you'll take the post?"

"With pleasure," Guy said, and put out his hand. The Mongo took it. Under the fat, his grip was like steel.

"You see," he said smiling, "how far you have already come. Now for you this shaking hands no longer has any importance—"

"No," Guy said. "A fellow grows up, Mongo. Can't stay a fool kid all his life. . . ."

"Good!" the Mongo Joã laughed. "Now I'll have Ungah Gulliah show you to your new quarters. . . ."

"Don't you think I'd better go back aboard for tonight?" Guy said. "I've got my clothes aboard, and a couple of sea chests full of books which I prize. In fact, it's going to be quite a trick to get them off, heavy as they are—"

"Don't trouble yourself about it, Dom Guy. I will send word to Captain Martinez that you have been stricken with what looks like yellow fever; and under the circumstances, you'd best be left with me. Should he insist upon investigating, I'll have Manómassa, my Ju Ju man prepare a potion that for twenty-four hours will produce all the symptoms of a hopeless case, but will disappear without a trace thereafter. I assure you that the head physician at Edinburgh could not tell the difference—"

"That won't be necessary," Guy said smoothly. "Scared as Cubans are of yellow fever—"

He lied deliberately, secure in the knowledge that Joã da Coimbra had never been to Cuba. Actually, most Cubans were holders and sometimes victims of, the hard-headed belief that yellow fever was a disease of newcomers, to which they, by long acclimatization, were immune. But he was sure that Miguel Martinez would not investigate, for the simple reason that the captain of the *Aerostatico* was a party to the plot.

Two hours later, Ungah Gulliah knocked upon his door. He opened it, and she came in, followed by a parade of stalwart blacks, bearing the two great sea chests and his bag. Guy thanked her gravely in Mandingo; then, after she had taken her leave, opened one of the chests, and took, without looking at the title, a book from it. He crossed the cabin and lay down on his bed, which, like all African beds was a leveled-off heap of mud, covered with leopard skins. The pillow was a block of wood, carved to receive his head. It was surprisingly comfortable.

Lying there, he leafed through the pages of the book, *Dante's Inferno*, reading idly, without much interest, until his eyes fell upon the lines from Canto Seven, Fourth Circle:

"But the stars that marked our birthing fall away
We must go further, deeper into pain,
For it is not permitted that we stay . . ."

He lay there a long moment, staring at the words. Then he straightened up, thinking: Yes. My stars have fallen one by one, Cathy and Pa and Pili, and each star track streaking the sky, going out into nothing, marked some kind of birthing for me—out of childhood, out of believing, out of even hope. And it's no good to stay—not permitted—keep moving, go on, further, deeper, into—

He closed the book almost reverently. He had, suddenly, the feeling that the words were going to haunt him. He shook his head angrily to clear it of such thoughts. That final line was nonsense, even if it had survived for more than two thousand years. What man didn't have bitter memories? He had had Cathy stolen from him; seen his beloved father murdered; loved and lost Pili; suffered terrible hardships and dangers at sea. . . .

He thrust open the door and went out into the blinding sun, seeing the crowds of blacks rushing toward the square. He followed them, pushing his way through the circle they had formed until he was a scant yard away from the two scowling muscular young Negroes, who stood there, glaring at one another. Beside them, in his hideous mask of wood and ivory, under his plume of vulture feathers, Manomassa, the Ju Ju man stood, holding a whip of bullock hide in one hand, while in the greyish pink palm of the other lay a pair of cowrie shells. Without a word, he tossed them in the air, studied the way they fell, and then, in a wild outburst of gibberish, handed the terrible whip to one of the youths.

Stoically the other folded his arms and turned his back. The crowd spread out, giving his opponent room. The lucky one swung the whip out behind him, then brought it whistling around across his enemy's back, with such force that the other fell to his knees, the stripe opening like a knife wound, the blood streaking his back. Again. Then again. Fifteen times, without a sound, a tremor, a grimace of pain escaping the suffering black.

He straightened up now, and turned; the panting whipper passed the whip over to him, and turned his back in his turn, to receive fifteen lashes that left his back as bloody raw as his enemy's. . . .

The third turn was sickening, leaving no unbroken flesh into which the lash could bite. But they kept it up, turn and turn about, until, at last, the first man lay on the ground, unable to move, while the cheering crowd lifted the victor to their shoulders and bore him in triumph to his hut.

"Lord God!" Guy said to Ungah Gulliah. "What in the name of hell fire do they call that, Ungah?"

"A duel," Ungah Gulliah said. "Young master sabby duel? White man fight 'em, too. Only with guns. Bad, 'cause one man gotta die—"

"That one's going to die, or I miss my guess," Guy said.

"No. Ungah fix him up," Ungah Gulliah said. "Be good like new two, five day."

"But what were they fighting over?" Guy demanded.

"Beeljie," Ungah Gulliah said simply.

"Beeljie!" Guy said. "But I thought she was the Mongo's wife!"

"Is. Mongo wives big joke. Him too fat, too old, too much whiskey, gris-gris. All them boys take him wives, and him don't know. Sleep from whiskey. All new babies black now; boys make em big belly all him women. 'Cept Beeljie. She won't choose. That's how come them boys they fight em prove em who's more brave more strong, make em good hot loving in the dark. They fools. Beeljie won't choose nohow. . . ."

"Because she loves the Mongo?" Guy said.

"No. 'Cause she waiting for cupy white man gone over sea. But I think she be happy now. 'Cause I think him done come back. You want I tell her you here—you one damn fine pretty white man, Guy?"

"Ungah, do you mean," Guy whispered, "that all this time, she—"

"Wait for you, yes. Don't never talk 'bout nothing else. How you tall, how you good, how you take her 'way from here when you come. I tell her, yes?"

"But—" Guy said, "but—her baby?"

"Dead. Mongo kick her in belly one time drunk. Baby come too soon all dead. Pretty—'most cupy baby, hair like straw, eyes like sea. Damn bad. And she won't choose, so no more baby. Waiting for you come back. . . ."

"But the Mongo?" Guy said.

"Can't make em no baby him no more. Him big fat tub of guts, no man. Don't even try love em up he wives. Know he can't, so no more try—"

"You mean—never?" Guy said.

"Sometimes, maybe yet," Ungah admitted grudgingly, "but wives em give him things in him grub make em him sleep, so he can't bother 'em. Suphiana, his old wife, first number one, she let him sometimes 'cause she already old, ain't got em no warrior in the town. But mostly him don't bother. Eat'n drink'n smoke the dreamy grass; and no make em love. The others got em young hot strong boys in the town, 'cept Beeljie and now she got em you, yes?"

"I don't know," Guy said. "The Mongo is my friend and I don't want to—"

"Hah!" Ungah said scornfully. "Him smoke Bangi, dreamy grass, him sleep. Then Beeljie come. Him not know. Tonight she come, you wait. . . ."

Deeper, further into—

He lay there in the dark, sweating, peopling his private hell with the images of his shame. But it had been a long time, a very long time; for after Pili he had seldom been able to accept purchased love. He had grown beyond that. But Beeljie. God, Beeljie. How was she now, four years later, eighteen nearly nineteen what was she like all mahogany burnt teak and purple wine, how?

Then the door opened, and she was there.

He jack-knifed up upon his narrow bed, and she, collapsing to her knees, seized his rough hands in hers, devouring them with kisses, bathing them with her tears.

"Beeljie, no!" he choked. "I—"

But rising up slowly, surely, she stopped his mouth with hers, and the sweet, soft underflesh of her lip and probing tongue tip started the hammers within his blood, smashing against the fiery anvil of his heart.

She was beautiful. The word has no meaning; but all it once meant before careless tongues and pens debased it, she was. Oriental and languid, the dusk of a tropic night, a python goddess writhing slowly. Wonderfully warm and trembling as he entered into

Africa.

Further, further, deeper, deeper into

Pain.

For it was that, too; the line of demarcation between pleasure and its twin being broken through, until the stars fell away finally into daylight; and she rose, trembling, and stole out of there. . . .

For it was not permitted that she stay.

15

THE rainy season had come and gone, just in time, Guy was sure, to preserve what was left of his reason. During the entire month of April, it had rained day and night, without letting up for a single instant. The sound of it, drumming on the mongongo leaves which the natives used to thatch the roof, was a slow and insistent kind of torture. Mildew formed on everything made of leather. He saved his books by scraping their morocco bindings vigorously, and setting them on end to dry in a circle around a charcoal brazier. But he lost three pair of good boots which simply rotted away. Because he had been so preoccupied with saving his scanty treasures of the mind, he neglected the simple comforts of the flesh. The loss of the boots was a serious matter. He had only one pair left; and, when these were gone, his feet and ankles would be without protection from the insects and the pit vipers with which the region abounded. The Negroes seemed to know instinctively how to avoid snakes; for though they padded barefoot through the tropical rain forest, he never heard of one being bitten. He would have to wait until the next slaver put into the mouth of the Pongo, and hope they would sell him a couple of pairs of seaboots—if, indeed, they had his long and narrow size aboard. It wasn't a pleasant thought.

The worst part of the incessant rain was the effect it had upon his spirits. He sank into a moody despondency, from which not even Beeljie could arouse him. He cursed himself for forty-seven different kinds of a fool for ever coming to Africa. But he employed his enforced idleness well. He perfected himself in Soosoo and Mandingo, learned to speak comprehensible, if sadly ungrammatical Arabic—which wasn't much of a handicap, since the Mohammedan Negroes' own command of their priestly tongue was a good bit less than perfect—and set up the first real system of bookkeeping in Pongoland.

For Joã da Coimbra's business methods existed in a state of abysmal disorder. Had it not been for the teeming wealth of the country, he would have failed years ago. But so great was the richness of Africa, that the big mulatto had managed to go on in comparative prosperity, though his neglect of his accounts and his stores was total. He was being robbed in a thousand ways by his underlings; not because he was stupid, or even because he did not realize what was going on, but because he did not care.

Da Coimbra, Guy realized was too near white to live in the rain forests of central Africa. Though his black heritage enabled him to survive better than a white man could have done; the Caucasian part of his ancestry made him a prey to the dark and bitter moods, the slow erosion of will, of force, of character, that nearly always destroys the European in that green hell, where no white man ought to even try to live. In him the process was slower, that was all. In the end, the huge mulatto would be finished, too, falling before the slow doom that Africa's old and bloody gods inflict upon all intruders.

I, Guy thought bitterly, will have to get out of here. Make my pile fast, then go. If I stay here, I'll die—or go crazy. There's a thing here that's too strong. Don't know what it is —but it's here. . . .

He had rid himself, in part, of one major worry. From Manomassa, the Ju Ju man, he had procured, indirectly, of course, through the good offices of Ungah Gulliah, a bitter white powder, which was reputed to have a contraceptive effect. He dosed his and Beeljie's palm wine with it. Whether it was really effective, or whether that dreadful climate had so depressed the bio-chemical processes of his body as to render him largely sterile, he could not be sure; but the fact was that month after month went by without Beeljie's becoming pregnant—much to his relief and her sorrow.

"Mongo ruin poor Beeljie," she wept. "Kick em in belly and no more baby! Beeljie sorry. No give Bwana Guy man-child, no. Maybe him better take him number two girl. Beeljie cry, but Bwana can do."

"No, Beeljie," Guy said kindly. "I'm content with you. I don't want a child. When I go away to my own country, I couldn't take him. My people don't like mixed bloods. It would be bad for him. . . ."

"Master no go long time yet?" Beeljie whispered fearfully. "Him go, Beeljie die. . . ."

"Not for years," Guy said. "Don't worry about it, Beeljie. . . ."

And with that poor comfort, she had to be content.

Guy no longer worried about the Mongo Joã's discovering his liaison with Beeljie. Nightly the Mongo went to bed drunk, or overcome with the fumes of bangi, the dreamy weed, the plant that Europeans call marijuana. He could understand da Coimbra's lessened interest in sex. Gluttony, drunkenness and narcotics—combined with that climate—diminish a man's vital forces. Even he, young as he was, sparse and spartan as were his appetites for food and drink, completely unaddicted to narcotics, as needless to say, he was, sensed a certain diminution of his need. Africa is for Africans; the stubborn whites who insist upon staying pay a terrible price for their hardheadedness. . . .

In May, the weather cleared; but the butterflies came. Guy had never imagined that anyone could hate the lovely, fluttering insects that nearly all year round bejeweled the tropic air. But, before May was out, he hated, loathed, despised them. For, in May, two of the smaller species, one black, one white, began to swarm. They came by the thousands, then by the millions, then by billions. They shut out the sky completely. They got into everything, contaminating the food with their small, furry bodies. Masks of mosquito netting had to be worn day and night to keep them out of mouth and nostrils. Eating became a very nearly unendurable torture. Sleep was brought on only by exhaustion, as the netting over the beds was so thick as to shut out most of the air. Birds died from over-feeding, and the village reeked with the smell of their rotting bodies. People died too; not too many, but in significant numbers, from eating bad food and drinking the foul water from which they had fished hundreds of the beautiful little insects.

Then, in June, they were gone, as quickly as they had come; and life became normal again. That is, if life is ever normal in central Africa. In the jungle, the leopards coughed. A woman came into the compound, holding her torn belly together with her hand, but with a foot of mangled intestine, which escaped her blood-slimed fingers, protruding. She took five screaming hours to die, and nothing the Ju Ju man could prepare eased her pain. The blacks went out, led by Guy, and after a week's hunt they killed the leopard, just as he leaped out of a nine-foot-deep deadfall with a full grown goat in his jaws. But there were other leopards. And genets. And pythons.

At night, the beasts and the insects who are the lords and rulers of Africa, and the thousand different varieties of birds, each with a cry more harsh and discordant than the rest, made the dark hideous with their din. No great city was as noisy as the jungle, Guy discovered, nor anything on earth as terrifying.

Almost daily the gunshots echoed from the wooded hills, and the barkers raced out to meet the caravans, "dashing" them with tobacco, powder, rum. Because the Mongo was wise enough to be more lavish with his generosity than the other factors, his barkers nearly always won out over those of the other factories. Guy made a mental note of this astute practice, determining to put it to his own use when the time should come. The barkers' signal guns would be heard, and hours later they would appear with a caravan in tow. A true caravan, not merely a coffle; for in this region there were many other things to trade beside slaves.

The caravans wound down out of the hills, the bearers carrying bundles of hides on their heads, sacks of rice, jars of palm oil, beeswax, honey, liquid butter, the great curving tusks of elephants, bundles of smaller pieces of ivory, bunches of bananas and other tropical fruits, vegetables, leather pouches of gold dust, and many other central African products that Guy could only guess at.

After the bearers came the guards, armed with muskets, assagais, and spears, leading the coffles of slaves, bound throat to throat with liana vines. Behind the slaves would come a herd of bullocks, succeeded by a flock of goats, and these by another of sheep. After the beasts, the women of the caravan marched in a demure line; and last of all, some warrior came, leading a tame okapi or an ostrich, or some other rare beast intended as a gift for the Mongo Joã.

By the middle of summer, Guy had learned the trade so well that he took over the negotiations with the white slavers entirely. He was fair, courteous, and accurate; so his profits and those of the Mongo, grew. More and more da Coimbra also allowed him to deal with the caravans and the coffles from the interior. Then, late in July, he revealed his reasons:

"You'll do," he said. "You've exceeded my hopes. Now I can take the trip to Europe I have been deferring these ten years. Keep the books well, Guy; and see that none of the town bucks enters my harem. Should you stray in that direction yourself, do so with discretion. I am not a jealous man; and those wenches bore me to tears and beyond. But the customs of the country demand that I kill you should you be caught. So be careful. It would be a pity if I should be forced to at least banish you over a question that interests me not even slightly—"

"Don't worry about it, Mongo," Guy grinned. "I still haven't acquired a taste for dark meat—"

"Then I'll have to try to bring you a little French girl, as I promised. Frenchwomen are—interesting. It shouldn't be too difficult; for no more materialistic people ever existed. A small display of generosity, and your petite Jeanne will follow where I lead—"

"If you like," Guy said carelessly. It didn't seem worth serious discussion. That any white woman, European or not, would consent to be seen in the burly mulatto's company, seemed to him a possibility too remote to think about. Before da Coimbra embarked in his small sloop sailing southward towards the Congo, where he was sure of meeting a French vessel, Guy had forgotten the matter completely.

In a very little time he had forgotten more than that. August came in with a blazing sun, and the rains failed completely. The near-by tribes began to drift into Pongoland, begging for food. They, themselves, were without meat for days on end; which in that land of abundant game was a real hardship. Guy organized several hunts; but the catch was sparse. The slaves in the barracoons grew thinner by the day, so that he was forced to dispose of them to the Yankee captains at ridiculous prices. He got so sick of plantains, yams, vegetables and fruit, that he swore he'd never eat greenstuff again as long as he lived. By the end of August, he had to send out word that he would accept no more slaves, for the simple reason that he could not feed them. And the whole of September had to pass before the fall rainy season would begin.

He would have been hard put to stand it, had it not been for Beeljie. Night after night, with a moon as big as a quarter of the sky spilling liquid silver over the dry and dusty jungle, and the blue bullikookoos crowing raucously from the tree tops, she came to him, bringing with her—peace. For her, he felt a great tenderness, combined with both pity and shame. But not love. And this not for the reasons that earlier had held him apart from Phoebe, but, because at twenty-five, he was a man grown, and master of himself. When he should love again, it would be forever. So he did not permit himself to love Beeljie, though as a person and a woman, he knew she was fully worthy of his love. He could not, knowing it was no good. He knew with bitter clarity the impossibility of bringing this child of Negro and Arabic parentage back to the world of white men. Within his own psyche, he held all the ugly limitations of his people, he had mapped within his own Caucasian soul the narrow frontiers of their charity and their comprehension. No—the leaving was the lesser evil; better the knife-sharp severing of this warm and perfumed tropic tie, than the slow wearing out of love under loneliness, rejection, protracted pain. . . .

She lay in his arms, while the great bats squeaked and whimpered in the heavy dark; and seeing the purple wine of her lips, the midnight veiling of her lashes, the small pulse beating in the burnt-teak darkness of her throat, he felt like crying out his grief, his shame—

Outside, startlingly close, a Bolozi leopard coughed in the dark. Guy lay there, listening to the sound. So bad was the dry season that the great cats were driven to prowl around the villages in the night, turned man eaters by the lack of game. They heard them every night now, and in the mornings saw their spoor. But they didn't hunt them. They stayed locked in until dawn, and listened to the terrified bleating of the goats; hoping the hunger-maddened cats would not climb the stockade walls.

I'll have to do something about that, Guy thought. Tomorrow I'll take some of the boys and go out. And I won't come back 'til I've wiped every one of those spotted devils out, and stocked the village with meat as well—

There was some comfort in the thought. It enabled him to turn his mind to practical things, pushing aside the problem of Beeljie, which had no answer nor any solution. He lay there planning his great hunt, until, at last, he fell asleep.

They moved out from Pongoland in the first light of morning, Guy leading the procession, followed by his gunbearers and the long line of the beaters. They carried supplies for a week's trek, for Guy meant to go far beyond the local hunting grounds, now deserted by the game with which they usually abounded. Walking along, he felt a sudden lift and surge of mood. He lifted his eyes toward the canopy of dusty leaves, filtering out the sun. A hornbill croaked, ominously. He quickened his pace, going on.

In the first five days of the trek, they killed three leopards, old and battle-scarred cats, down to skin and bones from the lack of game. But of eatable beasts they saw no sign, with the sole exception of a pigmy antelope, a dik-dik no bigger than a hare. They killed and ate it, dividing it with scrupulous fairness, so that each man took one bite and it was gone. They were not hungry, actually, simply sick of their enforced vegetarianism. Guy's bearers ate well, better than he, in fact; for though they invited him to join their feasts, one look at a pot full of snails, lizards, frogs, grasshoppers and grub worms, over which they were smacking their lips in gusto, ended completely whatever appetite he had. The camp cook was diligent in his efforts to tempt his master to eat. The fifth night, he set before Guy a stew that was superb. Guy had eaten a large portion of it, when a tiny skull, exactly like that of a newborn infant, floated to the surface of the thick liquid in the pot. Guy clapped his hand over his mouth and fled for the nearest bush. The cook followed him, disappointment and solicitude in his eyes.

"Bwana no like monkey stew?" he said.

"Hell, no!" Guy roared; then seeing Nimbo's disappointment, "Look, Nim—it's too much like eating a child. . . ."

"Baby good, too, bush niggers say," Nimbo said gravely. "Only him tabu our people. We go, me'n Master to Biribi, big Ju Ju, no long time, half day march. Biribi fix. We catch em plenty meat, yes, Bwana come?"

"Yes," Guy said. "Right now, I'll try anything—"

Biribi, the jungle wizard, lived in a cave. He was, of course, like all the Ju Ju men, an outrageous fraud, complete with ebony mask, and vulture feathers and an extensive vocabulary of gibberish. For several pounds of tobacco, and a bottle of rum, he made big Ju Ju. First he killed a chicken, extracted its guts and mingled them with a brownish substance that Guy strongly suspected was animal dung. Then he smeared the sticky mess all over Guy's and Nimbo's faces.

"You must no wash," he said solemnly in Mandingo, "until

209

you find game. The Furtoo must lead the party; and he must not speak. You will cross three rivers and come out on a plain. This will take you two suns. On the plain will be many buffalo. They will not flee. You will catch all the meat you need—if these things are done. . . ."

Feeling like the biggest fool in the world, Guy followed these instructions to the letter. They marched two days with Guy leading, without opening his mouth. He didn't wash the smelly mess off his face. They crossed three rivers. And at nightfall they camped on the edge of a rolling savannah, dotted by small and scattered trees.

In the morning, they were awakened by the lowing of the buffalo.

It was, of course, pure coincidence, Guy told himself, as his bearers prepared his guns. But he had been in Africa long enough to be no longer sure of that. And the longer he lived in that dark land in which natural law, and pure science were endlessly and effortlessly negated, the less sure he would become.

In the first volley, they dropped three young and tender cows. Then as the bearers passed him a fresh gun, he saw an old and war-scarred bull lift his head and sniff the morning air.

He lifted the gun and waited. The light was poor, and the old bull was facing him. He knew better than to try a shot like that. There is no beast in Africa meaner than a buffalo, nothing that moves more fearless. Lions, themselves, leave him strictly alone. He has no natural enemies, except his own kind, when the younger bulls in the mating season duel him to the death for the possession of the cows. This one, obviously, had survived many such duels—and remained king.

A head-on shot at a charging bull buffalo, Guy knew, was difficult to the point of near impossibility. The brain pan is protected by an armored bone where the great horns overlap the forehead. When the bull puts down his neck to charge, this same bone boss protects his chest. Since not even an elephant gun in the 1840's had the impact or the penetrating power to bring him down once he started charging, the only chance was a side or flanking shot before he began to move.

Guy and the bearers began to work their way slowly to the side. They were all sweating, though the morning was cool. Guy remembered the body of the woman who had stumbled upon a buffalo cow at the watering hole near Pongoland. They had had to scrape the purplish mass of shredded flesh and bone up out of the earth into which the cow had pounded it, with shovels. There had been no other way of lifting the remains of the woman. They had not even been sure at first that this pulpy mass of flesh and guts and brains and bone splinters had ever been human. But for the hair and teeth and shreds of cloth that Manomassa picked out of the mud for his own purposes and showed to Guy, it might as well have been the remains of any of the larger animals.

He prayed the wind wouldn't shift. The buffalo's eyes are notoriously poor; but the keenness of his sense of smell is very nearly incredible. They had nearly reached a fair vantage point, when the tick birds nestling on the old bull's scarred and shaggy hide exploded into flight. At once, without any snorting or pawing of the earth, the bull charged, coming on at express-train speed. Guy put a ball into his neck, aiming over the horns, trying to break the vertebrae. The bull didn't even slow. Another shot clipped splinters from the bone boss; causing the bull to lift his head momentarily. In that exact instant, Guy snatched another gun from the bearer, and slammed home a shot full into the old bull's chest.

That was all he had time for. The buffalo crashed into them, hurling one of the bearers high into the air, knocking Guy and the other one aside with tremendous force. Then he went on through. Twenty yards further on, the animal's knees buckled, and he slid to earth with such force that he ploughed up a furrow with his chin. He lay there without moving.

But when Guy tried to get to his feet to see if the bull were dead, he found he could not. His left leg was broken very cleanly in two places. The pain hadn't come yet. Instinctively, he raised his hand and wiped his face. The sticky mess came off on his fingers. He stared at it solemnly.

Maybe, he thought, if I'd given that witch doctor another bottle of rum, he'd have warned me about this, too. . . .

When, after making bamboo splints for Guy's leg and the gun bearer's arm, they dressed out the old bull, they found the third shot had gone through his heart. But he had gashed open one man's hip, broken the bones of two more, and traveled twenty-five yards before surrendering to death.

They had plenty of meat now. They had a feast of liver, tongue, hearts, and succulent steaks from the three cows. Then they salted down the meat of the four beasts and started home, carrying Guy and the bearers in tipoys. It was pure hell. Every jolt ran red hot knives through Guy's broken leg. But they made it finally, arriving at the edge of Pongoland on the first of November, to find the air saturated with mists.

But it did not rain. The dry season was gone, yet all they had was this super-saturated mist that hung on for weeks. It was enough, of course, to bring the animals back to the old hunting grounds, and make the plants grow luxuriously. All in all, it was the best and most comfortable rainy season they ever had.

On Christmas day, 1843, Joã da Coimbra returned to Pongoland. He had lost forty pounds. He was dressed in the latest European mode. His eyes were clear and sparkling. He seemed twenty years younger.

And to his arm there clung, looking up at him with eyes big with adoration, the chicest, most petite Parisienne imaginable in this world.

16

IN THE next two weeks, Guy Falks very nearly lost his mind. His leg was bad enough; but this—this was absolutely not to be borne. For one thing, the Mongo lodged tiny, elfin Monique Vallois, not in his seraglio with the other women, but in his own quarters. He went no more to his harem. He presented to all the world the fatuous portrait of a middle-aged man in love. For two weeks he did not come near Guy's house, where that tortured young man sat, with his broken leg resting on a footstool, and raged like a wounded lion.

"But why?" Beeljie whispered. "You love em Furtoo girl, Bwana? Beeljie no sabby. You never see her, you. How come you crazy mad? You love her, tell Beeljie and I go—"

"I don't love her!" Guy howled. "I don't give a damn if she drops down dead! But she's white, Beeljie, white! Can't you understand? And that burr-headed dung-colored nigger has got no right to—"

"Bwana him white," Beeljie pointed out. "And Beeljie her black, most like. So why?"

"Oh Christ!" Guy grated. "Get out of here, will you! Get out before I kill you!"

Beeljie fled. Guy sat there in the thick darkness. His all too vivid imagination kept conjuring up a portrait of Monique, white and naked, enwrapped in the Mongo's dark and burly arms. It made a great sickness in him. He had never seen Monique Vallois; he hadn't the faintest idea what she was like; but at the thought of her and the Mongo, his vitals seemed to dissolve into water. . . .

Finally the Mongo came to see him.

"I heard about your accident," the mulatto said affably. "I am sorry, Guy. Been meaning to pay a call upon you; but I've been—busy. . . ."

Guy sat there, gripping the arms of his chair and glaring.

"Since," da Coimbra went on, "there are no secrets in Pongoland, I don't have to explain matters to you. I suppose you have some justification in thinking that I am a man of little word. Perhaps I am; but this was not of my doing. I acquired the petite Monique—for you. I had no idea that a man of my age or girth would interest her. It seems I was wrong. She was not concerned with age nor bulk, nor—"

"Color?" Guy grated.

"Color?" the Mongo said. "No. Why should she be? That is of no more importance among civilized people than it is among—pigeons, say. And the French, with all their faults, are civilized. I am sorry for your sake that this happened. For my own, I must confess, I'm glad. It is nice to have a woman one can talk to—though the rest does have its relative importance—"

"Get out of here, Mongo!" Guy screamed at him. "For God's sake, go! I don't want to kill you, but by heaven, I'll—"

"I doubt that you could," da Coimbra said calmly, "but it saddens me that you want to. I thought you'd outgrown this thing which makes the Anglo-Saxon peoples such backward, savage children. I see you haven't. I am truly sorry. . . ."

"Savage children!" Guy whispered. "You, half-African son of a bitch! You use that word! You dare!"

"My people are savages," Joã de Coimbra said quietly, "but then they've had no chance to be aught else. Yours, my choleric young friend, have had that chance—and rejected it, perhaps because their souls weren't big enough. And that, Guy Falks, is truly sad. . . ."

"Get out!" Guy whispered.

"Very well. But before I go, I must tell you what I came to. The driver ants are on the march—for the first time in seven years. They might by-pass the village, or they might not. In any event, you'd better have a couple of your Negroes prepared to move you. In the morning, after they'd passed, incapacitated as you are, we'd find you neatly dressed in your clothing, with that broken leg still outstretched and not a shred of flesh left on your bones. I'm told it's a singularly unpleasant death—so take care. . . ."

Then he was gone, out into the driving mists.

Two days later, the whole village of Pongoland was ready to march, waiting only to see what direction the ants would take. Ungah Gulliah, with the savage's admiration for pure force, told Guy the history of this true king of the beasts, this small insect, less than a quarter of an inch long, which is lord absolute of the African earth. Every five to seven years, she told him, under conditions of extreme humidity, the ants began to march. By the tens of billions, by the trillions. And everything that cannot flee their path dies. Everything. An aged lion, crippled by rheumatism. A wounded elephant. Snails, caterpillars, snakes, scorpions. All tethered or corraled beasts, no matter what their size or strength. The aged and infirm among men, if the more able do not bear them away. After they have passed, the skeletons of their victims are found as clean as though the flesh had been boiled away. Cleaner. White and dry. . . .

The workers among the driver ants are blind and sexless. The few males can see. The queen is twenty times the size of her subjects, so fat she cannot walk and must be dragged along by the workers. She is a terribly efficient egg-laying machine, producing her offspring by the millions. She is, also, the only female in her tribe.

Guy listened idly to Ungah's story of their savagery; how only the spiders escaped, by suspending themselves from blades of grass by a thread so fine the ants dared not descend it. But he was not thinking about ants. What he was thinking was that the time had certainly come to leave Pongoland forever. But, before he went, he had a thing to do: he had to see Monique Vallois, talk to her. Beeljie? That, too, was better broken now. Perhaps she would believe him dead. It would be far better if she did.

He remembered, wryly, that during the first two weeks of December, he had, with Beeljie's supple assistance, managed the act of love several times, despite his leg. And without precautions. He dismissed the worry; in his present state of health the chances of any results from their love-making were slight indeed. . . . See Monique, make her his generous offer, then go. Another month or two of recuperation in one of the coast factories, and he would be ready to begin his own.

"Ungah," he said suddenly, "will you take a note to the Furtoo wife of the Mongo for me? In secret, of course. The Mongo must not know. . . ."

"Of course, Bwana," Ungah said.

His French was rusty from long disuse. But its defects aided him. He managed to impart, unintentionally, such an air of mystery to his message, that Monique, being all woman, and what was more, all Frenchwoman, came.

She slipped into his hut, and stood there, staring at him. She was tiny, doll-like, exquisite, elfin, with a gamin's face that broke every rule of beauty, and yet resulted in something better than mere loveliness. Her facial bones were prominent, her mouth enormously wide; her eyes eclipsed her tiny face. But they were wonderful eyes, big with remembered pain.

"You 'ave wished to see me, M'sieur?" she said. Her voice was low and throaty, softer than a caress.

"Yes," Guy said in French. "I have wished to see you, Monique. And now that I have I am glad. . . ."

"Zut, alors!" she laughed. "And me, too. But why? Is it, I think, a little indiscreet that I have come here. My husband, the Mongo, he would not like it, I think—"

"Your husband?" Guy got out.

"But yes. We have married ourselves before we have parted from France. Is it that this is so very strange, M'sieur?"

"Look, Monique," Guy said, "I haven't been able to save much money. But I'll pay your passage back to France and give you enough money to open a little business in the bargain. A milliner's shop, say, or even a dress salon."

She stared at him in helpless astonishment.

"But why?" she said. "You do not know me at all and—"

"I know you enough. At home, you can make a proper marriage and—"

"But I have made a proper marriage! In the church. I had flowers and a veil and—"

"Monique! I don't care how you did it; it is never proper for a white woman to marry a nigger!"

"Ah, so?" she said. "Now you begin to anger me a little, I think. Who are you, M'sieur, that you presume to speak so of my husband?"

"Doesn't matter who I am. I'm white, and that's enough. Maybe you've never had an easy life, but even that is not justification for—"

"Assez!" Monique spat. "Enough! Perhaps now you will permit me to tell you something, M'sieur. I married my husband because he was kind and good to me and I love him. His skin is very soft, and its color is nice. It was this that made me notice him at first. I have seen so many, many men like you. You are white. So, M'sieur, is the belly of a fish. And the fish does not puff himself up with pride over a simple fact of nature. Some men are white, some yellow, some red, some black. These are all but colors, and they are not important. They are just interesting—as the various kinds of flowers are interesting. But in the end, they are all men, with love and hate and pity and pain in their hearts, they are the little children of the good God, who loves them all—equally. You have well understood this which I have said?"

"I understand that you are hopeless."

"If by 'hopeless,' you mean I will not leave the man I love because you do not like the color God has given him, you are right, M'sieur. In this you go too far. I do not, myself, particularly like this color of yours, but I would not presume to tell your wife to leave you because of it. That would be too much. And now, I go. With your permission, M'sieur, may I say that I am very sorry for you? You could be nice, if you could free your heart—and let it grow—"

She turned, too late. For the Mongo Joã stood in the doorway, staring at her. He was trembling all over; and he could not speak. But he dominated himself finally. When he did speak at last, his control was admirable.

"Come, my dear," he said softly. "It is very late. Good night, Mister Falks. I trust you will sleep well. . . ."

Guy, of course did not sleep at all. He lay down on his mudheap bed with his pistols by his side. He lay like that for two hours. Then he heard the babble of voices rising all over the village, and the sound of running feet. He got up and hobbled to the door, using his bamboo crutches. The door was locked, not with his own latch on the inside; but with a tremendously heavy log of ironwood inclined against it. He drew back and threw his weight against the door. It did not budge and he fell to the floor, in agony from his broken leg. He got up, tried again; but with the same results. He lay on the floor, hearing the terror-laden shouts, the cries quavering on the night air.

Then, just outside, he heard Beeljie's voice, screaming his name. He heard her hands slap against the log, the rasp of her breath as she tugged. Then she screamed. And two dark, guttural voices cut through her cries:

"Do not fight, woman! Come away. The Mongo has condemned him. He dared to touch the Furtoo woman, so he must die. Now come—the devil ants are already here!"

He heard her, lost, despairing, screaming his name. Then the screams were shut off, muffled, as though someone had clapped a hand over her mouth. He lay there gathering his forces; then he got up and went to the window. They had barred that exit, too. He came back to the center of the room. His guards had fled by now, he was sure of that. No man could stand in the path of the driver ants. He sat there, thinking. Then, with a slow smile, he picked up a musket and hopped to the back wall. Standing on his good leg, he swung the musket against the mud and wattle wall. The butt went through with the first blow. He kept it up until the hole was large enough. Then he began to worm his way through. It was awkward work. He pushed and tugged, until at last he dragged himself through the opening, falling so clumsily on the outside that his bad leg was under him. The pain of it made him pass out completely.

He came awake with the sensation that someone was stabbing him all over with white hot needles. He lay there a long moment, and then he knew what it was. He tried to pull himself upright, but he could not. He had left his crutches inside. He turned over and began to crawl. The white hot stabs increased. He was a very brave man; but this was one hell of a way to die. He got three yards, then the slashing, stabbing mandibles of the ants overcame him. He lay in a pool of them, thrashing about and screaming.

It was by his screams that Beeljie found him. She was small and slight and not very strong; but she got him out of there; she lifted him, dragged him, praying to the white man's big Ju Ju up in the sky, praying to all the dark and bloody gods of Africa. And one or the other of them answered her. Perhaps even both. For there are no false gods if one believes in them enough; and each man carves his private fetish in his own image, shaping it in his own ugliness, or ennobling it with his truth.

She got him to the higher ground, out of the path of the ants. They lay there, panting; and then they heard more screams. They moved to the edge and looked down. Something was struggling down there—something, or someone—and there was nothing they could do. The screams died into gurgling moans—then into silence. They lay in each other's arms, and wept over their helplessness.

In the morning, Beeljie went down to the deserted village —for the ants had passed on now—and got Guy's crutches. She brought, too, his money belt, and his pistols. Then the two of them went down the trail toward the river and the sea. But on the spot directly below the place where they had lain, they found the skeleton of a woman, still clad in beads and bangles; chained by one foot to a log.

"Ungah!" Beeljie shrieked. "Ungah!" Then she collapsed to her knees beside the pitiful rack of bones, her body torn by a storm of weeping.

"How—how do you know?" Guy whispered.

"Bangles! Ungah's bangles, Bwana! But why? Why Mongo he kill em so?"

Guy didn't answer her. He couldn't. But he knew. Clearly and perfectly, he knew. Because poor Ungah had taken his note to Monique. Nothing more. For that she had died in an agony inconceivable to the minds of men who had not, like himself, experienced the driver ant's bite. . . .

Beeljie had plastered him all over with a poultice of tobacco leaves to draw out the stings. He felt much better now. At least his body did.

But there was no name for that which festered within his heart.

17

ON THE twenty-first day of June, 1852, Guy Falks sat on the piazza of his slave factory, Falkston, and talked with Captain James Rudgers, who sat sprawled out lazily in a bamboo chair. The years in prison had marked Rudgers. Guy didn't know by what means the company had secured his release, and he didn't ask. If the captain wanted to tell him, he would; besides, it wasn't really important, anyhow.

From where he sat, Guy could see the ocean. Just beyond the dark masses of the cotton silk, baobob, tamarind, and raffia palm trees, he could see the masts and spars of the *Volador*, James Rudgers' vessel; and, crawling like black insects over that vast expanse of sparkling waters toward it, the canoes of the Kroomen, loading the slaves. James Rudgers should have been aboard, supervising the loading. It was a measure of what the years in prison had done to him, that he sat there on the piazza, and let his mate do the job.

"You lucky bastard!" he growled.

"Lucky?" Guy said. "Why?"

"Look what you've got: an easy life, a nice woman to take care of you—"

"Which woman?" Guy grinned. "Seems to me I've had a dozen off'n on since you first started to put into Falkston. . . ."

"Beeljie," James Rudgers said flatly. "Those Portuguese quadroon gals don't count. They come and go; but Beeljie really keeps you going. . . ."

"Reckon so," Guy drawled. "I get damned sick of her sometimes. But I am used to having her around. Don't see why that makes me so lucky. . . ."

"You are though. Biggest factory on this part of the coast—richest factor in Africa—"

"Third richest," Guy corrected him. "Pedro Blanco and da Souza are still ahead of me. . . ."

"Doesn't matter," Rudgers said. "You'll catch 'em. Folks are saying that you've got over a million dollars scattered about in banks in London and New York. . . ."

"People make a mighty heap of loose palaver," Guy said dryly.

"Knowing you," Rudgers said, "I'd bet they're guessing under, not over—"

He was right. Guy Falks, at that moment, had a quarter of a million banked in London—in pounds, not dollars. And distributed among various banks in Boston, Philadelphia and New York, he had seven hundred thousand dollars more.

"Funny," Captain Rudgers mused, "how life is. One man's star rises, another's sets. You've heard what straits the Mongo's in?"

"Yes," Guy said. "Little Monique's a damned expensive proposition. . . ."

"It's not that. Before you started operating, he could afford her whims. She's a nice woman. And that kid of theirs is mighty damned fine. . . ."

"I heard."

"There just isn't room on the Pongo for two factories the size of Falkston and Pongoland. And you don't leave the Mongo anything but the culls. . . ."

"I don't make the caravans come here," Guy pointed out.

"Don't you? You 'dash' bigger than anybody else, Blanco and da Souza included. You spend more money on *colungees* than any five other factors put together. You pay more than anybody for your niggers. So naturally you get the best—"

"Which I then sell at better prices. It's only good business, Cap'n. But it's more than that. The Mongo's business methods are pitiful. All his niggers rob him blind. He can't or won't keep books. I'll bet he hasn't taken an inventory since I left there. . . ."

"Don't doubt it. But speaking of nigger hanger-ons, you've got a mighty flock of them yourself. Which reminds me: your headman here is the twin brother of another chief back in the bush, isn't he?"

"Yes," Guy said. "Flonkerri is the twin of Flamburi, who lives way up the river behind the Mongo's domain. Why?"

"Because I saw the other one, Flam—Flam—"

"Flamburi."

"Flamburi holding mighty close palaver with the Mongo the other day. Wouldn't put it past his nibs to stir up any bad blood existing between those twin images of ugly sin in the hopes that you and Falkston might get caught in the middle. . . ."

"You're way behind, Cap'n," Guy laughed. "He's already started. Flon and Flam, neither one of 'em being older than the other, and their Ma not remembering which one came first, nor the midwife, had to split the chieftainship between 'em. So now the Folgias have got two Dondas. That made trouble from the first. To ease things up, Flonkerri came down here and asked me to let him settle on the place with his bunch—"

"And you let him. Why?"

" 'Cause the Folgias, for all that they're as dumb as old hell, are first-class fighting men. Don't have the cold intelligence of the Ashanti—who are bloody geniuses, for all their being niggers—nor the blood lust of the Dahomeans. Trouble with them is that they try to make up with pure guts what they lack in brains. I've seen 'em charge Fulah and Mandingo caravans with assagais and spears. And those Mohammedan tribes have been using firearms ever since the Berbers and Arabs converted them, so the Folgias get slaughtered. But they keep right on coming. I don't have to worry about that. If a bush war breaks out, I'll lead 'em. . . ."

"So you think there's going to be a war?"

"Yes. Between the two halves of the same tribe, which is a pity. Flonkerri and his bunch have tripled their wealth since they came here, while Flamburi's crowd have been gnawing genet bones. Jealousy, Cap'n, is mighty bad Ju Ju. . . . "

"Especially with the Mongo to stir it up," James Rudgers said.

"The Mongo's being even cuter than you think," Guy said. "He's sent us a Trojan horse. Name of Mukabassa, a Ju Ju man. Supposed to be a present from Flamburi to his brother. Ugliest black bastard you ever did see. Cross-eyed. But he's some Ju Ju all right. Ever since he came here all hell has popped loose. The cattle get sick. One of the kids went blind. A big, husky warrior lost his mind because he was convinced he saw the spirit of death, all wrapped up in white fire, in the jungle. Flonkerri's number one wife miscarried last week. Life-long friends are getting into brawls and knifing each other. And all this because of ol' Mukabassa—"

"Old what?"

"Mukabassa. Hell of a name, isn't it? Fits him, I think. I've told Flonkerri a dozen times to run that Ju Ju son of a bitch off the place. Only Flon's scared. Reckon I'll have to do it, myself. . . ."

"Well, as long as you're warned," James Rudgers said.

Guy walked down to the landing with the Captain, where the Kroomen waited to take the old New Englander aboard the *Volador*. The Captain shook hands with him.

"Take care, boy," he said. "I want to see you when I come back next trip. . . ."

"Don't worry, Cap'n, I will," Guy said.

After he had gone, Guy went back to the piazza. He sat there, thinking about the gathering danger. What da Coimbra was up to was perfectly clear. By sowing dissension among the Falkston Folgias, he hoped to weaken their fighting prowess and then incite Flamburi's jealous faction to attack and burn the factory.

Actually the situation was a good deal worse than even Guy knew. For Mukabassa was doing more than merely stirring up the Folgias of Falkston; he was slaughtering them. Whenever Flonkerri, Donda of the Folgias, sought from him the reason for the series of disasters that had fallen upon the tribe, the Ju Ju man had one pat and ready answer: Somebody was putting the evil eye on Flonkerri's people. There were trials almost every day; and already five people had died of drinking the sassy water—a poisonous concoction made by boiling the bark of the gedu tree—in ordeal trials to prove their guilt or innocence. Mukabassa, of course, made sure that nobody was proved innocent.

As the ordeals were staged in the jungle beyond Falkston, Guy knew nothing of these quasi-judicial murders. Nobody dared tell him. They knew too well his outspoken hatred and contempt for the Ju Ju men and all their works. On the other hand, so great was the power of superstition over their savage minds, they didn't dare disobey Mukabassa, either. By such means was the Mongo Joã weakening Guy's defense. . . .

Guy saw Flonkerri coming toward him. Flonkerri was a tall and stately black, well-muscled, and still young. But now his face was twisted in purest grief. Great tears sparkled on his ebony cheeks.

Now what the devil? Guy thought.

Flonkerri glanced quickly in every direction before he spoke.

"Us take walk, Bwana?" he said at last.

"Right," Guy said, and stood up. The two of them walked across the compound and into the jungle at the other side.

Flonkerri looked about him, fearfully.

"Nobody here," he said at last.

"Speak up, man!" Guy snapped. "What the devil's bothering you?"

"It Kapapela, Bwana. Mukabassa got her locked up."

"What!" Guy roared. "How in the name of living hell fire could Mukabassa lock up your number two wife? You mean you let him lock her up! God damn it, Flon, how many times have I told you to run that old fraud out of here?"

"Had to, Bwana. Mukabassa say Kapapela she put 'em eye on Nikia, make em baby come too soon all dead. So tomorrow Kapapela her got em drink em sassy wood, prove em she bad she good. But I scairt she die, me. No like. Them others all die. Five men, women die. . . ."

"Damn it all! You mean you've let Mukabassa murder five people, and you didn't tell me! Flon, I got a good mind to take a cat to your black tail!"

"Him big Ju Ju," Flonkerri whispered. "Him only give em sassy wood. They own black hearts kill em, yes. . . ."

"Look, Flon," Guy said flatly. "Gedu bark is poison. Like a pit viper's bite. You give anybody enough boiled gedu bark, and he'll die, period. Innocent or guilty, he'll die. Christ, man! Use your brains, if you have any! Those Ju Jus save the people they want to save—those whose relatives have bribed the evil bastards—by giving them only enough gedu bark water, or sassy wood if you want to call it that—to make 'em sick. That's all there is to it. . . ."

Solemnly Flonkerri shook his head.

"Bwana no sabby Ju Ju. Big medicine. Sassy wood only make black hearts choke. Clean hearts beat too strong and—"

It was hopeless. Guy knew that. Between the two of them lay a barrier of centuries. He was terribly fond of Flonkerri; but he felt like strangling him. Only that wouldn't solve anything either. He remembered Kapapela the last time he had seen her. She was something out of the Song of Songs, slender as a palm tree, nightshade velvety. Her close-cropped wool fitted her delicate little head like a cap. Her little shoe-button nose and softly pouting lips were the epitome of African beauty. Hell, Kapa was beautiful. With all his prejudices, even he could see that. And tomorrow she was going to die because this big, black burr-headed ass she had married was so afraid of Ju Ju medicine he didn't dare save the life of the woman he loved more than life. . . .

As though echoing his thought, Flonkerri said:

"Kapapela die—me die. No can live without her—"

"Wait!" Guy said. "Look, Flon—if I can prove that white-man's Ju Ju is stronger than Mukabassa's, do you promise to run him out of here?"

Flonkerri's eyes flamed.

"You make me bigger medicine, Bwana, I take em assagai, open him up teeth to belly, yes!"

"That's won't be necessary," Guy said. "Come on, we'd better have a chat with His Nibs. . . ."

Mukabassa stared at Guy out of his evil, crossed eyes.

"Bwana want make em white man Furtoo medicine 'gainst

Mukabassa Ju Ju?" he growled. "Bwana no sabby what him say!"

"I savvy all right," Guy said flatly. "What's more I savvy that I've got more than a bellyful of you, you murdering black bastard! You'n me are going to make big medicine—twice. The first time, when I prove your sassy water can't do a damn thing against mine. The second will be right after: when I prove to you that even Papa Damballa's on my side. . . ."

At the mention of the serpent god, Mukabassa turned ashen. But something, pride in his craft, perhaps, made him rise to the challenge.

"A'right," he said. "How Bwana want to prove em all that?"

"I want the girl for ten minutes before you give her your sassy water. I'm going to give her mine, first. You can watch me do it. In fact, you can make yours triple strength, and it still won't work. Then after that, you'll see—"

"A'right. But I think it Bwana who gonna see. Gumbye, Bwana. . . ."

Guy stared at him, his eyes filled with icy contempt.

"Come on Flon," he said quietly. "You'n I have things to do—"

He led Flonkerri out into the jungle until they came to the gree-gree grove sacred to Damballa, the snake god. Then he cut a forked branch from a nearby tree. He stood there holding it and frowning. He had forgotten the principal thing: What the devil did you carry a pit viper home in, once you'd caught him?

"Flon," he said. "Run and get me a couple of skin bags. Big ones, like the women carry water in. Can do?"

"Can do, Bwana," Flonkerri said, and was off, running easily and well. He was back in ten minutes with the bags. When he saw what Guy was going to do, his glistening ebony skin turned ashy grey.

Guy stepped into the grove, confident that his stout boots would protect his feet. As always, it was swarming with the vipers. He thrust the forked stick deftly, pinning one of the ugly snakes to the earth; then very calmly bent and picked it up, holding it just behind the head, so it could not turn to bite him. It wrapped its sinuous length around his arm. With his right hand, he unwound it.

"Open the bag, Flon," he said.

The big Negro did so, and Guy dropped the serpent in, tail first. Flonkerri slapped the bag shut, and tied it with a leather

224

thong. Five minutes later, Guy had caught another viper, and placed it in the second bag. Flonkerri's eyes were wide with wonder. This was big Ju Ju indeed.

"What Bwana do now?" he said.

"Big medicine," Guy laughed. "Take 'em home. Tomorrow, you'll see. . . ."

Back at the factory, he searched in his tool chest until he found a pair of stout pincers. Then he stood there, studying the matter. There was a way to milk a snake of its venom; but he didn't remember what it was. The medicine wagon "doctors" back in Mississippi had done it with rattlers and cotton-mouthed moccasins before their exhibitions. They let the snake bite something, and then—that was it! They hung the fangs in an inflated pig's bladder. But he didn't have a pig's bladder, or anything like it. Just then he saw a flock of chickens crossing the yard. A chicken would do—if the viper could be prevented from drawing back after striking.

He went out into the yard and caught a plump pullet. He tied her by one foot to a stake. Then, taking his forked stick in his left hand, he unlaced one of the bags and dumped the pit viper out on the ground before the pullet. The snake struck at once. Guy pinned him down with the stick, with his fangs still sunk in the pullet's flesh. Then holding him like that, he began to press the poison sac just between the serpent's beady eyes. When he was sure he had emptied it into the dying pullet, he caught the viper's head between his thumb and forefinger, and withdrew it, keeping the mouth open. Even now, he knew, the slightest slip was damned dangerous, because the viper had probably retained enough poison on his fangs to lay a man up for weeks. Taking the pincers, he yanked out one of the long, curving, yellow fangs, then the other. The viper was absolutely harmless now, because it is only through the hollow fangs that he can inject his venom into his victim. The rest of his teeth are solid, and serve only to hold his prey until the venom does its deadly work.

He picked the snake up, and put it back in the bag, marking the bag with his pocket knife. Then he called one of the native women and ordered her to weave two long narrow baskets, with a hinged cover on one end. He told her to leave the lattices fairly open so that the vipers could be seen. Four hours later, when she had finished them, he put the harmless viper in one, and marked it with an almost imperceptible piece of raffia. Then he placed the deadly serpent in the other. As an afterthought, he buried the dead pullet for fear someone might eat it.

At noon the next day, howling and dancing, his face hidden by a hideous Ju Ju mask which Guy thought rather improved his looks, Mukabassa came, leading poor Kapapela. Her hands were tied behind her with liana vines, and a loop of the vine had been twisted around her slender throat. She was half dead of fright.

"Don't worry, Kapa," Guy said gently. "My medicine is stronger than his. . . ."

He got no further.

"What's going on here?" a crisp feminine voice demanded.

Guy turned, and saw Beeljie standing there, staring at him, and with her, a white woman almost as tall as he was. He had never seen Prudence Staunton before; but this, indisputably, was she, for the very simple reason that she was the only white woman in the entire territory. She was, at that time, twenty-six, or twenty-seven years old. And, though Africa had not been kind to her, she, clearly, had dominated it. He did not, at that moment, or indeed until much later, realize that Prudence had her own distinctive kind of attractiveness. What struck him at the beginning, was the serenity in every line of her.

And, realizing the simple faith upon which it was based, that very serenity was to his skeptical mind, the most piquant of provocations.

He studied her with almost insolent slowness. The details were not, in themselves, striking. She was almost too slender, with a kind of boyish slimness that somehow was curiously feminine. Her blue eyes had wrinkles in their corners from too much staring at the sun. Yet the wrinkles added not age to her eyes, but a certain imperiousness. He had the contradictory feeling that upon some other, different occasion, those same lines could crinkle into good humor. Her hair was dark golden, clubbed softly into a bun on her slim, sunburned neck. Her mouth was wide, and surprisingly full-lipped, revealing the fact that there was great warmth under that exterior aspect of cool control. Her eyebrows and lashes had been bleached almost white by the sun, and were startling against the rich, golden tan the same sun had given her.

The details were not striking. But Prudence Staunton was.

"I asked," she repeated dryly, "what on earth is going on here?"

"Nothing much," Guy drawled. "Me'n this big time Ju Ju man have got a little wager going. He's going feed this wench some sassy wood—"

"But you can't let him!" Prudence snapped. "Sassy wood is a deadly poison!"

"You aren't telling me anything I don't know, Miss Staunton," Guy said calmly. "Still—as a sporting proposition—"

Prudence's eyes flashed sapphire flame.

"What kind of a man are you, Mister Falks?" she snapped. "You mean you'd gamble with a human life?"

"That is, granting that niggers are human," Guy said, baiting her; "which I don't. Besides I'm a better Ju Ju man than this child of ugly sin. The girl won't die. I guarantee it."

"Why, you—" Prudence got out.

"Look, Pru," Guy said flatly, "you're getting a little tiresome. Now stand back like a good girl, and don't interfere. Beeljie, honey, hand me that bottle. . . ."

Beeljie gave him the bottle of tarter-emetic without a word. If he had told her to cut her own throat, she probably would have done that, too, just as quickly, and unquestioningly.

"Open your mouth, Kapa," Guy commanded.

Kapapela did so, hope beginning to dawn in her eyes. Guy poured the nauseous concoction down her throat. Then he turned to Mukabassa.

"Your turn, big Ju Ju man," he said.

Mukabassa lifted the bowl full of boiled gedu bark to Kapapela's lips. Out of the corner of his eyes, Guy saw Prudence tensing to spring. He caught her just as she did so, pinioning her arms.

"No you don't," he said flatly. "A wager's a wager; and down here we deal from the top of the deck. . . ."

"Let me go!" Prudence shrilled. "Let me go!"

"I better tell you one thing, Pru," Guy mocked. "Down here at Falkston we've got just one rule: I speak, and people listen. 'Specially women folks. Damn it all, Pru, keep still!"

Kapapela swallowed the poison bravely. The townspeople gathered around her, staring at her in breath-gone fascination. Suddenly, before a half minute had gone by, Kapapela doubled up, and vomited the poison out upon the ground.

"She'll be all right, now," Guy said. "Gedu juice has to stay down at least ten minutes to work. Can I turn you loose now?"

"I—have—never—" Prudence gasped, spacing the words,

"encountered more brazen effrontery in—all—my—life!"

"Then, Pru," Guy said, "you've got a lot to learn . . ." He saw Flonkerri fingering his razor-edged assagai. "No, Flon," he said. "Me'n Mukabassa have got another test. We're going to call on Papa Damballa to show you who speaks true mouth. Nibiri, bring the snakes!"

"And you a white man and a Christian!" Prudence said.

"That white man part is all right," Guy said solemnly, "but I'm not sure about the Christian business. I'm an African by adoption, ma'am; and it appears to me that neither Jehovah nor Jesus ever got cross the Atlas Mountains. . . ."

Prudence stared at him with frank curiosity.

"You mean you believe in this Ju Ju rot?" she said.

"Yes'm. Don't you? Seems to me I've just proved it works; which is more than you Bible pounders have ever done with your brand. You've been washing niggers in the Blood of the Lamb for two hundred years, and they've stayed just as black and ornery as ever, far as I can tell . . . Got 'em, Nibiri? Now hold 'em up like a good girl, so all the people can see. . . ."

The Negroes recoiled a step or two from the caged vipers. Guy took the cage with the raffia bit on the top, and held it out in his left hand. Then he put his right hand against the hinged door.

"Bwana!" Beeljie wailed. "Bwana, don't! Bite em you, you die!"

"Don't you worry your pretty head, Baby," Guy grinned. "Me'n Papa Damballa are real close. Nothing'll happen to me. . . ."

"You mean," Prudence whispered, "you're going to put your bare arm in a cage with a pit viper?"

"Yes'm," Guy drawled. "Doesn't the Good Book say that faith can move mountains? I've got a mighty heap of faith in old Papa Damballa. This won't hurt a mite. . . ."

He thrust his arm boldly into the cage. The viper struck at once from a half coil, fastening its back teeth in Guy's arm. Guy heard Beeljie's high, despairing wails. But Prudence didn't make a sound. He half turned. She was staring at him with calm curiosity.

"Defanged the creature, didn't you?" she said easily. "Neat trick, Mr. Falks. . . ."

"You," Guy grinned, "are all right, aren't you, Pru? I'd thank you if you didn't let on, though. . . ."

"Don't worry about that," she smiled. "Any method at all

that will stamp out this Ju Ju business has my hearty approval. . . ."

He put his other hand in the cage, and forced apart the viper's jaws. The natives crowded around him, staring at the welter of tiny blood drops on his arm.

"Bwana no die?" Beeljie whispered.

"Not for forty more years," Guy chuckled.

He turned to Mukabassa, who was trembling like an aspen in a gale.

"Now you, big Ju Ju man," he said; and handed the witch doctor the other cage.

Mukabassa took one look at it, and whirled, already running.

Flonkerri flew after him, gaining on him with every bound.

"Let him go, Flon!" Guy called. "Just see that he doesn't come back!"

Flonkerri stopped. He turned back to Guy.

"No kill em, me?" he said dolefully.

"No," Guy said. "He's gone into the woods. Esamba will catch him tonight and blow out the light behind his eyes. That's punishment enough. . . ."

Flonkerri came up to where Kapapela waited, and smiled at her. He put his arm about her slender waist. They walked away together. The sight of it made a good feeling in Guy. He turned to Prudence Staunton.

"Now," he said gravely, "may I somewhat belatedly welcome you to Falkston, Miss Staunton? As the Fulahs say: My house is your house. . . ."

She did not answer him at once. She stood there staring at him with frank and open curiosity.

"Well?" Guy mocked. "Do I pass inspection?"

For a moment, her eyes were troubled.

"I'm sorry," she said. "I have been taught better manners, Mr. Falks. You see—it's just that I haven't seen a white man, except my father, since I was seven years old. . . ."

"And now that you have seen one?"

She smiled at him coolly, completely mistress of herself.

"All judgments are based upon comparison, are they not, Mr. Falks?" she said. "And having had no materials upon which to base them, how can I judge?"

"You, Pru," Guy said solemnly, "are purely a Philadelphia lawyer. But damn my soul, I like you! Come on up to the house. . . ."

"Thank you," she said. "And, if you'll permit me, I'll attend to your arm for you. I've had quite a bit of experience with snake bite. . . ."

She knelt by his chair in the living room, and opened the wound with his own razor, which Beeljie had sterilized at her orders. She pressed firmly around the incision with her fingers, causing it to bleed copiously.

"Don't think there's any poison," she said crisply; "but it pays to make sure. If there is, the blood will wash it out. There now, I think that does it. . . ."

She looked up at Beeljie.

"Girl," she said in Swahili, "where are the clothes for the bandages?"

"She speaks English," Guy said.

Prudence's gaze fixed itself upon Beeljie's face. Since her encounter with the Timbo woman that afternoon at the landing, she had paid her no more than the normal attention that she always accorded Africans. But now, seeing the deep hurt in Beeljie's eyes, she knew. Absolutely, and finally, she knew.

But what held her there, rooted to the floor with pure astonishment, was her own reaction. It wasn't an unusual thing, she realized. In fact, this practice of concubinage with native women was the final reason why, despite their scarcity, she had never met a white man in Africa. Holding her too precious, too pure to be offended by the sight, her father had always left her behind on his rare trips to the factories and trading posts of the Slave Coast. The trips themselves had been made, at least in part, for the express purpose of preaching against this practice. His efforts had been useless. He knew before he started out that they were going to be; but he held it his Christian duty to make them.

She got up, very slowly.

"Bandage it yourself," she said to Beeljie. The sharpness of her own tone shocked her. She hadn't meant it that way.

"Yes, Memsahib," Beeljie said humbly.

She needed time to think, Prudence realized. And she couldn't, with his great dark eyes on her like that. She had the feeling that his gaze penetrated her; that he knew exactly how she felt. . . .

Which, the remorseless honesty her father had instilled in her told her, was neither shock nor outrage over this flagrant violation of the Christian code of morals, but pain—bitter, female, jealous pain.

230

I don't know him, she thought furiously. What I said to him was true: I have no basis for comparison, because father kept me so sheltered. And he's a slaver, a dealer in human flesh. More than half infidel. I cannot tell whether he is ugly—or as beautiful as a pagan god, which is how he seems to me. Father should have known better! He should have taken me with him. Then I would have known other men of my race, and not be standing here helpless—already half in love with —this stranger I met less than an hour ago. . . .

Guy smiled at her.

"The world," he said gently, "is a mite different—outside the mission walls. . . ."

"I see it is," she said flatly, "but I'm going to disappoint you, Mr. Falks. My father is the preacher, not I. Your life is your own business, as far as I'm concerned. . . ."

"Is it?" Guy said. "I don't think so. I'm a great believer in human brotherhood. And I am disappointed. I was looking forward to having my soul saved by such an attractive missionary. But now you've got me puzzled: just why did you come here, then?"

"My father sent me," Prudence said slowly. "There's a bush war flaring up around the Mission—and he's seen what Dhiakiar's savages do to women. I didn't want to come; but he promised me that if the situation became really acute, he'd send a messenger down here asking for your help. Would you send it, Mr. Falks?"

"Gladly. Your pa's quite a man from all I've heard. To my mind, the harm he's done by trying to introduce a religion that never was designed for Africa, has been more than made up for by the sanitary practices he's brought in, by his teaching the Bumboes a little cleanliness, and curing their ills. As a doctor, he's first-rate. Sent him a few patients, myself. . . ."

"In other words," Prudence said icily, "you're concerned with their bodies, not their souls. That's understandable. Healthy Africans fetch better prices, don't they, Mr. Falks?"

"Right," Guy said. "But I'm being remiss in my obligations as your host. What would you like for dinner, Miss Staunton?" Prudence stood there, her cheeks flaming.

"I apologize," she said at last. "I'm your guest, after all. Sorry you had to remind me. My manners have been abominable. Please forgive me, Mr. Falks. . . ."

"There's nothing to forgive," Guy smiled. "Come, I'll show

you about the place, while the cook prepares your favorite dish. What is it, Miss Staunton?"

"Favorite dishes," she said sadly, "are a luxury that mission people can't afford. Just carry on as usual, Mr. Falks."

"Very well," Guy said. "Shall we go?"

18

THE moon was caught in the cotton silk trees, silvering all the sky. A wind came in from the sea, making the trees dance so that they shredded the light, giving everything motion, inquietude. A flock of monkeys scampered through the tamarinds, chattering. A bullikookoo crowed raucously. Then it was still, except for the roll and thunder of the surf setting up its answering rhythm in her blood.

She lay there on her back, staring at the ceiling. The wind talked darkly in the baobob trees, flickering alternating patterns of leaf shadow and moon silver over her face. She was sure that she could feel the alternation like the strokes of a child's grass whip, flickering lightly, teasingly, across her flesh. A lizard scampered across the patch of moonlight reflected on the ceiling by the mirror, and was gone in a rustling.

And Prudence Staunton lay there clenching and unclenching her bony fingers in the darkness and trying not to cry.

I must not think, she told herself, I must not. He is the opposite of all I've dreamed of: an unbeliever, a trader in human flesh—a wicked, cruel man . . . No . . . he could have let his warriors kill that witch doctor, and he didn't. He's got goodness in him—only he fights it down. I could help him, oh, I could help—

Only he doesn't need me. He's so strong—so terribly strong, and there's neither doubt nor humility in him. If I could only make him see—make him give all this up—what wonders we could do together if that strength of his were turned to the service of the Lord. I'd be so happy, then—because I don't need comparisons any more. He's as handsome as I thought him—so tall, with those devil's eyes and a mouth half mocking, half tender—

She sat up suddenly, and swung her long slender legs down from the mud-heap bed. She was clad only in a chemise; for among all the objects to be found at Falkston, there was not one nightdress, and she had forgotten to bring her own. She crossed over to the mirror and sat down before it. She didn't have to light the palm oil lamp; because that side of the room was washed in moonlight until it was as bright as day. She sat there, staring at her reflection in the glass. She had good bones, and with a little more flesh she would have been pretty. But she didn't have that flesh, and she felt that she would never have it. . . .

She sat there, hearing surfpound treerustle simianscamper batsqueak; hearing deeper, wilder, fiercer in her own blood, the voices of Africa's dark and awful gods.

He's right! she wept. He's right! They never got across the mountains! Neither Jehovah nor good and gentle Jesus! Africa's no place for Them never was, never will be. It belongs to Ju Ju, Damballa, Bolozi, Esamba—to all the black and terrible gods that gibber in the night—

And I—

She stiffened suddenly, hearing Beeljie's voice crooning a soft love song. It hung on the perfumed, tropic dark, low and husky and sweet. She sat there listening to it, the scalding hot and rebellious tears running down her cheeks.

It is not fair, not fair . . . She's a black African savage and she's got—him. While I—while I—

She put her hands behind her, jerking the loose cotton chemise tight across her breasts, trying to mold it to her form. She clamped her mouth tight shut, leaning forward, staring at what she could see of herself. She had a surprisingly good body, for which the proper clothes could have done wonders. Had she been born one hundred years later, her slim, boyish figure would have been considered very smart.

She reeled back, appalled at the realization of what she was doing. She whirled away from the mirror and began to dress very rapidly. When she was fully clothed, she went out into the moon-silvered night.

She stood there, near the end of the piazza, staring out over the dark shapes of the trees that fringed the shore, at the broad moon track, dazzling upon the dark waters. She did not know how long she stood there—not thinking, not moving, just—being, surrendering to the night, letting its great peace enter into her—when something, not a sound really, less than

a sound, a feeling, perhaps, a sudden heightening of consciousness caused her to turn; and she saw the end of his cigar,
glowing like a red star in the shadow of a tamarind tree.

He came forward to meet her, out of the tree shadow into
the light of the moon.

"Couldn't sleep, Miss Staunton?" he asked calmly.

"No. And you?"

"Obviously not," Guy said dryly.

"Why couldn't you?" she asked, avoiding the use of his
name. She didn't want to call him Mister Falks again.

He studied her a long time before he spoke.

"Do you want me to make polite noises," he said, "or shall
I tell you the truth?"

"The truth," she said firmly.

"I haven't seen a white woman in a little more than
twelve years," he said. "To have one as my guest—particularly
a woman as young and attractive as you are—is, frankly, disturbing. But it's more than that—"

"More?" she echoed.

"Much more. I'm not a man of any great nicety of scruples,
Miss Staunton. But I've never met a missionary's daughter
before. I've got the feeling that your religion is mighty real
to you—and that's just the trouble—"

"Why should it be a trouble?" she said.

"Because, but for that, I'd proceed on the assumption that's
never failed me: that all women are sisters under the skin.
Never met one yet who was permanently damaged by the
discovery that she was human after all. But you are different,
Pru—I mean Miss Staunton—"

"Call me Pru," she said gently. "I like it—I was a little
sorry, when you remembered your manners and began to be so
formal. Pru sounds so friendly. . . ."

"If you will call me Guy. You are different, Pru. Most people give lip service to their God. When the chips are down,
they can always find reasons for forgiving themselves for things
they condemn in other people. But I'm not sure about you. I
think maybe you couldn't forgive yourself if you ever stepped
down from that pedestal on which your Pa has placed you.
Maybe you'd be badly hurt if you ever found out that there
was blood in your veins and a mite of human passion in your
heart. . . ."

As I have already found out, she thought bitterly; but she
didn't say that. Aloud she said:

"I don't know how to answer that, Guy. I was brought up in Africa—and I haven't had the advantages of a mother's love and training. I know that women aren't supposed to say certain things, nor even think them, really. I've shocked my father no end, at times, by what seemed to him outrageously free speech. So it's made me shy of expressing myself. I don't really know how a lady is supposed to talk. . . ."

"With me," he said, "you can say any damn thing that pops into your little head, Pru—"

"All right. I warn you that I'm awfully blunt. It seems to me that what you're saying is that if you weren't afraid of my religious and moral scruples, you would attempt to make me your—your mistress. Is that right?"

"Exactly," Guy grinned. "Go on, Pru—"

"Then I'm awfully glad you are afraid of them," she said.

"I see—" Guy said dryly.

You don't see, she thought bitterly. You don't see at all. When I go back home, I shall tell father to lock me up with nothing but bread and water for a month to punish me for my sinful thoughts. What I mean, Guy is—if you tried, I'd resist you with all my strength. Only I'm not sure of that strength any more. You are an awfully attractive man. I thought at first that I felt this way because I hadn't seen any others; but now I know you'd stand out in any group. And, if you tried, you— God help me!—might succeed. I know that. And that would be the most awful thing that could happen—

He stood there waiting, unwilling to break into her thoughts.

Because I would hate you then for having shamed me, she reasoned painfully, and hate myself for being so weak—

"No," she said aloud, finally, "I don't think you really see, Guy, or even understand. Which is why you must send me home tomorrow. . . ."

"Home?" he said. "Are you that afraid of me, Pru?"

"Afraid?" she whispered. "Yes. But of both of us, Guy. Dhiakiar's savages are less dangerous than this, I think. They can only kill my body. I believe that's a great deal less than— the destruction of—my soul. . . ."

It was still, there in the moonlight, a long, slow time. Then Guy sighed, a little.

"All right, Pru," he said quietly. "You win. Only you must stay here until your father sends for you. I'll keep my horny hands off of you. I promise you that."

She stood there looking at him; and the tears were there,

bright and sudden in her eyes.

"Thank you," she whispered. "I hope you'll believe me when I tell you that this is the emptiest victory I ever won in all my life. . . ."

Then, with enormous dignity, she turned and walked back into the house.

She stayed the whole month, during which the threatening bush war simmered on the verge of outbreak. The only reason that it had not flared up was that Guy, by ridding Falkston of the Mongo's Trojan Horse, Mukabassa, had made da Coimbra uncertain of his chances of success. It was, for her, a month of purest hell. Had Guy broken his word, she would have been fortified by her sense of outrage. But he did not break it. He was matchlessly polite, treating her with bland kindliness, making no reference by word, gesture, or innuendo, to their strange, brief encounter.

At the root of her anguish was the fact that what was for her the obvious solution to the problem, apparently never even occurred to him. She pictured him a thousand times, kneeling before her, saying: "Marry me, Pru—and I will give this all up for your sweet sake. I'll stop slaving, become a Christian, live uprightly with you before my God. . . ."

Finally, she could stand it no longer. Without a word to Guy, she went out into the native compound, and having, naturally, a perfect command of most of the dialects of the region, hired from Flonkerri an escort of five stalwart warriors to take her home again. The Donda insisted that she wait until a tipoy, that typical African conveyance, consisting of a comfortable chair swung from two poles borne on the shoulders of four bearers, could be made for her. As this was a matter of no more than two hours' work, and would easily be ready for her departure at dawn, she accepted the suggestion gratefully.

She went back into the house and lay down, fully clothed, on her bed. She did not sleep. An hour before dawn, she got up, and sitting down before the mirror, penned her farewell note to Guy. Then she picked up her bag, and tiptoed to his room. She prayed that Beeljie would not be there. And hers, being the prayers of the righteous, were answered.

Guy lay sprawled out on the leopard skins, fast asleep. A light coverlet covered him from the waist down, but his upper body was bare. She stood there, frozen, staring at his powerful form, seeing the great scar that Kilrain's sword thrust had left upon his massive shoulder, the crescent of fang scars which she incorrectly attributed to a leopard, on the back of his left hand, his dark face in sleep relaxed into a noble, masculine beauty that was more than she could bear.

She put the note on the table beside his bed, and turned to go. But at the last moment, the longing in her became too great, dominating her will. She bent swiftly, and kissed his sleeping mouth.

His great arms swept up, locking her in his embrace. His eyes came open, the eyes of a hunter, instantly clear.

"Why, Pru!" he laughed. "Nice of you to drop in. . . ."

"Let me go! You hear me, Guy Falks, let me go!"

"Nope," he chuckled. "You gave me a kiss. I aim to pay it back—with interest. . . ."

He sat up then, and found her mouth. He kissed her a long time, lingeringly, tauntingly, expertly. When at last, he drew away, her face was as white as death, her cheeks flooded with tears of shame.

"Guy," she whispered. "You—you're a great hunter, aren't you? And a sportsman?"

He frowned at her, then his face relaxed.

"Reckon so," he drawled. "Why, Pru?"

"I've heard my father say that there's nothing worse than shooting tame and tethered ducks," she said. "Do you understand me, Guy?"

"Yes," he said. And opening wide his arms, he freed her, as one frees a captive bird.

"Thank you," she whispered, and got up from there. As she passed the table, her skirt swept the note off onto the floor. A trifling accident. But of such trifles is tragedy often made.

For, when Guy got up in the morning, as always, he tossed his coverlet onto the floor. It covered Prudence's note. And not until nightfall, when he returned from a tour of inspection of his defenses against sudden attack, did Beeljie who had found it as she cleaned his room, give it to him.

By then it was far too late to send a party after her. From Flonkerri, Guy learned that she went accompanied by an armed escort. Still, a nagging sense of worry tugged at him during the whole of the next week. It sharpened terribly when Flonkerri came to him with the news that Pru's escort had not returned.

He was just about to order the Donda to form a war party, when he heard Flon's guttural expression of surprise. He turned then, and saw the people at the landing: a tall white man, surrounded by a little group of blacks. The Negroes were holding the white man up. Apparently he could not stand.

Guy and Flonkerri went down to the landing, running. That the white man was Pru's father, Guy hadn't the slightest doubt.

The Reverend Obadiah Staunton swayed there, supported by two of the Folgias who had formed part of Pru's escort. He had taken a spear-thrust in the shoulder. The point had gone all the way through. The clumsy bandage was soaked with blood.

"Howdy, Reverend," Guy said gently. "Looks like you could use a mite of help—"

"Don't worry about me," Reverend Staunton said tiredly. "Help my people. Dhiakiar's taken them off—the ones his murderers didn't kill. If you've got the men, Mr. Falks, I'd appreciate—"

"Right," Guy said crisply. "But first we'd better get that wound attended to. That shoulder looks right bad—"

"No!" the missionary thundered. "There's no time! Don't you understand? Dhiakiar's taken—"

"I know," Guy said. "But we can ransom them later, come—"

"You don't understand, sir," Obadiah Staunton said. "Dhiakiar won't ransom prisoners. His people are really back-bush. They—they'll eat them!"

Guy stood there staring at him. Then he saw the death and hell in the missionary's eyes.

"Pru?" he said.

"Dead," Reverend Staunton said, speaking in the flat, dead-level calm of pure shock. "One of your Folgias shot her—at my command. She—she didn't suffer, son. . . ."

"At your command?"

"Yes. I've seen what Dhiakiar's people do to women. She wanted me to do it, but I—I couldn't . . . And there wasn't—any hope. . . ."

Guy measured him with his eyes. When he spoke, his voice was like splintered flint.

"*You* escaped," he said.

"I was rescued—by these Folgias of yours. The ones who came with Pru. Dhiakiar's brigands were carrying me away to the stake. They figured I had a couple of hours of resistance to torture left in me. I wanted to spare Prudence that, sir—and worse. . . ."

"My apologies, Reverend," Guy said. "Let's get you up to the house, man. . . ."

"Wait," Reverend Staunton said. "There's something I've got to know. Can you trust your Folgias, Mr. Falks?"

"Implicitly," Guy said. "Why?"

"Because the Folgias are mixed up in this. Prudence told us that you have Flonkerri and half the tribe here. It's his brother, Flamburi, who's the cause of all the trouble. . . ."

"No love lost between them," Guy said. "Go on, Reverend—"

"Flamburi stole the youngest wife of his uncle, Tamarrar. That's what started it. I've labored and labored to stamp out polygamy—"

"What you're laboring to stamp out is human nature," Guy said dryly; "and that, Reverend, is a losing proposition. Get to the point, man. What happened?"

"Tamarrar attacked Flamburi's village. The battle was a draw. So Flamburi called in Dhiakiar and his filthy cannibalistic swine. Now, what began as a minor bush war has gotten completely out of hand. The most dreadful things have happened—"

"I know," Guy snapped. "I know how niggers fight. Just tell me one thing, Reverend—where are they?"

"Near the Mission, I think. They burned it. I had a French priest as my guest. They—they disemboweled him. They cut his servant into pieces—and made off with the children—"

"What children?" Guy growled.

"The pygmy children Père Tissot had with him. He was going to take them back to France to help raise money for the Catholic Missions—"

"But," Guy pointed out, "there aren't any pygmies in this part of—"

"I know. Père Tissot was up from the Congo. Doesn't matter. God, I'm tired—"

"Take him up to the house," Guy commanded.

Half an hour later, he had Flonkerri and his warriors rounded up and started the march upriver toward the Mission. It was two suns away, walking; but they couldn't use canoes against the current. Coming downstream, breasting the rapids, and carrying the canoes around the cataracts, Reverend Staunton's party had been able to make it in a day and a half.

Marching along at the head of his black legion, Guy's thoughts were black and bitter. Poor little thing, he thought; she was holding out for marriage and I—I didn't care enough to give her a chance. She'd be alive now; but for that—alive, and maybe even happy. Might have made me a good wife—who knows? Even if she wouldn't have, anything would have been better than that lonely dying—alone and surrounded, in a burning Mission, with a bullet through her head, like a crippled horse—at her father's own command. . . .

But it wasn't any good to think about that. The crying need now was for haste. By now the captives could well have been cut up into bloody bits and wolfed down the gullets of Dhiakiar's cannibals. For that reason, Guy and his war party were traveling light, without either food or water, living off the country. In the jungle, except during one of the rare droughts, that was not only possible, but easy.

He had armed as many of the Folgias as he could with muskets; which he had forbidden them to use except in battle. With game as thick and plentiful as it was in the jungle, their bows and spears were good enough to keep the party well supplied with meat. And powder and ball couldn't be replaced so far from the coast. Besides, the jungle afforded other kinds of food.

Without even slackening their pace, the warriors cut mongongo leaves. Crossing a clearing by the waterhole, they kept stooping to gather the little yellow mushrooms that grew there. They wrapped the mushrooms in the leaves and added nuts of the kola tree. They gathered some greens, leaving others that seemed to Guy identical. They gathered caterpillars, termites, grub worms. They robbed a bee hive in a dead tree, by making a hole below and dragging the honeycombs through it, wrapping them in their universal carrier, the mongongo leaf. Just before dark, some of the warriors left the party, and made their way to a salt lick. When they came back, they bore four red antelope on their shoulder.

They made camp. The first thing they did was to wrap each squirming caterpillar and grub worm in a bit of leaf and placed them close enough to the fire to toast. Then they boiled the toasted insects in palm oil. They looked almost exactly like shrimps. And knowing the filth that shrimps generally eat, in comparison to the variety of clean leaves that formed these worms' diet, Guy figured they were probably a good bit more hygienic, though the very idea had revolted him before. Prepared this way, the caterpillars didn't look revolting. In fact they looked damned good. So when he was offered this delicacy, he didn't hesitate. He took one of the grub worms between his thumb and forefinger and popped it into his mouth. It was delicious. Thereafter he ate the caterpillars and grubs with good appetite. But he balked at the termites. Their looks didn't please him.

The rest of the meal, broiled antelope, mushrooms, plantains and green stuffs, was conventional enough. He finished off his meal with kola nuts and honey. He saw the Negroes filling their pipes with what he guessed was bangi. He didn't try to stop them. If they wanted to smoke marijuana, let them. He was aware that the moralist's profession is the most futile of all.

He lay down by the fire, but he could not sleep. What was troubling him was the fact that although they had detoured around Pongoland, they had encountered a group of the Mongo's people. By now, da Coimbra knew he was absent from Falkston with his warriors. And that was bad.

Flonkerri came over, and squatted on his heels beside him. The Donda seemed disposed to talk. Guy didn't discourage him. It was a good chance to find out what they were up against.

"Tell me about Dhiakiar," he said.

"Bad," Flonkerri said, using the English word since there was no word in the African tongues to describe this quality. "Eat people."

"I know that. What I want to know is what is he like?"

"Big. Ugly. More ugly than Mukabassa. Dirty. Sleep with him mother."

Among Africans, Guy knew, incest is the most detested of crimes. Dhiakiar must be degraded indeed.

"I don't believe that," Guy said. "His own people would kill him if he did such a thing."

"Him Ju Ju, Herfera, tell him do it. Say him win em battle, if him spill em own blood. So Dhiakiar take em own baby, break him head 'gainst doorpost. And him win. So when Herfera tell him, him go back in mother's womb, him never die, him do that, too. Since then arrows, spears don't touch him. Herfera big Ju Ju."

"When I catch this Herfera bastard," Guy said, "I'll show you just how big he is."

"Bwana big Ju Ju," Flonkerri grinned. "Even snake no kill.

But always Ju Ju more big. Maybe Herfera medicine more strong—"

"Oh, hell," Guy said tiredly. It was useless, and he knew it. No man in one lifetime could conquer the superstition of a thousand years.

At nightfall of the following day, they reached the burned-out Mission. All around it there were plentiful evidences that the savages had not left the vicinity. But neither threats nor persuasion could induce the Folgias to scout the jungle at night. Bolozi or Esamba would catch them sure, they declared, and blow out the light within their heads, leaving them gibbering idiots, if not dead men.

"You are gibbering idiots!" Guy howled. "If there were a real man among you—"

Flonkerri stepped forward.

"I go with Bwana," he said. "Us scout jungle. Come sun, we lead warriors to bushman camp—"

That wasn't much; but it was better than nothing. They stole through the jungle, following the fresh-cut trail. Two hours before dawn, they came upon the bushmen's camp. They climbed high into a cotton silk tree, and looked down upon it. What they saw was—horror.

The bushmen danced about a pile of maimed and bleeding captives. Every so often, another warrior appeared, and hurled another victim upon the pile. . . .

"Flon," Guy whispered. "Go get the others. Leave me your gun. You can do all right with that assagai, and it would be fatal to make noise anyhow. If you meet one of those bloody devils, don't give him time to yell. Cleave his head to the teeth. Get going now!"

"I split him to his belly," Flonkerri growled. "Gumbye, Bwana—I bring boys!"

He didn't make a leaf rustle, going down the tree. But it wouldn't have mattered if he had broken off whole branches. The bushmen kept up such a savage din, that any noise quieter than a gunshot would scarcely have disturbed them.

Guy sat there, watching. The men fell back, now, and the women danced. Their faces were smeared with white clay and human blood. No more hideous collection of harpies ever shocked human vision than these bushwomen. They fell upon the pile of captives, each one selecting a victim. Then they began to torture the victims with a cruelty indescribable in any language spoken by man.

Guy closed his eyes, but that didn't help. He could hear the screams of the tortured captives, and the bushpeople's fiendish yells. He leaned back against the bole of the tree, and let the world revolve dizzily around him. He was thirty-four years old now; he had seen enough cruelty to last any man a lifetime; but this was too much. When he straightened up at last, he saw that the trees were coming clear, as the sky faded out of blackness into morning. An eternity later, while the bushmen were still gorging themselves upon the flesh of their victims, Guy heard a twig crunch below, and Flonkerri and the warriors were there.

He climbed down the tree and joined them. He was grey and trembling.

"No shooting," he croaked. "Use steel. Somebody give me an assagai. . . ."

One of the warriors passed over the razor-edged African sword.

"All right," Guy said. "Surround them. Don't yell. Don't make a sound until we're onto them. And don't," he added flatly, "take prisoners. Not even women. If there are any living prisoners in those huts, save them. But as for those bushmen—kill them all."

So it was done. They swarmed out of the jungle like black ghosts. The bushmen were too gorged and stupefied by rum to put up much of a fight. Guy and Flonkerri advanced side by side, cutting down the bushmen like so many sheaves.

"That Herfera!" Flonkerri panted, pointing with an assagai which from point to hilt dripped blood. Guy saw the Ju Ju man howling and dancing, brandishing spear and shield. He crossed to him in two bounds, knocking aside the Ju Ju's spear thrust with the flat of his blade. Then he lifted the assagai and brought it down whistling. The Ju Ju man threw up his oxhide shield; but the blade went through it like a heated knife through butter. Herfera dropped, dead almost before he struck the ground.

"Look, Flon!" Guy roared. "See your big Ju Ju man!"

He looked around him for a new foe; but there were no more left to strike.

Flonkerri and his men held the big wench who had led the women. And now, for the first time, Guy could see that her kinky wool was grey. Another group held a powerful, struggling bushman. Dhiakiar, Guy guessed, and his mother. He knew how his Folgias would put them to death. By inches—

with a degree of invention that even the bush people might have envied. But he didn't stop them. Mercy is not an African word.

They found the pygmy children, alive and unhurt in one of the huts. Guy guessed it was their size that had saved them. So tiny were they that the bushmen had had a superstitious fear of killing them, he reasoned. They were a rich, burnt-chocolate color, and perfectly formed. To his astonishment, they could both walk and talk. What was more, they understood and could speak Kingwanna. The boy, Nikiabo, was eight years old; Sifa, his sister, was six. Guy would have sworn that neither of them was more than three.

They left the dead to the kites and vultures, and hurried back to the Mission. For some reason, most likely because they had planned to use them, themselves, the bushmen hadn't touched the Mission's canoes. As they were shoving them off into the headwaters of the Pongo, Flonkerri touched Guy's arm. His black face was twisted with fear.

"What's the matter, Flon?" Guy growled.

"Flamburi not here," Flonkerri whispered. "None me brother people there. Where they, Bwana? White man Ju Ju say they join em bushdevils. But no there. Where they, Bwana?"

"Good God!" Guy murmured; then: "All right. Move!"

They didn't stop to eat or rest. They shot rapids no man had ever made before. They carried the canoes around the cataracts at a dead run. Not even darkness stopped them.

So it was that they reached Falkston just before morning . . . Or where Falkston had been. For it wasn't there any longer. Nothing was there but ashes and embers, some of them still smoldering.

And the dead.

Guy searched among them. There was no sign of Beeljie. He was about to give up, when he heard a moan in the underbrush. He plunged into the thickets, lifting his torch. Kapapela crouched there, bleeding from a great gash over her left eye. Beside her, the Reverend Staunton lay dead, his skull crushed by a war club's blow. It was, Guy realized, a merciful death.

"Beeljie?" he croaked.

"Mongo took her 'way, him," Kapa said.

The Mongo was prepared for them. His stockade was barred and locked. Guy was glad now that they hadn't wasted powder and ball on the bushmen.

244

"Climb the trees!" he commanded. "Pick 'em off from above! Flon, you got any fire arrows?"

"No, but me make em, Bwana," Flonkerri said.

"That round building to the left of the long one is his powder magazine," Guy said. "Set it afire. It blows—and he's done. Get moving now—"

They swarmed up the trees. Flonkerri's people were good marksmen. Guy had taught them. And the only shooting da Coimbra's blacks had ever done had been into the air, to welcome coffles. Half of the Mongo's men fell at the first volley. Guy saw Flonkerri climbing up a tree with his bow, and arrows with blobs of pitch on their heads. Behind him climbed another black with a pan full of live coals.

Then he saw the little hut made of raffia palm. It was as dry as tinder. He guessed at once what was in it. But it was on the other side of the stockade from the magazine. He didn't have to stop Flonkerri. The Donda could blow up the gunpowder without setting the hut afire.

He saw the first of the firearrows arcing the night. The second. The third. Flonkerri was a damned fine archer and the target was big. All three lodged in the thatched roof of the magazine. It leaped into flame, but Flonkerri continued to send the firearrows into it. The Mongo's people were scattering now, screaming.

Then it went, in a slow-rolling, belly-deep boom that scattered flaming fragments all over the barracoon. The storehouse caught and blazed merrily. But, miraculously, by the direct intervention of God, Guy was sure, the little hut had been spared. The Mongo was done now—or should be.

Only he wasn't. He appeared in the square, brandishing a torch.

"Guy Falks!" he bellowed. "Call off your dogs! If you want to see Beeljie alive again, call them off!"

It was then that Guy shot him. Low. In the belly.

The Mongo reeled and fell on this face. Then he stretched out his hand and picked up the torch. He started to crawl—toward the hut.

Loading a muzzleloading musket on the ground is a task. The average rate of fire maintained by crack troops was two shots every three minutes. And Guy Falks, sitting high in a baobob tree, had to pour in powder, fumble with the patch, ram home the ball and put a percussion cap in the lock, before he could even aim. He was a crack shot; but his hands trembled so that he missed the Mongo completely. Da Coimbra continued to crawl.

Guy had to do it all over again. By the time he had the clumsy weapon reloaded, the Mongo was only yards away from the hut. Guy lifted the musket. Then he lowered it again. The mulatto's head, the only sure way of killing him instantly, was too difficult a shot.

The spine, Guy thought. I've got to break the spine—

He fired. He saw the Mongo jerk. Then, in a slow, nightmare dream of action, the big mulatto's arm came back, holding the torch. Back, back, back, until the ache in Guy's jaws and lungs made him realize he was screaming.

Then the Mongo threw the firebrand. It turned end over end, crawling through the air with agonizing slowness to fall, to fall—

Just at the edge of the hut. Close enough. Guy saw the tongue of flame lick hungrily up the side.

Then he was falling, scrambling, slipping down the tree.

"Flon!" he roared. "A log! Get a log! We've got to smash the gate in!"

He lost precious seconds making them understand. An age, an eternity, before they found a suitable battering ram. They ran toward the gate, smashing the log against it. It held. Again. Again. Again. And between the thuds now, he could hear her screaming.

The gate gave finally. He dashed through the opening with Flonkerri at his side. The two of them entered that mass of flames, and dragged out the writhing, moaning, flame-wrapped object, that had been—

A real and true part of his life. He rolled her, slapping at the flames.

"No good," Flonkerri said. "Her dead, Bwana—" And Guy saw that the big black was crying. From that moment on, he loved him like a brother. Beeljie lay still in death. There were chains about her feet. The post to which the foot irons had been fastened had burned through, and that was the reason they had been able to drag her out.

Guy sat down on the singed earth and stared at her. The tears ploughed white furrows through the soot on his face. He sat there crying as only a strong man can cry the tears of brine and blood, the gut deep tearing.

Then he got up and walked toward where Monique Vallois knelt, cradling her dead lover's head in her arms and crying.

19

HE REALIZED, a month later, when he had recovered enough to think about it, that the terrible events of June had somehow freed him. He had all the money he would ever need; enough to buy twenty-five plantations the size of Fairoaks. Even if he had had any desire to stay, the slave trade was already ceasing to be profitable, not only for him, but for every factor on the coast. For the International Squadron had added fast paddlewheel steamers to its forces. Not one slaver in ten was getting through now. The fastest clipper afloat couldn't outfoot a steam cruiser. So he didn't rebuild Falkston. He merely waited for Captain Rudgers to put into port again.

On Christmas Day, 1852, he stood on the deck of the *Volador,* watching the sailors drop anchor before Regla. He looked down at Nikiabo and Sifa, resplendent in silks and turbans, standing at his side, staring in awe at Havana, the first city they had ever seen. He patted their tiny turbans fondly, for he had developed a great affection for this shining, doll-like pair.

"Come, Nikia, Sifa," he said gaily. "We'll go ashore now—"

"Yes, master," the pygmies chorused. By now they spoke English very well indeed.

He spent three weeks in Havana, stopping with Don Rafael Gonzalez, and visiting all his friends. The pygmies in their silks and satins were the wonders of the city. Last of all, he paid a call upon Captain Tray and Pili. He could do that now. In the sixteen years since he had seen them he had learned a great deal about life, and even a considerable amount about women. One of the things he had learned came vividly to mind when he saw Pili for the first time after all those years: women always lie about their ages. And Pili was no exception. In 1835, when she had told him she was thirty, she had actually been thirty-five. Now she was fifty-two, fat, comfortable, matronly, her black hair streaked with grey. And Captain Tray was a bumbling, toothless old man.

It was, in a way—tragic. And funny. He wondered what the hell he had been expecting, anyhow. But as he rode away from there to take the schooner for New Orleans, he was conscious of a vast sense of relief.

He had only to go forward. There was nothing left behind.

20

WITHIN one hour of his arrival in New Orleans, that fifteenth day of February, 1853, Guy Falks had changed, or at least modified, all his plans. Since the day his father had brought him the fox-hunting coat, he had had a deep seated appreciation for good clothes. In Cuba, he had been able, as the adopted son of a great planter, to indulge this harmless vanity; but Africa is no place for niceties of dress. He had, of course, during his three weeks' stay in Havana, commissioned several suits from one of that city's fine tailors. But now, standing in the grandiose lobby of the St. Louis Hotel, he saw that they were hopelessly outmoded. Havana drew its fashions, not from London or Paris, but from Madrid; and in the Spanish capital, styles changed with relative slowness.

Men no longer wore skin-tight trousers. The Prince Albert frock coat had appeared. Men lounged about the lobby in sack suits, came in out of the driving February rains in box-coats, burnooses, and raglans. For the first time in his life he saw the rounded hat called the bowler, or billycock, in England, the melon in France, and the derby in America. Many of the loungers in the lobby wore turned-down collars. The stock had vanished, to be replaced by the cravat, by an earlier version of the scarf that twenty years later would widen and puff into the Ascot, and by the narrow bow tie wrapped around stiffly starched high collars.

Only his hat and his waistcoat were right. Men still wore high beavers, and gay, embroidered waistcoats. Nor had their boots changed much. But jeweled stickpins and gold watch chains flourished. What startled him most, was the number and variety of whiskers that adorned the faces of the New Orleanais. When he had left the States, in 1835, only old men had been bearded. Now, nearly everybody sported some form of hirsute adornment. Whiskers separated by a shaven chin in the Dundreary style were popular. The Creoles favored the mustache and imperial. Instead of being shaved off just below the temples, the sideburns (though they wouldn't be called that until General Burnside's name, reversed, would be given them during the war) had crept downward to the point of the chin, and even looped around it in some instances in the form of a small beard that looked for all the world like a fur muff.

He turned to the desk clerk.

"Who's the best tailor in town?" he asked. "I've been away from home one hell of a long time. Appears to me I'd better get me some clothes. . . ."

"Ah," the clerk said; "that explains it. Begging your pardon, sir; but until you spoke, I thought you were a foreigner. The best tailors, beyond all question, are Legoastier and Sons. They're quadroons; but no white tailor in generations has been able to match their skill. If you like, I'll send a boy—"

"Do that," Guy said. "Tell them to trot over their best fitter and a selection of materials. I feel like a freak!"

"I think it's your little blacks everybody's looking at, sir. Real fancy articles. You could name your price for them in New Orleans. Always a market for the unusual, here. How old are they? I'd say five or six; but there's something about them that looks older—"

"Boy's twelve," Guy said. "The wench is ten. And they're damned nigh as big as they'll ever be."

"Then they're dwarfs?" the clerk said.

"Pygmies. From the Congo. Let's see that suite, now—"

"Yes, sir!" the clerk said, and tapped his bell. "Pygmies! I never thought I'd see—"

The fitter from Legoastier arrived that same afternoon. Guy ordered a Prince Albert, various trousers, a raglan, three sack suits, morning coats, evening dress, three dozen shirts of the newest mode; everything, in fact, that he needed, including twelve dozen cravats and bow ties. Moreover, by paying double, he got the assurance that the morning coat, two pairs of trousers, and one of the sack suits would be delivered by the seventeenth, along with several shirts, and cravats.

When they were delivered, he donned the sack suit, adjusted

his newly acquired derby at a jaunty angle, stuck a cigar in his teeth, and sauntered forth to make further purchases, taking, of course, Nikiabo and Sifa with him—

And thereby succeeding with astonishing ease in doing what he had only thought about trying to do. He found Phoebe. Or rather, the pygmies found her for him.

For the two tiny blacks caused an immediate sensation. Crowds followed them wherever they went, staring and asking questions. It got so bad, finally, that Guy took them back to the hotel, accompanied all the way by the curious mob.

He was just about to mount the stairs when a man touched his arm. Guy turned, angrily.

"I beg your pardon, sir," the man said. "I'm Tom Henessey of the 'Picayune.' I know you're a bit put out by all the attention your dwarfs have been attracting; and I don't blame you. But I'd like to do a story about them. They're real news, sir, and I don't think a gentleman like you will object to a fellow's earning his daily bread—"

"All right," Guy said shortly. "What do you want to know?"

"Do you mind if we go up to your room and talk, sir? It will be more private that way—"

Guy considered the matter. The best way to get rid of the man was to give him his story. And it was much better to talk in the privacy of his suite than in the lobby crowded with curious onlookers.

"Come along, then," he said.

At the sight of the suite, the St. Charles' largest and most luxurious, the reporter's eye goggled.

"Who are you, sir?" he asked, "a nobleman in disguise, or something?"

"We came up here to talk about the pygmies," Guy said flatly. "May I offer you a drink, sir?"

"Don't generally indulge so early," Henessey said; "but I reckon a snort of whiskey would sort of dry the damp out—"

Guy crossed to the sideboard, and poured out two glasses of Scotch.

"Now, Mr. Henessey," he said. "What do you want to know?"

The story when it appeared in the next day's "Picayune," bore some relation to the few simple facts that Guy had told the reporter. But Henessey had given his imagination ample rein. What the front page box bore was a romantic story of the multimillionaire traveler, "Colonel" Guy Falks, who during one of his voyages in darkest Africa, had saved the pygmy children from savage cannibals at the risk of his own life. There was a full description of Nikiabo and Sifa, down to their exotic dress; but the rest of the article was devoted to an equally detailed description of "Colonel" Falks, his bearing, his manners, his looks, his princely wealth, and even his luxurious suite. There was a half column of speculation over the sources of his income and comments by all the clerks, from whom he had made his purchases, upon the expensiveness of the articles bought; a statement from an official of the Bank of Orleans that the "Colonel" had presented letters of credit for more than fifty thousand dollars on the day of his arrival. The banker refused to be quoted by name, which saved him from having his neck wrung by Guy Falks. Apart from the bogus title, it was all true, except for the emphasis the reporter had given it. Guy, of course, had refused to comment upon the sources of his fortune. Southerners might buy and work slaves; but they didn't associate with slave traders. Not even ex-slave traders.

Three hours after the paper hit the streets, a bellhop appeared at his door with a note. He tore open the envelope and read:

> "Dear Mister Guy,
> If you be the man who used to be my friend, come to see me at number twelve Rampart Street. I sure hope you is. Be mighty nice to see you agin after such a long time. I a widder now. I got a little boy four years old. I wanted to come to the hotel when I read about you in the paper, but it don't seem right. Don't want to cause you no trouble. But come to see me, please. I purely pining to see you agin."

It was signed, "Phoebe."

The writing was large and clear, like that of a child.

Guy tipped the bellboy five dollars, thereby adding to the legend that was beginning to form about his name in New Orleans. Then he donned his hat and coat; picked up his heavy, gutta percha walking stick with the gold head, and went downstairs leaving the pygmies behind. Five minutes later, he was sitting in a hansom cab, heading for the ramparts.

Number twelve was a neat white bungalow of the type that rich New Orleans gentlemen usually built for their quadroon placées. He paid the hackie and dismissed him. Before he could even knock, the door was opened for him.

"Lord God!" Phoebe whispered. "Lord God, but you's done changed!"

So, Guy reflected sadly, had she. She was thirty-four years old, a year younger than he. But she looked older. She was thin. And years of sorrow had left their handwriting on her face.

"Come in, Mister Guy," she said timidly.

"Guy, to you," he said gruffly. "God, Phoebe, I—"

They sat and talked, sitting in conscious mourning over the invisible corpse of the dead past. For there was no going back to what had been, and both of them knew it. The boy of seventeen who had tried to save the sixteen-year-old Phoebe from being sold into shameful servitude was forever gone, metamorphized into this taut and fine-drawn man of teak and iron. The girl no longer existed; there were only traces of her in this thin and sorrowing woman who had endured the ending of both dreams and hope. There was, in that tastefully furnished little room, a finis as complete as death itself and more tragic; for they both lived on to mourn for what might have been.

She had been the mistress of three wealthy Orleanais in those eighteen years. The first of these, Hently Davis, the man who had bought her at a Natchez auction, had lost his fortune through unwise speculation, and had been forced to sell her with the rest of his goods and chattels. The second, Manfred Beuhler, a fat and brutal German who had bought her from Davis, had taken her to his upriver plantation, from which, being unable to support his drunkenness and beatings, she had run away. Apparently, Beuhler had not even troubled to look for her. The third, a young Englishman named Wilcox Turner, had treated her not only with kindness but with such exquisite consideration and courtesy, that in the end she had learned to love him.

She had become his common law wife. He had had no other mate. He would even have taken her to the city's parties and balls; but Phoebe, knowing, as this newcomer did not, the abysmal depths of American prejudices, had dissuaded him. He had lived openly with her in this cottage and fathered her only child.

More, he had given his son his own name, acknowledged him, and made a will making him and Phoebe his heirs. But, after the stranger's disease, yellow fever, carried him off, some dubious American "cousins" appeared, and contested the will. Turner had been very wealthy. And the "cousins" were white. That was enough. Phoebe had been supporting herself and her son for three years now, by taking in sewing. She had become an expert seamstress; but her earnings were pitifully small.

She told him all this very simply, and with great dignity. Nothing in her tone conveyed the slightest hint that she hoped for anything from him.

"May I see the boy?" Guy said quietly.

Phoebe rose without a word and brought little Wilcox Second, in. He was a beautiful child. Like most octoroons, Wilcox was white, not only in color but in features. His head was covered with a mass of soft blond ringlets. His eyes were long-lashed, enormous, and blue. He was exactly the sort of blond cherub that advertising firms print on calendars. In fact, he was almost too pretty to be male.

"Shake hands with the gentleman, Willlie," Phoebe said.

The child hung back, timidly.

Then Guy reached out and took him in his arms. He sat there, holding the boy, and thinking. He was a man who had a need for sons. And at thirty-five, he had neither home, nor wife, nor child. It was time to be moving, going on. Now, more than ever, he had things to do.

But first he must pay his debt to the past; discharge his obligation toward his memories.

"Look, Phoebe," he said, "you got any objection to living up North?"

"Up North?" she echoed. "Don't reckon so—I can live most anywheres; but why do you say that Mis—why do you say that, Guy?"

It was hard to eliminate that Mister. Especially when talking to this—stranger.

"Because I'm going to stake you to a new life," Guy said flatly. "It would be a living crime to bring this boy up as a nigger. He isn't. Got a drop or two; but when it's been bleached out this far, I can't see where it makes a difference. I'm going to send you two to New York. When you get there, if anybody asks you—you're Cuban, or Mexican, or any damn thing but nigger. Northerners can't tell the difference—"

"Southerners, neither," Phoebe chuckled. "Mister Wilcox uster to take me to Virginia Springs with him every summer, 'cause folks didn't know us, up there. Right in that there big

253

hotel. Signed me as his wife. Lord, Lord, Guy, many's the time I had to hold myself to keep from laughing out loud when them white ladies chatted with me about how trifling good-for-nothing their niggers was getting to be—"

"Good," Guy said; "but this time, the game's going to be for keeps. You're going to live like a well-off widow, Mrs. Turner, whose husband died and left her money. It'll be hard at first to act like white, but you'll learn. You always were smart. Listen to the way people talk, and imitate them. My bankers in New York will pay you money every month. What do you say to that, Phoebe?"

"You ever going to come to New York—Guy?" she said slowly.

"Once in a while," he said. "Whenever I can—"

"Then I says, all right," Phoebe whispered, "and thank you mighty kindly—long as I can see you—once in a while—"

He lingered in New Orleans even after his clothes had been delivered. He could not explain why, even to himself. It was as though, now that the near certainty of achieving all his ends was upon him, he was seized with a lassitude, born of a certain nameless dread. He had to exorcise that fear, bring it out in the light of day, examine it. But when he described the shape of it finally, gave it definition, clarity, it only increased, paralyzing his will.

Jo Ann. By now she was twenty-nine years old. What was she like? They had loved each other as children; even Jerry and Rachel had understood that they might marry some day. But now the mountain peaks of time reared up between them, cloudy with the mists of years. Perhaps the body of love would lie dead between them. He had lived too long, and suffered too much. . . .

He thought about it, listening on that twenty-seventh night of February, to tiny Adelina Patti filling the opera house with golden sound. The music moved him, though he heard it with a half attentive ear. During the entr'acte, a sudden terror seized him. Had Jo Ann waited? She had meant her childish promise; but no promise is proof against loneliness and tears. And in a land where a girl begins to fear spinsterhood at twenty—

He stayed on for weeks, witnessing the near-riots over the arrival of Lola Montez, that incredible dancer, whose charms had caused Ludwig I, King of Bavaria to make her Countess Landsfeld, and who, with one bigamy trial behind her, was maintaining the life of continual scandal that had made her the darling of the international set. The gay blades fought in the streets with the puritanical elements who wanted to ban her New Orleans appearances. He sat in the courtroom and listened to her trial for assault and battery, after her admirers had beaten the amorous prompter of the theatre, who had returned the kick she had given him with interest—thereby enabling himself to live out a lifetime of fame as the man who kicked Lola Montez. He laughed with the rest when the irrepressible Lola lifted her skirts in open court to display the bruises on her thigh. Life was not dull in New Orleans. . . .

He listened, without comment, to the fiery talk of secession, of war. He could not have commented in any case; he had been too long apart from things. He read *Uncle Tom's Cabin,* which had been published the year before. It left him with the unshakable conviction that Mrs. Stowe had never seen, or at least had never talked to, a southern Negro in her life.

Then there was April and the perfume of early flowers drifted down the wind. He felt something striving to awake within him. Each day the feeling was stronger. Then one morning, he awoke and said:

"Nikia, go downstairs and tell the man to send the boys up to pack my things. We're leaving today—"

All the way upriver to Natchez and beyond, he felt the excitement stirring in his blood. And as the ponderous paddle wheels of the steamer backed water, slowing her, sliding her into the landing before Fairoaks, he was like a man with ague.

The Negroes came flocking to the landing, greeting him, staring at the pygmy children, seizing his trunks and valises, laughing, shouting, until, quite suddenly, an older black recognized him, saying:

"Marse Guy! God Awmighty, hit's Marse Guy!"

The ragged black children raced ahead of him to the house, babbling:

"Hit's Marse Guy! Marse Guy done come back! Marse Guy—"

She was waiting for him by the time he gained the gallery. She was tall, willow-slender, exquisite. The kind of a woman a man dreams about as he listens to the ceaseless thunder of the African rains upon the mongongo leaves. She stood there, staring at him, her face as white as death. Wordlessly, he took her in his arms.

He heard a cough behind him, and turned. Kilrain Mallory stood there, grinning at him maliciously.

"Oh, well," Kilrain said; "this time, all right. For old time's sake. But in the future, Guy Falks, remember that we Mallorys don't cotton to men who kiss—our wives. . . ."

21

ANOTHER man, a lesser man, would have fled at once, attributing his flight to pride. But pride was exactly what Guy Falks had. And it was precisely this quality in him that held him there during the next two weeks. That, and his own sense of justice. He had been gone from Fairoaks for eighteen years; and, as he put it to himself, clearly: After all, boy, what the hell did you expect?

He rode out alone at the end of those two weeks, mounted upon a black, sired by Demon out of one of the grey mares. He wanted to put distance between himself and the house, sort out and examine his memories of Fairoaks, so that he might discover precisely how it had changed. For it had, and in no obvious way that a man could take hold of with a glance. At first, he had been willing to attribute this sense of strangeness, of darkly brooding sadness which hung over that house and that land he had vowed to make his, to his own altered point of view. The eyes of a man of thirty-five, and those of a boy of seventeen are totally different. But it was not that entirely; it was much more than that. . . .

The damned place is haunted, he told himself. Phantoms stalk the halls; the ghosts of old sins, old injustices, and of— very present grief. . . .

Or was he wrong about that, too? Her self control was perfect; if it were self control. Her blue eyes rested upon his face with calm friendliness; her voice, speaking, was wonderfully serene. She had felt no need to explain, or even recount the circumstances surrounding her marriage to Kil. Nor, when he came to think about it, was there any such need. A child of ten gave her solemn promise, unasked, to a boy of sixteen. Hardly an event of world-shaking importance. People, family, friends had held the assumption that they would one day wed. But assumptions, anybody's assumptions, even his own were neither cause nor effect. Tragedy was a cause: his father's lusting after another man's wife; paid for in blood. Time was a cause: eighteen years of separation, without a letter, a word, a note to bridge the gap. Kilrain Mallory was a cause: gay, laughing, debonair, strikingly handsome, very male. There were too many causes. And only one effect: this aching void in the exact center of his universe, widening out to engulf even his future, leaving him purposeless and without plan. For in his mental shaping of his coming years, he had always linked Jo Ann and Fairoaks together. The one implied the other. He could buy Fairoaks now, twenty-five times over. That is, he had the money to buy it. But why should Kilrain sell it? Why would any man, married to Jo Ann Falks and master of Fairoaks, sell out and move on?

And if he did—what then? Guy Falks would stride the ancestral halls, bereft of wife and child, bereft, indeed, of any reason for ownership, for possession, that made any sense at all. Say—my grandfather built it. Say—it was stolen from my father by the man who later murdered him. Say—it is rightfully mine. . . .

The only thing that is rightfully any man's, he thought savagely, is six feet of earth—and he'll soon be disputing that with the worms. . . .

The only purpose for which Fairoaks had been built, had already failed: the siring of sons, the founding of a dynasty. Jo Ann and Kilrain had been married ten years, and there was no child. And he, Guy Falks, had lived past the savage hungers of his youth. His mind ruled him now, his iron will. He would not accept any fair face or lissome form, merely to supply himself with a mate. He had the feeling that he was going to be damned hard to please from now on; that the final woman in his life must emerge unscathed from the sternest test of all: comparison with Jo Ann.

Riding out alone, now, he felt curiously let down; like a man who has girded himself, donned shield and buckler, hefted his sword; and gathering all his forces, has sallied forth to strike—foes no longer there, dissolved into mist and cloud, vanished mockingly into air. He had spent eighteen years in

257

accumulating his great fortune, which now, finally, could buy nothing that he wanted, nothing to still his aching need: a home. A wife. Sons. . . .

There was something that clawed at the back part of his mind, struggling to come clear. And now, suddenly, seeing the fences that separated Fairoaks from Malloryhill; it burst blindingly out into the light. A man, any man at all, brings home his bride proudly to the home of his fathers—if he has a home. And Kilrain had, or should have, Malloryhill. Alan Mallory was dead. Kilrain was his sole heir. Why then, in the name of everything unholy, did he live at Fairoaks, depending, as it seemed, upon the bounty of his bride?

There was no answer that he could think of; but the means of answering it lay readily at hand. He lifted the black over the fence in a soaring jump, and headed for Mallory Manor. Kil's overseer or the Negroes would know. He had only to ask and—

Then he saw something else; one of the things he had been trying to define, brought now by contrast into stark relief, the way that Fairoaks had changed. Malloryhill was beautifully kept. It was clipped, pruned, white-washed, planted by expert hands. What had struck him at Fairoaks, then, had been— neglect. Not a total, or even obvious neglect; but rather a falling off from the high standards that Rachel, and later his father, had imposed. Things were falling into place now; the puzzle was beginning to solve itself. Kilrain lay abed each morning until after eleven o'clock, and let Brad Stevens, his overseer, run the place. And Fairoaks could not be managed like that. Nothing of importance ever can; laziness and sloth are qualities that life punishes pitilessly. Of course, young Stevens was fairly good, as overseers go. His family had always followed that trade. His grandfather, old Wil Stevens, had been Ash Falks' overseer; his father had worked at Malloryhill. But you didn't leave plantations like Malloryhill and Fairoaks entirely up to overseers; due allowance has to be made for human nature; and no man ever cares for another's fields the way he would his own.

The manor house of Malloryhill was sparkling. The Negroes were clean, sharp, alert. Guy had scarcely dismounted when a tall, grey-haired man descended the stairs from the gallery to greet him. This one had competence written all over him; his grey eyes were as opaque as ice, and very nearly as cold.

"Good day to you, sir," he said. "Whom have I the honor of addressing?"

His mode of speech brought Guy up short. Overseers simply didn't talk like this. Nor dress like this, either.

"I'm Guy Falks," he said, and put out his hand; "a neighbor—or rather an ex-neighbor, back on a visit. I presume you're the new owner?" This was a shot in the dark; but it struck home.

"Hardly," the man said. "You might call me the supervisor. Not the overseer, sir, for I have four of them working for me. Yes, supervisor describes it. My name is Willard James; I was appointed by the Bank of Natchez to take care of this place until a purchaser can be found for it. That, I'm afraid, is going to be a difficult proposition. It's too big; and, if we split it up piecemeal, its location makes it difficult for any established planter to tie the parcels into his present holdings, so—"

"You mean," Guy said, "that the Mallorys no longer own it?"

Willard James permitted himself a brief, wintry smile.

"You have been away from here a long time, haven't you, Mister Falks?" he said.

"Eighteen years," Guy said. "I used to live at Fairoaks—"

"I know," James said. "May I offer you a drink, sir? Or even a simple repast?"

"Both," Guy said. He needed time. Getting information out of this human iceberg wasn't going to be easy.

As they mounted the stairs, Mr. James turned to him.

"You're stopping at Fairoaks now, aren't you, Mister Falks?"

"Yes," Guy said, in a chagrined tone. "How did you know that, sir?"

"The Negroes. When a man appears from nowhere, dressed like a prince, and accompanied by two black dwarfs in turbans and silks, he is hardly hiding his light under a bushel, sir. Besides, all people have to do in this godforsaken place is to attend to one another's affairs. It's an addiction I don't share—"

"I should have guessed as much," Guy said dryly. "Now, how about that repast, Mr. James? I'm starved. . . ."

Willard James ate sparingly, and drank less. Nor did the little he drank loosen his tongue. Finally, in desperation, Guy put the question to him directly.

"Don't you know?" James answered quietly. "I should think

he would have told you. You and he are old friends—"

There was a strong undercurrent of distaste in his tone. Guy guessed that Willard James didn't approve of Kilrain Mallory or his intimates.

"He didn't," Guy said. "Perhaps the subject was too delicate to be discussed even between—friends. . . ."

"Perhaps it was," Willard James said. "Would you like a toddy, Mister Falks?"

Guy laughed aloud.

"I've met some close-mouthed people in my time," he chuckled, "but you, Mister James, have got 'em all beat a mile. Why won't you tell me what I want to know?"

"It's hardly my place to," Willard James said serenely. "The thing's too involved in Mallory's personal affairs. Now, if you were a prospective purchaser for this place, I'd be obliged to explain the situation to you in detail. Otherwise—no."

Guy stiffened. Why not? Malloryhill was one hell of a fine plantation. And he couldn't let the race of Falks come to a barren, futile end because of the lack of any one woman, no matter how lovely, or how fine. . . .

"All right," he said. "I am a prospective purchaser. Hell, I'm more than that; I'm a definite purchaser, if the terms are right. For God's sake, man, speak up!"

"Well," Willard James began slowly, "if you're as sincere as you seem to be, I guess I can speak after all—"

Then the supervisor told him. Only the bare outlines, of course; but enough for any man knowing Kilrain Mallory to fill in the details. Guy summed it up, starkly, in a phrase:

"You mean Kil whored and gambled away his birthright, don't you, Mr. James?"

"That is—harsh, but true," Willard James said judiciously. "Even, perhaps, less than the truth—"

"What the devil do you mean by that, sir?"

"He married that sweet and gentle child to save his skin," James said flatly. "And in less than six months from now, he will have rendered her penniless—and homeless as well. She'll stick by him; more's the pity. He doesn't deserve that kind of loyalty. I," he went on, a note of icy fury entering his tone, "have met some worthless bastards in my time; but Kilrain Mallory takes the cake!"

"You mean that he—?" Guy said.

"Has piled up a mountain of debts against Fairoaks as well. Gambling losses; gifts of jewelry to his mistress—"

"His mistress!" Guy exploded. "Married to Jo Ann and he—"

"Some men are not monogamous by nature," James said calmly. "In fact, most men aren't. But I think the majority of us have sense enough to appreciate a truly good woman when we find one, and curb our appetites in order not to jeopardize what we have. Kilrain Mallory, unfortunately, hasn't that much sense. Not even that much taste. When we go to Natchez, I'll present you to the woman. I'm sure, after seeing her, you will understand his reasons even less than you do now—"

"All right, name it—"

"Name what, Mister Falks?"

"What you want for this place. I'll write you a check, right now!"

"It is not what I want," James said quietly. "We'll have to go down to Natchez and talk to the president of the bank. And I wouldn't be fair to you if I didn't tell you that in my opinion the notes outstanding against Malloryhill are worth more than the plantation is on today's market. But, if you still want to cover them, you'll get clear title—"

"And Fairoaks?" Guy said.

"Even worse. We hold only part of them. We've been steadily buying up his paper at a discount from creditors—who, quite justifiably, despair of ever collecting—because the two adjacent spreads of land would make a worthwhile investment, even so. In a few more weeks, we should have them all. But there's one strange thing about the matter—"

"What's that?" Guy growled.

"Apparently there are no notes outstanding against the house, nor the grounds on which it stands. All the rest of the plantation, yes. As you can see, from a business standpoint, that hurts matters. The best part of Fairoaks is that house. Few buyers would be interested in the plantation without it—"

"You," Guy said quietly, "write Natchez this afternoon and tell them to get those notes. All of them. I'll take care of the house, myself. When you've got them, let me know. I'll take both places off your hands—and price, Mr. James, is no object—"

"I know it isn't." James permitted himself a tight-lipped smile. "I've a very fair idea of how much you're worth, Mr. Falks."

"How the devil could you?" Guy said.

"We have—ah—means of finding out such things. Don't be annoyed; it's just business. There's hardly a man in the state who could afford to take this burden off our hands at one stroke. We were a bit concerned over the difficulties of selling these parcels piecemeal. So, when you appeared upon the scene, with your beturbaned dwarfs and trunks galore, I took it upon myself, as an official of the bank, to investigate. I was about to tender you an invitation to visit me; but you anticipated my action. At any rate, I'll have definite information for you in a month to six weeks. Will that suit you, sir?"

"Perfectly," Guy said. "Thank you, Mister James."

"Thank *you*," Willard James said. "Goodbye, Mister Falks—"

Guy did not return to Fairoaks that day. He rode up to the farm that Alan Mallory had presented to his mother and Tom. As he more than half expected, the place was a ruin: windows broken, sagging steps, half the fields gone to weeds; and no evidence anywhere of rational care.

You can get 'em out of the hills, he thought bitterly; but you sure can't get the hills out of them!

He found Tom, finally, sleeping under a tree, the mule and plough waiting patiently in an unfinished furrow. There was not a Negro on the place, nor any sign of feminine occupation. Where the devil were his mother—and Matty? It had been a long time—long enough for Charity to have—but Matty? He bent down and shook Tom, hard.

"Hawrumph!" Tom muttered, the fumes of rotgut whiskey rising into Guy's face. He stepped back and planted a swift kick into Tom's ribs. That did it. His older brother came up into a sitting position, blinking like a drunken owl. Only, owls were supposed to be wise birds, Guy reflected with disgust.

"How come you hafta go'n kick me, Mister?" Tom whined.

"Because you need it, you drunken swine," Guy said flatly. "Tell me: where are Ma and Matty?"

"Ma died of the lung fever, five years ago," Tom said; "and Matty—God! You—you're—"

"Guy. Get up from there. Let's go back to the house and pour some coffee into you, so you'll talk sense. So poor Ma's dead, eh?" Try as he would, he could not awake in his heart any more than the faintest ghost of regret, such as he might

262

have felt for a stranger, whom he had known—slightly. As I knew Ma, he thought, or even less. Living always in Pa's shadow—in the shadow of a giant. For Pa was that—even his follies and his sins were outsized—

He reached down and yanked Tom to his feet.

"And Matty?" he growled.

"She run off with a trader in niggers a year after you left," Tom said. "Heard from her for a while—from up in Kentucky. Lexington, it 'pears to me. Then the brats kept coming; one every year, and sometimes, two. So she left off writing. Reckon she all right, though. Ain't heard that she warn't—"

"All right," Guy said. "Come on."

The interior of the house was worse than the outside. It smelled of sweat and dirt, and spoiled food. The bed hadn't been changed in a year, Guy was sure. The house had not been swept or dusted in five. There was not an unbroken chair in the place. Clumsily, Tom got the fire going and put the battered coffee pot on. Then he sat down in one of the rickety chairs, and stared at his younger brother in frank admiration.

"Lord God, but you're fine!" he said. "Reckon them duds cost you more'n I make in a year—"

"Considering what I've seen of the place," Guy said dryly, "I reckon they do. Haven't done a single damned thing that I told you, have you? Sold off the niggers; ate your way through the stock; planted cotton to the front door, instead of stuff you could eat; spent the money from it on gut-rotting swill and a cheap whore or two, instead of keeping up the place; made such a pig of yourself that no decent filly would have you—and now look at you; just look!"

"I tried," Tom whined. "Honest to God, I did, Guy . . . Jest don't seem to have the knack . . . Things have been rightly hard. Say, Guy—rich like you be now, could you—?"

"Not a cent. Not a dirty copper. But I am going to do something for you, if only because we're kin. I'm going to have my own place in a month, or six weeks. Then I'll send a gang of my niggers up here every day to clean this place of brush and work it for you, under a capable overseer who'll know how it ought to be done. I'll get a wench to be your house keeper—a yellow wench, about twenty-eight or thirty, young enough to keep you away from the village whores. I'll have the place cleaned up and whitewashed. And this time you'll keep it that way, because I'll be around to kick your wormy tail if you don't!"

"Gosh, Guy, thanks," Tom muttered.

"Skip it," Guy said. "I've got to be going now—"

"You going up there to Kentucky and look for Matty?" Tom said.

"Hell, no!" Guy snapped. "It's a pity you didn't get yourself lost as well—"

The way back to Fairoaks led through the Mallorys' up-river plantation. It, too, was well kept; but there was something a trifle less professional about the work. Malloryhill was coldly perfect, the evidence of an expert hand. But love had gone into this planting, more love than knowledge; enough to win out over that lack. . . .

Half an hour later, he passed a tall young man sitting on a horse, overseeing a gang of slaves. He noted, with some surprise, that the man had no whip coiled around the pommel of his saddle; and yet the Negroes were working rapidly and well. He touched his hat in salute, and the young man lifted his own broad-brimmed hat in answer. His hair was blond. There was something familiar about him.

Guy cantered on for another hundred yards. Then, suddenly, he yanked the black about, and raced back toward the group.

"Fitz!" he called out.

Young Mallory stared at him.

"I'm afraid you have the advantage of me, sir," he began; then: "Guy!—Guy!"

Guy reached over and seized Fitzhugh in a crushing hug. Then he sat back, staring at this young man, now twenty-eight years of age, grown tall and brawny; the only trace of the delicate, scholarly boy left in him was the serene candor of his great blue eyes.

"Don't reckon I've been so glad to see a body in a coon's age," he said gruffly, partially to conceal the emotion that young Fitzhugh always awoke in him; thinking with renewed conviction the same thought of eighteen years before: why couldn't Tom have been like this?

"Nor I," Fitz said contentedly. "Come on up to the house, Guy, so we can really talk—"

"Can't leave your hands like this," Guy pointed out. "They won't hit a lick at a snake the minute you're out of sight. . . ."

"Not my hands," Fitz said proudly. "They work whether I'm here or not. Right, boys?"

"Yassuh, Marse Fitz!" the Negroes chorused triumphantly.

Guy thought he had never heard so much love in so many voices in his life. He's got it, he thought; don't know what it is, but he's got it. No wonder the place looks so fine. I don't know why, but even as a kid, everybody loved him, even Kil. And it's not just charm. Reckon it's because he loves everybody, really loves them, and there's nothing more appealing than that—

They rode up to the house. It was very neat and freshly whitewashed; the yard before it was a sea of flowers. But as soon as he entered, Guy saw there was not, nor ever had been, a woman here.

"Aren't you sparking a gal, boy?" he said.

"Yes," Fitz answered, and blushed almost like a girl himself. "Grace Tilton. Don't suppose you know her. When you left, she was only three years old—"

"Know her folks. Good, upright people. When's the hitching going to be?"

"I don't know," Fitz said sadly; "as soon as I can clear this place of debt—another two years, I guess. . . ."

"Kil?"

"Well—" Fitz hesitated.

"I know the story, boy," Guy said flatly. "Malloryhill and Fairoaks. No reason why he should have overlooked this one. . . ."

"It's a kind of sickness," Fitz said. "This mania of his for gambling. Don't reckon we should hold it against him, Guy. There's things a man can't help—"

"Never had much Christian charity," Guy said, "so let's not talk about Kil. You got any drinking whiskey, son?"

"Of course," Fitz said, and pulled the bell cord. The maid servant who appeared was fat, and middle-aged. Apparently Fitzhugh did not share the usual Mallory vices. "Get us the whiskey, Mae," he said.

"Yessir, Marse Fitz," Mae beamed. "Right away, sir."

"You've sure got a way with niggers!" Guy said. "Don't reckon I've ever seen the like—"

"It's simple," Fitz smiled. "I treat them like what they are—human beings. There's not a blacksnake whip on the whole place. If they want to prowl about at night, I let them—all they want. I don't overwork them, and I feed them well—"

"There's more to it than that," Guy said.

"Yes, I suppose there is. When they get a lazy spell, I simply look them in the face and tell them I'm ashamed of them.

265

That they've disappointed me, and hurt my feelings. Lord, Guy, I've seen a thirty-year-old man cry like a baby because I mentioned I was maybe going to lose the place after all, what with the trifling help I have. They—they're so easy to reach by kindness, perhaps because they've had so little of it. . . ."

"Could be you've got a point there," Guy said. "But you aren't, are you?"

"I'm not—what?"

"About to lose the place? I'd be glad to stake you. Heck, Fitz, call it a wedding present. The deeds, free and clear. What do you say, boy?"

"Thank you very much; but, no, Guy. I've got to do it myself. You understand that, don't you? It'll be more mine, that way. So Grace will know I did it all alone—for her. I don't mean to be a stiff-necked fool, but—"

"No—not a fool, boy," Guy said gruffly.

They sat there sipping the bourbon and branch water.

"Left the books, eh Fitz?" Guy said. "Settled down to man's work—"

"No," Fitz said gravely. "Books are man's work, too, Guy. Perhaps they're where it starts—the real stuff of humanity, I mean. Plowing, chopping cotton, driving slaves—are occupations maybe higher than a beast's, but not much. But what a man smears on canvas, hacks out of stone, scrawls on a page —these are the things which make him 'but little lower than the angels, and crown him with glory and honor.' Because these are his way of reaching up, Guy, out of his blood lust and his animal cruelty, out of his stupidity, and his littleness, toward wherever God is—"

God? Guy thought bitterly; where was He the night that Beeljie went screaming out of life? Where is He ever in this darkling plain without either justice or hope?

But he didn't say that. It wasn't the kind of thing you said to men like Fitzhugh Mallory.

"Come," Fitz said, "I'll show you my library. It isn't very much, really; but I think it's what keeps me hoping, really— going on. 'For we are such stuff—' "

" 'As dreams are made on,' " Guy went on: " 'And our little lives are rounded by a sleep—' "

Fitz grinned at him.

"Sort of a bookreading man, yourself, aren't you, Guy?" he said. "For all your talk—"

"Reckon I am," Guy said sheepishly.

266

He did not go back to Fairoaks that night. He stayed on and the two of them talked the night through, in one long blaze of excitement, striking sparks from the swordplay of their minds; which was a rare thing in that intellectual desert in which they lived. A man has hungers beyond those of the flesh; they were, both of them, starved for talk like this; thoughtful, free of dogma, rapier-like in its thrust and parry. They argued about everything: secession, the possibility of war, the mental capacity of the Negro, the existence of God, the meaning of life, itself. They shouted at each other, pounded upon the table, poured out a great quantity of thunderous nonsense, and even a tiny spark or two of original thought. They went to bed at last in the dawn, hoarse-voiced from all the shouting, thoroughly pleased with themselves and with each other. It was a friendship that would last a life-time, because they needed each other. A man always seeks, and sometimes finds, the brother of his soul.

Guy slept late that next morning, a thing he had not done in years. He woke with the sunlight in his eyes, knowing instantly where he was, and yawned and stretched luxuriously. I'll get my things, he decided, and move over here. Batch it for the next month with Fitz; give him a hand about the place. Better that way. The less I see of Jo Ann, the better—

He had his coffee in bed, then dressed and went out on the porch. He sat there lazily, enjoying the sun, until he saw Fitzhugh riding in from the fields. Then he was standing up, his brown eyes widening in pure astonishment; for on both sides of Fitz' roan there bounded, playful as kittens, the dogs. Those dogs. For there was no mistaking that Shetland pony size, the dark tiger brindle of their glossy hides, the lambent flame in their eyes. They saw him now, and raced ahead, silently, the short hairs on their backs rising, flattening themselves out for the attack. But Fitz called out to them:

"Down Tiger! Down Beauty!" They stopped in their tracks, obediently.

"You did it!" Guy breathed; "you caught 'em! How in the name of living hell—"

Fitz swung down from the saddle.

"Unlike you and Kil," he laughed, *"I* have brains. What do you think of my beauties, Guy?"

"Magnificent," Guy said. "I'm eaten up with envy. But for God's sake convince 'em that I'm friendly, or I'll have to pistol them when you're not around in order to save my hide!"

"Come Tiger, Beaut!" Fitz commanded. "Shake hands with the gentleman."

The two big brutes approached, and squatting on their haunches, offered Guy their massive paws. He shook hands with them, patted their great heads and scratched their ears. The male, Tiger, reared up suddenly, placed his paws on Guy's shoulders, and licked his face. In that position, the mastiff was nearly as tall as Guy was.

"You see, he likes you," Fitz grinned. "You've got nothing to worry about, now."

"Nothing," Guy groaned, "except to figure out a way to steal them from you. If you knew how long and hard I tried to catch me a pair of this breed!"

"I do know," Fitz said, glancing briefly at Guy's scarred hand. "Kil told me. I haven't bred these two yet; but when I do, you can have your pick of the pups, a male and a bitch, to establish the breed at your place. They're some dogs, all right. . . ."

"But how did you do it?" Guy demanded.

"Brains," Fitz teased, "and some luck. You see, they kept coming back at intervals during all the time you were gone. Kil and I tried to capture a pair, for a while, until he got more interested in—other things. About seven years ago, they disappeared and didn't show up again until about two years back. The pack always stayed small. I think that hunters must have killed them off. But two years ago, they came back —an old male, and a young bitch ready to whelp. I kept tracking them, hoping that some way would occur to me to trap them—"

"Obviously one did," Guy said. "Go on, Fitz—"

"No. A way didn't occur to me. I found the way—in a book, Guy. The memoirs of an old fur trapper. Ever hear of a deadfall?"

"Yes! I've caught leopards with them in Africa. Now why in the name of everything unholy, didn't I think of that?"

"No reason why you should have. We haven't any big, fur-bearing animals in Mississippi—except a few bears—so we never developed the idea. Anyhow, it worked, partly. The male and the bitch were in the pit, and the pups, because they'd been born by then, some in, and the rest yelping about the edge. The catch was I couldn't get those ugly brutes out of there. Had to shoot them, finally. Then I went down into the pit and brought up the three pups that had fallen in. I picked out these two from the bunch, and drowned the rest. Hated to do it; but I just couldn't afford to raise 'em all—"

"Damn your hide," Guy said. "You've made me feel let down. I'd been looking forward to doing this job myself. But anyhow, boy, I'm going to hold you to your promise about those pups. Another thing: Any objection to my becoming your star boarder for a while? I can stay on at Fairoaks as long as I like, but—"

"Of course not! Glad to have your company," Fitz said; then: "Jo Ann, eh? Bad business, Guy—"

"I know. Reckon the best way to put temptation behind me is to get out of sight. Main reason I'm buying Fairoaks is for her. But I'm putting it in my name. That way, he won't have anything left to borrow on, so he'll have to straighten up, I reckon, and hoe his own row—"

"He won't," Fitz said flatly. "He can't, Guy. It's the way he's made. He'll go on to mortgage the house, next, and the blacks. . . ."

"Then I'll buy the house and the niggers in, too," Guy said.

"I wouldn't, if I were you. Jo Ann won't live off your charity. Kil—yes. He'll take anything from anybody, but Jo Ann—no. You should know that. Especially not from—you."

"What's so special about me?"

"You were her first love," Fitz said quietly. "I know she wasn't anything but a baby, then; but she loved you, truly. Now, she loves Kil—really loves him—in spite of all he's done to destroy her affections. Which is a pity. Because there are some situations the rules don't cover. This is one of them: two people very nearly perfect for each other, kept apart by what men call morality. Doesn't make sense. It would be a hell of a lot more moral for Jo to run away with you, than to let my no-good cousin destroy everything she owns, and her, too, finally; because she'll stick to him out of a mistaken sense of loyalty—"

"You said love," Guy pointed out, dryly.

"I did, and I do. But there are limits. Jo's not happy, Guy. She's tremendously kind, understanding, and—loyal. But she demands, at least, loyalty in her turn. That's one thing that could change the picture. She doesn't know about his women. He's got sense enough to stay out of the quarters. If she ever found out about that big, blousy wench in Natchez, say—"

"You're suggesting that I tell her?" Guy said. "What the hell do you think I am, Fitz?"

Fitzhugh sighed. "Nor can I. Reckon we're prisoners, Guy, both of us. We've got to do it by the book. The right thing in the right way. Why can't the right thing be done the wrong way, sometimes, Guy? What difference would it make, as long as good was achieved?"

"Because," Guy said slowly, "the end is shaped by the means. Play it dirty—and it comes out, dirty. Inevitably. Reckon that's the answer to the age old plaint: 'Why do the wicked prosper?' The answer is, they don't. We only think they do because we insist upon equating material prosperity with happiness. Pure nonsense. A man can be richer than Astor, and be unable to buy anything with all that money that counts, not a bloody, damned thing to ease the hell inside his heart—"

"Listen to the preacher man!" Fitz laughed.

"End of the sermon," Guy said cheerfully. "I'm going to bring my two little niggers with me, too. Hope you don't mind—"

"Not at all," Fitz said. "Delighted to have them. Got anything else over there? Crocodiles, lions, tigers?"

"Nope," Guy laughed. "Those miniature devils are enough. You'll see. . . ."

The first person he saw, as he entered the grounds of Fairoaks again, was Brad Stevens, the overseer. The young man cantered over to his side, and took off his hat, respectfully.

"Begging your pardon, sir," he said. "If you got two minutes, I'd like to talk to you. Been waiting for the chance to see you alone ever since you came back. . . ."

"All right, Brad," Guy said, "but why all the mystery? You've had dozens of chances to talk to me—"

"Never alone, sir. There was always somebody around; and this ain't a thing I could tell you, even in front of the niggers—"

"Speak your piece, boy," Guy said.

"I'll make it short, sir. Miss Jo Ann and Mister Kilrain don't own Fairoaks, sir; not rightly. You do, Mister Falks."

"Look, son," Guy said kindly, "I've known that all my life. But not having any way to prove it—"

"That's just the point, Mister Guy! You can prove it. All

270

you've got to do is to take the next boat down to Natchez and go see my Aunt Martha Gaines—"

"Rein in a bit, boy. What the devil has your Aunt Martha got to do with my proving I own Fairoaks?"

"Everything, sir! You see, she's my Pa's oldest sister; and my grandpa, Wil Stevens, lived with her at Gooseberry Hill, her husband's place, after he got too crippled up with rheumatiz to work at Fairoaks any more. Your grandpa, sir, wrote him letters from time to time. They was real close, you know—"

"And those letters?"

"Prove your grandpa never disowned your Pa. Ash Falks was trying to find Mister Wes most up to the day he died. My aunt says that will must be a forgery, sir, and—"

"Wait a minute, Brad," Guy said quietly, "there's a lot in all this that doesn't go down so easy. First of all, why didn't your aunt speak up before now?"

"Because she wasn't here, sir, and didn't know about what happened. She lived at Gooseberry Hill with old man Gaines 'til he died two years ago. Then, cause she didn't want to go on running a plantation at her age, she sold it, and moved to Natchez. She opened the Martha Gaines Boarding House for Gentlemen down there. You go to Natchez and stop with her, and she'll give you all them letters, sir. She plumb nigh hit the ceiling when Pa told her that your cousin Gerald was the owner, and—"

"Strange she didn't know. . . ."

"No, it ain't. How could she? Gooseberry Hill is way the hell down south in Louisiana, sir. Below New Orleans. She'n my Pa warn't no hand at writing letters. A few words every other year 'bout their miseries in the back and such like. But when Pa heard from her that she'd moved to Natchez, he took me down there to see her. That's when it all come out."

"I see," Guy said. "But one thing more, lad. Why are you telling me all this now?"

"Hard to put down into talk, sir," the overseer said slowly, "but I reckon it's this way: I been hearing about Fairoaks all my life from my Pa. And living at Malloryhill, I was always over here. Used to see you'n your pa riding together. Anyhow, I always did pine for the chance to oversee it when I got old enough. When I got that chance, I felt mighty fine. In a little while, I got to love the old place. Reckon I sort of aimed to spend my life here just like Grandpa. So I just don't cotton to the idea of its being sold off piece by piece to strangers when a real, honest-to-God Falks is right here at hand, with all it takes to run it right, not to mention the fact that it's his anyhow. So I hope you'll go visit my aunt, sir. She's rightly old, for all that she's spry as the dickens. I wouldn't wait too long, if I was you—"

"I won't," Guy said. "You keep your lip buttoned, son; and you've got that job for life, with better pay. . . ."

He rode up to Fairoaks, and ordered the blacks to pack his things. Then he sought out Kilrain and asked the loan of a wagon and a driver to take them up to Fitzhugh's place. Kil gave the orders cheerfully.

"What's the matter, old boy?" he mocked. "Don't we feed you right, or something?"

"It's not that, Kil," Guy said evenly, "and you know it. . . ."

"Reckon I do," Kil grinned. "You're a smart cuss, Guy. Smart enough to learn by other folks' experience—maybe even by your Pa's. . . ."

"Smarter than you at any rate," Guy said quietly. "Smart enough not to waste my life and goods in riotous living— and to value a treasure when I see one, which you don't, even when you have that treasure in your hands—"

"Thus sayeth the preacher!" Kilrain laughed. "Where are you going now?"

"To say goodbye to Jo Ann," Guy said, "with—or without your permission, Kil—"

"Go ahead. There's one thing you're forgetting, Guy. I have nothing to worry about. Jo Ann is nothing like her mother; nothing at all—"

There was no answer to that one, so Guy attempted none. He walked away from Kil, thinking: I *am* getting into the bad habit of preaching. Fitz said so, now Kil. And I've been bastard enough, myself, not to have the slightest right at all to—

He found her on the gallery. Her blue eyes were grave and sad.

"You're leaving us," she said quietly. "Would it be unbecoming of me to ask—why?"

"No," Guy said, "but damned unbecoming of me to answer. Besides, I reckon you know why. . . ."

The pain was there, bright and sudden in her eyes.

"Yes," she said, with enormous dignity, "I suppose I do, Guy. And I'm sorry—truly sorry. But nine years were an

272

awfully long time for a girl to wait—without a word. No—don't go yet. There's one more thing that must be said: I love my husband. I know that he's a wastrel and a gambler and a ne'er-do-well. But I love him. I suppose you know we're going to lose Fairoaks as we've lost Malloryhill. We're trying to keep the house and a few acres of land. If that goes, Kil will have to leave; and I—I'll leave with him. There—I've said it. But I had to make you understand—"

"That I have no hope?" Guy said. "I understood that from the first. What I don't understand is—"

"What, Guy?"

"Why you love him so—"

"How could you, not being a woman? It's many things: he's gay, and tender, and good to me. And loyal—that's the principal thing. He has never looked at another woman. He knows, I think, that's the one thing I could not, would not stand—the only thing that would ever make me leave him. So—what on earth are you doing, Guy Falks?"

"Praying, I reckon," Guy said. "Forgive me, Jo—"

"What an odd thing to say. Why were you praying, Guy?"

"For the strength to go back into the wilderness," he said in his dark, rich voice. "For the will to put Satan behind me. Damn it, Jo, there are some temptations that just shouldn't be put upon a man—"

"I—I don't understand you," she whispered.

He smiled at her then, bleakly.

"Thank God, you don't," he said, and turning, left her there, walking toward where Nikiabo and Sifa waited by the wagon—forgetting even to say goodbye.

She watched until the wagon was out of sight, before she shaped her thought.

"Nor upon a woman, either," she murmured. Then very quietly, she went back into Fairoaks' cool and shuttered darkness—into, perhaps, a shadow greater than she knew.

THERE are times in the life of a man when all roads run seemingly towards an end; when the goal is within his reach, his fingers curving now to grasp it. But these are also the times of the ribald gods, demon sprites of chance and fate, the upsetters of applecarts, the interveners between kiss and lip. And at just such a perilous period in his existence had Guy Falks arrived now, as he went down the gangplank of the *Prairie Belle* at Natchez, with Willard James that June day in 1853.

By sundown he had it all: the deeds to Malloryhill; every note outstanding against Fairoaks; even the letters of his grandfather to old Wil Stevens. More, he and James had called upon the county clerk, and examined in his presence the original will leaving Fairoaks to Gerald Falks. The most cursory examination comparing it with the old letters, showed the signature to be a forgery. One of the letters that Martha Stevens Gains turned over to Guy was dated the same day as the will, thus providing conclusive evidence against the only possible doubt—that age and illness had caused Ashton Falks' hand to tremble.

"There's only one thing to do now," Willard James said. "We'd best show this evidence to Judge Greenway, and open a suit against Gerald Falks and his heirs to repossess your property. Incidentally, Guy, if you'll return the notes against Fairoaks to the bank, we're honor bound to give you back your money. Kilrain Mallory made those debts against a security he did not own. Therefore, since we bought them from his creditors in an effort to get control of the property, the loss is ours—"

"No," Guy said. "I'll keep them, thank you."

"But that doesn't make sense, Mr. Falks," the county clerk pointed out. "You own Fairoaks; there's no reason for you to assume Kilrain Mallory's debts!"

"There is a reason," Guy said, "a very private reason. Let's leave it like that, shall we?"

"I understand," Willard James said slowly. "I even approve, though it goes against my grain as a business man. Nevertheless, I'm going to give you some advice, Guy Falks, which I hope you'll take. All right, you don't want to prosecute her father, or deprive her of her home. That's very noble of you. What you do want to retain, however, is sufficient control over these holdings to prevent this blackguard she married from robbing her of the place by his folly. Am I right?"

"Perfectly," Guy said dryly.

"Then present this evidence to Judge Greenway. Mr. Montrose, here, and I, will serve as witnesses. You don't have to prosecute. You can ask the Judge to hold off even the State's very legitimate case against Gerald Falks for the crime of forgery, because of the culprit's age, and infirmity. The word of the injured party carries great weight in these cases. You won't have the deeds to Fairoaks; but you will have a legally unshakable document attesting to your right to them; and these, coupled with Mallory's notes, if you insist upon keeping his paper, will take care of any eventuality that could possibly arise. . . ."

Guy considered the matter.

"All right," he said slowly; "and it's not just sentimentality, Will. I want to make damned sure that Fairoaks doesn't pass out of the family. Kil and Jo Ann have no children. Nor do I—yet. But I mean to marry, if for no better reason than to make sure that my grandfather's dream of the Falks of Fairoaks doesn't vanish from the earth. Jo can keep the place, while she lives. But afterwards, I want to know that sons of mine will live there. Come on, let's go see the Judge. . . ."

Judge Greenway proved difficult. A fiery and upright man, he was all for clapping Gerald Falks into jail at once. If, Guy thought, he gets so heated up over forgery, what would he do if I showed him that plugged powder flask? Dueling's murder, anyhow, under Mississippi law; but if this here Judge saw that flask, he'd stretch Jerry's neck before night. . . .

"Look, your honor," he said, "let's put it this way: I just don't rightly cotton to that idea of the sins of the fathers being visited upon the heads of the children. And that's who'd chiefly suffer in this case: the innocent. I'm mighty fond of Jo Ann Mallory. We've been friends all our lives. Jerry Falks is old, sick, and ready to die. So we clap him into the hoosegow, and dispossess the Mallorys; then what? We turn a woman, who didn't have a damned thing to do with the original crime, out to starve. I don't need Fairoaks, now. I've got Malloryhill. All I want to make sure of is that my sons get it in time. If I, the injured party, would like to see justice tempered with a little mercy in this case, why the hell shouldn't you?"

"Runs counter to the law," Judge Greenway growled. "But I'm willing, Mr. Falks, since you seem to be. Montrose, you call my clerk, and we'll draw up a document setting forth the facts as you've presented them. The document, with the evidence attached in the form of those letters and the will, make a rock-solid basis for any suit you or your heirs might want to make in the future. But, blast it all, it's highly irregular!"

"But not illegal," Willard James said.

"No," Judge Greenway said. "It's legal as all hell!"

"Guess that about ties everything up," Willard James said, as they left the Judge's chambers.

"No," Guy said, "there's one thing more. I want to see the woman. It's none of my damned business; but I want to see her. Curiosity killing the cat, I reckon. Can't help craving to see the filly that Kil prefers to Jo—"

"You'll be disappointed," Willard James said; "but anyhow, come on. . . ."

They noticed, as they walked, that the streets were covered with handbills; great playbills plastered the walls. Guy read them idly, those playbills which were going to come close to changing his life. They were, of course, nothing but an exceedingly crude publicity stunt, arranged by Edward Mulhouse, the greatest showman and impresario since Barnum. In effect, under the heading of "Great Steamboat Race ! ! !" they managed to give the impression that the professional rivalry of two great opera singers, Giulietta Castiglione, and Norma Dupré, was going to be settled by a steamboat race. Now this was a notion so exceedingly outlandish, that Guy and Willard James both stopped and studied the playbill with some care. The small print told the story: how a mistake had been made in the bookings of the St. Charles Theatre in New Orleans; and neither diva being willing to relinquish her rights, they had both agreed to the proposition of a certain sporting gentleman of their mutual acquaintance—that they both leave Cincinnati on the above date on different boats, the *Queen of Natchez* and the *Tom Tyler*. The first singer to arrive in New Orleans was to get the first two-weeks' run at the St. Charles, and the loser the second. Both craft would put into Natchez for fuel; citizens wishing to complete the journey southward aboard either, could purchase tickets now at prices called reasonable in the playbills, but which Guy found vastly inflated.

Guy turned to Willard James.

"You believe that?" he said.

"Of course not!" James laughed. "I know Mulhouse. He's simply building up an audience for his diva. I must say she's worth it, though. I heard her last year in New York. . . ."

"Which one?" Guy said.

"Castiglione, of course. The Frenchwoman is a minor, supporting singer. There isn't any rivalry between them. There couldn't be. Castiglione is the finest voice since Patti. Quite a girl. First opera singer I've ever seen who doesn't run to beef. . . ."

"You mean she's slender?"

"I mean she's—gorgeous. Found myself waiting at the stage door, roses in hand, an old fool among all the young blades. She accepted my invitation to dinner. I was damned flattered until she told me why—"

"Why?"

"Because I was sufficiently decrepit to appear harmless. She was sure she wouldn't have to fight me off, like she would have had to with one of those young bucks. She was right. She didn't. After having that ice water poured over my vanity, I didn't have the spirit left to make an attempt. I'm afraid I bored her—horribly. But she was very kind. Just the faintest trace of an accent—and that trace, fake—"

"You, Will," Guy laughed, "have unsuspected depths! You say her accent's fake?"

"She was born on New York's east side to an Italian fruit vendor and his wife. Now, of course, her birthplace's been revised: Firenze, I believe. She did study voice in Italy; that's true enough. But an Italian doctor I know in New York told me it's her Italian that's accented, not her English."

"Will James, the lover!" Guy roared. "Who'd have thought it!"

"I've always suffered from a certain severity of manner," James said sadly. "It's not my fault. I was engaged once, but the girl died. My friends quipped that I froze her to death.

So I threw myself into banking and finance, with planting as a sideline. I'm a planter's son, you know. And I'm damned good at both. But with women—no. I've become resigned to bachelorhood. . . ."

"We'll have to do something about that," Guy said. "Come along. . . ."

The house where Elizabeth Melton lived was not far out of town. It had the advantage of privacy. They got out of the cab and walked down the path to the door. But before they could knock upon it, an explosion stopped them.

"It's all your fault, Kil Mallory!" Liz Melton screamed. "I want to know what you're going to do about it!"

"Nothing," Kilrain said tiredly. "Liz, I—"

"Nothing!" Liz' shriek was ear-shattering. "You get me with child, and you say you'll do nothing! Why you miserable, low down, stinking, rat-bastard, I'll—"

"The lady's vocabulary," Guy whispered, "is choice, to say the least—"

"Oh, come off of it, Liz," Kilrain said. "I come down here once a month at most. Who's to say what goes on when I'm away? You, my dove, were no languishing virgin when I met you. I've got five dollars that says you don't know who the brat's pa is, yourself!"

"Gallant, isn't he?" Guy grinned.

"We'd better go," James whispered. "The moment's most inopportune—"

Another shriek drowned his words. They started for the gate. But, before they reached it, the door burst open and Kilrain flew out, with Liz behind him, swinging a hatchet at his head. Willard James stepped aside with amazing decorum. Guy did the same thing, but with less grace. He waited until Liz had gone by him, then he seized her from behind, pinioning her arms.

"Leave him be, Liz," he chuckled. "Can't you see the bastard's not worth killing?"

At the sound of his voice, Kilrain whirled. He stood there helplessly, staring at Guy Falks.

"You spy!" he said at last. "You filthy spy! I reckon now you'll rush back to Fairoaks to tell Jo Ann—"

"You know me better than that, Kil," Guy said calmly. " 'Pears to me you've got troubles enough without my adding to them. Will, take the ax away from her. Murdering this mangy polecat won't help her case at all. . . ."

"Oh, Mr. James!" Liz blubbered, "you know what he's done? He's got me that way and—"

Guy studied the woman. She was a big blonde, not a day under thirty. She was coarse, corpulent, drink-ravaged, the very announcement of feminine vulgarity. If she were pregnant, as she claimed, he was certain it hadn't been an accident. She had achieved the expectant state voluntarily—with Kil, or with someone else, and turned to him because of his reputation for great wealth.

Kilrain was talking again.

"If," he granted, "you set foot on my place again, Guy Falks, I'll have my niggers cane you and throw you off! If you come within a mile of Jo Ann, I'll pistol you like a dog!"

"My," Guy said mildly, "he does talk big, doesn't he, Will? Look, Kil, there's a couple of things wrong with those statements. First of all, you can't throw me off your place, or have your niggers cane me, because you haven't any place, or any niggers either. Ever see these before?"

He took Kilrain's promissory notes out of his pocket and held them out. Kilrain recognized them at once, all the color draining out of his florid face.

"Where the devil did you get those?" he whispered.

"Paid off your debts," Guy said, "on both plantations. Reckon you'll have to get used to the idea of our being neighbors, Kil; because I'm taking over Malloryhill—"

"And Fairoaks?" Kilrain got out.

"You can stay," Guy said, "as long as you behave yourself. Work the place, and don't make any more debts against it. As my guest at Fairoaks, you sure Lord can't use it as security against any new loans. Stay out of Natchez. You've got yourself a good woman, and you damned well can't afford two, now—"

"You mean," Liz burst out suddenly, "that he ain't really rich?"

"Honey," Kil laughed bitterly, "you've been barking up the wrong tree all the time. Reckon you'd better find yourself another pappy for lil' Nell, 'cause I ain't got two coppers to jingle together in my jeans!"

"Oh!" the woman cried, "you lying, mangy—"

"That's enough, Liz," Willard James said icily. "There are gentlemen present, you know."

"Let's get back to your second bright remark about shooting

me," Guy said. "Beyond the fact that you have no grounds, I might remind you I'm a pretty fair hand with a gun, myself. So don't tempt me, Kil—"

"All right," Kilrain said. "I guess you've got me sewed up in a croakerbag, Guy. But man to man, I want to make you a real sporting proposition. You've been over those notes?"

"Yes," Guy said.

"Then you know there's not one note outstanding against the house, or the grounds it stands on. So here's my proposition. I'll wager you the house and the grounds against those notes you hold. Winner take all. One poker hand—draw or stud. What do you say, Guy?"

"Why should he?" Willard James said, "when he already—"

"Hold it, Will!" Guy said warningly. "Let's leave things as they are. The answer to that proposition, Kil—is, no."

"I knew you weren't a sport," Kilrain sneered.

"Reckon I'm sport enough, Kil," Guy said dryly; "but I won't gamble with Jo Ann's future. As long as things are like they are, you can't leave her homeless, since you don't have anything left to pawn. So forget it."

"You take mighty tender care of my wife," Kil said. "If I thought—"

"But you don't," Guy said. "You know better. Come on, let's have a nice, quiet drink somewhere, and forget the hard feelings, shall we?"

"All right," Kilrain said sullenly. "Come on, then—"

"What about me?" Liz Melton wailed.

"Aw, to hell with you!" Kilrain said. "Come along, you two!"

On the way to the bar, Kilrain noticed, apparently for the first time, the handbills littering the street. He bent and picked one up. He read it rapidly, and the glow of the incurable gambler appeared once more in his eyes.

"Now here's a real sporting proposition!" he chuckled. "Are you willing, Guy, to bet on which one of those opera singer's boats'll get to New Orleans first?"

Guy looked at him, coolly.

"What are the stakes, Kil?" he said.

"Five hundred dollars. I can raise that much. Come on, boy, what do you say?"

"All right," Guy said evenly. "To show you I can be a sport, I'll take that bet—and give you first choice. Take your pick, Kil. . . ."

"The *Tom Tyler!*" Kilrain said at once, "and lil' Castiglione. They say she's one hot number!"

"Done," Guy Falks said.

"Good!" Kilrain said. "Now come on, Guy!"

"Come on where?" Guy said.

"To buy ourselves tickets on the boats. I'm going to ride down the river with my Guinea Warbler! Bet she'll be a different girl by the time we get to New Orleans . . ."

"All right," Guy said. "It might be fun at that. What about you, Will?"

"Oh, I'll come along for the ride," Willard James said.

Although the race was only two weeks off, there were still plenty of tickets left for the down river trip. The citizens of Natchez differed from the New Orleanais in this: they could take their culture or leave it. And mostly, be it said, they left it. Guy was able to get a stateroom aboard the *Queen of Natchez* for himself and Willard James with the greatest of ease. Kilrain had equal success in procuring accommodations on the *Tom Tyler*. Guy wondered where Kil got the price of his fare. He guessed he had won it gambling.

The same night, the three of them sat over their drinks in a Natchez tavern. Kilrain was as affable and friendly as it was possible for a man to be. And as drunk, though it didn't show at first.

"Sorry I lost my temper this morning," he said thickly to Guy. "But it's no fun being caught with your trousers at half mast. Thought you came around snooping on purpose—"

"I did," Guy said flatly. "I was curious, Kil. Wanted to see the woman that could wean you away from Jo Ann. But I didn't come to get something on you in order to use it against you. I just wanted to see this Liz Melton, that was all. . . ."

"And now that you have?" Kilrain said mockingly.

"I don't understand it. I just plain don't understand it—"

"That's because you're in love with my wife. Wait a minute! Don't start bristling on me. Facts are facts, no matter how unpleasant they are. A man can't help how he feels; and I don't hold it against you. No reason for me to. In your way, you're too strait-laced to try to do anything about it. In the second, angel that Jo is, it wouldn't do you any good if you tried—"

Guy could see Willard James' face tightening in disgust.

"Look, Kil," he said patiently, "don't you think this is one

281

hell of a conversation for two men to be having? Even two friends, which, in a funny way, we still are?"

"Yes," Kilrain said drunkenly. "It's goddamn bad taste. But then my taste's notoriously bad. Liz proves that—"

"Since you feel like talking," Guy said, "tell me about it. How'd you get mixed up with—that?"

Kilrain threw back his head and laughed aloud.

"That!" he chuckled. "Funny how right 'that' is. Hell, I've known her for years. Never interested me much. Jo—drove me to her. Jo's so—so immaculate. So patient and dutiful. Disapproving of the hell and ginger in me, but never saying anything. Hell, boy, I want me a woman who pants and sweats and screams and bites—you understand. Want her to smell like a woman, not like soap, perfume, and rice powder—"

Willard James stood up, his face working.

"If you don't mind, Guy," he said, "I'm going for a walk. I feel the need for—air."

Kilrain grinned.

"Sit down Mr. James," he said. "You've no call to act so high and mighty. The sins of the flesh are one thing; but they stack up a damn sight better to most men's viewing than living off folks' life blood. . . ."

"That's enough, Kil," Guy said icily. "Sit down, Will. I can handle him."

"Then I'll leave him in your hands, Guy," Willard James said, "but they'll have need of washing, I think." Then he stalked out into the night. There was, Guy decided, a hell of a lot to be said in favor of Will James.

"All right, Kil," he said, "this has gone far enough—"

"It's a pity," Kilrain said morosely. "Jo's too good for me. You're more her kind. Don't reckon I ever loved her, really. She was always too much like one of those painted plaster angels they hang up in the Catholic church to suit my taste. But now she's stuck with me—and she deserves better. But she'll never leave me. Even after I lose Fairoaks, for I will lose it, with my gambling blood'n rotten luck, she'll stick. She'll go hungry; but she'll never bend her proud head. And one day she'll come to hate me—if she doesn't already, in secret. I couldn't stand that, Guy! I couldn't stand—"

And the tears were there, clouding his bleary, bloodshot eyes.

"Come on, Kil," Guy said. "I'll take you home, now. . . ."

Nothing was simple in life; nothing at all. How the hell can you hate a man, he thought bitterly, when you pity the bastard so?

He spent the better part of those two weeks getting settled at Malloryhill. Willard James and Fitzhugh helped him. The three of them had become fast friends. The banker, for all his forty-eight years, and his appearance of having been carved from river ice, was a decidedly likable person once you got to know him. The two weeks were marred by two incidents, the first one more humorous than serious.

They came in from the fields one day, to find one of the housemaids writhing in agony on the floor. All they could get out of her between her screams was:

"Nikia put a hoodoo on me! Nikia put a hoodoo on me!"

Guy summoned the two pygmies.

"Now, what the hell's going on?" he demanded.

"She slap me, Bwana," Sifa said; "so Nikia him give her the eye. Night time come, Esamba eat her brains, leave her one big damn crazy fool!"

"Nikia—" Guy said.

"No, Master!" Nikiabo said defiantly. "She one mean bad bitchy old gal!"

Nikia, Guy thought with wry amusement, was learning Mississippi Negro dialect damned fast.

"Take it off of her, Nikia," Guy said.

"You mean you believe in this nonsense, Guy?" Willard James asked in pure wonder.

"Did you ever live in Africa, Will? You believe in the Resurrection, which is a thing you've never seen. I've seen Esamba blow out the light in people's brains. God damn it, Nikia, take the Ju Ju off!"

"No!" the pygmy spat.

"All right," Guy said, then switched into Swahili. "You have lost the strength in your right arm, oh Nikiabo! Your right leg is crippled. You can no longer lift your arm, or walk!"

"What—what the devil are you saying, Guy?" Fitzhugh whispered.

"I put a bigger Ju Ju on him," Guy said calmly. "Watch this: Nikia! Lift your right arm!"

The pygmy tried. Beads of sweat stood out on his ebony forehead; but he could not lift his arm.

"Now walk!" Guy roared.

The tiny black took one step and crashed to the floor. He lay there, crying.

"Take it off, Bwana!" he wept. "Take off the Ju Ju! I be good! I take Ju Ju off bitchy nigger gal!"

"All right," Guy said; then in Swahili: "The curse is gone, Nikia!"

At once Nikia got to his feet. He ran over to the prostrate girl, and stood there jabbering away, making cabalistic motions with his hands.

The girl stopped screaming. She relaxed into motionlessness. Then, her eyes wide with terror, she leaped to her feet and fled from the room.

"I," Willard James whispered, "feel the need of a drink. A good, stiff drink!"

"Me, too," Fitzhugh croaked. "Guy! How in the name of living hell—?"

"Don't ask me to explain it," Guy said solemnly. "I can't. All I know is that it works—"

The second incident was quite another thing. Guy was out in the section nearest Fairoaks, when he saw Jo Ann come riding up to the fence. He moved over to greet her, then he saw her eyes. They were—ice.

"Kil told me," she said, "that you have covered all his debts. I see you've taken over Malloryhill. That is, of course, your right—"

Guy sat there on the black, looking at her.

"Go on," he said quietly.

"If you had dispossessed us," Jo said, "I'd have called you a scoundrel and a swine. But Kil tells me you have no intention of putting us off the place—"

"I haven't," Guy said. "So what does that make me, now?"

"A subtler kind of swine, I think. You have no right to do this, Guy Falks! Why must you hurt him so?"

"Lord God, Jo," Guy said, "I never thought—"

"Oh, yes you did! That you could wound him in his pride as a man. Or else cause me to despise him for being weak enough to accept your bounty. But it won't work, Guy. You can take over Fairoaks, too. We're leaving!"

Guy sat there looking at her, the pain moving in his eyes.

"Where will you go?" he asked. He saw from her confusion that she had not thought of that. "I asked you where will you go?" he repeated. "What will you use for money? Who'll take care of your father, even if you go to work—as a governess or a lady's companion? Because Kil won't work. There's nothing he knows except planting. That leaves him one opening: to take the job of overseer on somebody else's place. Think he'll accept that?"

All the color fled from her face.

"Oh! Oh, you—"

"If he'll even leave," Guy went on imperturbably, "which I doubt. Have you asked him? I can see you haven't. I'd suggest you'd better. Yes, Jo, go ask Kil how he feels about taking my bounty, as you call it. Find out if his pride—the pride you think he has—is wounded enough for him to leave. Go on. And next time before you come to accuse me, be sure of where you stand . . ."

"Oh," she said again, "you are a swine, Guy Falks! And not even a subtle one at that!"

The next time Guy saw Kilrain Mallory was the morning that they waited for the *Queen of Natchez* and the *Tom Tyler* to put into the landing below Natchez. Early as it was, Kil was already drunk. Drink was fast becoming his only refuge.

"What's the matter with you, boy?" Guy said, not unkindly.

"Women!" Kilrain said morosely. "Guy—she hasn't spoken to me in a week! And you know why?"

"No," Guy said softly.

"Because I won't agree to leave the place. Says a real man wouldn't consent to live off a friend's charity. Maybe she's right; but what can I do? I don't know a blessed thing but planting. What does she expect me to do? Hire out as an overseer?"

I would, Guy thought clearly, coldly; before I'd accept the slightest favor from anybody. But you haven't got that, have you, Kil? Reckon you never were anything more than breath and britches.

"Told her, 'Guy won't put us off. Good ol' Guy won't put us off.' So she ups and screams at me: 'Don't you ever mention that blackguard's name to me as long as I live!' God, boy, what'd you ever do to her?"

"Heaped coals of fire upon her head, I reckon," Guy said.

"Don't understand her. You give us a fighting chance, and 'stead of appreciating it—"

"Forget it. Tell me, Kil, what do you intend to do about the fair Liz? Doctor Morris says she really is in the family way—"

"Nothing," Kil spat. "How the devil do I know the lil' bastard's mine? That there Liz is the biggest whore in the whole state of Mississippi!"

Guy stood there looking at him.

You poor devil, he thought. You poor, poor devil. Haven't got a hope left, have you? Nor a prayer. Reckon it'd be better all around if the *Tom Tyler* gets there first. . . .

It might have, but for Kilrain Mallory. After spending most of the day in vain attempts to attract Giulietta Castiglione's attention, he made his way to the engine room. He called the engineer aside and showed him a roll of bills big enough to choke a horse. Most of the roll was made up of newspaper cut to size; but the engineer saw only the few twenty-dollar bills that Kil had wrapped around the outside. Kil peeled off two of them and gave them to him.

"What's this for, sir?" the engineer said.

"A few miles above New Orleans," Kil said, "you tie down the safety valve. Get us a long lead before you ease it off. Do what I say, and you get the rest of this. This here's one race I don't mean to lose!"

"But sir—that's awful dangerous!" the engineer said.

"If the pressure gets too high, ease her off. But win this race, and you get yourself this wad!"

Then he went back out on the deck.

As they came abreast of La Place, a tiny Creole village some miles north of New Orleans, Guy and Willard James were standing on the deck of the *Queen of Natchez*, chatting with Norma Dupré. The diva was a fine woman, a big, healthy Norman peasant girl. She was blonde and rosy, and strikingly good-looking. She was exactly the type of woman who would have appealed to Kilrain, at least physically. But there was nothing vulgar about her. She was simple and good. Except for the fortune, or misfortune of being born with a lovely coloratura soprano voice, she would have made some sturdy Norman farmer a good wife, and presented him with at least twelve sons.

She was delighted to be able to speak her native tongue

286

with someone. The French that Doña Pilar had taught Guy, for all its American accent, amazed her. She declared it much better than her own rustic, Norman French.

Guy saw that Will was feeling out of things, so he switched into English.

"We're leaving the banker here out on a limb," he said. "Let's talk American for a while, Mademoiselle—"

"Le banquier?" Norma said in French; and a shrewd sparkle came into her little blue eyes. She was all French peasant despite her voice. "Is it that he is then—rich?" she said.

"Enormement! Besides, he's terribly struck with you, Norma—" Which was true. Ever since the beginning of the voyage, Willard James had been devouring her with his eyes.

"Ah, so? Then I will be very, very nice to him. The singing, it grows tiresome, you understand M'sieur Guy—and a banker—"

"Bless you, my children!" Guy chuckled. He leaned forward, close to Will's ear. "Careful, boy," he whispered, "you've made yourself a conquest. See that you handle it right. . . ."

To his vast amazement Willard James actually blushed. Well, I'll be damned, Guy thought. Maybe I've yanked old Will off the shelf at that!

He strolled forward, leaving them there. The two packets were very close together now, panting downstream, hurling their four great plumes of black smoke hard into the heavens; their big sidewheels digging in. The prow of the *Queen* was perhaps a yard ahead. Then, over the eight or ten yards that separated the steamboats, Guy saw Giulietta Castiglione for the first time. She was standing on the *Tom Tyler* deck. Edward Mulhouse was with her—and Kilrain Mallory. She looked very annoyed. But even in her wrath she was the most beautiful thing Guy Falks had ever seen in all his life. Her hair was black—which was to say nothing. It was more than black. It was inky, the darkness on the deep before God spoke and light was. And her eyes—were blacker than that. Which wasn't possible; but they were.

Her lips were like the wine of her ancestors' native Tuscany. And her figure under that tight-fitting bodice—

He kept staring at her. At that moment, Jo Ann Mallory vanished very silently out of time and mind.

Just look at her! he thought. She acts like she was getting set to explode—

The moment he shaped that thought, he was sorry; for it was at the exact instant that the *Tom Tyler* blew.

He watched it in a frozen horror that slowed the terrible things happening, in the fractional parts of seconds, into a nightmare crawling. He saw the thick hunk of iron, part of the walking beam, he guessed, hit Kil Mallory in the small of the back and sweep him overboard. He saw Giulietta open her mouth to scream; but the blast lifted her and hurled her into the river between the two packets. He saw Edward Mulhouse wrapped in a mist of scalding steam. But he didn't see anything more, for he was already out of his boots and jacket and hat, diving very cleanly for the spot where Giulietta struggled in the water.

He almost fetched bottom; it took him a lung-cracking age to claw his way to the surface. In two swift strokes he reached her, and wrapped his fingers in the foaming midnight of her hair.

"Now just you relax," he panted. "Don't fight me, and we'll be all right—"

To his relief, she obeyed instantly. He saw Kilrain in the water a few yards to his left. Kil was pinned under a mass of wreckage. Only his head was above water. His face was white with despair.

"Hang on, Kil!" Guy shouted. "I'll be back in a minute!"

"Don't leave me!" Kil shrieked. "Don't, Guy!" Then, his voice choking with rage and fear: "You bastard—letting me drown so you can get Fairoaks—and Jo! Damn you, Guy! Damn you! Damn—"

Five strokes brought him to the *Queen's* side. Eager hands reached down for them both. Guy could hear the commands:

"Stop the larboard! Stop the starboard! Set her back on both!"

Then Giulietta was lifted up and away from him. Hands grasped at his shoulders.

"Turn me loose!" he roared. "I've got to go back for Kil!"

He whirled, splashing. The distance was nothing: six or eight yards. He was there in seconds, clawing at the wreckage.

He saw then why Kil didn't sink. A piece of the deck was under him, buoying him up. Ropes hurled from the steamer snaked into the water around them.

"You—you," Kil gasped. "Let me drown, and you got Jo—and Fairoaks. And you can't do it . . . You're just too damned white. . . ."

Guy treaded water, and stared at him. That was very probably true; but it didn't matter, now.

He eased Kilrain out of the wreckage, and looped a rope around him. He saw that Kil was being dragged rapidly through the water toward the *Queen*. Then he looked around for other people to save. He got two more out before the *Queen*'s boat got to work. After that, he had nothing more to do. They dragged him up on deck and he sat there trembling and coughing up the muddy water he had swallowed. Somebody handed him a bottle of whiskey. It made a good burning, going down.

People crowded around him, all talking at once. Then a Negro steward was working his way through the crowd.

"Mister Falks, suh," he said, "Miss Castiglione is axing to see you—"

"All right," Guy said. He got up woodenly, and followed the Negro. Pools of water dripped sullenly from his clothes. His hair was a matted mess; he stank to high heaven with the river's muddy stench.

They had put Giulietta in Norma Dupré's stateroom. She had gotten out of her clothes, and was wrapped in one of her colleague's robes. It went around her, twice. Norma and Will James were there with her.

She got up as he came in, and stood there, staring at him. Then she came up to him, and took him by the arm.

"You know," she said, and her voice, speaking, was liquid music, the loveliest sound that Guy Falks had ever heard; "I've changed my mind. When I asked them to send up the man who had saved me, I was going to give him a kiss—and thank him very nicely for having saved my life. But now—"

"But now, I don't even get my kiss?" Guy said.

She hung back, smiling at him. Her smile was something to see.

"Oh, yes!" she said, "but for another reason—a far better reason. Before it was just gratitude—but now it's—"

"What is it, Giulietta?" Guy asked, his voice deep.

"Happiness," she said gaily, "at my luck. I would gladly be blown into the river twice a day, if I could be saved—by you!"

"By me?" he got out. "I'm pretty thick-headed, I reckon. Because I just don't understand—"

She came up on tiptoe, her mouth inches from his own.

"Didn't anybody ever tell Guy Falks," she whispered, "that he is the most gorgeous male creature in the world?"

He went with her to the hospital in New Orleans to visit Edward Mulhouse, wrapped in grease-soaked bandages from head to foot like a mummy, to ease the terrible scalds he had sustained. Afterwards, they called upon Kil in another room. Guy had seen that his injured friend—for Kil was that after all—had the best of everything. Only the best was not enough. For Lucien Terrebonne, the doctor, stood beside the bed, and said in French, knowing that Kil would not understand:

"He will never walk again, this gentleman here. From his hips on down, he is totally paralyzed. . . ."

"How sad!" Giulietta whispered, and took Guy's arm. "Come, Guy—we'd better go now—"

Guy took her back to the Hotel St. Louis, where they were both staying. Norma was not in her room. She was out with Will James—as usual.

"Giulia," he whispered.

"No, Guy," she said, "not here. Listen, my tall and impatient lover—and I will tell you a thing. In the Vieux Carré there are little apartments to be had for a song, are there not? With a little maid in apron and cap. Where one lets down a bucket on a rope with money in it for the greengrocer and the butcher from the gallerie?"

"Yes," Guy said, "that's true—all right."

"Then if my tall and beautiful lover were to sally forth and find such a place for himself and *tua moglie,* who would know? Especially since we cannot open until Edward is well enough to manage things—weeks from now—"

"Giulietta—" Guy croaked.

"I will tell you another thing. I—I am impatient, too! So go!"

He had the little apartment on the third floor of an old building on Royal Street, before night. The mulatto maid in apron and cap. The pail on the rope for buying things from the merchants down below without having to stir from the house. Then he rushed back to the hotel.

Willard James and Norma Dupré were there. They were beaming.

"Guy," Willard said proudly, "we—we're going to be married—"

290

"Congratulations!" Guy flung back over his shoulder, as he dragged Giulietta from the room by one arm. "Come on, Giulia!"

"You weren't very nice," Giulietta pouted, as they climbed into the hansom.

"I'll be nice tomorrow," Guy promised, "or the day after—"

She stood in the little sitting room, looking around. She turned to the mulatto maid.

"You will go downstairs," she said, "and bring us up some cheese and cakes and fruit and wine. Much wine. You will place them here upon this table—and then you will go away. For three whole days and nights. Then you will come back. But not before. *Tu comprends ça, cherie?*"

"Yes, ma'am!" the girl giggled. "I understands all right, me! Y'all throw down that bucket on a string, and I'll put the stuff in it and not even come back upstairs!"

"Good!" Giulietta laughed, gaily. " *'Voir, ma petite*—'til three days!"

"Sure you don't want four, ma'am?" the girl cackled. "He look awful strong this gentleman, him!"

Giulietta looked up at Guy, mischievously.

"In three days," she said, "he will look all wilted like an ancient salad that has been left in the sun. For I, too, *ma petite,* in some ways, am very strong!"

23

Guy stood on the gallery of the little apartment, and looked, not down at the quiet street below him, but upward at the stars. It was a very warm night, and as it was nearly one o'clock in the morning, the city was very still. The night sounds rode in upon him: the far-away, soft clip-clopping of hooves upon cobblestones; the muted jingle of harness; the song of a pensive drunkard, coming late to his home, hanging mournfully upon the air; the slam of a door, somewhere nearby, in some house, in some street. . . .

He had made the one concession to conventionality of slipping on a pair of trousers; both his feet and his chest were bare. He folded his great, muscular arms across his chest and stood there, feeling contentment curling soft and warm down to the very marrow of his bones.

Behind him, through the open door, he could hear Giulietta splashing about in the slipper-shaped tub. People ordinarily didn't take baths at one o'clock in the morning; but as he had already learned, to his delight, what people ordinarily did, and what Giulietta Castiglione did, bore no relationship whatsoever.

Then, suddenly, all the night was silvered with the purest sound he had ever heard. He stiffened, feeling icy fingers racing up and down his spine. No human voice could make music like that: a violin, perhaps, or a cello; no, not even those; they had not this roundness, this purity, this utter absence of edge. She was simply running a scale, her voice changing in midflight from cello, to flute, to violin to—nothing could do that! Nothing and nobody. But Giulietta could. He knew he was listening to one of the great voices of the age, indeed of any age. The scale stopped; she swung into "Robert, *toi que j'aime*," from Meyerbeer's *Robert le Diable;* singing it with such haunting tenderness that he, who had not wept since the night Beeljie died, found himself blinking furiously, feeling a rough-edged stone bigger than half the world at the base of his throat, shutting off his breath. . . .

She broke off suddenly.

"Guy!" she called out gaily. "Come scrub my back!"

He went into the kitchen where the tub was. She lay back against the tub in a mountain of suds, the air heavy with the perfume she had poured into the water with a reckless hand. She smiled at him, lazily, and stretching out her hand, gave him the sponge.

"Lean forward," he growled. She did so, slowly; and he swept the sponge over her shoulders and back, while she held her hair upward out of the way with both hands.

"Sing that again," he said; "that—that song you were singing just now. . . ."

"No!" she laughed. "To hear Castiglione, Signor Guy, one must pay!"

"All right," he grinned. "How much?"

"A kiss—no! Not a kiss; because kisses between us never end with kisses, do they, lover mine? And now that I'm all clean and smell nice— Wait; I'll think of something else. Now hand me the towel. . . ."

She stood up, and stepped out of the tub.

"There ought to be a law," Guy said thickly, "against your ever putting on clothes!"

"Ah?" she said, "but that would not be nice, I think. Would you like for all men to see—what is only—yours?"

"Hell, no!" he laughed. "Far as I'm concerned, when we go out, I'd like to drape you in a mother hubbard, and ten yards of veiling. . . ."

"Not that. For then you would not have the pleasure of seeing the envy in their eyes—"

"Envy!" Guy said. "What those hombres are thinking about when they look at you, they ought to be horsewhipped for— maybe even shot."

"And what were you thinking about when first you saw me, —that did not also merit a whipping?"

"No," Guy said slowly. "Funny, but I didn't think about— this. I just thought: How beautiful she is—how wonderfully, perfectly beautiful—"

"For that," Giulietta whispered, "you get your kiss! There and there—and there! Now let us go out upon the gallery, and look at the stars."

"Like that?" Guy gasped.

"Why not? It is very late, and everyone is sleeping. I love to feel the night air on my skin. It is cool, with such a lovely coolness—come on!"

She seized him by the hand and ran through the little apartment. He followed her, in wonder, and in joy. They stood upon the little balcony, with their arms around one another. She cradled her head against his shoulder. He could smell the perfume in her hair.

Funny, he thought. I'm scared. I'm happy, too happy, so I'm scared. This is too perfect. It can't last. Nothing so god damned beautiful ever does—

"Guy," she murmured, "you said you did not think—of this. Why?"

"Don't know. But I didn't. Reckon I thought you were too lovely to be real. . . ."

"But I am real," she said. "Very real. Just, different from most women, I suppose—"

"By God, you are!" Guy chuckled. "Tell me, Giulia, how did you manage to escape the vapors and the faints and the plain damn bitchiness of being a woman? I never met a woman like you before. I didn't know they existed. . . ."

"They are—rare," Giulietta said. "I was lucky. My uncle saved me. My father's brother. He was a musician, a very, very bad musician; but he loved it. One day, when I was very little, he heard me sing. So he stole me from my parents and started to train my voice. He knew they'd never part with me otherwise—"

"You say he saved you," Guy said; "from what, Giulietta?"

"From stupid things that make no sense. From being ashamed of my body. From the curious idea that a good woman has no feelings. I loved my uncle. He was a vagabond and a drunkard and a good-for-nothing. But he was very wise. He scoffed at all of the things that most people believe in. 'Giulietta,' he used to say, 'men run from those good women who keep their hearts packed in ice. But no man ever left a woman who keeps him laughing all day, and busy all night.' Besides, I like being loved; I like to love. And how is one to express what one feels? By singing a love song?"

"Yes," Guy said, "when they can sing like you, yes!"

"True," Giulietta said. "Singing makes me happy. But not so happy as being in your arms. Singing, and the other things, the kissing, and playing at love, are like the overture. But there must be the grand finale, no? So I love you with my body, and I am not ashamed. Our bodies were made for that— to delight each other. And how you do delight me, my Guy! Ai-yeee—"

"What ails you, Giulia?" Guy said.

"I have talked too much—of love. Turn me loose, Guy—"

He did so and stepped back, staring at her wonderingly. She wheeled without a word, and fled into the house. He stood there staring after her, frowning, thinking: Now what the devil—?

Then he heard her voice, darkly golden, soaring up from the bedroom, softly, sweetly, with so much warmth, tenderness, invitation, singing:

"Deh vieni, non tardar, o gioia bella—"

He had never even heard of Mozart's *Le Nozze di Figaro;* he knew only a few words of Italian; but the invitation in Susanna's aria as Giulietta sang it, was unmistakable. Besides, the words were very much like Spanish:

"You must come, do not delay—"

But he delayed all the same, even after he understood it. It was such a delight to hear her sing.

That next morning, riding toward the hospital in the little wickerwork trap he had rented, he kept watching her out of the corner of his eye. Her face was still—very still, and sad. He saw suddenly, a tear steal from beneath one eyelid.

"Giulia," he asked, in alarm, "what ails you?"

She turned to him, clutching his arm convulsively, burying her face against his sleeve.

"I'm afraid!" she sobbed. "Oh, Guy, I'm so afraid!"

"Of what, little Giulia?" he said gently.

"Of—of losing you!" she wept.

He threw back his head and laughed aloud—mostly from the relief that she, by sharing his very private fear, had negated it.

"Just how do you aim to lose me, Giulia, baby?" he chuckled. "Shot gun? Poison? An ax?"

She tilted her face toward his, her black eyes misty.

"No," she whispered. "You will leave me. . . ."

"Good Lord Jesus!" he exploded. "What a silly idea!"

"No, it is not silly. Tell me, Guy, do you wish to marry me?"

"Of course," he said at once.

"Oh!" she wailed. "You see! That was just what I was afraid of!"

He sat there, staring at her. "I'll be damned if I can understand you," he said. "You talk like you love me; you damned sure act like it; yet when I say I want to marry you, you—"

"I know," she said. "I am difficult to understand. I love you. I think that when you do leave me, I shall kill myself. Wait! Do not interrupt me. But I cannot marry you, however much I want to; and I do want to, Guy—oh, I do!"

"Why can't you?" Guy growled. "Are you married already or something?"

"No! If I were, I should not look at you. I am not a cheat. It is all entirely your fault! You are just too much man!"

"This," Guy said dryly, "is getting clearer by the minute. . . ."

"Listen. If I married you, you would want to take me to live upon that farm of yours, no?"

"It's not a farm. It's a plantation. But apart from that, yes."

"And I, if I married you, would want you to go with me everywhere. Rome, Milan, Paris, Venice—wherever I go to sing. And this you would not, could not do. You could not be dragged over the world like a—a doll. Nor could I bury my voice upon a farm. Whom would I sing to, there?"

"To me," Guy said.

"With all my heart. But it is not enough. My uncle used to say a voice like mine is born only once in a hundred years. And that it does not belong to its accidental possessor; it belongs to the world. . . ."

"I'm a part of the world," Guy said.

"A very, very small part, for all that to me you bestride the mountains, and hide your face among the clouds. You have not the right to ask this of me, nor I, to give it—"

"So," Guy said bitterly, "the three days were enough, Giulia?"

"No! Not three days, nor three lifetimes. It is just that, being what we are, we can only be together by one of us destroying the other. Bury me upon a farm, to sing to the cows, and I would die. Drag you about the world, a puppet on a woman's string, and you would be offended to the core of your manhood. You'd come to hate me. And that would destroy me, too. . . ."

"So," Guy said bleakly, "what do you propose?"

"That we stay together all we can. Before we open at the St. Charles, I would like to visit your fa—plantation. You have said it is lovely, and I want to see it. After that, I hope you will go away with me—like we are now, untied by any connection except the love we bear each other. Then, when you have tired of me, there will be nothing to stop you from leaving. . . ."

"Or vice versa," Guy said.

"Never. I shall tire of you the night they put the pennies on my eyes. Not even then. I think you will hear me always in the wind and the rain, singing the saddest love songs in the world, so long as you have ears to hear. . . ."

"You're a strange little creature, Giulia," Guy said tenderly.

"I know. And I know another thing now. I have never loved before, even though I thought I had. And my lover, my heart, I shall never, never love again; for I am yours forever—with you, or apart. . . ."

"Let us not talk nonsense, Giulietta," Guy said.

"Nor any more sadness!" she said, all gaiety again. "Come, let us go see poor Edward, the mummy!"

Mulhouse was much better. But they had not yet taken off the bandages which covered all his face except his eyes, so

296

he could not talk. And the one-sided conversation was decidedly a bore. Guy could see the impresario watching him
speculatively. It made him damned uncomfortable.

But when they went to visit Kilrain Mallory, it was worse.
For Jo Ann was there. Her eyes were red from weeping, but
her dignity and her control were superb.

Guy presented Giulietta to her; and even as they shook
hands and murmured polite acknowledgments, the very air
crackled with tension. Two words, and they already despised
each other with cordial female malice. And for no reason that
he could see. Jo Ann, at their last meeting, had called him a
swine. Moreover, she was married to—this poor, bedeviled
half of a man.

She dropped Giulietta's hand as one drops a live snake, and
turned to him, an excess of warmth in her tone.

"I want to thank you, Guy," she said, "for saving my husband's life. . . ."

"He," Giulietta said in unfeigned astonishment, "is your
husband?"

"Of course," Jo Ann said. "What did you think, Miss Castiglione?"

"I—I don't know. Forgive me; but aboard the *Tom Tyler*,
he seemed so—so very unattached. . . ."

"To some women," Jo Ann said icily, "all men seem unattached, until they can remedy the situation. . . ."

"True," Giulietta smiled. "But, fortunately, tastes differ.
As for your husband, the chief reason I thought him unmarried is that I could scarcely imagine a woman's being sufficiently interested in him to bother—especially not so attractive a woman as yourself. . . ."

"Oh!" Jo Ann gasped. "I have never—"

"Girls," Guy chuckled, "you aren't being very nice. And if
you don't stop it, I'll take my cane to the pair of you." He
turned to the still figure on the bed. "How do you feel, old
man?" he said gently.

"Like hell," Kil growled. "I haven't any pain; but that's
what's bad. If I could even hurt, there'd be some hope. God,
Guy! What are we going to do now? Me crippled up like this
with that place to run. . . ."

"Jo'll manage," Guy said. "All she's got to do is to keep
after young Stevens. Fairoaks is a good producer, and—as for
those debts—" He took the notes from his side-pocket, and
tore them across. "Here," he said, and tossed them on the bed.

297

"Here's something to get well on, boy—"

"God damn it, Guy," Kilrain choked.

Jo Ann stood up suddenly and came over to where Guy sat.

"I wish we didn't have to accept this—this gesture," she said. "My pride tells me it's wrong. But we do. There's no way out. Forgive me for what I said that time. I was wrong."

Then, with a quick sidelong glance at Giulietta, she bent and kissed him, not upon the cheek, as he fully expected her to, but on the mouth.

The next instant, she was spinning around under Giulietta's far-from-gentle grasp. Before Guy could get to his feet, Giulietta had slapped her, stingingly, across the face. Jo stood there, staring at her, all the color gone from her face, except the widespread print of Giulietta's fingers, whiter than the rest, at first, then slowly turning red.

"You are not to kiss him!" Giulietta spat, "not even in this mockery of gratitude. He is mine, you comprehend, all mine, and any woman who touches him—"

"Giulia," Guy said evenly, "that is quite enough."

"No," she wept. "It is more than enough! It is too much! When I came in here, I saw how she looked at you! They are all alike, these icy blondes! So cold to look at, but underneath—"

"A woman," Jo finished for her quietly. "I apologize, Miss Castiglione, for having kissed your—your lover. I'll even forget that slap. As you said, tastes differ—and so do standards of behavior. Mine, my dear, do not permit me to descend to the level of a public brawl. I wish you joy of him; for though tastes do differ, if I may quote you once again—in this, at least, yours is very good."

Giulietta took a backward step. She stood there looking at Jo Ann, her face piteous.

"I am ashamed," she whispered. "I have behaved badly. And you have made it worse, by behaving well. It is with this that you Nordics have taken over the world—with this *sang-froid*. We can never manage it, we Latins. We have the sun in us and music and wine and fire. We are always singing—or storming. It is a weakness, I think. Will you forgive me, please?"

"Gladly," Jo Ann said, "if only because you love him. For you do, don't you? You really do. . . ."

"Yes," Giulietta said. "So much, so very much!"

"He deserves that," Jo said. "I only hope you'll make him

happy. Malloryhill has lacked a mistress for a long time—"

"I—" Giulietta began, but she could not finish. Under Jo Ann's steady gaze, she faltered, and turned away.

"Guy," she said, "will you take me home now?"

"All right," Guy said. "Be seeing you all—at home—"

Kilrain raised himself up on both elbows and gazed at them.

"You lucky, lucky bastard!" he said.

Guy knew that when he took Giulietta up to Malloryhill, he was, in the classic Spanish phrase, going to arm the biggest scandal in the history of the state. But he did not care. He was responsible to no man; nor Giulietta to any woman. Besides, he reckoned that the possessor of a voice like hers was not bound by the rules that afflicted ordinary mortals. So ten days before the date that the pitifully scarred Mulhouse had announced for the opening at the St. Charles Theatre, they descended from the steamboat at the Malloryhill landing. The five days that they stayed there were a time of unalloyed delight. They rode together over the plantation, wandered hand and hand together in the garden, watched from the great gallery every night as the river swallowed the moon. Giulietta was delighted with Nikiabo and Sifa, the pygmy children. She begged Guy, if he should decide to travel with her, to bring them along.

In the afternoons, she practiced her opening rôle, that of Lucia, in Donizetti's *Lucia di Lammermoor,* accompanied by Hans Heinkle, a young German musician from that grave and peaceful Bavarian group, who in 1850, after two years of wandering as refugees from the Revolution of 1848, had suddenly and unaccountably settled in the swampy, unclaimed lands north of Fitzhugh Mallory's place.

So, throughout the long afternoons, Malloryhill echoed with golden sound. Guy, who, apart from some feeble attempts by the vapid daughters of neighboring planters, the hymns of the church, and the Negroes' Spirituals, had never heard any real music in his life, realized at last how much he had missed.

Giulietta was enchanting, delightful, divine. He was sure that no other man had ever known a woman such as this, who in the slumberous darkness, loved him like a pagan goddess, chanting in that soft, golden loveliness that was her voice: "*Andante molto calmo,* oh my heart! *Lento, lento—Allegro moderato,* my love—*sostenuto—Allegro con spirito*—ah, now!

299

Molto vivace; allegro vivo—like a *glissando*—ah, now! Finale, grand finale! Ah!"

"What the heck do you think you're doing?" he laughed, when at last he could speak; "directing an orchestra?"

"Ah, *si!* And what lovely, lovely music we make together, is it not so, my love? Our overture to immortality, I think it is, no?"

But it had to end, finally. And it did upon a twisted note. The day before he was to take her back to New Orleans, he was sitting on the gallery, listening to her practicing in the parlor, when Jo Ann Mallory rode up to the house. He got up and went down the stairs.

"I suppose," Jo Ann said dryly, "that that woman is still here."

"She is," Guy said calmly; "Any objections?"

"None. It's not my business. But, Guy, you can't fly in the face of public opinion, so! I know she's lovely; but surely you have common decency enough to marry her, and not—"

"I've asked her," Guy said quietly, "but I've got a rival I can't lick—"

"A rival?" Jo said. "He must be a pretty poor figure of a man, to let you do—this!"

"Not a man. Her voice. She can't give up her career. And to follow her all over the world, I'd have to leave—this—"

"Then you're a fool!" Jo Ann said angrily. "If she really loved you, she'd—"

"Wait a minute, Jo," he said gravely. "Come with me—"

He led her up the stairs. As they reached the gallery, Giulietta swung into the haunting aria, where Lucia, already mad, imagines that she has married her Edgar; her voice joyous with a pitiful, false joyousness, soaring up, the notes crystalline pure, incredibly lovely:

"*Al fin son tua, al fin sei mio*—At last I'm yours, at last you're mine—" making the very air tremble with a kind of suppressed sadness that was absolutely insupportable.

"God!" Jo Ann whispered. "It—it kills you, doesn't it? It tears you apart!"

"What right have I to put a stop to that, Jo?" Guy said; "tell me, what right? For Malloryhill or ten thousand Malloryhills, or whether I have sons or not? Go on, tell me!"

"None," Jo said humbly. "And what is worse, you'll never give her up. Just listening to her would be enough—even if she weren't so damned beautiful!"

300

"Jo—" Guy said.

"I'm sorry. I shouldn't have said that. I—I'm not sure of anything anymore. When you came back so suddenly. I was—disturbed. I admit it. But I had Kil then, and I did—do love him. Now—"

"Now?" Guy said.

"I'm more disturbed than ever. Confused. Only I have nothing to be confused about, have I? I have Kil—or what's left of him; and you have—her. So I guess it's goodbye now, for keeps—"

But it wasn't.

For on the night of that opening, Guy sat through the first opera he had ever heard in all his life. He had covered her dressing room with roses, so many that the wardrobe mistress had to take most of them away to give Giulietta room to change. He sat there, listening to the miracle of her voice, and knew absolutely and finally in his heart that she could never truly belong to him; that she belonged to the world, and to the ages.

By the last act, he was sure of it. He sat motionless through the mad scene, frozen by the anguished, terrible power of Giulietta's singing, her great acting, as superb almost, as was her voice.

When she reached the final, pitiful, *"Spargi d'amaro pianto, il mio terrestre velo—"* he echoed the words, for she had taught him their meaning: Yes, cast upon this grave a flower, upon the tomb of our love, Giulietta mia; but there will be weeping, as long as I live there will be weeping, in my mind and in my heart—

He called for an usher, and sent him for a pencil; then upon the back of the program, he wrote:

"Goodbye, little Giulia. I cannot take you from this, nor drag behind you like a weight, interfering with this magic of yours. It is better so. Forgive me, knowing that you have my love for ever." He signed it simply, "Guy."

Then he left the theatre. An hour later he was already aboard an upriver boat.

Two days later, the opera company closed its run, when its prima donna, Giulietta Castiglione collapsed upon the stage in the midst of Act Three. But Guy did not know that. He only learned it five months later, when he received the letter written by Edward Mulhouse from New York.

By mutual, unspoken consent, he and Jo saw little of

each other during those five months. In fact, during the last of them, they saw each other not at all. But on that final, fatal day that Elizabeth Melton, visibly pregnant, descended upon Fairoaks to seek out Kilrain, Jo came to seek Guy Falks.

It had been a bad day, from the beginning. In his wheelchair, Kilrain had been moody, snappish; Jo quarrelled with him and with her father, crying:

"Oh, for heaven's sake, Dad, go back upstairs and leave me alone!"

"All right," Gerald Falks quavered. "But I did it all for you —got you this place, even if I will be punished in hell for what I did and—"

"Oh, shut up!" Jo Ann said; and Gerald fled. An hour later, a Negro announced Liz Melton.

She was drunk.

"I want to see Kilrain Mallory," she declared flatly.

"I'm afraid you cannot," Jo Ann said. "He's very ill, and—"

"Ill! He ought to be! Getting me in the family way like this and leaving me without a penny—"

Jo Ann stared at her.

"You're saying," Jo Ann whispered, "that my husband is— responsible for your condition?"

"You're damned right he is, dearie," Liz said; "and I'm going to see that he pays and pays and pays, 'til he won't having nothing left, not this house, not this plantation—not even no pink and white milksop like you! Got to acknowledge my child, take it to live here, bring it up to its proper place in the world, or—"

She stopped, staring upward at the head of the stairs. Kil sat there in his chair. Then, very slowly, like a sleepwalker, Jo Ann went up those stairs. She stood on the landing with him, looking into his face. What she saw sickened her.

"So," she whispered, "it's true, isn't it, Kil? You—you wouldn't even leave me that. I believed in you that much— in your absolute fidelity. It sort of made up to me for all the rest: the lying, the drinking, the gambling. . . ."

"Jo—" Kilrain's voice was naked anguish.

"Don't worry. I won't leave you. But only because—I can't. If you weren't a cripple, I'd—"

"Jo, for God's love!" Kilrain wept.

"No, Kil. Not for God's love. Not for anybody's love. I'll stay, and I'll take care of you. I'll even be outwardly kind. But, don't mistake me, Kil Mallory—however gentle I am in the future, considering all the things you've robbed me of, the life you're robbing me of now, never forget that I hate you with all my heart!"

"So, you rat bastard!" Liz cried from below, "you've already got what's coming to you! God don't love ugly and——"

Jo had turned at the sound of her voice. She heard at the last second, the desperate scrape of the wheels on the carpet. She whirled, her hands outstretched to him. The tips of her fingers touched the back of that chair. Then it was gone. He flew past her, the wheelchair crashing and bounding on those enormously high stairs, turning over, losing one wheel; and he, falling out, rolling, bumping, turning over, came to rest finally at Liz Melton's feet.

Finally. For when Jo Ann reached him, the shrill echoes of her own voice crying, "Kil! Kil!" still hanging terribly on the air, the blood was already pumping out of his mouth. In a voice gone taut, toneless, almost without sound, she called the Negroes to her aid. She did not even notice Liz Melton's flight.

They carried him upstairs to his bed; and one of them rode for the doctor. She watched beside him, wiping his still face with a damp cloth, until two hours later Doctor Hartly got there.

The doctor's examination took scarcely a minute. He straightened up silently, sadly.

"I'm sorry, Mrs. Mallory," he said, "but your husband is—dead. . . ."

Jo got up without a word and went down the stairs. She called for her mare, mounted and rode over to Malloryhill. What she was going to say to Guy Falks when she found him, she had no idea. As it turned out, she said nothing at all.

For Guy Falks, with the pygmy children beside him, stood on the deck of an upriver steamer bound for Cincinnati, where he could get rail connections to New York. On the morning before, when he had received the letter, he had ridden at once over to Fitzhugh's place and asked that young man to watch Malloryhill for a few days, until he could get a wire off to Willard James, still honeymooning with his Norma in New Orleans. Will, he knew, was free to run the place for him as long as he had to be away.

He held the letter in his hand, reading it for the hundredth time:

She has lost twenty pounds. She hasn't the strength to

sustain a note. She does not eat or sleep, or take an interest in anything. We are supposed to sail for Europe by the end of this month. For the love of God, Mr. Falks, come to her, and save the world a glorious voice! I am not a moralist. I don't care what your relations were, or will be. I only know that on her opening night in New Orleans, she sang as I have never heard her sing before or since. I have promoted opera all my life; but that night I found myself crying openly at the miracle you helped her perform. Beyond the fact that if you let her die—as she will—you will be a murderer, you can not deprive millions all over the earth of a voice that occurs once in centuries. You know about her collapse upon the stage the night after you left. I found your note. Your sentiments were noble, but foolish. I beg you, I beseech you, come!

Edward Mulhouse.

Fifteen days later, New York opera goers gave Giulietta Castiglione fourteen curtain calls for her incredibly moving performance as Lucia. They would have given her more. But the curtain rose for the fifteenth time upon an empty stage.

Giulietta was no longer there. She had flown to the wings, and hung there, weeping hysterically, in Guy Falks' arms.

24

Guy sat by the window of his bedroom in the Royal Arms Hotel in Berkley Street, London and looked out at the grey mist of the rain. I'll tell her tonight, he thought grimly. But he knew he wouldn't. In fact, he had no need to. She knew. She had known from the very first, not being a fool, that it would have to end one day. And the whole of the time since they had sailed from New York in November 1853, to this bleak day in February 1856, they had been preparing themselves for the inevitable end.

She was wrong about one thing, though, Guy mused. I haven't come to hate her. I love her just the same—no, more. Only I can't stand this idleness. I can't. She's busy and successful and happy, while I—I have wasted damn near three years—for what?

But that wasn't true, either. The three years hadn't been wasted. By the mere fact of the incessant journeys, Florence, Rome, Milan, Venice, Nice, Bordeaux, Lyon, Paris, Vienna, Munich, Berlin, the last faint trace of his rustic beginnings had been rubbed off him; he had, without knowing it, without ever thinking about it, become polished, courtly, a man of the world. For idleness has its uses; particularly when it is combined with the sort of intellectual hunger that Guy Falks was born with. He had haunted the museums and galleries in all the great cities, becoming something of an expert upon the Renaissance painters; he read prodigiously; and, due to Hope Branwell's early discipline, his choices were generally good. And he knew, by now, at least from the standpoint of a cultivated listener, a good bit more about music than Giulietta would ever learn. For to her, the world of music began and ended with the opera; while Guy, discovering through her its magic, had gone on from there; discovering the symphony, the chamber music assemblies, the concert artists of the piano and the violin. He tried to take Giulietta to hear them; but usually she was too busy, too tired out from her incessant practicing; and, most of all, just not interested enough. "The human voice," she declared dogmatically, "is the perfect instrument. The rest bores me—"

Why the devil doesn't she come? he thought; weather like this— But the same weather had not stopped him from seeing a great deal of London: the Tower, Westminster Abbey, Madame Tussaud's Waxworks, both the National Gallery in Trafalgar Square, and the National Portrait Gallery in Saint Martin's Place, Windsor Castle—in fact, all the chief tourist attractions. He was a very frank and diligent tourist, for he was aware that he might never again have this opportunity.

He knew where Giulietta was: over at Covent Gardens, practicing for her London opening in the rôle of Gilda in Verdi's *Rigoletto*. For even then she had found her niche, the thing that was to earn her world-wide fame; she, Castiglione, was going to specialize in the works of Giuseppe Verdi. They had met the composer in Venice, in 1854. Verdi had been just forty-one years old at that time; and both Guy and Giulietta found him immensely sympathetic. But Giulietta's interest in Verdi was not based upon mere personal liking; she had very sound instincts as far as opera was concerned, and she knew genius when she saw it—or rather heard it.

Guess I'll go out, Guy thought; God knows when she'll be back, and even walking in the rain is better than sitting here moping. Hope she remembers to keep Nikia and Sifa wrapped up. Poor little beggars; this is no climate for them—

He got up and took his great coat, his hat and his umbrella from the closet. As he was going down the stairs, a thing started working inside his mind, more a feeling than a thought: London—funny how familiar it is. As though I had known it, always. I walk through streets I've never seen before; yet every stone of them cries out to me. I stand before doors with my hand almost poised to knock—knowing that if the people in those houses were to open to me, a stranger, I would walk into rooms whose shabbiness, poverty, dirt I would find unbearable; but which I would accept, because they were the shabbiness, poverty, dirt—

Of my grandfather. No. He was a lord; the son of a baronet. Strange—those letters that Martha Gaines gave me. Surely a baronet's son should have expressed himself with more felicity of phrase. Old Ash's spelling was Lord awful, and—

He stopped dead, there upon the stair. He had been in London for two weeks, and this had never occurred to him. Two weeks of wandering about the city, the country from which the clan of Falks had sprung; and he had not thought to go back to his origins, to seek out, to explore—the reasons for what he was.

He went on down the stairs, and knocked upon the door of the manager. If anybody in London could inform him about the doings and whereabouts of the greater or lesser nobility, the manager of the Royal Arms could. He was almost the original inventor of snobbery, having that pristine appreciation of his betters that is the hallmark of the born lackey. He had, also, that other lackey's trait of thinly veiled insolence toward people whose social position was not high enough, or whose origins seemed to him uncertain.

He stood up as Guy entered his office, for he had long ago learned that the very finest form of insolence is excessive politeness. Besides, it afforded him a certain amount of protection on those occasions when he guessed wrong. Which, be it said, he very rarely did; he had a very accurate nose for the delicate aura of generations of birth and breeding, and that fine, faint aroma of decay which usually accompanies them. It was precisely this in Guy which puzzled him: the breeding was there; the decay, wasn't. So he had been forced to base his interpretation of the situation upon Giulietta, which, for him, vastly simplified matters. Because to the manager of the Royal Arms, there were some distinctions which didn't exist. Opera singer, chorus girl, prostitute, were synonyms in the dreary narrowness of his mind.

"Yes," he said, waiting the precisely inacceptable limit, before adding, "sir?"

Guy didn't even notice. He was too intent upon his errand.

"Are there any people named Falks in London?" he said.

"Why, yes," the manager said. "I should imagine that there must be hundreds of them—sir. Are you searching for a long lost relative?"

"Exactly," Guy said. "My grandfather came from England. His name was Ashton Falks, Sir Ashton Falks; from a place called Huntercrest, in Warwick County. Just like to know if the family still exists—what the devil ails you, Mr. Denton?"

"I—I didn't know, sir! I had no idea—if there is anything you are not satisfied with—the rooms say, or the service, I'd be glad to—"

"No," Guy said blandly; "everything's fine. All I want is a simple answer to a simple question: Is any member of that family still alive?"

"Of course, sir! There's Sir Henton Falks, Bart. M. P., O.B.E., V. C.; his wife, Lady Esther—she was a Forbes, you know, the Duke of Forbes' daughter; young Henton, Second, the heir; his brother, Brighton, though they do say he's going to take the cloth—customary, you know, in second sons; Lady Mary, the only daughter—and some cousins who are—very rich, but not titled. Went into manufacturing—a pity. . . ."

"Fine," Guy said. "Now tell me—where do they live?"

"At Huntercrest, naturally. Though this time of the year they're sure to be at their townhouse. It's in Kensington, Earl's Court Road, I believe. If you'd like to send them a message, I'd be glad to—"

"No, thank you," Guy said. "I'll just drop in on them."

Denton stared at him, his face twisted into an expression of frozen horror.

"But, sir!" he gasped. "That simply isn't done!"

"I know," Guy said. "It's one of my favorite pastimes,

Denton—doing the things that aren't done. You ought to try it sometime. It'll do things for you, broaden your point of view for instance. Anyhow, thanks—"

His card, with the magic word "Falks," opened their door to him; that, and the butler's whispered, "obviously a gentleman, sir—"

Sir Henton turned to his wife.

"Well, Esther?" he said.

"I don't know," Lady Esther said. "You say he's American, Rawson?"

"Yes, m'Lady," the butler said, "from his accent, definitely; but, if my lady will permit the observation, I'd say he was educated abroad. His manners are much too good for an American—"

"Show the beggar in, Rawson!" young Henton laughed. "He's probably a New York confidence man. If so, we're in for a lively evening, which I, for one, should appreciate."

"Do, father!" his fifteen-year-old sister said. "He sounds so mysterious!"

"Very well, Rawson," Sir Henton said. "Ask the gentleman to come in. . . ."

Guy was, of course, flawlessly dressed. And his contacts with the younger nobility of the continent had been extensive—for the very good reason that they considered the season on young and lovely opera singers, single or married, escorted or not, open all year round. In learning to fend them off, good humoredly and with grace, Guy had acquired a social poise that stood him in good stead now.

"I hope you will pardon the intrusion," he said calmly, with a slight smile, "at least long enough to permit me to explain the purpose of my visit—"

"I know," young Henton laughed, "you're a long lost cousin from America!"

"Henton!" Lady Esther said severely.

"I don't know," Guy said. "That's what I came to find out. . . ."

"Please do sit down, Mr. Falks," Lady Esther said. "You were saying that you are a relative of ours?"

"No, my Lady," Guy said. "I said that I didn't know if I was. It's just barely possible. My grandfather, Ashton Falks, and my granduncle, Brighton, came from a place called Huntercrest, in Warwick County. Beyond that, I know little. In my grandfather's house, in Mississippi, there are two walls filled with pictures, some of them dating back to the Restoration. To me, some of the faces have the strongest kind of resemblance to you, sir," he nodded toward Sir Henton, "and even to your son, here. The ladies—that is more difficult to say—even then flattery was more important than verity in portraits of women. There are no papers, no documents. Some jewels, of course; but I don't imagine that they prove anything. . . ."

"Hmmmn," Sir Henton mused. "There was some sort of a story about a shipwreck off the coast of Carolina—back in 1780 or '85, I don't recall which—"

"Not a shipwreck, father!" Mary said excitedly. "Piracy! It's all down in the family chronicles. Greatgranduncle Percy was appointed to the governorship of Antigua, one of the islands in the Caribbean. He sailed with his whole family: his wife, who was called Mary, like me, and his two sons, Ashton and Brighton. That was during the time the American colonists revolted against the Crown—"

"Good riddance," Henton II said. "They were a bad lot, if you ask me—"

"Nobody asked you, Henton," his mother observed mildly. "Go on, Mary, dear—"

"Well, for some reason, they sighted land off the Carolinas, hundreds of miles north of where they should have been. Navigation wasn't very exact in those days—"

"It wasn't that inexact," Guy pointed out. "I've always felt they had some other reason for being so far north—"

"Perhaps they did," Mary said. "We're related to the Tarletons, too, on the distaff side. And Banastre Tarleton was leading cavalry in the Carolinas. Or maybe they had some message for Lord Cornwallis— Anyway, Greatgranduncle Percy's craft, the *Mermaid*, was attacked by an American privateer and crippled. Then a storm came up, and it sank. According to the records, it sank with all hands. Does your grandfather's story have any connection with that, Mr. Falks?"

"Yes," Guy said. "My father told me that my grandfather was shipwrecked off the coast of South Carolina, near the Georgia line. My grandfather and his brother had a terrible argument about the family pictures, Ashton wanting to save them, and his younger brother thinking that pictures were a foolish thing to save. As all that part of the coast was in the hands of the Revolutionary army, they had no way of making connection with the British forces. Apparently they got to like the country, for they stayed on. My grandfather ended up in Mississippi and became immensely wealthy; but until he died, his proudest boast was that he was the son of a lord—"

"Hmmn," Sir Henton said. "Huntercrest. The missing pictures from the North wing. Shipwreck. It appears to me, young man, that we very definitely *are* kin—"

"Good," Guy said. "I'm glad that's settled. I'm very glad to have met you all. Now, if you'll forgive me, I have to be getting back to my lodgings. . . ."

"No, you don't!" young Henton said. "I think you're far too clever for me to permit you to walk out of here without our having come to some agreement about the main point—"

"What main point?" Guy said.

"The one you're so elaborately overlooking," Henton said. "That if you can prove this rather fanciful story, either your father, if he is living, or yourself, if he is not, should be sitting there in my father's chair. For our great grandfather was your supposed great grandfather's younger brother, as you obviously already know. And in England, younger brothers don't inherit, not as long as the holder of the title has living sons. So I want to know what you propose to do about your claims?"

"Nothing," Guy said calmly. "Why should I?"

"Not even to become Sir Guy Falks, Bart. of Huntercrest?" Sir Henton said.

"I've never seen Huntercrest, sir," Guy said slowly, "but I rather imagine, from what I have seen of English estates, that either of my two plantations is quite a bit bigger, and a great deal more productive. I'm not saying this in order to boast; but rather to clarify matters. My father is dead. I'm unmarried. I have interests in America which preclude my ever thinking seriously of moving to England or anywhere else. The title is an adornment, I can do without . . ." He turned to young Henton.

"I hope you'll believe me, sir," he said quietly. "I came only out of simple curiosity. A man sometimes likes to know what his roots were. . . ."

Henton II stood there, staring at him.

"By God, I do!" he said suddenly, and put out his hand. "I'm very glad to know you, Guy Falks. By the way, do you do any shooting?"

"A bit," Guy said. "Why?"

"Then you're invited up to Huntercrest for a go at partridges, as soon as the weather clears. You'll be here that long, won't you?"

"I imagine so," Guy said. "Thanks for the invitation. I beg your pardon again for having intruded. A very good night to you all. . . ."

"No intrusion at all," Sir Henton Falks said. "You're welcome at any time. . . ."

When he got back to the Royal Arms, he heard, before he even turned the key in the lock, the voices of Giulietta and Edward Mulhouse screaming at each other from the sitting room. He knew what the argument was about, for it had been going on between them, with scarcely a pause, for a year. On March 6, 1853, at the Teatro la Fince, in Venice, Giuseppe Verdi's *La Traviata* had opened, and closed with a resounding thud. Mulhouse, all impresario, was not going to risk Giulietta's soaring reputation for continual success on an opus that every respectable critic had damned to hell and beyond. And Giulietta was determined to sing the rôle of Violetta, which, since the opera was based upon the famous *La Dame aux Camélias* by Dumas, *fils*, gave her both the opportunity to wear stunning modern gowns, and to die nobly and self sacrificingly of tuberculosis on the stage. Like all prima donnas, Giulietta loved death scenes. She carried around in her purse a clipping from a French newspaper, in which the critic swore that she had made the stone statues decorating L'Opéra de Paris weep at her death scene in Bellini's *Norma*.

"It failed! It failed! It failed!" she was chanting now. "Of course, it failed! But did it ever enter that thick, utterly tone-deaf head of yours, Eddie, to ask why?"

"I know why!" Mulhouse growled. "No opera audience is going to accept a piece of modern dress! They want spears waving, armor clanking, silks rustling."

"Hello," Guy laughed, pushing open the door. "I could hear you two all the way to Piccadilly Circus. Giulia, you've too fine a voice to risk it screaming at Eddie—"

She jumped up and kissed him, hard.

"Come, love," she laughed. "You must help me convince this stubborn mule of an Eddie who will not listen to reason. . . ."

"But *La Traviata* did fail," Guy pointed out, mildly.

"You, too! I think I'm going to slap you, Guy Falks! Only

you would slap me back twice as hard; and on where I sit instead of the face. . . ."

"I'm glad you realize that," Guy said with mock gravity.

"Oh, I love you!" she said irrelevantly, and kissed him again. "Now, where was I?"

"Somewhere in the middle of *Traviata,* coughing your lungs out," Guy teased; then he sobered. "By the way, how are the pygmies?"

"Fine. The doctor says it's just a cold. He says that there are quite a few blacks in London and they don't die of consumption as you seem to fear. I gave them castor oil, orange juice and brandy, and put them to bed. They'll be all right tomorrow."

"Good," Guy said. The two little blacks were very dear to him.

But Giulietta was not to be deterred.

"Listen, both of you," she said, returning to the fray with new fervor, "*Traviata* failed because they gave Violetta's role to Salvini-Donatelli, who is as fat as a cow, no a hippopotamus who can't sing, looks hideous in her clothes; and who, naturally, made the audience laugh when she was supposed to be dying of consumption. For Salvini they should have had sense enough to change the script and have someone shoot her! Not even that. It would have been unbelievable that the bullet could reach her heart through all the lard. Now, take me—"

"Gladly," Guy murmured.

"Later," she teased; "when I have done arguing. I could put some blue powder on my cheeks for the death scene; stop eating long enough to lose a few pounds—"

"Don't you dare!" Guy growled. "I remember how you looked when I came to New York."

"Your fault," Giulietta said; "I was trying to die, so I could haunt you!" She turned to Mulhouse. "I could do it, Eddie, I could! And *I* wouldn't fail!"

"It's that modern dress business I'm afraid of," Mulhouse groaned.

"Why," Guy said, "don't you just put the damned thing back a couple of centuries, Ed? That way you could have all the swords, silks, ruffles and laces you want—"

They both stared at him.

"You know, Guy," Edward said suddenly, "that's one hell of a fine idea!"

Giulietta seized him about the waist and began to romp

312

around the room like a wild Indian, singing the drinking song "Libiamo," from *Traviata* with purest joy.

"I'll be on my way," Edward said, smiling his painful smile out of his terribly scarred face.

Poor devil, Guy thought. No woman would ever have him now—

Giulietta leaned over and kissed his scarred cheek.

"You are going to do it, aren't you, Eddie?" she said.

"I think so," Mulhouse said. "With Guy's idea about the costumes, and your looks and voice, perhaps we'll save Signor Verdi's opera for him, at that—"

"Now," Guilietta said, after Mulhouse had gone, "I can begin to kiss you very seriously as I have wanted to all day. But first tell me where you have been. I think you have been making love to some long-legged English blonde."

"*Questa o quella!*" Guy began to sing; "*per me parisono—*" He had heard so many rehearsals of *Rigoletto* that he knew most of the arias by heart. The Duke's aria fitted very well here, with its mocking idea, "this woman or that one, they're all the same to me!"

"Ah, so!" Giulietta said, hands on hips, tapping her foot in mock wrath, "but just remember love, that '*La donna è mobile! Qual piuma al vento!*'"

"You win," Guy laughed. "I can't fight operatic duels with you, Giulia. But if you ever do try being changeable as the wind that blows—"

"What would you do, Guy?" she said seriously.

"I don't know. Leave you, probably—"

"Guy, you would like to—to go home, wouldn't you? Tell me the truth, love—"

"Yes, Giulia," he said sadly. "I would like to, very much. Only—"

"You are afraid I will starve myself again? Or cut my throat or take poison?"

No. I'm only afraid that you might be—unhappy—"

"Guy—"

"Yes, Giulia?"

"Take me into the bedroom, and love me to sleep. Then go, before I wake up—"

"Lord God, Giulia, I—"

"I want you to go. I can't bear seeing you like you've been these last months. So restless—so sad. . . ."

"You *want* me to go?"

"Yes. I want you to be happy. Perhaps the crippled one is dead by now. She will be waiting, at any rate. I know women. And that one loves you—terribly. That is why I hated her so!"

"But what—what about you, Giulietta?"

"I—I will manage. I am stronger now. I have my music, and that is my life. It was not enough the night you left me in New Orleans. It is not enough, now. But I think it could come to be. After the pain has dulled a little—if it ever does—"

He stood there, looking at her, seeing the tears bejeweling her sooty lashes.

"Oh!" she wailed; "take me, Guy! Now, now—so that I will not think of it! Now, while I still have strength a little . . . oh, Guy, please!"

But, in the morning, when he was dressed, she was unable to maintain her pretense of sleeping. She came up on one elbow and stared at him, her face whiter than death.

"Guy," she said, "leave me the pygmies, won't you? I love them so; and Edward says they're good publicity. Do you mind?"

"Not at all," he said, and bent to kiss her. But she drew away from him.

"No, Guy," she said. "Inside I am like crystal vibrating to the highest note ever made. Touch me, and I will shatter into tiny, tiny pieces—"

"All right," he said. "Goodbye, Giulia—"

"Goodbye, my heart," she whispered. But the moment that the door closed, she whirled, burying her face in the pillow, the sobs escaping from her lungs, like someone ripping a heavy cloth apart with their hands. . . .

Outside the door, muffled as they were, he heard them. He stood there, listening to them a long time. Then, because he had to, he went down the stairs.

He did not go home at once. He was, strangely, a little afraid to. He went, instead, up to Huntercrest. It gave him a feeling of reverence to walk those Tudor halls, and look at the very places, religiously kept bare, from which those pictures had been lifted down for that fatal voyage so long ago. He shot partridges and pheasants with young Henton Falks. They also rode to the hounds, and indulged in steeplechasing. Guy's skill at these activities won Henton's admiration forever.

He took Guy over to a neighboring estate, and introduced him to Lady Maude, his fiancée, a fair and fragile girl who was the last of her own august line.

"Guess I can get married after all," Henton laughed, "since you don't want to dispossess me. I'd be in an awful spot if you did. For there's nothing so unemployed as an unemployed nobleman, Guy. . . ."

"Throw in Lady Maude, and I'd do it," Guy teased; "but there's fat chance of that. You'll write me from time to time, I hope?"

"Gladly. But only if you'll promise to answer."

"Shake on it, then," Guy said.

The world had changed since his youth. Then, an Atlantic crossing took forty-five to fifty days. Now, a crack mail steamer, still equipped with masts and sails, of course, made the voyage from Liverpool to New York in fifteen. When he had left Fairoaks at seventeen years of age, if a man wanted to go anywhere in a direction a river didn't run, he had to walk or ride horseback, or take a creaking stagecoach. Now, the railroads reached the Mississippi river at ten points. New York to Saint Louis took two days; Saint Louis to his plantation, Malloryhill, took not quite four by fast river packet. Twenty-one days after he had left Liverpool, he was home again. The very thought of such speed made him a little dizzy.

The plantation was so beautifully kept that he knew Willard James was still there. He had written to no one. It would have been useless in any case; because, due to his constant wandering about, their letters could never have reached him.

Willard and his Junoesque Norma greeted him with evident pleasure. They had one son, Nathan, a sturdy youngster a year and a half old. This fact gave Guy renewed hope. He was almost thirty-eight now; but Will James, more than ten years older than he, had managed parenthood. And old Ash had become a father at fifty-two.

They talked about everything—except Jo Ann. Fitzhugh had cleared his lands of debt, and he and Grace were to be married in June. People were mightily riled up about the anti-slavery agitation from the North. Secession talk was getting louder.

315

Finally Will James got around to the subject closest to his heart.

"I don't suppose, Guy," he said, "that I could persuade you to sell me Malloryhill. Norma and I have gotten very fond of it—Besides, with a son growing up—"

"I haven't any deep attachment to Malloryhill," Guy said slowly; "but, if I sold it, I'd feel honor bound to offer it to Fitzhugh first. It would be a pity to have it pass out of the family, if you see what I mean. But, for another thing, Will, where would I go in such a case? I've been rootless long enough—"

"You? Why to Fairoaks, of course. I naturally assumed—"

"I'm not taking Fairoaks away from Jo Ann and Kil," Guy said flatly. "I thought we had all that straight. As long as they live, they can—Lord God, Will, you having a fit, or something?"

"No," Willard said. "You didn't know. I suppose you never received a single one of my letters—"

"How could I? Wandering about the way I did—Just what are you trying to tell me, Will?"

"Just a suggestion. That, after dinner, you ride over to Fairoaks. Kil Mallory died—in an accident, the very day you left here in fifty-three—"

Guy stared at him.

"An accident? But that's just not possible! Kil was flat on his back and—"

"No. He had improved enough to get about in a wheelchair, by then. You know those long, curving stairs at Fairoaks? It seems the chair got away from him at the very top of them. He died instantly. Fractured skull, Hartly says—"

Guy sat there, still looking at him.

"You believe that, Will?" he said.

"No. I think he killed himself. Hartly was sure he would never walk again. But I am also sure of one thing, if that's what you're thinking; his wife did not—rid herself of him that way or by any other means. Beyond the fact that she is not that kind, I saw her nails broken off to the quick, and the marks they made in the wood of the chairback, raking for a hold, trying to save him. So—go to see her, Guy. After all, it's been nearly three years; and I," Will grinned, "have a selfish interest in the matter. Perhaps, after you're settled down at Fairoaks, I can persuade you to sell me Malloryhill, after all!"

Thereafter, Guy Falks proved conclusively that his youth was behind him. He ate a leisurely dinner, with good appetite. He answered all Norma's questions about Giulietta. He had bathed before dinner; but he went back upstairs, and shaved himself with some care. He dressed in a riding habit he had had made in England. Then he rode over to Fairoaks.

When she came down the long stairs on which Kilrain had died, he saw that she was not wearing black. Not being a hypocrite, she had never worn it. And he saw something else, too; in the nearly three years since he had seen her last, she had gathered from somewhere, an inner serenity, a deep and abiding peace.

She put out her hand to him.

"I'm very glad to see you, Guy," she said calmly. "When did you arrive?"

"This morning," Guy said. "You've changed, Jo—"

"And Giulietta?" she went on serenely. "She is well, I hope?"

"Very," Guy said. "At least she was when I saw her last—twenty-one days ago. . . ."

Jo Ann's blue eyes widened. When she spoke, there was an almost imperceptible tremolo in her voice. Another might not have heard it; but Guy's ear was very trained by then.

"She's not with you?" she said.

"No. We parted—by mutual consent. The same thing: her career, against my hunger for—a home—"

"I see. You've had dinner, I suppose? I can offer you coffee and a liqueur. Come, let's sit in the little parlor and talk. . . ."

She moved away from him, cool, remote, serene. It was a thing absolutely not to be borne. He put his hands upon her shoulders, and turned her very gently about until she was facing him. He drew her to him, not suddenly, or savagely, but just as gently, his gaze fixed upon her face. It was very white. . . .

At the very last moment, she closed her eyes.

25

"Guy, let's keep it simple this time," Jo Ann said. "I had my gorgeous wedding before. Papa spent a fortune on it. And it—didn't work out. . . ."

"You were happy enough with Kil," Guy said.

"Yes—I was. For the first few years at least. And even after that, I was more or less—content—until you came back. Kil was actually a very nice man, Guy. You—you don't mind my talking about him?"

"Not at all; if you want to—"

"I want to; but not because I miss him. I think it's just a way of—of leading up to some things you—you ought to know, that you had a right to—"

"Why do you hesitate and stammer so much, Jo?"

"Because I'm terrified of you! I'm so scared that my teeth are chattering!" She whirled suddenly, and buried her face against his sleeve. "Oh, Guy—don't marry me! You—you mustn't! I'll be such a disappointment to you—just—just as I was to Kil!"

He pushed her away from him gently, and tilted her chin upward with his hand. Then he kissed her, tenderly, tasting upon her cold and trembling mouth, the salt of her tears. She managed, finally, a pallid smile.

"That's better," he said quietly. "It's just a case of nerves, Jo. You've been through an awful lot. I think I'd better go home now, and give you some time to yourself—"

"No!" she wailed. "Don't go! I—I need you here. Sit beside me, and hold my hand. But don't look at me. When you do, I cannot talk. Your eyes give me the shivers. You have that Falks quality about you, like your father had. You walk into a room—and the air crackles with unseen lightnings; you speak, and there are the echoes of thunder—it's true, Guy! Now I know why my mother—"

"Let's not talk about that," Guy said.

"No. There are other things to talk about. I thought you were never coming back, so—I married Kil. I didn't love him, then. I didn't know what love was. Afterwards, I learned to—or at least I convinced myself that I did. I tried to be a good and dutiful wife; but—"

"You were," Guy said.

"I tried. But I failed him in some way I don't even understand. He would look at me, and I could see the disappointment in his eyes. I'm trying to be honest and fair, Guy. Kil was weak, never really wicked. I understood that. I forgave him over and over again for the gambling and the drinking, because they were, in a way, my fault. If I had been a different kind of a woman, freer, gayer, he wouldn't have—"

Yes, he would, Guy thought; and it wasn't your fault. When a man has been brought up on nigger serving wenches and white trash whores, he develops a kind of fear of decent women. I think that Kil had so much respect for you that it made physical love difficult for him. I think he'd separated the two things in his mind. You were his white angel, so the act of love seemed a kind of a profanation to him, almost a blasphemy—

But he didn't say that . . . In 1856, a man couldn't talk about such things to a gently born lady.

"And with you, it'll be worse, Guy . . . You're so terribly, frighteningly male! More than Kil ever was. It scares me. I know you're very gentle and patient, but—"

"But what, Jo?"

"But most of all, I'm afraid I—I cannot be what you want . . . Or even give you the child you're pining for. It would be a crime if the race of Falks vanished from the earth because of me! Kil and I were married ten years and we never had a child—"

"Could have been his fault," Guy said.

"No. He—he had a baby by that—awful Liz Melton. A little girl. They say she—she looks just like him!"

"I doubt it. Knowing Liz, I'll wager she didn't know who the guilty party was, herself."

"It was Kil, all right. People say the child is beautiful. But it's more than that. I'm thirty-two years old, Guy. In a woman, that's awfully old. Maybe you should find yourself a younger girl and make sure—"

"The risks are the same," Guy said. "When you married Kil, you were nineteen, and it made no difference. Besides, a younger girl would have one major drawback from my way of looking at things—"

"What drawback, Guy?"

"She wouldn't be—you," Guy said.

She kissed him then, suddenly, shyly.

"Thank you for that, love," she said. "Oh, Lord, but there are so many things between us!"

"There is nothing between us, absolutely nothing at all."

"Oh, yes there are. Ghosts—of old sins, old hatreds—of the dead and the living, Guy. My father killed yours—over my mother. You know, Guy, he seems absolutely terrified at the thought of my marrying you—especially since he knows we'll live here—"

"He needn't be," Guy said mildly. "When my father was dying, he made me promise that I would never harm Jerry. All those ghosts are far better laid to rest, Jo."

"Yes. If it can be done. Only they haunt me. Kil—and the way he died. Your—Giulietta—"

"You shouldn't worry about her, Jo. She's out of my life for good—"

"Physically, yes. But out of your heart and mind? I doubt it. I wonder if she will ever be. She was so beautiful, Guy. And gay and talented and interesting in so many ways. I'm so afraid of the comparisons you will make after we are married. I—I'm just not up to competition with one of the most famous women in all the world—"

"I don't make comparisons," Guy said, "nor contrasts, which is the better word as far as the two of you are concerned. You'll be my wife, Jo. I've loved you all my life. Now I've come home—to you. And I won't be put off by the imaginary phantoms in your mind!"

"I'm not trying to put you off, love," she said gently. "I'm just trying to be honest, so you won't be too disappointed with me. If you did go away now, I don't think I could bear it. But I've said it all, now; and I feel better. When do you want it to be?"

"That's for you to decide, Jo."

"Is—two weeks from now all right, Guy? It will take me that long to have a simple wedding gown made. Pink—for happiness, since I can't wear white any more—"

"Two weeks are just fine. Where do you want the ceremony to be held, Jo?"

"Here at Fairoaks. I'd like us to start our life together where

320

we will end it. Not too many people. Just Willard and Norma, and Fitzhugh and Grace. My father will have to take part for convention's sake. Of course, if you want to invite somebody—"

"No, but let's take a short honeymoon. To New Orleans, say—"

"No! Not New Orleans! That's where you—"

"Where I what, Jo?"

"Spent your honeymoon—with her. For it was a honeymoon, even if it was a sinful one!"

"In love, there are no sins," Guy said, "but it doesn't matter. Where would you like to go, then?"

"To New York, I think. I've heard so much about it—"

Where, Guy thought wryly, I spent my second sinful honeymoon with Giulia. But you don't know that, so it'll be all right. Lord, but it would be hard to find a major city where —Jo's right. That's one ghost who's going to haunt me—

"Fine," he said. "Now I'd better be getting along, love. There are a few matters I have to arrange. After all, it is my wedding, too. . . ."

What he had to arrange would have been of much less importance to a different kind of man. But at the very core of Guy Falks' being, his father had instilled a respect for tradition, for family, that nothing, as long as he lived, was ever able to shake. The mere fact of being a Falks was his *raison d'être;* the idea of aristocracy, his religion.

Therefore, what he proposed to do did not seem to him an intolerable invasion of other people's affairs, but a simple rearrangement of circumstances to put them aright. Malloryhill had belonged to the Mallory family for generations. Fitzhugh was the last surviving Mallory; therefore Malloryhill must be placed in Fitzhugh's hands. That Fitzhugh might not even want the huge plantation never entered his head.

Guy was determined that the old order must prevail: Falks at Fairoaks; Mallorys at Malloryhill. If he had been called upon to explain his reasons, he would have found himself at a loss to do so. To him, they were self-evident, requiring neither explanation or justification. He didn't even think about them. What he was thinking about with great concentration, was the method of bringing them about.

By the time he reached Malloryhill again, he had it all worked out in his mind. Willard James wanted to become a planter again in his own right. Moreover, he had the money to purchase a plantation. Guy's hope, then, was that he could persuade Will James to buy the old Mallory Place for enough money to enable Fitzhugh to purchase Malloryhill from him. He didn't need the money; he was perfectly willing to give Fitz and Grace the plantation for a wedding present; the trouble was that he knew they wouldn't accept it. The whole thing presented a thorny problem: Will wanted Malloryhill, and Fitz, Guy strongly suspected, was very nearly perfectly content where he was. The only discontented person in the whole complex situation was Guy Falks. He had created the problem himself; and, by God, he was going to solve it.

It was a tribute to his force of character that within the space of one day, he accomplished it. He had, of course, two formidable allies whom he had never even thought about, much less counted upon: Norma James, who found Malloryhill too grandiose for her simple peasant's taste; and Grace Tilton, who born of yeoman farmer stock, had an invincible determination to go up in the world.

"Well," Fitzhugh sighed ruefully, "the old place is plenty good enough for me; but since Grace is determined to be a fine lady, reckon I'll have to give in. Mighty decent of you, Guy, to agree to accept the same price for Malloryhill that Will gives me for this place. Only it looks suspiciously like charity to me—"

"It isn't," Guy said quickly. "This place, on less acreage, produces the same crop as Malloryhill. The only difference is the house. And it's worth that small sacrifice to me to have you and Grace as next door neighbors. Not that I have any objection to Will and Norma, mind you; it just seems to me more fitting to have Mallorys once more at Malloryhill—"

"Thanks," Fitzhugh said. "By the way, Guy, I've got a wedding present for you. Beauty whelped a month ago. When you come back from your honeymoon, I'll send you the two pups I promised you. You want to pick 'em out, now?"

"Damned right I do!" Guy said. "Come on, boy, let's take a look at the little critters—"

The wedding was a solemn one. Jo Ann wept all during the ceremony; and Norma and Grace joined in her tears. Gerald Falks gave his daughter away for the second time, with the aspect of a man marching to his own doom. In 1856, Gerald was in his early sixties; but he looked twenty years older than

322

his actual age. He was palsied and trembling, his hands twisted into talons by rheumatism; his face was grey, his eyes jerked with fear as he looked at Guy Falks.

Guy noticed these things about him, then dismissed them from his mind. He was far more troubled by another thing: while Norma James' tears were those of remembered joy, and Grace's of anticipated bliss, his bride wept out of—fear.

What did Kil do to her, he thought bleakly, to make her like this? She looks like a young girl faced with ravishment. I've had my problems with women before, but never this kind. What the hell is a man supposed to do with a woman who is at bottom afraid of men—and terrified of love?

He possessed within himself the answers to his own questions; but he did not know he had them. Cathy had taught him some of the answers; Beeljie even more; but it was Giulietta who had shown him finally how perfect love can be when it unites body and spirit, combining taste and delicacy with a warm and healthy sensuality in which there is no element of shame. He was extraordinarily well equipped to solve the problem that Jo Ann Falks, child of her age and her upbringing, presented him. But he did not know he was, so his wedding was a bleak and solemn thing.

They departed from the house in a shower of rice and old shoes, racing for the landing in Guy's little trap, followed by the wagon-load of their luggage. All around them, the Negroes ran, shouting and dancing with joy. At the landing, the steamboat waited; Will James had journeyed all the way to Natchez to reserve the bridal suite for them. The passengers lining the decks, having been advised by the captain, were also armed with bags of rice. At the sight of Guy and Jo, they set up a welcoming cheer and started throwing rice in their turn.

Everybody wanted to stand them drinks; but Guy fended them off good naturedly, with: "Later—when the little lady has had time to change—"

After the porters had placed the luggage in the suite and departed, happy with the enormous tips that Guy had given them, Jo Ann stood there, facing her husband. She was trembling and her face was very white. But she didn't say anything.

"I," Guy said cheerfully, "am going below to have a drink with the company. Slip on your traveling suit and join me when you're ready, Jo. It's not a good idea to keep apart from the folks. It'll only put mischief in their heads. And they do dearly love to tease new brides. But a little good humor and sportsmanship will fix that—"

He could see the relief flooding her eyes. Damn, he thought, I've got my work cut out for me all right. . . .

It took her more than an hour to get up enough courage to join him. But once she did, it began to get better all at once. The passengers were sympathetic. Long-married women offered her matronly advice about how to please and keep her man. The men eyed her enviously; for her very failure, unconscious as it had been, to enter fully into the physical aspects of love with Kilrain, had left her with a curiously virginal, extremely youthful look. The most feline guess, by the worst cat abroad, was eight years short of her actual age.

By the time they sat down to supper, much of Jo Ann's fear had left her. After all, she thought; it wasn't so bad—with Kil. I didn't like it; but then most women don't, from what I've heard. I mustn't disappoint him, though; I mustn't—even if I have to pretend—I won't show that I'm afraid. I suppose that Giulietta, being foreign, was different. I'll bet she was like some low women I've heard about who—who like it . . . Even more than men, some of them. They—they're lucky! Since it's necessary; since men are that way—since we must have a child—Why shouldn't a woman like it? Only it used to disgust me a little. And I loved Kil. But Guy—so silent— so terribly male. I'm so afraid.

"Drink your champagne, Jo," he said gently. "It helps. . . ."

"You think I need help, Guy?" she said.

"Yes. You're terribly nervous. And you shouldn't be. I'm not a wild beast. In fact, I think you'll find me a remarkably patient man—"

She leaned over and took his hand.

"I don't want you to have to be patient, love," she said. "I want to be your wife—in all ways. What I'm really afraid of is—disappointing you. . . ."

"You won't," he said, and lifted his glass. "To us, Jo—"

"To us!" she echoed, and downed the champagne at one draught.

He smiled at her from above his barely tasted glass, and signaled the waiter to fill hers up again. Wine, he thought gaily, has its uses. . . .

By the time supper was over, she was floating in the bosom of a soft and rosy cloud. He danced with her, holding her close. She cradled her pale blond head upon his shoulder, her lids drooping tenderly. The matrons looked at them with misty eyes.

But the whirling sweep of the waltzes, combined with all that champagne was too much for her.

"Take me upstairs, Guy," she whispered. "I—I'm so dizzy!"

He led her away, oblivious to the knowing smirks of the men, and the sentimental tears of the women. In the state-room, she wound her arms about his neck, and kissed him, babbling:

"I'm not afraid, Guy! I'm really not afraid!"

He helped her off with her clothes, an act, which, but for the champagne, she never would have permitted. Her chaste nightdress with its oceans of ruffles, and buttons rising to the throat, lay untouched upon the chair. As for his nightshirt, he had never even taken it out of his valise . . . She was willow-slender, snowy. And if her body had not the singing perfection of Giulietta's midnight and golden, highlifting, deep curving figure, it was, none the less, lovely. . . .

He was gentle, patient, tender, and, more important, expert. At thirty-eight, with years of experience behind him, he was marvelously controlled, being in no hurry at all. . . .

She lay there, looking at his dark head making nightshadow against her snowy arms; and all her blood went singing through her veins in slow and slumberous measure.

My husband, she thought; really my husband—the first I truly ever had. For Kil—wasn't. And if this means I'm a low woman, Lord how low I'm going to be! They're wrong! Wrong and fools! This is what a woman's born for—to have a man who can make her body scream inside from too much joy . . . I—I think I fainted. No—I died and came alive and died again—how many times? Lord, the things I said! He must think that I—no. He knows better than that. He must have seen how surprised I was that I could—I'm a woman, now. Finally, after all these years—

She bent and kissed his sleeping mouth ever so gently, so as not to awaken him. But he woke up just the same, and lay there, smiling at her.

"You know, Jo-Baby," he said. "You're really quite a girl!"

"Don't talk!" she said, her voice lazy, throaty, warm.

And he didn't.

At least not until the river lay golden in the sun.

26

DURING those next four years, while the slow, dogged retreat of the forces of moderation, of compromise, of good sense quickened gradually into utter rout; while the demagogues took over, the fanatics, the hounds of glory driving the Nation ever closer to an unnecessary, stupid, and fratricidal war, Guy and Jo Ann Falks were very nearly perfectly happy. Guy rode his broad acres, brought the Fairoaks greys back to their former fleet fineness, established the great breed of mastiffs on the place, and concerned himself little with talk of war. For it was to them, as yet, but talk. They had other concerns more pressing to them then the far-off questios of peace and war. They were haunted by Gerald Falks' all but invisible presence in their house, his terror of Guy, which was driving him slowly toward insanity; and, most of all, by their failure to have a child.

"Oh well," Guy said to his weeping bride, "it's still a mighty heap of fun trying!"

But that was scant comfort to her. Fitzhugh and Grace, married in the Spring of 1856, had now, four years later, two fine sons called Preston and Walton. Norma had presented Will James with another child, a daughter, Francoise, despite the fact that Will was now in his late fifties. From England came the exultant letters, announcing, in 1858, the birth of Banastre Falks, who would one day be Lord of Huntercrest, and again in 1860, of Lance, Henton II's and Lady Maude's second son. But tall, virile Guy Falks and his lovely bride had, after nearly four years, no child at all.

To Jo Ann's timid suggestion that they adopt a son, Guy said flatly, "He wouldn't be a Falks. It's the blood that counts, Jo: can't you understand that?"

In her desperation, Jo was driven to consult the inevitable wise old slave woman who was a fixture of every great plantation. Aunt Ruth shook her kerchief clad head and declared:

"You eat yourself some eggs, child. Lots o' eggs. Feed 'em to the master, too. Oysters when they's in season. And tomatoes. All them things helps. Don't know why they does; but they helps. . . ."

When for the fifteenth time in succession, eggs appeared upon the supper table, Guy was almost driven to repeat his father's act of hurling the platter out of the window. But he was far more controlled than Wes had ever been; so he merely growled: "Eggs, again?"

"I know," Jo said sadly. "But Aunt Ruth says—they help. They build up the body so that—"

"You think *I* need building up?" Guy said.

"I don't know—I think it's my fault; but, after all, Guy, with the irregular kind of life you've led—"

"Blast and damn, Jo!" Guy roared. "There's nothing wrong with me!"

"But how can you be sure, Guy?" she said.

He stared at her bleakly.

"I can't," he said at last. "Maybe you're right, Jo—"

She got up from her chair and came around the table to him. She put her arms around his neck and whispered:

"I'm sorry I said that, Guy. I know how much you want a son. It's not your fault. I—I am useless to you. You should leave me! You should—"

"Hush, child," he said gently. "You've always complained about my lack of religion; but it seems to me that it's you, now, who's questioning the will of God—"

And it was that very night, strangely, that Jo Ann conceived. Counting backwards, afterward, she was sure of that. Two weeks later, when the usual evidences of her continued sterility failed to appear, she said nothing to him. She would not have in any case, for in 1860, women did not discuss such things with their husbands. Besides, beyond the question of feminine delicacy, she feared that she might be mistaken. A few weeks later, when the secondary symptoms appeared: nausea in the mornings, cravings for wildly exotic foods in the middle of the night, nervousness, she was beside herself with joy. She knew perfectly the meaning of these oddities, because she had discussed the whole matter very thoroughly with Grace Mallory and Norma James.

"I'll tell him now!" she exulted; "today, I'll tell him!" She got up from bed, slipped on a robe, and went in search of Guy. In so doing, she passed her father's room. Gerald's door was open, which struck her at once as being extremely odd. Ever since their return from their honeymoon, Gerald had kept his door locked and bolted. When she had demanded why, her father's quavering answer was: "He'll kill me in my sleep one of these nights! I tell you, he'll—"

"Oh, for God's sake, papa, hush!" she had said disgustedly; and dismissed the matter from her mind. But now the door was open wide, and Gerald knelt beside the fireplace, poking at the fire. Then he turned, and resumed his efforts to break open the box—Guy's box, which he kept in his study, and which contained—papers of importance, was all he'd ever told her.

Gerald's efforts were hampered by his rheumatism, which had already twisted his hands into something resembling the talons of a bird. But his knife blade forced the lock finally, while she stood there wondering why she did not interfere. Then he took the papers out and started to read them.

She moved then, walking very quietly until she was directly behind him. Reading over his shoulder, she took the papers from his all but useless hands. He whirled, startled; then, wordlessly, he fled past her and down the stairs.

At the bottom of them, Guy Falks stopped him.

"Look, Jerry," he said quietly, "what did you do with my box of papers? I know you took it; it wouldn't interest anybody else. Come on, tell me what you did with it?"

"Burnt it!" Gerald cackled with insane joy. "Now you've got no proof—"

"Oh yes he has, papa," Jo Ann said from the head of the stairs. "All the proof he needs . . ." She came down very slowly. Her face was white, but she wasn't crying. "Yes, papa —the proof that you were a liar and a forger and a thief. That you stole Fairoaks from his father. And I—God help me—I, all the time he was allowing me to live here with Kil, paying our debts—debts he didn't have to pay because Fairoaks was already his—thought it was a scheme to—Oh, forgive me, Guy!"

"Doesn't matter, Jo," Guy said gently. "I'm just sorry you didn't realize that the only action I ever was capable of taking as far as you were concerned, would always be for you, never against you. If it weren't like that, then the word love has no meaning; and honor makes no sense—"

"But they do make sense, don't they, Guy?" she whispered; "which is a thing my father never understood. But there's one thing that's beyond me: Why, among papers as important as these, did you keep an old, broken powder flask with a block of wood carved to fit inside it?"

"That's one question I won't answer, Jo," Guy said. "It's a thing you're far better off not knowing. Now, if you'll give me back my Pandora's box—"

"I'll tell you!" Gerald said in high glee. "I was very clever, child! That big bastard, Wes—"

"Shut up, Jerry!"

—"was much too good a shot. I couldn't let him win. I couldn't! You understand that, baby? He'd taken your mother from me and—"

"Jerry—"

"Let him talk, Guy!" Jo Ann said. "Let him spew it all up—every bit of it!"

"So I had to kill him. He didn't deserve to live. He didn't. I had to kill him, and not risk getting killed myself. So I plugged that powder flask so it wouldn't hold more than six or eight grains of powder—less than half of a normal load. I tried it out, first. I stretched an old shirt tight in a frame and shot at it from twenty-five yards. The ball didn't have force enough to go through that cotton shirt, so I knew I had him!"

Jo stared at him.

"Oh, I was clever! I arranged for Wes' pistol to be charged from the plugged flask. That way, although he hit me fairly, I wasn't hurt, while he—"

Jo Ann's eyes were big with horror.

"You mean," she whispered, "that, in addition to all the other vile things you are, you are also a murderer—a despicable, cowardly murderer!"

"Jo," Guy said. "Let him alone. Can't you see he's paid enough—even for that?"

"No!" she wept. "He hasn't paid! Your father begged you not to take vengeance upon him. But nobody asked me not to! And I have reasons for vengeance as grave as yours, Guy Falks! He robbed me of my mother; brought me up in this house of silence and evil; surrounded me with a—a way of life, an atmosphere I had to escape from—so I married Kil. That was his fault, too! He has cost me everything: my youth, my happiness, all the years I could have spent with you if you hadn't been driven away—"

"Nevertheless," Guy said gravely, "he has paid. I much

prefer my eighteen years of exile to what he has had to live with day and night, inside his mind. He's mad, now, Jo; and that's punishment enough for any man. Besides, you can't take vengeance upon your father. The means for doing so just don't exist. For one thing, you haven't got the necessary evil in you. For another, we are shaped by our every act, for good or ill, Jo. So to revenge yourself upon this old monster, you would have to become a monster in your turn. And I just don't cotton to the idea. Don't reckon being married to a monster would be much fun—"

"I—I shouldn't have told you!" Gerald quavered. "Now you'll both go to the sheriff and—"

"No, Jerry," Guy said; then, turning, he took the box from Jo Ann. "Here," he said, and gave it to Gerald. "Take this upstairs with you. Tear it up, burn it. I don't need it anymore. Don't know why I kept it, anyhow. A man never needs such things—not if he is a man. You grow beyond violence, beyond hatred even, if you grow at all. You learn finally—"

"What, Guy?" Jo Ann whispered.

"That the only person capable of damaging your immortal soul—if you have one—is you, yourself. What other people do to you, is not important. It's how you respond that counts. Either you strike back, lash out in a fury, get down in the mud with them and wallow, becoming in the act as much a swine as they are—"

"I—I called you that once," Jo Ann said.

"Or you can learn the only acceptable answer—"

"Which is?" Gerald mocked.

" 'Father forgive them, for they know not what they do.' I forgave you a long time ago, Jerry. It's you who's got the harder part, maybe the hardest of all—learning to forgive yourself. And I don't think you'll make it. Take your toys and run along now. I'd like to talk to my wife—"

"Guy," Jo Ann said solemnly, after Gerald had scurried upstairs; "how can you think like that? I know these are the teachings of Our Lord, but—"

"It doesn't matter who taught them," Guy said calmly; "Jesus or Buddha or Lao T'zu. What's important is that they're correct. And the hardest one is that business of self forgiveness. It's a heck of a lot easier to forgive other people, Jo. For most of us, when we look inside our hearts, find things that it's a rough go to pardon. Most of us, like I said to Jerry, never quite make it—"

"You mean to say that you—?"

"Have done things for which there is no pardon on earth or in high heaven," he said slowly; "especially since I cannot, without hurting innocent people, rid myself of the effects for which I did them. 'Offense's gilded hand shoving by justice,' I reckon—at least for now. It'll catch up with me one day—But let's drop this nonsense. I've got a problem that only you can solve—"

"If I can, Guy," she said.

"The last time I was down in New Orleans, I saw notices posted up before the new French Opera House—you know, that one that Gallier built last year—"

"Yes," she whispered; already knowing what he was going to say.

"Giulietta's opening there next week in *La Traviata*. I want to hear her sing that rôle. And I would like for you to go with me for many reasons: First, because you've never really heard her sing—"

"And second," Jo said quietly, "because you don't want me to think that you're going to spend the night with her once you get to New Orleans. Either that, or—"

"Or what, Jo?"

"Or you're afraid you might be too tempted, and you want me there to protect you from yourself—"

He grinned at her, mockingly.

"Could be, you're right," he said. "Will you come along, Jo?"

"Of course, silly! If you think I'm going to let that warbling vampire get her hands upon you again you're crazy. There's just one thing I want from you, Guy Falks! You send somebody over to Malloryhill to tell Grace to lend me that little yellow seamstress of hers. Fortunately I've still got that shot-silk I bought in New York; I never had a dress made of that material, thank goodness! And I never even let Kil see mother's jewels, so—"

"You don't have to compete, Jo," he said. "You're stuck with me—"

"Every woman's life is one long competition, love," she said. "Besides, you've got it backwards: you're stuck with me—far more than you know—"

"What do you mean by that, Jo?" he said.

"Tell you—after New Orleans. Anyhow, thanks, Guy—"

"Thanks, for what?"

"For not just taking 'a business trip' as most men would have done. You won't be sorry. Now kiss me and get out of here and send someone for that girl!"

The French Opera House, designed by Gallier, and erected upon the uptown lake corner of Bourbon and Toulouse Streets in 1859, was indisputably the finest opera house in America.

It was, Guy realized from the sparkling excitement in Jo Ann's blue eyes, a sight to see. He, who had witnessed like occasions at the principal palaces of music in the old world, tried to see it now through her unsophisticated eyes: the landaus, victorias, hansoms, traps, surreys, sulkies, even buggies, rolling up to the door to disgorge the gorgeously bejeweled and gowned Creole grande dames, escorted by their gentlemen in strictest formal evening wear. Top hats, opera capes and canes flourished; the swift, sibilant rush of French filled the air; the titter of laughter; the heady aroma of perfume. . . .

Jo looked at Guy, standing beside her, his top hat collapsed in his hand, his opera cape lined with white silk, his tail coat and braided trousers made by London's finest tailor; his stiff-bosomed shirt snowy, whiter even than the spreading sweep of snow at his temples. He was taller by half a head than the tallest of the French Creoles, and by long odds, her heart told her, the handsomest and most distinguished man there. She looked at her own lovely shot silk gown with disquietude. Was it all right? Good Lord but these women were fine!

When the curtain rose, Jo Ann caught her breath. She remembered that Giulietta was lovely; but she was not prepared for how almost unbelievably beautiful the prima donna was. She threw a sidelong glance at Guy; but his face was grave, impassive, perhaps even a little sad—she could not tell. But Giulietta, as Violetta, was singing her first aria now, in which she declares that frivolity is the best medicine for her illness; and Jo Ann forgot her fears, forgot everything, in fact, under the spell of that matchless voice.

Only twice during the entire three acts did Jo escape that spell long enough to feel a renewed onslaught of disquiet. The first time was near the end of the first act, when Giulietta sang the haunting, *"Ah, fors' é lui*—perhaps it is he—" the man who could fill the emptiness of her life. When she reached the last of the aria, where Violetta concludes that this happiness can not be for her, that it is only a hopeless dream; Giulietta looked directly toward their box. Lifting her gold-en-crusted opera glasses, Jo Ann saw clearly and unmistakably in the glow of the footlights, that the tears in her eyes were real. It was damnably disturbing. . . .

The second time was worse. In the middle of the second act, when Violetta has already renounced Alfredo at his father's plea, unable to control herself at the sight of her lover, she sings the passionate: *"Amami, Alfredo, amami puant 'io t'amo*—Love me, Alfredo, love me as much as I love you," Giulietta strode deliberately front and center, ignoring the obviously flustered and annoyed tenor, and sang the aria directly to Guy, never once taking her eyes from his face. The applause was thunderous, stopping the act dead. And Jo Ann sat there in cold misery, crying very quietly at the sight of the puzzlement and hurt in her husband's eyes.

And, at the entr'acte, the usher brought her note, inviting them both to join her—and her husband—for supper in their suite at the St. Charles. Jo saw Guy's face tightening a little; then wordlessly, he passed the note over to her. At the sight of those words, "my husband," Jo could barely repress a cry of joy. She looked at Guy tenderly.

Poor old dear, she thought; you believed she'd go on pining for you, forever. How little you know of women! We all mean well, with our oaths of undying devotion; but they don't last until sundown. Maybe it's better that way. Life does have to go on. Even our fickleness is a means to that end. I— I'll tell you about—our son—tonight. That'll make it up to you, make you forget this creature's playacting. . . .

When the curtain rose again, she surrendered happily to the spell of Giulietta's voice . . . Then it was all over, the applause, the bravos, the dozens of curtain calls. With the languid grace of pure triumph, Jo Ann Falks stood up, and allowed her husband to slip her velvet cloak about her.

"Shall we accept this invitation?" Guy growled. He was, Jo could see, thoroughly out of sorts.

"Of course, love," Jo smiled mischievously. "I wouldn't miss this particular supper for anything in the world!"

But, as it turned out, her anticipated triumph was neither unmixed—nor pure. For the husband so laconically mentioned in Giulietta's invitation proved to be none other than the aging, bald, terribly scarred Edward Mulhouse. Anybody else but Giulietta would have realized the utter impossibility of inviting a man, whose mistress she had been, to have supper with her and a husband who had been a witness and a confidant of the whole former affair. To invite her ex-lover's wife as well, was simply begging for an explosion.

Yet, strangely, nothing happened. In five minutes, all three of them were, if not perfectly at ease, at least in accord upon the obvious point that you couldn't expect Giulietta Castiglione to either think or behave like anyone else on earth. Even Jo saw that this was no piece of subtle female malice. Giulietta simply wanted to see Guy Falks once more; to talk to him, to devour him with her eyes; and she quite honestly didn't give a tinker's damn whether his wife or her husband approved or not.

"Ah, but you are more gorgeous than ever!" she said. "That white hair at the temples becomes you. So distinguished, I think . . ." She turned to Jo: "Forgive me, my dear; but you have him all the time, and Eddie has me all the time; so be nice and sweet and talk to each other and let me have him all to myself this once!"

"All right," Jo said, "as long as you give him back, Miss Castiglione—ah, I beg your pardon—Mrs. Mulhouse—"

Edward Mulhouse smiled his painful smile.

"I'm used to it," he said dryly. "Besides she only married me out of pity—"

"That, no," Giulietta said. "I think it was the other way round. No other man would put up with my tantrums, my sulky moods and vile temper without beating me half to death, or leaving me. Eddie is very sweet and I do love him. Besides he's so nice and ugly that I don't have to be crazy jealous of him as I was of—Guy. And," she got up and came to Jo and looked her over critically, "you suit your husband, Mrs. Falks. You're very pure and sweet and controlled, while I am most disorderly. Any babies, yet?"

"No," Jo said quickly. "Not yet—"

"A pity. He loves children so. While I cannot stand the wet-bottomed, yowling, snotty-nosed, smelly little beasts. The only children I ever loved were those cute little blacks, Sifa and Nikia—"

"That's right, by God!" Guy said; "Where are they, Giulia?"

"They are—dead," Giulia whispered. "Do not look at me like that, Guy! I took good care of them! I did all the things you told me: fed them, kept them warm. Didn't I, Eddie?"

"Yes, she did, Guy," Edward said. "She took wonderful care of them. It wasn't her fault—"

334

"Then what happened?"

"Sorcery, witchcraft, black magic—I do not know!" Giulietta said. "Nikia cursed Sifa—and she died of his curse. Then he willed that he should die, too. So he did! I swear, Guy, that is God's own truth!"

"I know it is," Guy said sadly. "Nikia was one hell of a good Ju Ju man. But what I don't understand is why he cursed Sifa. He loved his little sister more than life. . . ."

"She—she dishonored him. We were in Paris—and you know the French. They have little or no distaste for a black skin. Well a cute little page boy, about fifteen years old, at L'Imperial, thought it would be fun to seduce Sifa. After that, we had a five-months run in Rome; and before long it became apparent that Sifa was protruding in the middle. Nikiabo went wild. He stormed at her in that gibberish of theirs until she confessed. Then he drew himself up to his full four feet, and said—"

"How the devil do you know what he said, Giulia," Guy interrupted, "since I know damn well he said it in Swahili?"

"Sifa told me. He said: 'As this moon shall wane, so also shall you wane, my sister! And when there is darkness over half the world, you will die!' And she did. I got doctor after doctor. They said it was mesmerism, hypnotism, superstition, fear. But she was dead of it just the same, the first night there was no moon."

Guy could well believe it. He remembered the hypnotic arts that Biribi, the last Ju Ju man at Falkston had taught him. If the victim believed enough, or even respected the practitioner enough—

"And then?" he prompted.

"He sat by her body and chanted his death song. He sat there, all night, singing it. At dawn, he stopped singing. I ran into the room, and there he was—without a mark on him, dead beside his sister—"

"I don't believe that!" Jo Ann said. "It's just not possible! Nobody dies because of curses or—"

"You think so, Jo?" Guy said in his deep, grave voice. He felt the dark deviltry rising in him, his old impatience with the serene belief of most people that their own cultures hold all there is of truth. Besides, he was in a thoroughly bad humor, any how. He loved his wife dearly, but he had seen her earlier enjoyment of his discomfiture when they had received Giulietta's note. And there were other reasons, which he didn't even understand. He enjoyed the feeling of mastery; and these last few days, Jo had been slipping away from his grasp. She seemed to have some secret which negated his control of her. And he didn't like it.

"You think so?" he growled. "Look into my eyes, Jo. Straight into them. Keep looking, don't waver. Now. Now. Now. That's perfect. You're sinking down. The lights are dimming. It's growing darker, darker, darker—you are in the jungle. It is night. The leopards are coughing about you—"

"No!" Jo Ann shrieked. "No, Guy, no! You can't leave me here to be devoured! Even if you want to be rid of me, you can't! Because of the child, Guy! Because of your son, I'm carrying now! You can't—can't—"

He snapped his fingers before her glazed eyes. Very slowly they came clear again.

"Jo," he said brokenly, taking her in his arms, "I'm sorry. That was rotten of me. Is it true what you said about—the child?"

"Yes, love," she whispered. "I'm glad to be back! That jungle was awful and—Guy! You—you can do those things! Who—what are you, Guy? What am I married to?"

"The devil out of hell," he said sardonically. "But don't worry about it, Jo. For:

> 'This rough magic, I here adjure . . .
> I'll break my staff,
> Bury it certain fathoms in the earth
> And deeper than did ever plummet sound
> I'll drown my book—'

"Come, love, we better be getting out of here . . ."

"But the supper?" Giulietta wailed.

"Sorry, Giulia," Guy said. "Some other year—"

Then, putting his arm about Jo Ann's waist, he led her from the room.

Eight and one half months from that date, their son was born. Guy named the baby Hunter, after Huntercrest, the Falks' ancestral home. But it was not until they placed the squalling, red-faced mite in her arms, that Jo Falks lost her fear that it might be born with cloven hooves—or horns.

336

27

" 'ALL the world's a stage,' " Guy Falks often quoted to himself from the Bard, " 'and men and women are merely players. They have their exits and their entrances. . . .' "

So it was with him, in the Spring of 1884, with his life nearly all behind him; poised now, he liked to think, before the last grand exit, watching fondly as the younger players trod the boards. Some of them had already found their rôles; and all of the new generation of the intimately linked clans of the James, Mallorys and Falks were making their presence felt. Preston Mallory, Fitzhugh's and Grace's eldest son, had married Françoise James, Will's and Norma's daughter. Walton, the younger Mallory boy, was proving himself truer to type than his father. His flair for fast horses, wenching, and gambling made him seem more like the departed Kilrain than like Fitz. Yet, Guy knew, there was much good in the boy. He was great-hearted and gay, with no malice in his soul at all. The last of the Mallory children, little Trilby, born just a year after Fitzhugh's return from the war, was a pure delight; a blond and laughing sunbeam of a girl.

The Mallorys were fortunate in their children. It was left for Guy and Will James to be drawn together in their old age by their common problem: sons completely beyond their father's comprehension. The problem was similar: Nathan James, sired by a man whose brain was like a rapier blade, was a big, awkward, silent boy, lost in a private world of his own, painfully shy, bumbling in action, clumsy in speech. "A good boy," people said; "but he'll never set the Mississippi afire. . . ."

Hunter Falks was neither bumbling, awkward, or shy. Blond and handsome as a Norse god, he was a crack shot, champion rider, expert boxer, swordsman, swimmer. He was a fine scholar, having already taken honors at Oxford, where Guy had sent him to study along with his British cousin, Lance.

He was all those things; but despite them all, he was slowly breaking his father's heart.

For Guy Falks' son was a stranger—as different from his father as the moon is from the sun. The love between them was an intense and painful thing. Guy discovered how much his son loved him on one fall day, when he damned and blasted Hunt for missing a shot at a stag, so close that a child could have hit it, blindfolded.

"Again!" he roared. "What ails you, Hunt? You're a damned sight better shot than I am, yet—"

"Dad," Hunt said quietly. "We'd better have this out, I guess. I've been trying to avoid it; but I can't, anymore. Look, Dad, please don't be too disappointed; but I—I hate hunting. I always have, and I always will. It seems so rotten cruel to shoot beautiful, helpless things like that stag. . . ."

Guy had stood there, looking at his son. So many things were coming clear in his mind.

"Reckon there are a good many things you don't like, aren't there, son?" he said.

"Yes, Dad. All kinds of sports: riding, shooting, fencing, swimming, boxing. I'm sorry, sir—but they've always seemed to me—well—children's games; and not fit occupations for a man . . ."

"But mooning around with that Catholic priest, Father Schwartzkopf—is a fit occupation for a man, eh, Hunt?" Guy snapped at him.

"Yes, Dad—the things of the mind, and of the soul—are. . . ."

"I see." Guy said bitterly. "All right, Hunt—you can hang up your gun for keeps—and all the other toys connected with the children's games. But what I don't understand is how a boy who is so damned good at sports, better than I ever was, could—"

"Dad," Hunt said, his tone vibrant with pain, "have you any idea what it cost me to get that good?"

"Then why did you?" Guy grated.

Hunt looked at his father a long, slow time.

"For—you, Dad," he said.

Guy had left Hunt to his own devices after that. But it was a hard thing to live with. The worst part of it all was the feeling, amounting almost to conviction, that Hunt's engagement to Trilby Mallory was also a part of that painful and embarrassing dutifulness. Hunt simply didn't act like a man in love. Both Guy and Fitzhugh had their hearts set upon that match; but Guy was resigned to seeing it broken any day, now.

For consolation, he turned more and more to his daughter, Judy, born the same day as Trilby, thus giving rise to his and Fitzhugh's private joke that their daughters represented the last sparks of energy left in two tired old men—energy it had taken them full five years of forced abstention, while in the service of the Confederacy, to accumulate.

Judy was Guy's physical and spiritual image; so they got along famously. He had great plans for her. During the War, as Captain of the Confederate Privateer *Meridian,* he had coaled in English ports and renewed his acquaintance with the British branch of the Falks' family. He was mightily taken with young Lance, Sir Henton Falks Second's younger son. Lance had the verve proper to a Falks; he always had some Music Hall queen in tow. He knew intimately the history of every Derby winner since the race had been established. And he was the best wing shot, either over the dogs or before the beaters, that Guy had ever seen. Besides which, he was keenly intelligent, a matter he was at some pains to hide. Best of all, from Guy's point of view, was the fact that, as the second son of a titled family, under the laws of primogeniture, his chances in England were slight. Guy saw in him, transplanted to the States, the perfect husband for Judy.

So it was, that after thinking it all over, Guy set sail for England once again, in the spring of 1884. He meant to arrange things for good and all. What he did not know, in fact could not know, was that he had deserted his family and his friends, precisely when they needed him most.

On the eighteenth of September, 1884, Jo Ann Falks sat on the great gallery of Fairoaks talking to Grace Mallory. The talk between them was grave and slow, for what they were confronted with was a problem that neither of them knew how to solve.

"People," Grace said dryly, "put a mighty heap of store by the value of age and experience; but here you are, sixty years old, while I'm fifty-one, and neither of us has learned enough sense nor gumption to handle this situation in all that time. . . ."

"What does Fitz say?" Jo Ann asked.

"Fitz! You know him; he's worse than useless. Always looking on the good side of folks. But I tell you, Jo—there's something mighty funny about this Wilcox Turner. Can't put my finger on it; but it's there. And I'm bound to say that a good deal of the trouble is your Hunt's fault. If that boy had even half the get up and go about him that his father has . . . Can't you talk to him? He's such a nice boy; and I'll tell you frankly that Fitz and I have our hearts set on Trilby's marrying him. Guy, too, from what Fitz says. Everything was just fine, what with the children seeming so devoted to each other, until the mysterious Mr. Turner put in his appearance. Rich as all get out, smoother'n silk, talks like a college professor; but, after he's been talking two hours, it suddenly dawns on you that he hasn't said anything. You still don't know who he is, who his folks were, how he came by his money, what profession he follows, if any—nothing! He can get out of answering questions he doesn't want to slicker'n anybody I ever did see. . . ."

"And little Trilby?" Jo said.

"Is much too smitten with him. Thinks he's finer than a showboat with a steam calliope. And smooth as he is—oh, Jo—I'm scared!"

"The best laid plans of mice and men," Jo said. "Guy and Fitz all but signed the marriage contracts for our children even before they were born. Then what happens? Trilby and Hunt go along dutifully with their parents' plans; but only dutifully; and, of course, this New York slicker has to show up to ruin things. As for your Walt and my Judy, put them together for five minutes and they're fighting like cat and dog. . . ."

"That's healthy," Grace said. "They'll end up by fighting their way into love. . . ."

I doubt it, Jo Ann thought. You don't know my Judy.

"Speaking of fighting," Grace was saying; "if Hunt would only show a little—"

"He won't," Jo Ann said quietly. "He can't, Grace. Just hasn't got it in him."

"He's always mooning around with that big oaf, Nathan James. Poor Will! What a burden that boy must be to him. . . ."

"Nat's nice," Jo Ann said, "just quiet—and slow. He and Hunt get along because they're both so peaceful that they don't get on each other's nerves. Françoise is the same way; yet she's made your Preston a very good wife. . . ."

"I was opposed to Pres' marrying Françoise James," Grace said; "but it turned out much better than I expected. Just goes to show you. Maybe we hadn't ought to worry about Trilby's being so interested in Mr. Turner—"

"I wish Guy was here," Jo Ann said. "He'd know what to do—"

"Bet your sweet life he would!" Grace said. "Most decided man anybody ever did see. Lord, it's getting late! You must have a million things to do for Hunt's birthday tomorrow. . . ."

"I do," Jo Ann said. "I was just about to ask you to excuse me—"

As she entered the kitchen, where Aunt Ruth was hard at work, the first thing Jo saw was her daughter, Judy. At eighteen, Judy Falks was stunning. Her father's spitting image, people said. She was—with the reservation that Guy's dark good looks had been softened by her femininity into a beauty which troubled Jo Ann more than a little.

"Judy," Walt Mallory groaned, "reminds me of a powder barrel with the fuse already lit! If she'd only pay me some attention—"

Judy turned and kissed her mother's faded cheek.

"Inviting all the usual crowd, Mother?" she drawled.

"Yes," Jo Ann said. "Preston and Françoise, Nat, Walt, Trilby, the Clive girls—we need them to have enough partners for the boys, because I had to invite the Mallory's house guest, though I must say I don't like him—"

"Wilcox Turner?" Judy said languidly. "I think he's positively charming. Most interesting man I ever did see. So smooth—"

"Too smooth," Jo Ann snapped. "Don't you go and get interested in that New York slicker! In the first place, he's far too old for you. In the second, nobody knows a thing about his background or his prospects—"

"He says his mother is an old friend of Dad's," Judy said. "From New Orleans. If he even looked a little like Dad, I'd think—"

"Judy!" Jo Ann said.

"Oh Lord, Mother, don't be so pious! I know that Dad was quite a gay dog in his day—"

"Your language," Jo Ann said, "is most unbecoming, Judy. How many times have I told you——"

"At least a million. Waste of breath, Mother, dear. You can't change my ways any more than you could change Dad's. I wish he'd come home. Always chasing off to England to visit those tiresome British cousins of his——"

"Since you don't even remember them," Jo said, "how do you know whether they're tiresome or not? I found them very nice."

"Tastes differ," Judy said.

"You're absolutely impossible," Jo Ann said. "I'll be glad when you're married and off my hands!"

"No such luck, Mother. I'm afraid you're stuck with me. Whom could I marry? The next person I catch trying to matchmake between me and that grinning idiot, Walt, I'm going to take a buggy whip to! Of course," she added insinuatingly, "there's always Mr. Turner——"

"Don't you dare!" Jo Ann cried. "Nobody knows anything about him, and he's forty if he's a day!"

"Thirty-six," Judy corrected imperturbably. "Seems to have enough spending money about him, if that's what's bothering you, Mother. And his manners are exquisite. Only trouble with him from my point of view is that he's far too interested in Trilby. My saintly brother had better watch out. Wouldn't be at all surprised if he found himself without a girl——"

"I——I've noticed that Trilby's paying a mite too much attention to him," Jo Ann said. "I wonder if Fitzhugh shouldn't send her away a while, or something——"

"Oh, for goodness sake, Mother! Can't you be a little sporting? Trilby'll get over it. And it's just what Hunt needs to wake him up. I do wish Dad would come home. I miss him so!"

"Your father," Jo Ann said, "is quite a man. See that you do as well, when you come to wed. . . ."

"That's just the trouble," Judy said soberly. "I compare every boy I meet with Dad—and they don't stand up. It's a hard test, Mother. Maybe I'm not being fair, though—'cause I didn't know him when he was young. How was he, Mother?"

"He was very much like he is now. A little cruder, of course. When I first met him, he talked like a backwoodsman——"

"Dad? I don't believe it!"

"He did, though. The first thing he asked me was to teach him to talk better. And he learned. Lord, how he learned!

342

He has never been to school in his life—though for a few years he had lessons with me. But he's better educated than any university graduate I ever met."

"You," Judy said seriously, "must have been beautiful, Mother. In fact, you still are, in a nice old ladyish sort of way. And you're a dear. I'm sorry I'm such a brat sometimes. For I do love you, Mother—so very much—"

"Thanks for that, child," Jo Ann said. "Come on, let's help Aunt Ruth with the things for the party. . . ."

"Oh, drat that party!" Judy said impishly. "But at least Mr. Turner will be here—and that's some consolation. . . ."

They were busy with the preparations when Hunt came into the kitchen.

" 'Lo, Mother," he said, and kissed Jo Ann. "Hi, Brat. Lord, Aunt Ruth! We aren't going to feed an army!"

"Knows how you young folks eats," Aunt Ruth cackled. " 'Specially them Mallory boys! And Marse Nat ain't no slouch hisself. How come you's home so soon, Marse Hunt?"

Only the old Negroes are worth anything, Jo Ann reflected sadly. The younger ones say Mr. and Mrs. now, and that grudgingly. Never Master. Of course, they are free—if anybody is ever really free in life—

"I was going to ask you the same thing, son," she said a little anxiously. "You didn't have a quarrel with Trilby, did you?"

"Hardly," Hunt said disgustedly. "I didn't even see her. She was out riding with the mysterious Mr. Turner. . . ."

"Why," Judy squealed, "he's jealous! Look, Mother, Hunt's actually jealous! Maybe he does have some blood in his veins, after all—"

"Guess you're right, Brat," Hunt said soberly; "I am jealous; I've taken little Trilby too much for granted it appears to me now. I'm beginning to realize how much it would hurt if I were to lose her—"

"So," Jo Ann whispered, "you do love her, don't you, son?"

"Was there ever any doubt about that?" Hunt said. "I'm not very demonstrative, Mother; but I thought that everybody—"

"Hunt," Jo Ann said a little desperately, "Did you ever *tell* Trilby that you love her?"

"Yes, Mother," Hunt said. "Why?"

"More than once? Hold her hand while you were saying it? Kiss her?"

"I've told you I'm not very demonstrative—" Hunt began.

"Oh good Lord, Mother!" Judy said. "Why don't we just shoot him!"

"Look, son," Jo Ann said quietly. "I'm sixty years old. Even now, quite often, your father tells me that he loves me. And I like it. All women do. You can't say it often enough. Women are so—so uncertain. They can't be taken for granted. Just let your father pluck a flower in the garden and present it to me as a thoughtful little token, and I'll spend the whole day, singing. Can't you understand? It's not enough that we know our men love us. We must be told and told and told! No matter how many times it's said, we never get tired of hearing it. I like Trilby. I think she'd make me a fine daughter-in-law. And if you let this Wilcox Turner—who is much too old for her, and who has something—well, odd about him —something I don't like—take her away from you; you'll disappoint me—sadly—"

"Oh, I know, Mother," Hunt said, "but what can I do? It's the way I'm made. I'm so doggoned shy. I don't suppose I would ever have gotten around to kissing her, but for—"

"Aha!" Judy said. "So you do kiss her, Huntie! Now, do tell!"

"Mother," Hunt said, "do we have to talk in front of the Brat?"

"No," Jo Ann said. "Come, let's go to your father's study. It's high time you and I had a serious talk. . . ."

"But, Mother," Judy protested, "I want to hear all about Hunt's love affair. He could use some sisterly advice. After all, these are modern times; and your point of view is so old fashioned!"

"You stay right where you are, Judy," Jo Ann said. "Aunt Ruth, if she leaves here, you follow her. And if you find her bending over the keyhole of the study, give her a good one with the flat of the skillet, right where she bends. You hear me?"

"Yes, ma'am. Be a pleasure. 'Cause if ever a living chile do need a walloping—"

"Aunt Ruth," Judy pouted. "You wouldn't dare!"

"Jes you try me, chile! Jes you try me!" Aunt Ruth said.

"So, Mother," Hunt said, "I had this crazy idea that I wanted to leave the world and become a monk. Produce a religious masterpiece like St. Thomas Aquinas' *Summa Theologae;* or St. Augustine's *Confessions.* Two people stopped me: Father Martin Schwartzkopf, who told me to pray and make sure I had a true vocation——"

"Hunt," Jo said. "You belong to that Church, don't you?"

"Yes, Mother. To me it is the noblest, the most inspiring, the most sublime——"

"All right. You don't have to convince me. I have nothing against Catholicism, as long as you don't go and try to convert me—or your father. If Protestants are automatically doomed to hellfire, we'll burn right merrily, thank you. But get back to the point, son. I reckon the second person who sort of stopped you was Trilby. Am I right?"

"Perfectly, Mother. And by the oldest method in the world. She—she kissed me. Then she said, 'Think you'll be able to give this up, too?' And I knew I couldn't. I was afraid. I thought I was risking my immortal soul for the sake of a woman. So I went back and talked to Father Martin. He told me that Christian marriage was a Holy Sacrament, sacred before God. Then I felt all right. . . ."

"And now?" Jo prompted.

"I'm going to ask her. Tomorrow at the party. We'll set the date for as soon as possible after father gets back. This is one thing, at least, I'm sure he'll approve of."

Some time before dawn, one of the giant mastiffs, which, along with the dappled grey horses that Ashton Falks had established there, were Fairoaks' pride, lifted his great, lion-like head and howled. It was a terrible sound, deep-voiced and sad. It hung on the night air like—

Like a promise of disaster, Jo Ann thought.

She lay there listening, while the four other bull mastiffs took it up, crying their age-old grief to the waning moon.

Then, one by one, all over the countryside, other dogs gave tongue, until even the mastiffs of Malloryhill were answering their cousins and descendants at Fairoaks. In between, the Fairoaks greys neighed shrilly.

And Jo Ann Falks lay there listening to that awful chorus and trembling.

Guy would call me a fool, she thought dumbly; but I'm afraid, afraid—

From where she sat, beside Wilcox Turner, Jo Ann could see Hunt dancing with Trilby. They were such beautiful young people—strangely alike in so many ways. They were both slim and blond, with rosy, fresh-scrubbed complexions. Trilby was tiny, a dresden china doll. Hunt towered above her, taller by half an inch than even his father. He had the lean-hipped, wide-shouldered body of an athlete. He had all the things which go into the making of a champion—except the fighting heart. Trilby looked sulky. She kept glancing over to where Wilcox sat. Nat James, on the other side of the room, was answering Eve Clive's bright chatter in disjointed mono-syllables. He was looking at Trilby with the eyes of an ador-ing dog.

Preston Mallory danced with Françoise, his wife. He looked sleepily content. Jo Ann could see he was getting fat. What was Guy's phrase for matrimonial stoutness? Oh, yes—*la curva de felicidad;* the curve of happiness. Walton Mallory was dancing with Judy. They were trying to imitate the Ne-gro's cakewalk. Oh, Lord, Jo thought; in another minute they'll be doing a buck and wing, or jumping Jim Crow—then I'll have to stop them. . . .

From their chairs, Willard and Norma James watched con-tentedly. Their marriage had been a good one. Their children were not headaches even if Nat was somewhat of a disappoint-ment to them. They had had a fine life. Fitz and Grace, sitting next to them, watched their daughter Trilby, dancing with Hunt, with unconcealed anxiety in their eyes.

Trilby kept looking toward Wilcox Turner. He was, Jo had to admit, something to look at. He was tall, distinguished, handsome in a curiously controlled, very Anglo-Saxon way. Trilby was all but signaling him to come and cut in. In des-peration, Jo engaged him in conversation.

"I don't want you to think I'm a prying old woman, Mr. Turner," she said, "but we would like to know something about you. I know it's different up North; but down here, everybody knows everything about everybody else. It's—just neighborliness. We reckon that decent folks have nothing to hide. . . ."

"Have I given you the impression of secretiveness, Mrs. Falks?" Turner purred in his deep, rich voice. "I'm sorry; I didn't mean to. I guess it's my English blood that causes me to be so reserved—"

"You're English?" Jo Ann said. "You don't have the ac-cent—"

"Of course not. I was born in New Orleans, and have lived in New York since I was four years old. I thought you knew all about me. After all, your husband was instrumental in my being able to make a start in life. . . ."

"My husband," Jo Ann said, "to my certain knowledge, has never so much as mentioned your name to me. . . ."

Wilcox Turner's face was genuinely puzzled.

"I must say that *is* strange," he said. "My mother talked so much about him—"

"Tell me about her," Jo Ann said.

"She was beautiful. Dark—rather Latin, like your daughter. The basis for her lifelong admiration for your husband, Mrs. Falks, was that he righted a flagrant case of injustice for her. My father was an Englishman residing in New Orleans. He was rather wealthy. When he died, some so-called relatives appeared, and contested the will. Because my mother was poor, and of humble origin, they won. But Mr. Falks, who apparently knew her family well, appeared in New Orleans in the spring of 1853, and did some keen detective work. Seems he proved that the relatives were not related at all. So my father's money was restored to us. We were able to live very well. I went to all the best schools, took my degree at Harvard . . . That's about all, I guess. . . ."

"No, it isn't," Jo Ann said. "What do you do?"

"I own a leather goods factory in Brooklyn. We make everything: ladies' handbags, footwear, luggage, saddles, harness . . . I hesitated to mention it, because I know how strong the Southern prejudice against people in trade is—"

"It's not that strong," Jo Ann said. "You could call yourself a manufacturer and be accepted everywhere—"

"I didn't know. For that's precisely what I am. My factory, if I may say so, without seeming to boast, is one of the largest in New York. But I was careful not to mention these things, because, as you can see, Mrs. Falks, I had a rather distorted idea of the South—"

"You should have mentioned it," Jo Ann said mildly. "When a stranger shows up down here, and conceals all information about himself, we start to think he's got something to hide. Tell me, Mr. Turner, why haven't you ever married? You're a good-looking man; you've got money; and you must be nigh onto forty—"

"I'm thirty-six," Turner said. "I didn't marry, because from

347

the time I got out of college until she died last year, my mother was an invalid. I'm afraid she clung to me rather desperately."

"I see," Jo Ann said. "One thing more, and I'll quit pestering you with questions: Why, considering that your mother and my husband were old friends, did you come to Malloryhill, instead of to Fairoaks?"

"Because," Turner smiled, "I was under the mistaken impression that it was where your husband lived, Mrs. Falks. Among my mother's effects, I found a letter or two from Mr. Falks—giving her advice about investments, counseling her to have a talk with his bankers, and so forth—and they were addressed from Malloryhill, except one letter from abroad. So naturally I went there, wishing to meet and thank our lifelong benefactor. When I asked for him, Mr. Mallory told me he was in England, and invited me to stop so graciously, that it never occurred to me that I was in the wrong pew. In fact, I had been there two days, before I accidentally found out that Mr. Falks had occupied Malloryhill for only a short while—and that he lived at Fairoaks. But, by then, I had met Trilby, so I was, understandably, reluctant to leave—"

"You know," Jo Ann said firmly, "that she's to marry my son?"

"I know that everybody assumes so," Wilcox Turner said, just as firmly; "but I also know that no one has taken the trouble to consult Trilby, herself, about the matter. She, Mrs. Falks, is not in love with your son. She told me so, herself. There has been no formal engagement. So, under the circumstances, I cannot hold myself guilty of breaking up anything. This engagement, exists only in the minds of the respective parents. Although, quite frankly, Mrs. Falks, to possess Trilby I'd most certainly adopt the ancient principle that all's fair in love and war, in this case, I don't have to. All I'm doing is to enter into a fair and open competition with your son—a very decent chap, incident ly—from which the better man will emerge victorious; and the loser, I think, should accept his lot with good grace. Now, if you'll excuse me—"

Trilby was standing before them.

"Aren't you going to dance with me at all, Will?" she demanded.

"Of course, darling," Turner said, and took her in his arms. They glided off. Wilcox Turner danced like a professional.

348

Better, in fact, than most professionals that Jo Ann had ever seen.

Oh Lord! She wailed inside her heart. Why doesn't Guy come home!

When she returned from the kitchen, where she had gone to tell Aunt Ruth and the maidservants to bring in the refreshments, Jo Ann saw at once that something was wrong. Grace Mallory's face was sick with worry. Fitzhugh was frowning darkly.

Trilby Mallory and Wilcox Turner had disappeared.

And Hunt.

Without a word, Jo went out on the gallery. The moment she reached it, she saw her son running from the direction of the garden. He came up the stairs three at a time. When he was close enough, she saw that he was crying.

"Hunt!" she got out: "They—they haven't—"

"Yes, Mother! She—she's accepted him—For the love of God, Mother, get out of my way! I've things to do!"

But she didn't realize what the things were. It was not until the next morning, when she knocked upon Hunt's door, determined to spur him on to a new attempt that she found out.

His bed hadn't been slept in. Two of his valises were missing from the closet.

And Hunter Falks was gone from the house of his fathers.

28

LIZ MELTON leaned over the bar of her tavern in Natchez Under the Hill and stared at the drink-sodden young man, lolling in his chair.

"I swear to God," she said in a hoarse, whiskey voice, "if he don't looka mighty heap like your Pa, child. Got planter's son written all over him——"

"He says he's from a big place upriver," Rose Melton said; "Fairwood, or something like that. . . ."

"Fairwood? Ain't never heard tell of it. Fair—Lord God, Rose, it wasn't Fairoaks that he said, was it?"

"Yes, Ma," Rose said; "now that you mention it, that was the name. Lord, Ma! That's the place you're always talking about!"

"Biggest, finest place on the river. And it ought to be yours! If your bastid of a Pa hadn't of gone and killed hisself. What that boy say his name was—Mallory?"

"No. Falks—Hunter Falks. Why, Ma?"

"Better'n better!" Liz cackled. "Been named Mallory, he'd be your brother—though that ain't possible neither, 'cause your Pa never had another chick nor child——"

Rose eyed Hunt speculatively.

"Must be awful rich," she said wistfully.

"He is! Look a here, baby—you found out if he's hitched or not?"

"No, Ma," Rose smiled luxuriously; "but I sure Lord aim to—now!"

Liz looked at her daughter. At thirty, Rose Melton was a sight to see. She shared neither her mother's—nor for that matter, her father's—fondness for drink. And this prudence, coupled with a native shrewdness that had caused her to be exceedingly sparing with her favors, had preserved her looks. "Iceberg Rose," the flatboat men called her. She had never married, despite numerous offers, for the very simple reason that her mother's eternal insistence that she was "quality" by blood, had instilled in her an ambition to rise in life that was absolutely ferocious. Considering the fact that an Under the Hill girl had about one chance in a million, if that much, of marrying above her station, her refusal from her eighteenth birthday onward to even consider the proposals of the men she could have wed was stubbornly unrealistic.

But she did have some things in her favor. From her father, she had inherited a certain fineness. Dressed in the proper clothes, she could have passed unnoticed among the wives and daughters of the great planters. No—not unnoticed; she was much too striking for that. She talked rather well; and even read an occasional book. She did not know that Southern great ladies seldom talked very well, and usually read nothing;

so she did these things, because her unshakable dream of one day becoming a great lady led her to believe that she would need them. She was fanatically neat and clean, partially out of disgust at her mother's blowsy sloppiness; and partially, believing herself of the elect, she felt that she must be that way. She was unaddicted to powder and paint, unlike nearly any other maiden in Natchez Under the Hill. If her clothes were bad, it was only because she had so few opportunities to observe how the better class women of Natchez on the hill dressed. In short, for Natchez Under the Hill, blond Rose Meiton, with her cat-like grace and imitation lady's manners, was really quite something.

"Now, don't rush things," Liz counseled nervously. "Them there quality is real finicky. They scare easy, and they're plumb, down right suspicious. You listen to me, child; I know. . . ."

"You, Ma," Rose said easily, "don't know which side is up, most of the time. Don't go telling me how to manage things, after the unholy mess you made of your own chances. I'm smarter by a long shot than you ever were, and I aim to prove it, right now—"

She walked over to where Hunt sat. He looked at her with glazed eyes, and stretched out his hand toward the whiskey bottle. It was very nearly empty by now. Rose's hand clamped down firmly over his wrist.

"I wouldn't drink any more of that Mr. Falks, if I were you," she said kindly.

"Why not?" Hunt demanded belligerently. "I've been a damn fool plaster saint all my life, and what's it got me? I ask you, what?"

"I'll bite," Rose said smiling. "What has it got you, Hunt?"

"Lost me my girl—that's what. Bored her to tears. So she's taken up with a smooth-talking New York tinhorn who—say, you're pretty!"

"Thanks," Rose said, letting the slow, throaty laugh bubble up from her throat. "I'm even prettier when you can see me clearly. Get up from there, and come on!"

"C'mon where?" Hunt said thickly. "Don't go trying any tricks, you hear?"

"No tricks," Rose said gently. "I'm going to take you over to my place, and pour black coffee into you, until you sober up. If I wanted to trick you, I wouldn't want you sober. Now would I?"

"Guess not," Hunt said tiredly. "You're pretty. Blond like Trilby. Different though. Wiser, I think. . . ."

"Oh, you'll find I'm a very wise girl," Rose Melton said.

Hunter Falks came awake slowly. He lay there, blinking, trying to bring things into focus in his mind. Where the deuce am I? he thought. The room was strange. It was neat, feminine, pretty. There were curtains at the windows. The dresser was covered with mysterious bottles and flasks. An aroma of perfume clung to everything.

His head ached damnably. Nothing made any sense. He remembered arriving in Natchez, wandering through the dives in Under the Hill, until shame at his inability to go through with his determination 'to go the limit' with the first prostitute he should encounter, had made him turn to whiskey instead. It had been a thing he was very nearly incapable of doing. The sight of the rouged and painted harpies who called out to him from the sidewalk cribs had awakened pure nausea in him. He had had a few drinks in other taverns before entering Liz' place; and now, he didn't even remember going there at all. He had no idea where he was, or how he had got there. He was just about to give the puzzle up and turn his face to the wall, when Rose Melton entered with a tray. He smelled the good smell of bacon and eggs and fresh-made coffee. He was, to his own surprise, quite hungry. Then he looked up from the tray to the girl who bore it, and all his hunger momentarily vanished.

She was clad in calico. Her blond hair was clean and shining. Her face was well scrubbed, and she was decidedly pretty.

"Here," she said kindly; "eat this. It'll do you good. . . ."

"Who're you?" he mumbled.

"Rose Melton," she said simply. "Don't you remember?"

"No," he said slowly. "I don't. Where am I, Miss Melton?"

"In my room. More exactly, in my bed. Still don't remem-.ber?"

"Good Lord!" Hunt whispered. "I didn't—?"

"You, love," Rose laughed, "were a perfect lamb. Every inch a gentleman. You objected violently to my undressing you and putting you to bed. I had to call in my mother to help me. Afterwards, I slept—with her."

"Thank God!" Hunt said fervently.

"Why?" Rose teased. "Am I so old and ugly as all that?"

352

"No," Hunt said. "You're very pretty. It's just that I'm glad that I wasn't—beastly. I shouldn't like to have offended you—"

"You, lambie-pie," Rose said fondly, "couldn't be beastly if you tried. Come on and eat your breakfast like a good boy. . . ."

"I'm sick of being a good boy!" Hunt burst out.

"That's silly. You shouldn't be. In you, it's becoming. You shouldn't try to change just because you've lost your girl. There are—other girls in the world—"

"Like you?" Hunt said, surprised at his own boldness.

"Like me," Rose said tenderly. "You're a very handsome boy, Hunt Falks. I hope you won't think me immodest if I admit that I'm somewhat taken with you. Any man who is as nice as you are when you're drunk, must be a pleasure to know when he's sober. I—I'm afraid I've known precious few real gentlemen—"

She spoke truer than she knew. All her instinctive snobbery, all her mother's teachings inclined her to respond to a boy like this one. She was not the first woman in history to be caught in her own trap. . . .

Hunt lay there, sipping the scalding coffee. He had already demolished the bacon and eggs. He felt much better, and new vistas were opening up before him.

"What," he demanded, as so many naive young men in similar positions have demanded both before and since, "is a nice girl like you, doing in a place like this?"

"I sometimes wonder myself," Rose said sadly. "The truth is, I was born here. My father died before I was born, and my mother had to open a tavern with the little money he left us, in order to make ends meet. . . ."

The truth was that Liz had opened her place, long after Rose's birth, with the bankroll of an incautious New Orleans sport, whom she had robbed while he was drunk—taking the money from the pocket of the trousers he had carelessly left on the foot of her bed. That had been in New Orleans. And Liz was in an upriver boat, bound for Natchez before the sporting gentleman ever woke up. With her windfall, Liz had opened her tavern and retired from the world's oldest profession with the maternal remark, "I got me a growing girl; don't want her to come up this way . . ." Since then her lapses from virtue, up to the time that age and fat had permanently insured her chastity by removing all traces of her former blowsy charms, had been few—and nonprofessional.

"In an environment like this," Hunt said pompously, "it's a wonder you stayed so nice. . . ."

"Look, Hunt, I want you to do me a favor," Rose said. "You get up and get dressed. Take yourself a walk. Wander all over town and ask anybody and everybody you meet to tell you what kind of a girl Rose Melton is—"

The proposition was entirely safe. While, had he known where to go, Hunt might have found a few young planters on outlying plantations who knew that Rose Melton was a good girl to have on a party, every single Under the Hill male could only tell him she was Iceberg Rose, the untouchable.

"I'll do nothing of the kind!" Hunt snorted, the very picture of outraged gallantry. "Why should I ask people a thing like that?"

Rose laid a gentle hand on his arm.

"Because I want you to, Hunt," she whispered. "I—I never met a boy like you before. I don't know how to say this—I'm so ashamed, but—"

"But what, Rose?"

"I—I'm afraid I've fallen in love with you!" Rose wailed.

He felt then, inside his heart, the swelling of a new and very manly kind of pride.

"Thanks, Rose," he said. "You don't know how good that makes me feel—"

He remained in Natchez for three more weeks, constantly at Rose's side. The jeers of the flatboat men, remarks like: "Looks like somebody's finally done melted the iceberg!" convinced him of her virtue. But, for all that, his pain over his loss of Trilby diminished very slowly. He hung back, politely, until Rose was finally goaded into playing her trump card. Under a moon that silvered all the river, she surrendered to him entirely. Or appeared to. Hunt had not enough experience to realize how skillfully she had provoked the event.

Afterwards, she lay crying very softly in his arms. The tears were real, to Rose's own vast astonishment. For Hunter Falks was not his father's son for nothing. She had never met a man like this one before, so clean, so fine, so matchlessly tender. She did not know at what point in the procedure her surrender became real, changed into participation, blazed into ecstasy.

354

But it had. She cursed herself silently, wailing inside her heart: I've gone and fallen for him! I have—Oh, I'm a fool; but he's so—so sweet!

But her voice, speaking, shaped nothing but lies.

"I—I've never done anything like this before!" she sobbed; "I—I'm ruined forever, Hunt! No decent man would have me now!"

She guessed shrewdly that Hunt would be unable to distinguish between virginity and the lack of it, and her gamble was an entire success, better even than she had anticipated. Hunter Falks was a highly educated young man; but as far as women were concerned, he had never even been promoted out of the first grade.

"I will, Rose," he said grandly. "I'll marry you any time you say—"

Then Rose made her only mistake. It was, considering the pride and vaulting ambition her mother had ground into her, an entirely natural one: Instead of seizing poor Hunt—whose entire experience with women consisted of one weekend at Lance's London diggings with a couple of Music Hall chorines whom that worthy and enterprising young man had procured for the two of them—and running to the nearest Justice of the Peace, Rose dropped her eyes and said:

"Thank you, Hunt, darling. I—I'm honored. Let's make it three weeks from now, if that's all right with you. Mama always promised me a big church wedding—and since a girl does this only once. . . ."

The mistake was major. For that very same night, Guy Falks arrived at Fairoaks. To that slim and silver-haired old man, who wore his sixty-six years as jauntily as he did his opera cape, three weeks were long enough to move a range of mountains. To dispose of what were to him the relatively small problems of Wilcox Turner and Rose Melton, was a day's work, or would have been if steamboats hadn't required a day and a night to ply between Fairoaks and Natchez.

He came into the house in great good humor. It was dark, and Jo Ann had her back to the candlelight, so he didn't see her face. He kissed her warmly, and began:

"Great news, Jo! I've finally persuaded Henton to let me bring Lance over here next year. The boy's at loose ends. He certainly wouldn't make a Vicar the way second sons are supposed to in England. Had a go at the army, but the discipline galled him. Likewise, the law. The only place he's really at home is on the land. And since his older brother, Banastre, will inherit, I thought—Good Lord, Jo—you're crying!"

"It—it's Hunt!" Jo Ann sobbed. "He's run away!"

"Name of God!" Guy roared. "What the blazes possessed him to do a thing like that?"

"T-T-T-Trilby," Joe wept. "She—"

"Calm yourself, Jo," Guy said. "Let's get this thing straight. What did that child do that made Hunt run away?"

"She—she's got herself engaged to—to a stranger! A man named Wilcox Turner—from New York. He came down here looking for you, and said—"

"Wilcox Turner. From New York. And he came here looking for me! Of all the simon-pure, brass monkey nerve! What was it that he said?"

"That—you were an old friend of his mother's. She died last year—and he came to thank you for all you've done for them—"

"Poor little Phoebe," Guy murmured; then, lifting his voice: "Henry—go tell Caliban to saddle me a horse!"

"But Guy!" Jo protested. "You've been traveling all day and—"

"Heck," Guy said, "a steamboat's downright restful. And I got things to do which won't wait—"

"Where are you going at this hour of the night?" Jo demanded.

"Over to Malloryhill. This Turner bastard is still there, isn't he?"

"Yes," Jo Ann said.

"Good. Now don't worry your pretty snow-white head. This is one wedding that won't come off . . . Fitz consented to it, of course?"

"Yes, Mr. Turner is apparently an upright man. He owns a factory in Brooklyn. Shoes and such. Showed Fitz his bank account. He's worth more than a half million. And you know, Fitz—"

"I know Turner even better. At least I know his background. And down here in Mississippi we still don't say 'Mister' when we speak of—niggers. . . ."

"Guy!" Jo Ann gasped, "you don't mean—"

"His ma was one of the Mallory yard children. Very light, of course. And the boy can't be distinguished from pure white.

Took after his pa, a poor damn fool of an Englishman, who——"

"He told me his father was English. But he didn't say any-thing—I knew it! Oh, I knew there was something wrong with that man!"

"There may not be," Guy said calmly. "Any boy with the grit and gumption to parlay the small stake they had into half a million is all right by my book. As long as he stays on his own side of the fence. What I can't figure is the amount of incredible gall it took for him to come down here looking for me——"

"Mister Guy," Henry said. "Your hoss is ready, suh."

"Thanks, Henry. Wait up for me, Jo. We've still got to figure out how to trace that fool kid of mine. . . ."

He saw, as he rode up to Malloryhill, the two of them sit-ting on the swing on the gallery. They got up as he came up the stairs.

"Uncle Guy!" Trilby said a little fearfully, "may I present Mr.——"

"I've had the pleasure," Guy said dryly. "Though your—friend probably doesn't remember it, since it happened when he was only four years old. Now be a good child and run get your father. Your friend and I have a very small crow to pick; or better still, a colored gentleman in the woodpile to skin—You heard me, Trilby, go get your father!"

"I must say," Wilcox bristled, "that I don't like your tone, sir!"

"You, Willie-boy," Guy drawled, "are hardly in a position to dislike anything. All I want to know from you is how long it will take you to get packed?"

"Packed?" Turner said. "But I haven't the slightest inten-tion of——"

"Didn't ask you what your intentions were. I asked you how long it would take you to get packed?"

"Let's get this thing straight, Mr. Falks," Turner said icily. "I don't frighten easily. I'm aware that you had your heart set upon your son's marrying Trilby, but——"

"But, nothing. That's beside the point. The point at issue, Turner, is that I'm going to make mighty damned sure that she doesn't marry you!"

"And just how," Turner said frigidly, "do you propose to go about it, Mr. Falks?"

"I don't propose to go about it at all. You're going to do it. I'm being very patient, Turner. You should know that down here in Mississippi, your people have had their necks stretched for far less. So actually, I'm being fair to you. I'm giving you a chance to get back up North with a whole skin. I'm not even saying anything to Trilby. You can make her any excuse you like. Or would you prefer that I tell her the truth?"

"And what," Wilcox Turner said, a little shakily, "is the truth, Mr. Falks?"

"That your mother was a quadroon. That you've got Negro blood in your veins. Not much—but enough. One drop's enough down here. More than enough from our way of thinking. . . ."

"My mother—" Wilcox whispered, "was—colored? Oh, God! I knew she was a little dark, but—Oh, God! Oh Dear God!"

Guy looked at him with real pity.

"You didn't know, did you?" he growled. "I'm damned sorry, boy. Thought it was funny that you had nerve enough to come down here looking for me. Don't take it so hard, son. There're some mighty fine colored folks. . . ."

"You don't understand! I—I've always hated blacks! Once a gang of us caught a skinny nigger boy in a blind alley and beat him into insensibility . . . And now you tell me—it was—my brother that I whipped—"

"All men are brothers," Guy said quietly. "As long as they don't try to become brothers-in-law, we can get along just fine. . . ."

The door flew open, and Fitzhugh, a dressing gown wrapped over his nightshirt, stood there blinking at Guy. Trilby was at his side.

"Turner's leaving us," Guy said. "The engagement's off, Fitz. He's just discovered that he's not quite qualified to marry Tril—"

"That's a lie!" Trilby cried. "I've always loved you, Uncle Guy; but now I say you're a mean, wicked old man! What did you say to him to make him—"

"Sorry, Tril," Guy said gently, "but that's one question I don't propose to answer—"

"Tell her," Wilcox Turner croaked. "It—it's the honorable thing to do; and I—I can't—"

358

"Yes, Guy," Fitzhugh said sternly, "it appears to me that you do owe us all an explanation."

"All right," Guy said tiredly, "but remember I didn't want to. Fitz, didn't Kilrain ever tell you about little Phoebe?"

"Why—yes. She was one of the Mallory yard children, and your—"

"Let's skip that part of it," Guy said. "The boy's been hurt enough. I don't believe in being unnecessarily cruel. He, it appears, didn't know—"

"What didn't he know, Guy?" Fitzhugh said.

"Phoebe was his mother, Fitz. But his behavior here has the very pardonable excuse that he didn't know she had colored blood. . . ."

"Oh!" Trilby gasped. "Oh, Uncle Guy!" She stood there like one frozen; not even crying yet.

"I'm sorry," Guy said sadly, "but you insisted—"

"I—I didn't insist!" Trilby got out; then she was hurling forward, hammering at Guy's chest with her two hands, "and you didn't have to tell me! You didn't! That way I wouldn't ever have known! I could have gone along all my life not knowing! And I'd have been happy, Uncle Guy! I would have been happy!"

Then, blindly, she whirled and ran into the house.

Two days later, the *Prairie Belle* docked at Natchez Under the Hill, and Guy Falks walked down the gangplank with Trilby Mallory on his arm. It had taken all his powers of persuasion to get her to come. To console her, he had rung in that old and quite erroneous bugbear of the possibility of her bearing a black child.

He—who had spent most of his life on a plantation, where the crop of mulatto babies usually exceeded the yield of cotton, pound for pound—should have known that no child is ever darker than the swarthier of his two parents. But in his defense it must be said that most people believe a great many things that run directly counter to the evidence of their eyes. His most telling argument, however, had been to play upon her really great fondness for Hunt. Guy painted a grim picture of his son's misery, waxed eloquent over the prospect of happiness that awaited them. It wasn't really difficult; an eighteen-year-old girl's heart is a tender thing.

He didn't know that Hunt was in Natchez. He merely guessed that he was. His broad experience told him that the first thing a heart-broken young man did was to head straight for the fleshpots, and the dens of iniquity. That, in Hunt's case, meant Natchez or New Orleans. And Natchez, being closer, was the logical choice.

It took them barely ten minutes to find Hunt. The Under the Hill section is very small. They came upon him, walking down a muddy street, his arm about Rose Melton's waist.

"All right, boy," Guy said calmly, "you can turn that filly loose, now. We've come to take you home."

"Oh, Hunt!" Trilby said. "Aren't you ashamed of yourself!"

"You should talk," Hunt said angrily. "You went and got yourself engaged to that New York tinhorn—"

"But I'm not engaged to him anymore, Hunt," Trilby said. "That's why I came to find you. . . ."

"You've broken with him?" Hunt whispered. "Oh, Trilby! Baby! Angel!"

"Hunt Falks!" Rose Melton spat, "you're forgetting something, aren't you? Do I have to remind you that we are formally engaged to be wed?"

"You—you got yourself engaged to—this?" Trilby gasped.

"Tril—" Hunt began imploringly.

Calmly Guy took out his purse.

"All right, sister," he said flatly. "How much?"

Then, in that moment, Rose Melton achieved real dignity.

"Not a cent, Mr. Falks," she said quietly. "My affections have never been for sale. And money won't soothe my heart. Nor anything else. Hunt—"

"Yes—Rose?" Hunt faltered.

"Are you going to stand by your word like a gentleman, or do you want to go with this simpering little china doll?"

"Rose," Hunt almost wept, "forgive me, but I—"

"All right," Rose said flatly, "but I'll tell you something— both of you. You'll see hell before you're wed!"

Then she turned very quietly and left them.

Don't like that, Guy thought. That filly's got grit in her craw. And women like her are capable of damned nigh anything. Then he dismissed the thought.

"Come on, you two," he said. "We've got a mighty heap of straightening out ahead of us. . . ."

The wedding, that spring, was a splendid affair. From top to bottom, Fairoaks was choked with flowers. Everybody who was anybody from New Orleans to the Delta was there. Guy remembered to chain up the big mastiffs just before the first of the guests arrived, which, in its way, proved as serious a mistake as the one Rose Melton had made. But it was an unavoidable one. To have had his guests devoured before the commencement of the festivities would hardly have lent a proper social note to the whole affair.

Father Schwartzkopf stood before the altar, waiting to perform the rites. Hunter had insisted upon a Catholic ceremony; and Guy, whose religious prejudices were very nearly nil, anyhow, had consented. He would have agreed to a Shinto wedding just as readily, for the simple pleasure of seeing Hunt wed.

Trilby came down the corridor on her father's arm, achingly lovely in her white wedding gown. All the women were crying, and Fitz' eyes were suspiciously moist. Among the men, Nat James stood like a man awaiting the executioner, the unconscious tears streaking his round face. Even Judy was crying now, a sight Guy had never expected to witness.

Damned wettest wedding I ever did see, he thought, as he and Jo joined Grace and Fitzhugh behind their children.

Trilby and Hunt knelt before the altar by the big window. Father Schwartzkopf began to chant the nuptial mass.

Guy heard suddenly, startlingly, the crash of breaking glass. He turned, aware as he did so, that every head in the house had turned towards that sound.

"Hunt!" the shrill voice screamed, "see how you like her now!"

Then the words were lost, all words were lost, all sound, all hope, in the shotgun's sodden blast. Trilby didn't even cry out. She just leaned forward as though she were bowing before her God, white, lovely, incredibly graceful, going down.

Guy, the moment the enormity of what had happened penetrated his shocked senses, was on his feet quickly. But he was, after all, sixty-six years old. Hunt was far faster. He had almost reached the window when Rose Melton fired again. He caught the blast full in the right side of his chest. The impact knocked him over backwards. Then Guy Falks, despite his age, was through that broken window, frame and all.

She didn't run. She stood there as the men took hold of her with trembling, outraged hands. Behind them, in the house, the women were troubling deaf heaven with their screams.

"Don't hurt her, boys," Guy said quietly. "Just tie her up. This is a thing for the law—not for us. . . ."

"String her up!" someone cried.

"No!" Guy roared. "It's my boy—and I say no! God damn it, men, hasn't enough happened here?"

He turned and hauled himself back through the window. Doctor Hartly was kneeling beside Hunt, working feverishly. Pierre Terrebonne, Doctor Lucien's eldest son, was working just as hard on Trilby. She lay, white as death before the altar, her head cradled in Nat James' big arms. Nat was crying hysterically, moaning:

"Trilby!—Oh dear Jesus, please!"

And Father Martin Schwartzkopf was gravely preparing to give Extreme Unction to them both.

Guy stood there helplessly, looking from Trilby to his son. Never in his life had he seen anything so bright as the blood upon that wedding gown.

Women crowded around Grace Mallory, holding her as she shrieked. Another woman was bathing Jo Ann Falks' face, trying to bring her to consciousness again.

Finally Jim Hartly straightened up, to face the wordless question in Guy's eyes.

"I don't know," he said humbly. "His right lung's full of rusty iron, Guy. The left one's been touched a bit, too. She loaded that old muzzleloader with nails, carpet tacks, bits of old scrap metal. He's a strong boy—and he might make it. But it'll call for a mighty heap of sweat and prayer. I'd ask the Padre to say one now, if I were you. . . ."

"Tell me the truth, Jim," Guy said. "What chance has my boy got?"

"Slight. Damned slight. If he makes it 'til tomorrow afternoon, I'll go in and clean some of that rubbish out of him— if he's up to it by then. But, as I said—it's in the hands of God—"

Guy moved woodenly over to where Doctor Terrebonne stood.

"How is she, Doc?" he croaked.

"Just fine," Pierre Terrebonne said. "The altar caught most of the slugs. She'll be up and about again in less than a month. I'd advise that they both be put to bed here, though. Wouldn't do to try to take her home. . . ."

Guy Falks aged visibly during that long night. The doctors had given Grace and Jo Ann sedatives, and ordered them to bed. Judy sat sleeplessly, watching over her mother. But Guy Falks and Fitzhugh Mallory paced that floor together, their lips moving in silent prayer. And in the garden, although they did not know it then, Nathan James paced the night through in his turn, staring up at the window of the room where Trilby lay.

"Buck up, Guy," Fitz said. "Trilby's going to be all right; and I'll bet the boy will, too. Couple of innocent kids like that—"

"In a way," Guy said, "it was Hunt's fault. If he hadn't got mixed up with that murderous little whore—"

"You're wrong," Fitz said. "Take it further back, and you could say, if Trilby hadn't gotten mixed up with Turner. Take anything far enough back, and you ultimately get to—God. No. Guy, I won't accept Hunt's guilt. He's a fine boy; and all he's guilty of is, once in his life making a very human mistake. And who among us hasn't?"

"Thanks, Fitz," Guy whispered. "I'm glad Tril's going to make it, anyhow—"

The operation, performed that next afternoon, on the dining room table by Jim Hartly with young Terrebonne assisting, was more than a man half Guy Falks' age should have been called upon to stand. To Hunt, himself, profoundly asleep under the influence of ether, it was far less troublesome. Nat James and both the Mallory boys gave Hunt their blood through transfusions, after both doctors had sternly refused donations from Guy and Fitzhugh because of their age.

Jo Ann, in a state of profound shock, had to be kept under sedatives, leaving Guy to sweat it out alone, except of course, for Fitz, who was, if anything, more nervous than Guy himself, and Father Schwartzkopf who knelt and prayed God to guide the surgeons' hands during the entire three hours it lasted.

James Hartly came out at last and stood there looking at Guy.

"He's not—" Guy managed at last.

"No," the doctor said gravely. "In fact, with any luck he'll pull through. But I'm going to have to give you some bad news just the same. There won't be any more Falks at Fairoaks, old man, after you and he have been gathered to your rewards—"

"But you said—" Guy got out.

"That he won't die. In fact, barring post-operative shock, or pneumonia, he'll live to a ripe old age. But—as an invalid. Marriage is out of the question for him. You know anybody in Arizona or California, Guy? Southern California, that is?"

"No," Guy said, "why?"

"Right lung's shredded. I'd have removed it entirely if I dared. Left's touched a bit, too. Within the next few months, or even years, the first bad cold he gets will be fatal. Mississippi is too damp. He's got to live in a dry climate. Sun and dry air will bring him back to a fair approximation of health. But he mustn't stay here, old man—"

"I have a suggestion," Father Martin said in his deep, grave voice. "I have a friend, Father Enrique Basco, who teaches at the College of Santa Clara in California. I met him in Rome. From what he tells me, the climate is ideal there. Hunt is a brilliant boy, and very well educated. They'd be only too happy to have an instructor of his calibre on the staff. If you like, Mr. Falks, I'll write Father Basco at once . . . How soon will he be able to travel, Doctor?"

"I don't know," Jim Hartly said, "but I want him out of here by fall, even if he has to be carried West on a stretcher. What do you say, Guy?"

"Why the living hell," Guy growled, "do you think you even need to ask a thing like that."

When, late in December, they received the first letter from Hunt, Guy knew at once what he was going to do. It was a wonderful letter, telling them of the improvement of his health, his joy in his work, his great love for California and his new life. It was filled with serenity, with a great and abiding peace. That same morning, Trilby appeared at Fairoaks, and tearfully asked Guy if he minded if she became engaged to Nathan James.

"Oh, Uncle Guy," she sobbed. "I'm so ashamed! It isn't as if I didn't still care for Hunt—I do—oh I do! But—"

"But you're young and have a right to your own life," Guy said, and kissed her. "Besides, it isn't my place to consent or withhold. Nat's a fine boy. I say, blessings on you both!"

And, as soon as she had gone, he called the servants, and ordered them to pack his things. And Jo Ann's. And Judy's. Then he sent a Negro scurrying over to Malloryhill with a note, asking Fitzhugh and Will James to keep an eye on things until their return.

When Jo Ann and Judy came downstairs to demand what on earth was going on, he said flatly:

"We're going abroad. All of us need a change, I think. And

Hunt's just fine. Here, read this letter from him. We'll have time to answer it before we go. . . ."

Jo Ann started to object; then, seeing his face, she realized how useless any protest of hers would be.

"All right, Guy," she said. "Reckon a trip would ease my mind. . . ."

Riding along with Lance Falks at Huntercrest, on that fair April day in 1885, Judy could hear voices singing inside her heart.

"Tell me about Fairoaks, Judy," Lance said. "Is it true that you all ride pearl-grey horses, and stride abroad accompanied by mastiffs as big as Shetland ponies?"

"Yes," Judy said. "Why, Lance?"

"It sounds fabulous. I'm aching to become a part of all that. Father's consented, you know. It wasn't hard. He's deuced sick of me—"

Judy sat there on the chestnut mare, her eyes alight with love and mischief.

"There's just one thing I want to know, Lance," she said with mock solemnity. "Are you marrying me for Fairoaks— or for myself?"

"For Fairoaks, of course," he teased. "Girls like you are tuppence the dozen. I wonder if even Fairoaks is worth it. . . ."

"It is," Judy said gravely, ignoring his banter. "Just wait 'til you see it. And now there'll be Falks at Fairoaks down through the years. . . ."

She did not, could not know, that actually Lance would be the first Falks to ever set foot upon the place. Or that the whole history of her family had been one long, glorious lie. It did not matter. If a man believes enough, even lies become true. . . .

She lifted her dark head then, and loosed a silvery shower of laughter.

"I say, Judy," Lance said, "what's got into you?"

"We," Judy laughed, "are a disgrace, darling. All the romances I ever read are filled with the stories of young lovers bowed down with grief because their fathers were forcing them to marry against their will. And here we are, with Dad being as cute as the dickens, trying in every possible way to throw us together just to make sure that there will be Falks at Fairoaks always—and what do we do?"

"Your father," Lance said, "has some rather decent ideas. I vote that we encourage him—"

Judy reined the mare in, closer to his side.

"You, love, had better start by encouraging his daughter, then," she said.

What's to become of

Miss Martha Mary Crawford

?

A Novel by Catherine Cookson
Writing as Catherine Marchant

Young, burdened with the responsibilities of the
household since the death of her mother, Miss
Martha Mary Crawford was growing more lonely
every day. But love was to find her—cruel and
demanding, fierce and sweet . . .

Two proud, deeply scarred people were soon to find
themselves overwhelmed by a love stronger than
either of them in an epic struggle of wills and
passion.

"Packed with human triumph and tragedy!"
                                            —*Columbus Dispatch*

A DELL BOOK $1.95

At your local bookstore or use this handy coupon for ordering:

Dell Bestsellers